Shaman's Blues

Mae Martin Mysteries, Volume 2

Amber Foxx

Published by Amber Foxx, 2014.

This is a work of fiction. Similarities to real people, places, or events are entirely coincidental.

SHAMAN'S BLUES

First edition. February 19, 2014.

Copyright © 2014 Amber Foxx.

Written by Amber Foxx.

Prologue

May 2010, Santa Fe, New Mexico

"Lisa, love, no, you can't, not yet—give me another week. A month. Something." Jamie Ellerbee parked his bicycle against the side of the coffee shop, phone in hand, as he undid the clip that kept his jeans out of the chain. He couldn't see a place to park in view of the window, and he'd lost or misplaced the lock as well as the helmet—the clutter in his place was unmanageable. After five months, he still couldn't bring himself to unpack much. Maybe he could take the front wheel in with him.

"I told you last month, this is it." His ex-girlfriend's voice took on a firm, teacherly tone. The one she no doubt used when a physics project was late or a test had been failed. They had met as high school teachers, music and physics respectively, and parted over his decision to leave the job. That, and the consequences. "I'm not managing your career any more. That was just to get you through the—the transition."

The transition from being a teacher to being a full-time musician, as well as the adjustment to no longer living with her. That was one long year, half of it without her. The year he fell off another rock.

"You've done it so well, love." He knelt to try to undo the quick release wheel with one hand while holding the phone with the other, and tipped the bicycle into an elderly man. "Oh Jesus, I'm sorry. Are you all right?"

"Jamie?" Lisa sounded puzzled.

"Hit some poor old—Sir?"

The man glared, slapping a hand across his crisp white pants as if swatting off a fly, smearing the bicycle grease. His dry, pale

1

face creased and furrowed, and his jaw worked. Something dark and jagged in the man, something wounded and bitter, seemed to grow.

"Here. For the cleaners." Jamie pulled out his wallet and handed the man a twenty. The man with the elegant but injured pants stuffed the money into his no-doubt money-filled pocket. Jamie returned his empty wallet to his worn-out jeans. "Lisa? Still with me?"

"On the phone, yes. In life, no. I told you, I'm with someone new now. I need to have a life with him, and I can't be putting in fifteen hours a week working for free. It's not a hobby. And I'm not your girlfriend. You're on your own. Time's up."

His heart raced, and anxiety rose up like a flock of birds. "You've been brilliant. You've helped so much."

"Thank you. But—"

The world grew narrow, darkness rising up from the sidewalk to wrap around him. "Just teach me how you've done it. Can we do that?"

"I already tried. You should have been paying attention."

Bloody prim and proper teacher again. "I wasn't. Sorry. I fucked up." The birds in his chest began to swirl and flap their wings. "Can you teach me?"

"No. Hire someone. Get a professional manager if you can't do it yourself."

"I'm broke."

"That's your problem."

"Lisa! Please, not yet."

"You're the one that quit his job, spent all his money on camping and climbing and biking gear and God knows what else. I'm done. Goodbye. You're a grown man. Act like one."

Act like one. It hurt, but she was right. He was almost thirty now, ought to be able to take care of himself. As Jamie turned off his phone, it dropped from his hand. Shaking. He couldn't go in and meet his friends in this shape. He had to get away before something broke, before his soul flew out the top of his head.

Still holding the wheel, he started to bolt, the crowd closing in on him, tourists as thick as a dust storm. One of them approached, a fat woman in pink shorts, holding his phone.

"Are you all right?"

She looked kind. Kind, worried, and even a little frightened, tiny chips and fractures in her field, the rosy glow pulsing and then breaking.

"Thanks." He took the phone, amazed that he could speak, as half a voice creaked out of him. "Yeah. I'll be all right."

"You sure?"

How bad was he acting? What had he done? The birds rose again as he nodded a silent *yes* to her and ran, half-blind, down an alley to the parking lot. No one around, just cars. Quiet. Leaning against the rough adobe wall of the back of a shop, he closed his eyes and let himself take a gritty slide into a squat on the ground, dropping the wheel. With a last, desperate trace of vision and strength, he pulled up Lisa's number over and over without dialing it, finally deleted it, and dropped the phone again. Time fell into a hole, a shaking, sweat-drenched void.

Abandoned. Cut loose. Hanging over What Next Canyon without a harness, looking at the next big fall.

Chapter One

On the second floor of the Healing Balance Store in Virginia Beach, Mae Martin-Ridley worked with a client in a small room with green tree shadows painted on the walls. The store was a sprawling emporium that encompassed a health food store, an organic foods café, and a New Age bookstore downstairs, with yoga classes, energy healing, and psychic services upstairs. Mae provided the latter two. Holding a plastic, feather-topped stick in one hand, and a quartz point in the other, the tall red-haired young psychic held still, eyes closed, while a sturdy woman of around sixty sat in the chair opposite, her face taut with worry.

Opening her eyes, Mae said in her soft Carolina accent, "Seen her, Ms. Harris. Got a real good look. She's all right. Hiding under a big ol' wrap-around porch with white stairs."

The client gasped, and her hand flew to her heart. "That's under my neighbor's porch. My goodness. Two doors down. Poor kitty's probably been there for days."

Mae handed the cat's toy back to the owner, and stood and shook her hand as Ms. Harris prepared to leave. "They do that, run close to home. You may have to crawl under and get her."

Ms. Harris pressed Mae's hand again. "Thank you so much."

Mae watched her go, and smiled. She'd made this woman happy. The final client at Healing Balance.

The final night on the East Coast. The end of what felt like a life. The beginning of the next. Mae wasn't really about to be reincarnated, but as she took a last look at her healing room, she felt she was getting close to it in one lifetime.

Sort of fitting to end up with a lost cat. Her first realization that she had a psychic gift had come with finding her mother's runaway cat. People were harder, but she could find them as well. She could find diseases and past secrets, too, see all sorts of things most folks

4

couldn't. Her husband—soon to be ex-husband—hadn't been able to make peace with this change in her when she accepted and began to use what her mountain granma had called "the sight."

A year ago, Mae had not expected to be a psychic, to be single, or to be moving again. Yet here she was. She said goodbye to the room, hoping someone else would make good use of it, locked it, and brought the keys down the hall to her boss's office.

Deborah, a light-skinned, freckled African American woman, dressed as always in colorful batiks that flattered her statuesque figure, rose from behind her desk and walked around to hug Mae. "We'll miss you here, Breda." Deborah made the psychics use working names that had more color and ethnic flavor. She'd given Mae an Irish-sounding name to go with her Celtic looks. "Never had anyone like you." She released the hug, accepted the key Mae gave her, and set it on her desk. "Will you be doing this kind of work in New Mexico?"

"I don't know. I'll be in college full time."

"How did I miss that? I thought you were moving to be near your father."

"I am. I get free tuition at the place where he coaches."

"That's wonderful. Studying—religion? Philosophy? Psychology? Anthropology? I imagine a healer could do all of that and learn from it."

"Exercise science, actually." Mae felt she was disappointing Deborah, but she loved her fitness work, loved sports and exercise, and wasn't a very spiritual or religious person in spite of her psychic abilities. "I'm gonna try to get some part-time work as a personal trainer, or in group fitness—"

"Mae." Deborah sat on the edge of her desk and sighed. "I'm sure you're very good at all that, but what a waste of your talents. Take some classes in these other fields, at least. You need to keep on as a healer and intuitive. You *have* to."

"I'll take some classes like that, sure. I promise I'll get back to the work. I just don't know when."

"You'd better. You'll be in a great place to do it. Lots of alternative healing going on out there. Where are you going to be in New Mexico?"

"Truth or Consequences."

"Oh, that's the little spa town, isn't it? With the hot springs?"

Mae nodded, and Deborah asked, "How far is it from Santa Fe?"

"I'm not sure. Looks like a long way on the map."

Deborah rose and went behind her desk, reached into a drawer, and brought out a lavender gift bag. It matched the walls of her office. "This is a goodbye present, to thank you for all you've done here, and to wish you a great trip, and to inspire you as a healer when you get there. A little music made in New Mexico."

She brought Mae the bag. Mae set it on the edge of the desk, reached in, and took out two CDs. Each cover had a picture of rock art in bare, awe-inspiring red desert land—petroglyphs of a flute player. One also showed a rock with ancient handprints on it towering above the hunch-backed flutist. The musician's name: Jangarrai.

"It's healing music," Deborah said. "A lot of our massage therapists and yoga teachers like to use it. I think you'll like it."

"Thank you." Touched, Mae put the CDs back in the bag and hugged Deborah again. "You're sweet to do this. But you've treated me so well here, I don't need a gift."

"You might not think I'm so sweet in a minute. I hope you don't have to rush out."

Mae had so few things, packing was easy. Only her clothes and books. All the furniture was her roommate's. "No, I can stay."

Deborah perched on her desk again, and Mae took a seat in one of the pastel armchairs.

"I have a little ulterior motive with my gift. We used to sell a lot of Jangarrai's music here. Our buyer in the bookstore says she can't order any more. He's supposed to live in Santa Fe, but he's coming up blank when we try to get hold of him. Web site's down, phone number doesn't work, mailing address doesn't work. Google him and all you get is old stuff, nothing more recent than April, and here it is August. It's like he dropped off the face of the earth. No new recordings for a long time. I hope he hasn't quit the music business—or died. I thought maybe you could locate him while you're out there. Your first piece of psychic work out West."

"You know I need to hold something the person owned or touched a lot to get their energy."

"He wrote the music, isn't that enough?"

"Not really. I work with feelings that I pick up through my hands. Best way I can describe it is like being a bloodhound getting a scent, except I feel their energy in what they touched. A recording or a picture doesn't work."

"Don't tell me that's it? Dead end? I've tried everything else. Have you ever *tried* to find a musician through his music?"

"No. But people have brought me voicemail messages, and videos and pictures, to find people or learn about them, and it didn't work."

Deborah stared, as if she didn't believe Mae, and then frowned, tilting her head. "As good as you are? You really couldn't?"

"I'm serious. It doesn't work with recordings. Isn't there some ordinary-world way you can find him?"

"I contacted the record label. They dropped him, he hadn't had anything new for so long. They say they always dealt with his manager and she doesn't answer, like her phone number changed or something."

"Did you try her?"

"I tried to look her up. She must be unlisted, and her old number is gone. The web site he used to have was really unprofessional and homemade. No pictures, no art, no videos, no downloads, just a place to order CDs and find out his performance schedule in Santa Fe. I think she must have been his girlfriend. I found her on Facebook and she answered, 'I'm not dealing with his stuff anymore.' She won't friend people who are trying to contact him. And he doesn't have a profile. It's gone. Like maybe she did that for him, too."

"I guess I could just ask around if I get to Santa Fe. This is weird. You'd think he'd have to be performing somewhere. What does he look like?"

"I don't know. Both his albums have the Kokopelli on them, the petroglyph of the flute player. Which is cool and very New Mexico and goes with the cedar flutes and all that, but I have no idea what he looks like. I guess you don't do a YouTube video if you've quit the business."

Mae rose, collected her gift, and said, "Sorry I can't connect with him through this. But I'll do what I can to find him while I'm there, even if I can't do it as a psychic."

"Thank you. We'll keep in touch anyway, of course, but call me if you locate him. We want more of his music. Once you hear it, you'll understand. Somebody that good can't just quit and disappear."

Driving west in the morning, Mae listened at first to one of the romance audio books her roommate had given her as a going-away present for the trip. The story kept her alert wondering what would happen next, but she found it absurd and unbelievable. The characters fought so much. Broke up over and over. To Mae, couples' conflicts were not romantic. There was nothing sexy about not getting along. And then the story wrapped up with *marriage,* as if that was some kind of happy ending. Her second divorce wasn't final yet, and she knew for sure she was never getting married again. Her idea of a happy ending would be getting over the unhappy one.

When the book wore thin, Mae switched to radio, but country songs reminded her of her husband, Hubert, who loved country music, and the twin stepdaughters she had to leave behind with him. She was truly alone and on her own for the first time in her life. No husband to be responsible for or to. No roommate to talk to. No children to take care of—the most painful separation of all. The loss ripped through her.

She put in one of the new CDs from Deborah, hoping that the healing music would help.

The melody at first was carried by a flute, with a didgeridoo droning in the background. Drums then began a complex rhythm, and the flutes faded, the melody taken over by a tenor voice chanting isolated words that didn't form a coherent lyric, creating a mood of descent and grief followed by transcendent joy, as the singer soared though an extraordinary range, a powerful and evocative voice like pure light and deep darkness. The vocal faded into tones without words, and then disappeared with the drums to let the melody be taken over again by flutes, underscored with the deep pulsing drone of the didgeridoo. Amazing. A kind of journey. Mae remembered from the liner notes that Jangarrai wrote all the music, played all the instruments, and did all the vocals. What a mind he must have, what a heart.

A new song began, two flutes in harmony. It had the quality of a lullaby, sweet and tender, music that held you in its arms and made you feel safe. Then it shifted to melancholy, a new flute, solo, with a different timbre, in another key. Same song, but sad now, and still heartbreakingly sweet. When the song came back to the lullaby, its brief trip to a darker place made the warmth of its return all the more welcome, giving a sense of relief, not just comfort. With all the turmoil in Mae's life right now, this music seemed to touch the center of it, both the places that hurt and her own powers to heal. Freedom found its way into the wounds, and life renewed from the inside out.

Sometimes she listened to the romance novels for variety, but the only thing that felt reliably good on the whole drive was Jangarrai's music. It saved her from missing Hubert and her stepdaughters so badly that she wanted to pull over to the side of the road and cry. Even when the music was sad, the sadness cleansed her. When it was uplifting, her heart followed the singer's extraordinary clear voice upward, and she felt like she could fly, leaving the broken history of her life behind to reunite with her father. Deborah was right—someone who created music like this couldn't simply quit and disappear. Yet he had.

Chapter Two

Mae dropped her suitcase onto the huge, firm hotel bed and answered her phone. Caller ID showed it was her father.

"Hey, Daddy. How are you?"

"I'm good, real good." After fourteen years in New Mexico, he still sounded like he was from North Carolina's Blue Ridge, as did Mae after that many years in the slower-drawling east. "How's my baby girl?"

His twenty-seven-year-old baby smiled at the endearment. "Ready to be there already. I'm more than halfway."

"Think you could handle a little change of plans?" She heard him walking, heard a door open and close, and then the sound quality changed. He must have stepped outside. "Had a little rainstorm, got a double rainbow on the mountains." A few steps. "The sky sure is pretty here. You've never seen anything like it."

"I will soon. What kind of change?" He couldn't be letting her down, could he? She had only recently got back in touch with him. Her mother had made an unspeakable secret of the reason for the divorce that had cut Mae off from him for half her life, and it had turned out to be something Mae could easily accept—her father was gay. They had talked and e-mailed a lot since finding each other again, but she had only seen him the one time he came out to visit. She hadn't even met his partner yet. "I'm still okay for school aren't I?"

"Of course you are, baby. It's nothing that big. We need some help."

Relieved, she asked, "What can I help with?"

"Our Santa Fe house. We started renting it out when I got the job down here. Furnished, with a big studio, good for artists spending some time there. It's usually worked out well. But we had a lady in there the past few months that we're kicking out."

"What'd she do?"

"First I have to explain that the house comes with a cat, Sweet-iepie. We found her hanging around the garden, and when we tried to take her to move down here, she was so scared of the car we left her there for our tenant to love. It's worked out nice for years—makes the house special that she comes with it. So the lease says no dogs. She can't be harassed by some dog."

"Did this lady have a dog?"

"And she smoked. Niall smokes, but not in the house. It's says *no smoking* in the lease, too. Rental agent went over it with her, figured we had a good tenant, and we hadn't been up." His footsteps slowed. "Didn't know how bad it was 'til we got a call. Our tenant travels a lot, seems, and had somebody stop in to feed Pie. Least she took the dog with her." A long pause. "The mess from the dog sounds like it's pretty bad. The cat sitter said it made her sick. Dirty kitchen, too, she said—really bad."

"That's awful. But Daddy, you can't want me to ..."

"I hate to ask you this, but we've got someone who wants to take it for a few months, visiting artist from Montana, and this place—it's gonna take a week or more to get it clean. I'm running a softball camp for young'uns, and Niall's got a gallery opening here—we can't do it. It's three hours to Santa Fe from T or C." Truth or Consequences was usually shortened to T or C. "We can't keep going back and forth. The windows are gonna have to be left open a lot, and Pie's all shook up and needs some TLC, so we need someone we trust to live in it and get it clean."

Mae tried to make room for the work in her mind. She had a few weeks before college classes started, but had hoped to use the time to find a job and spend some time with Marty and Niall. "And that's me?"

"We'd pay you what we'd pay the cleaning service, and a little something for meals out while you're getting it cleaned. You proba-

bly won't be able to eat in it for a while. We don't want some cleaning service person staying the night. There's some valuable art in the
house. And Pie is special. She needs someone to take care of her."

"So I'd go straight there?"

"Not quite. I'm heading up tomorrow and I'll meet you there.
But you'll meet Niall in T or C first to get into your place there.
Don't unpack much. Just meet my partner finally, and head on up."

"My place?" She thought she'd be staying with him while she
looked for a place to rent.

"Our other rental property. Gotta warn you it's not fancy, but
the price is right, for family."

"So I get the key, but I don't move in yet ... I go up to Santa Fe
and clean."

"That a *no* or a *maybe*?"

"It's a *yes*. I'm sorry. I'm happy to help you out."

"That's wonderful. I'll tell Niall. He's been having a fit about it."
A pause, the sound of footsteps crunching on gravel, then silence.
"And he's a little nervous about meeting you without me there. Don't
mind him. You'll love him when you get to know him."

*****

Descending from the desert mountains toward the long blue-green
curves of the Rio Grande, Mae drove to the center of the small city
and followed her father's directions to her new home. The house was
pea green, a former trailer in ranch-house drag, up the street from a
pastel purple house, in a mixed neighborhood of elegant adobes and
run-down trailers a few blocks from the river. Seeing a green VW
Beetle in the carport, Mae parked on the street. A large, hairy-barked
tree guarded the driveway, and another loomed over the tiny front
porch. Bizarre curly pods like a cross between rotini pasta and some
sort of larvae rained down from the trees, and the ground beneath
them was also littered with their thorns, one of which stuck through

the sole of Mae's flip-flop and poked her foot as she walked to the house. She leaned on the railing while extricating the thorn.

From a glaring corrugated metal outbuilding beyond the carport came a pale man who took skinny to its final destination. He had dark hair threaded with gray, wore thick-lensed glasses, and his posture curved into a kind of vigilant, head-forward slouch that made him look like a bird of prey poised for flight. Mae could see he must have been handsome when he was younger, before years of tobacco and dry air took the shine off him.

"Hey." She smiled and walked toward him. "I'm Mae. It's good to meet you."

Niall, hands in the pockets of old, baggy jeans, nodded, passing her on his way to the house. No handshake, not even a word. Nervous? More like rude. She stopped, another thorn piercing her shoe, and sat on the front steps to pull it out.

"What kind of crazy tree is that?"

"Mesquite." Niall patted the shaggy bark, and a largish brown lizard scrambled down the tree. "Thorns are bad. You might not wear those shoes. And you can't wear shoes in this house, I just redid the floors." He sounded as if she should be impressed and grateful. "*Bamboo.*"

Mae didn't know how to take Niall. He was from Maine, and maybe people up North were rude like that. Marty's sunny temperament had to explain how they had stayed together fourteen years.

"The last tenants were pigs. Hope it's not that bad in Santa Fe." Niall unlocked the front door after forcing the glass storm door to open—it seemed to stick a little. "I hope you're a good housekeeper."

"I am." Mae and Niall shed their shoes on a mat inside the door. The bamboo floors were silky and gleaming, in a room decorated with pointy-legged fifties furniture and a few of what Mae guessed were Niall's sculptures, masks and animals made from rusty recycled machine scraps, broken tools, and old horseshoes.

"It's wonderful," Mae said. "I'm gonna live with some of your work?"

"For now. Might sell it, though—the art, not the house. You've got the house 'til you graduate."

"Thank you." She felt relief, not only that she had somewhere to live, but that it came fully furnished with Niall's odd taste, making it so unlike her past home there wasn't a memory to haunt her. "What else should I know about it, besides not wearing shoes?"

Niall walked into the slate-floored kitchen, which featured a yellow fifties dinette set. "Don't lift the west side curtains 'til October. Floor gets so hot it hurts your feet. You got all your dishes." He opened and closed a few cabinets, showing her what was in them. "There's cleaning equipment in here and in the shed. No dishwasher." *Dishwashah.* "Your washing machine's in the shed, and it shakes like a son of a bitch, but so far it hasn't walked out the door. Clothes line—no dryer. Your clothes dry in a couple of hours, even three layers thick." He looked her over. "And you'll need long sleeves, a hat, and SPF 50 to hang 'em out, or you'll look like that lizard."

Was he being funny? Mae tried to take it as advice with humor, not making fun of how white she was, and thanked him.

Niall continued the tour, identifying rooms with a few unnecessary words. "Guest room." It had a flabby-looking futon. "Bath." It was tiny. "Bedroom." It had more fifties furniture, and a queen bed. Mae felt it. The mattress was firm.

Niall grinned. His first smile. "Planning something?"

"Sleep."

"So you say." He gave her a mischievous wink. "There are more men than women in New Mexico. And it's not because we're all gay." He opened the door beside the bed and took her out to the back steps. Shoeless, they didn't go down into the yard. The light was blinding after the darkness induced by thermal curtains in the interior. "Same key for both doors, and the hot spring is out here."

"I have a hot spring?"

"Yeah. You won't want the spring much at this hour, but it's nice at night. Get out under the stars in your birthday suit and soak."

Mae studied the back yard's tall red fence. There were gaps. "I think I'll wear a suit."

"You'll loosen up after a while. Meet some of the locals. Just keep the parties quiet. Those kids across the fence," he indicated where the red fence met with a stretch of corrugated aluminum, with improbably tall, small-headed sunflowers peering over it, "are like monks."

This was good news. "I don't give parties."

"You will. Your father was stiff like that, too, when we first moved here."

"I'm not stiff. I just don't party and fool around, that's all."

"Stiff. You need a good soak in the spring." Niall explained the switch and pump that would let the water from the deep spring emerge into a big metal tub in the yard. He gave her a crooked smile. "You'll get hooked on it. Be soaking with a glass of wine and a new boyfriend before you know it."

The yard was pale brown dirt spotted with odd small flowers and a few cacti near the shed. Ants ran across the red paving stones that led from the bedroom to the spring. A lizard scurried from one piece of shade to another. Mae felt a strange affinity for this plain, dry little space.

This was her home now. All alone, her own place, as much private personal space as she'd ever had in her life. A place where she would live by herself for years, happily solitary except for visits from her stepdaughters. She longed to be alone in it tonight, as excited as if she were the new bride in a romance novel moving in with her husband—moving in with herself. "No, no boyfriend needed. I'm psyched to be here all by myself."

They stepped back inside, and Niall locked the back door. "We've still never talked about the rent," Mae said as they walked toward the front.

Niall stopped and placed the keys into her hand. "Free."

"You don't have to do that. I'll get work, I can pay—"

"Free. Your mother wouldn't even take child support when she found out Marty was gay. Nothing. Wouldn't let you know where he was. He never got a chance, from when you were thirteen until now, to do a damn thing for you, and he wanted to. This is from us, from both of us." Niall walked down the hall to the front door and stopped, one hand on the handle. "But don't you frickin' dare think of me as your other father."

Mae couldn't help it—she hugged him. "Thank you, *Papa Niall*."

Niall pulled away with a growl that might have been a laugh. "Let me show you where all the tools are, in case you need to fix something. Then you'd better head for Santa Fe."

Santa Fe. She'd fallen in love with her new house, and she had to go clean another one.

"I'm supposed to take you to lunch." Niall locked the house, but not the shed. He pulled cigarettes and a lighter from his shirt pocket and lit up. "And being a Martin I suppose you want to walk."

"If it's not too far for you."

"Think I'm an old man? Just because I breathe poisons and don't exercise? Three blocks." Niall started down the driveway and Mae followed. She restrained the swinging, vigorous stride that she normally took. Niall walked at a snail's pace, smoking. It was hard to picture her athletic father with him. "I heard some things about you," Niall said. "You might get a kick out of this place."

"Why's that?

"The food's healthy, and the owner's psychic." He spat out a crumb of tobacco. "Or some of the fools that come to New Mexico as spiritual tourists think so."

Was Niall a skeptic about psychics and spirituality? "Daddy told you I'm—What'd he say?"

"That 'health nut' runs in his side of the family and psychic runs in your mother's." Niall gestured at a mauve-walled spa across the street. "This town is perfect for you on both counts. Santa Fe, too. T or C was a healing center way back when it was Apache lands, with all the hot springs. Still is. Good healers, and quacks, and plenty of suckers for both."

"You don't think I'm a quack, do you?"

"No idea. Just met you. But I think Muffie Blanchette is. Can't stand the woman." They paused at the main thoroughfare, Broadway. Approaching drivers stopped for them and waved. Niall waved back, and he and Mae crossed. "But the food is good, and I normally hate anything healthy or vegetarian. I have to give her credit on the décor, too. I can enjoy the place as long as she doesn't come around with her hocus-pocus. The one time Marty and I ate here, she kept her distance from us, but I could hear her yammering at the other people. Eat this, don't eat that, your aura needs this, your soul needs that. Bullshit."

The exterior of the building they approached was stucco, painted a startling pink, and with the inner recesses of the deep windows painted turquoise except for one, which was a dull gray. The door, all three colors, opened into a room like a restaurant in a 1940s movie, with dark wooden chairs, white tablecloths, and candles on each table. Off from this main dining area, a smaller room had curtained nooks, low tables, and cushions, some set up like bunk beds so the privacy of the diners was enhanced by the cushions' elevation. Another room off to the side had small round tables of crayon-bright colors and art from 19th-century children's books, as well as large papier-mâché sculptures of brightly striped tigers and zebras and a freakishly glowing blue donkey.

"Look at this." Niall tapped a sign that stood in a metal frame on a stand near the hostess's station.

Notice to Patrons: Bryan Barnes, a senior in Art and Theater at College of the Rio Grande, is filming his senior project here at Dada Café, a documentary on the restaurant as the theater of life. If you would prefer not to be part of the film please let your host or hostess know. If you are willing to be in it, please sign the consent form. Thank you for being a patron of the arts as well as of Dada Café.

The smiling henna-haired young hostess lisped around her gold tongue-stud as she offered a clipboard to Mae. "Will you be signing the release?"

"I don't know if I'm a patron of the arts or not, but I reckon I don't mind if somebody takes my picture." Mae signed the form. Niall signed as well, grumbling, and they followed the hostess through the elegant room and into the bright one, where she seated them close to the donkey.

"Bryan will be your server. And Muffie will be around to read your aura and make some suggestions."

Mae asked, "Bryan, the guy that's doing the film, is our waiter?"

"Yes. He got the idea from working here. I don't know if you know what Dada is." Niall started to speak, but the hostess went on. "It was an art movement based on startling you with nonsense, breaking up your preconceptions. Part of Dada in theater was the idea that the audience is as much a part of the show as the actors." She deposited two menus on the striped-and-dotted table. "But we don't serve Dada food, like fried roses or onion ice cream. Enjoy."

As the hostess left, a broad-hipped, large-busted, middle-aged woman strode in from the other room. She wore a tunic-style blouse with flowing sleeves and matching wide-legged pants in an extraordinary fabric, a walking work of art featuring sunsets against deep blue.

Her thick blonde hair swung in a crisp pageboy, her eyes were skill-fully made up behind wire-rimmed glasses, and her full lips, framed with a web of tiny lines, wore pink lipstick matching a shade in her sunset clothing.

"Here she goes," Niall muttered. "That's Muffie."

The blonde woman stopped at the nearest table, regarded the pa-trons seated there, and then placed her hands on the couple's heads and closed her eyes. "Less brown. More yellow." *Less brown what? More yellow ... vegetables?* Mae was confused, but the recipients of the reading didn't seem to be. Muffie intoned, "There's a residue ... the memories of chickens ..." Her voice had a raspy quality, pitched sur-prisingly low. She withdrew her hands. "Am I right?"

"Maybe," the man said, looking at his companion, who twisted her mouth and frowned. "Yeah, maybe."

Muffie looked at their menus, pointed out certain items, and nodded seriously. "*Do not* eat okra and cheese together. It will make a toxic sludge in your intestines that will clog your lower chakras. Take some lemon juice in the morning and filter it first. Remember, I'm always right." She moved on to Mae's table.

"Welcome, welcome." She homed in on Mae, and Niall rose, qui-etly announcing his intention to go have a *bee-ah* at the *bah*. Muffie ignored him, hovering over Mae. "First time here?"

Mae wished the psychic act she'd witnessed was Dada, but based on what Niall had said, it was meant to be taken as real. Muffie *looked* like she was acting, though. Close up, Mae could see that Muffie's face was smoothed to a flawless finish by foundation. Her elaborate eye make-up matched the blue of her outfit, and her cheeks, like her lips, echoed the rosy colors in her clothes. The effect was striking but unexpectedly artificial in someone whose restaurant emphasized healthy and natural. "Yes ma'am."

"I'm Muffie." The well-dressed woman took one of the empty chairs at the small table, reached over and grasped Mae's hand, and then paused in mid-handshake, frowning. She shook her head slowly and dramatically.

Puzzled, Mae asked, "Excuse me?"

Muffie held up her other hand, commanding silence, and closed her eyes. Her breath became loud and slow, her frown more pronounced. "Your circulation ... there's a blockage ..." She groped up Mae's forearm and gripped it, like a lobster claw's pinch. "There is canola oil in your system. Do you get pain here?"

"Only where you're grabbing my arm."

Muffie's eyes flew open. She let go. "That's the toxins."

"Ma'am, that canola oil scare was like an urban legend on the net, it's not—"

"I am always right." Muffie stood and walked behind Mae, holding a hand over her head. Mae didn't know whether she wanted to laugh or argue. Muffie hissed, "Shh."

Mae massaged her arm, waiting for the next pronouncement.

"Your aura," Muffie said, "is dirty." She pressed the hovering hand down onto Mae's head. "Your entire field needs cleansing. I recommend the spinach and squash soup. And you should get some sun. Let its vibrations and energy heal your light."

"The soup sounds good," Mae said. Muffie returned to the seat beside her. Curious how bad the advice would be, Mae asked, "But the sun ... Will my aura get cleansed if I wear sunscreen?"

"No, no, it blocks your pores, you need to dance under the sun, be one with it, bathe in light. Shake off your dirt in it. This is important. Along with the inner cleansing."

"Of my blockages."

Muffie nodded. "Your health is not good."

"I'm sorry to hear that. I've been feeling pretty darned excellent."

Enough was enough. This woman should not be getting away with this nonsense. Reaching a firm, well-muscled arm around to the back of the chair where she had hung her purse, Mae pulled out her business card case and opened it. She took out two cards and handed them to Muffie.

She watched the restaurateur go still and expressionless as she read. The first card said:

Mae Martin-Ridley
American Council on Exercise Certified Personal Trainer
and Group Fitness Instructor

Muffie sighed irritably. "Health does not come in the form of fitness." She regarded Mae as if she were a sad, benighted soul. "You exist at another level you can't see."

"But I *can* see it. The other card is me, too."

Muffie slid the first one behind the other, the one with deep green script on pale green stock, and images of trees bending over the words.

Breda Outlaw
Psychic, Energy Healer, Medical Intuitive
Healing Balance Center
Virginia Beach, VA

"Are you challenging me?" Muffie's eyes seemed to bulge. "Because if you are, you don't have to eat here. I'm always right."

"Bless your heart." Mae smiled. "I'm sure you think you are."

Muffie slapped the cards on the table, inhaled sharply, and marched back out to the main dining room. The other diners in the room looked at Mae, some with stifled laughter, others with disapproving frowns.

"About time someone took her on," Niall said with approval as he returned to the table, beer in hand.

An unusually tall, thin young man with light brown dreadlocks gathered into a ponytail of hair sausages arrived with a camera. "Hi. I'm Bryan. May I?" He aimed the camera at Mae's cards on the table. "I caught the rest on the camera that watches your table." He nodded toward a camera, one of several arrayed along the angle of the wall and ceiling. "But I need the close-up."

"Who's gonna see the film?"

"I'm entering it in a film competition in Santa Fe. But probably only the judges and my advisor, and maybe a showing on campus if my advisor likes it. Why?"

"My boss at Healing Balance liked us to have these working names, not our real names. I don't necessarily want anyone who does a web search for me as a personal trainer finding out I'm also this healer-psychic person. Not everyone respects that kind of work. I kind of like the two names being separate for the most part. Put them together on this film and it doesn't do so well for me."

"Sure it does, if you're good at both jobs. This is free advertising."

"You're in T or C now," Niall said. "Weird is normal."

As if Niall's comment meant Mae's permission, Bryan zoomed in on the cards, got his shot, and then let the camera hang from a strap across his body. "Can I get you anything to drink?"

"I want to see that scene before you show it on campus, if it gets that far. I'm gonna be a student at Rio Grande. I don't want to start out looking like a wacko. On the release form, look for Mae Martin-Ridley, that one's my legal name." Ridley was coming off soon. She had to get used to that. Bryan clasped his hands and bowed formally, nodding. "I'd like iced tea," Mae said. "Sweet."

"We never add sugar, but," he over-acted a conspiratorial whisper, "I'll bring you a ton of it."

"You sound like you're not into Muffie's advice."

"Muffie." Bryan almost giggled. He resumed his whisper. "She told me to detox with seaweed and," he looked to ceiling as if the other substance was inscribed there, "I think it was some herb, dandelion, maybe." Leaning on the table he spoke even more softly, "So I went out and partied hard, totally toxified myself," he winked, "and she said my aura was a hundred percent brighter."

"Does she know you think this?"

"I'm an actor. *You* have no idea if I think this." He straightened up and strode off, returning shortly with her drink, along with a sugar bowl that had feet clad in little pottery Mary Jane shoes, and a spoon with a Humpty-Dumpty figure on the handle. "Enjoy." He departed again. Mae wondered if he had a microphone picking up his own whispers.

"Good work," Niall said. "I'm glad you got rid of her. Maybe you can work somewhere here as a real psychic and shut her up for good."

"I hadn't planned on it." Mae put the cards back in her purse. She could still use the personal training cards, but she needed to drop Breda in the recycling bin, though Deborah would be disappointed. "I probably won't be doing that kind of work much while I'm going to school. It takes too much out of me."

Bryan glided up, notepad and pencil poised, and tilted his head expectantly. "Shall I recite the specials?"

They agreed that he should, and he went to great length to describe the virtues of each dish, its freshness, its freedom from animal cruelty, and Muffie's recommendation for the type of person who might benefit from it. Mae tried not to laugh at Niall's irritated expression.

As soon as they had placed their orders and Bryan left, Niall said, "The person who might benefit from those specials is her. People don't even look at the price when they hear it'll cure their stress or their *toxicity*. A lot of health nuts are suckers, and the spiritual tourists are worse."

"What do you mean by spiritual tourists? The place I used to work had a New Age bookstore and psychic readings, and sometimes the beach tourists would come see us."

"Not like that kind of tourist—more like coming here especially to have a New Age experience. You see even more of that in Santa

Fe. Christ, some people can't sort the wheat from the chaff. Can't tell shit from Shinola."

When Bryan delivered their meals, serving from a tray balanced on his shoulder, he said to Mae, "When you're done, would you please stop by the office? Roseanne Porter, the manager, wants to see you."

"About making Muffie mad?"

"More than that. Muffie *left*."

Chapter Three

"Best thing that could happen would be if she's gone for good," Niall said. "Don't waste time on her. Your father's expecting you in Santa Fe."

"I'll try to make it quick."

At the end of their meal Niall paid, brushing off Mae's thanks, and left to get ready for his upcoming gallery opening. Mae followed Bryan to the restaurant's office, a small room that contrasted with the décor of the rest of the place. She'd found that even the ladies' room was Dada, with a pink-and-yellow polka dot floor and zebra-striped walls, but the office was bland and white walled, furnished with an old metal desk and metal folding chairs, and a desktop computer. An elfin-faced, petite woman with short black hair looked up, her hands pausing on the keyboard.

"Rose, this is the psychic," Bryan said. "Or so her card says. You want the cartridge from the hall camera?"

"No, thanks. Get back on the floor. Your customers come first."

"You're so bossy, boss."

Her cat-like eyes flashed, and she leaned forward as if to scold, but Bryan left before she could. To Mae, Roseanne said, "Have a seat." She smiled. "I hear you really pissed off Muffie."

Relieved at the smile, Mae sat in one of the metal chairs. "Seems so. I had no idea she'd be so wacky. I thought she'd be a little on the fringe, but not that bad."

"Oh, it gets worse. I mean, she's had people change what clothes they wear so the colors fit their auras, change their cologne, shave their heads, all sorts of stuff to *tune their vibration*." Roseanne leaned back and dropped her small hands heavily on the desk. "And people love it. Even the ones that think she's a quack come to hear this crap for entertainment."

"I'm sorry I made her so mad, then. Am I the first? That's hard to believe."

"A few people leave if they don't like her. You're the first person who's claimed to be qualified to challenge her. I was wondering if you're a real psychic."

"I am."

"How do you work?"

"My granma was a folk healer in the Blue Ridge, used to lay hands on people and heal them. I take after some of her gifts. Usually I use crystals to help me. I don't see the future, I can only see where people are or lost pets—I'm good with them. And I can see inside folks' bodies when they're sick, or see the past to find how a problem got started. I don't always know what it is I'm seeing, but I can describe it. I do some energy healing, too. It's all related."

"So, I could have you check on a diagnosis Muffie gave me."

"Yeah, if you really wanted me to. I'm pretty sure it's all a load of bull."

"I think so, too. So that wouldn't work. You wouldn't find anything. I was looking for a way you could prove you're psychic."

"If I hold something that belonged to the person, I can see them. Answer some questions about them."

Roseanne looked around the bare office. "Everything in here is mine." She finally handed Mae a plate with a half-eaten muffin on it. "Tell me about the cook. Who made this?"

This had to be the strangest object she'd ever used for a psychic search. Mae held the remains of the muffin and closed her eyes. It was hard to concentrate. Voices and clanging and clattering from the kitchen intruded, and she could feel Roseanne's impatience. Breaking off the effort, Mae reached into her purse for the pouch of crystals she carried, took out a clear quartz point, and tried again. She sensed Roseanne fidgeting, but did her best to tune her out, focusing on quieting her own energy and tuning in through the crystal as well as receiving what came from the food in her hand. She set a goal, to find the person who made it, not the one who ate half of it.

Gradually the tunnel that told her she was entering a vision opened and carried her to a large, bright kitchen with stainless steel counters. A slender young man, his fair hair in a ponytail tucked back up under a chef's hat, measured flour into a mixing bowl, looking at a recipe, and then glancing at the woman who worked beside him, also in a chef's hat. She wore dark-rimmed glasses, and was as pink and round as he was wiry and pale.

Mae let go of the vision, and described the chef and the baker-in-training.

"And you've never met Nancy? Or Frank?"

"No. I just moved here about an hour ago."

"I guess that'll do. I wish I had something totally outside of this place for you to check on, though, something more unpredictable. Can you see what Nancy's doing right now?"

"I'd rather not. What if I end up seeing her in the bathroom or something? I don't like dropping in on people that way just to prove something. It's not fair for their privacy that I could just look at 'em. There has to be a good reason."

"Fine." Roseanne sounded exasperated. "You're ethical. I guess that's okay." She tapped her hands rapidly on the desk. "See, I want to investigate Muffie." She glanced into the hallway, walked to the door and closed it. "I don't want Bryan's camera getting this."

Mae waited. She didn't like Roseanne's attitude, but the idea of debunking Muffie appealed to her. Bryan was getting a lot of people on film who were being made into fools when they thought they were being serious and spiritual. Roseanne's request might be worth listening to.

"See, after she tried to read your aura and you said whatever you did, she came back in here and got her purse out of the desk and then she stopped in the doorway and took this kind of pose, nose in the air, like she's some diva in a bad opera, and she says, 'I have been dis-respected. Disregarded. Dismissed.' I wanted to laugh but I couldn't. You have no idea how often I have to do that. This job—God." Roseanne let out a groan, wrinkling her nose and hiking her shoulders. "Anyway, she says," she imitated Muffie's dramatic, deep voice and grand posturing, " 'This was my sign. It is time to ascend.' I could swear she was even getting right in front of the hallway camera to makes sure Bryan got it in his documentary—and then she leaves."

"Is that normal?"

"Wrong word with Muffie, *normal*." Roseanne returned to her desk and sat down again. "But for her it's not typical. She never *ever* leaves in the middle of the day. It had to be because of what you did. See, she's got these claims that she's always right, that she never gets sick, and that she can see what people need for their health by touching them. And that she can *ascend*. All thanks to Sri Rama Kriya." After typing something on her keyboard, Roseanne rotated her computer's monitor to face Mae. "This web site is Muffie's tribute to her guru."

The screen showed a garden with tall sage and lavender plants growing in it, against a background of pinkish dirt and pink-beige adobe walls. Text describing the wonders of the Ascended Bliss Center for Enlightenment and the teachings of Sri Rama Kriya struck Mae as vague babble, but the explanation of ascension got her attention:

Sri Rama Kriya teaches us how to choose our time and leave our bodies without pain or death, how to channel our spirits directly to the upper realms of energy and light. When you study Ascended Bliss, you are freed from the cycle of karma and rebirth, and from your body.

"This sounds like it's really mystical and spiritual, but then I tick her off and she's gonna leave her body? Sounds like she's taking her toys and going home. "

"I kind of hope she does, frankly. She's been driving me crazy for almost a year. I mean, I don't exactly want her to kill herself, but," Roseanne sped up, "this is a great place, or it would be if it didn't have her. The old Dada playbills at the bar are these amazing antiques, the whole concept is brilliant, and the business is thriving. T or C needs a good restaurant like this, and I want to run this place without her."

"Couldn't you try to buy it from her? I don't get why you need me."

"She doesn't answer her phone."

"It's been less than an hour."

"I know you think I'm jumping the gun. But she's usually glued to this place and to her phone when she leaves. After that speech about ascending, I think she's going to disappear. I don't think she'd claim that and then come back." Roseanne dumped the half-eaten muffin into her trash can. "If she doesn't come back, would you check her out for me?"

"If she doesn't come back, wouldn't you call the police and report her missing?"

Roseanne shook her head. "She could go to Santa Fe to study with her guru. She does that a lot."

"And she answers her phone then, right?"

"Of course. She's a control freak. She calls all the time when she's there and she answers her phone before it rings twice."

Mae slipped the quartz point into her jeans pocket, to remind herself to clean it before using it again. "I'm gonna be in Santa Fe myself. If I run into her, I'll let you know, but I don't see any psychic work you need done. Sounds like she's just sulking."

"Maybe. But ..." Roseanne hesitated, and then spoke softly. "I think a real psychic would be the one to find out if she—okay, I'm embarrassed to ask—if she really could ascend. Don't laugh. I don't know anything about yoga and meditation and all that stuff, but Frank and his roommate Kenny are really into it, and they believe her. They say there are yogis who can stop their hearts, and melt snow naked in the Himalayas, and levitate, and they really believe she could leave her body like that. They read all of Sri Rama Kriya's books."

Mae considered the possibility. She didn't know much about Eastern mysticism either. She had a book on meditation, but she had only read part of it. So far, skipping the whole death process hadn't come up. That didn't mean someone couldn't do it, though. Her own powers were considered impossible by a lot of people. Who was she to dismiss the strange and unlikely? Except, Muffie seemed like such a quack. That special powers could be *hers* was harder to believe than that such powers were possible. "So, you think that if you don't hear from her and she's not at her guru's place, that maybe she really ascended?"

"Maybe." Roseanne squirmed. "You could check it out, right?"

"I don't know. I reckon if I saw her in heaven or something—" Mae regretted her joke immediately as Roseanne's jaw tightened and her eyes grew bright and hard. It had been difficult for her to admit she had a shadow of belief in the ascension, and Mae had made fun of it. "Sorry. If she didn't have her body, I wouldn't see her. So far I've never picked up any energy or imagery from things that belong to dead people. If she left her body, I guess that'd be like being dead."

"So if you saw her at all, it would mean she didn't ascend, right?"

"That's my best guess."

"That's all I need. It'd save me looking like an idiot to the police, too. Missing woman just meditating." Roseanne shuffled through some restaurant business magazines on the desk, pulled out a catalog, and handed it to Mae. "This is Muffie's. This is where she gets all her clothes. She sits here and leafs through it and drives me up the wall spouting about the authentic style and the spiritual energy. The stuff costs a fortune, which doesn't seem too spiritual to me. She even tells people they need this for spiritual alignment, because of the organic cotton and bamboo, and the *vibration* of the art and colors."

Sanchez and Smyth, Fine Western Wear and Art Clothing. The first page of the glossy brochure showed some extraordinary cowboy boots in leather patchwork with imagery of cacti and mountains. They were priced at two thousand dollars. The following pages displayed belts, hats, dresses, pants, and silk-screened T-shirts with unique art on them, including the outfit Muffie had worn today. Every item cost more than Mae's entire clothing budget for a year. "She must be rich."

"Rich and crazy. Both of which mean she could take off at any time." Roseanne looked into Mae's eyes. "Take the catalog. So you can pick up her trail. And give me your card. She's up to something weird, and I want to know what it is. What if she's going to close the restaurant? Donate it to her guru in her will when she ascends? What happens to us? We love this place, everyone that works here."

"I can't help you with that. I told you I can't see the future. Just the past and the present. All psychics are different."

"Most of them are fakes." Roseanne turned the monitor back to face her way and studied the Ascended Bliss web site. "That guru might be fake, too. But what if he isn't? Take the catalog. If Muffie doesn't show up or call, I might need you. I know it seems crazy, but I think she was staging an exit."

Mae took another business card from her purse. They had the same cell phone number on them, and the same e-mail address. "I'm sure you understand you have to pay if I work for you."

"No problem. Psychic services are well within the scope of how Dada Café can spend some of its money."

On her way out, Mae stopped to look at the antique posters Roseanne had mentioned. The bar had dark wood and tall stools, and bottles lined up in front of mirrors. Between the mirrors hung framed yellowed playbills, some in French, some in English. The

plays had names Mae didn't recognize. *The Bald Soprano. Ubu Roi.*
"Can I help you?" asked the bartender.

"No, just looking at the playbills. I'm on my way out."

"You should look at the mirrors, too," the man said, as he poured
a shot of liquor into a glass. Mae moved a few steps over to follow his
suggestion. A fun-house type mirror stretched her reflected face into
absurd proportions. The bartender grinned. "Helps the audience remember they're part of the play."

At home, Mae pulled her car into the carport and opened the trunk.
She was eager to get to Santa Fe now, to see Marty and help him and
Niall with their rental house. Since they were giving her free use of
the T or C house, gratitude and love drove her to hurry. The only
things she wanted to unload before she left were her books and a box
of winter clothes. Removing the extra weight would make her car use
less gas, and she might need room in the trunk for something.

Watching the ground for mesquite thorns as she carried the first
box toward the house, she didn't see the owner of a cheerful male
voice that greeted her.

"Hi. You're our new neighbor."

She looked up to see a young man who looked to be in his late
teens, maybe twenty at most, around five foot five, stocky and mus-
cular, with short curly brown hair and multiple piercings and tattoos,
walking barefoot down the thorn-strewn driveway. He held out his
hand. "I'm Kenny. Frank and I live across the fence behind you. You
must be North and South's daughter."

"N—oh, Niall and Marty." The couple's nickname made her
smile. It described not only their accents but their personalities. Opposite poles. "Yeah. Marty's my daddy."

"He's a cool dude. Can I help with your boxes?" Kenny lifted a
box from the open trunk and followed Mae to the porch. "I helped

Niall do the new floors. He told me you were moving in." Kenny had no shoes to discard, and Mae wondered what Niall would think about those dirty bare feet on his perfect new floor. As if he knew, Kenny set the box down without stepping inside. "You probably haven't been shopping yet. Can I get you a cold drink over at our place? I'm about to do a green drink. Just blended some this morning. If you're new to the desert, you need some good things to drink. Get you adjusted."

Mae looked at the clock and at Kenny, and wondered if she should go. Niall trusted him, so she could. Did she have time? He was her back-door neighbor, and being so kind. "Thanks. I've only got a few minutes, though."

Kenny helped her with the other two boxes. Since the fence had no back gate, they walked around the block to a tiny white house with red trim, a house so small and unsteady-looking it was hard to picture anyone occupying it. To her surprise, the interior didn't look like a typical teenage male home. The shoebox of a room had only pillows, no chairs, no television, and several full bookshelves. In one corner stood a homemade altar, draped in bright orange cloth and decorated with a photo of a smiling, bald Indian man in a cheap metal frame, tiny figurines of Hindu gods, candles, and geode stones, their tiny cave mouths glittering with teeth of crystals. Tightly rolled yoga mats leaned against the wall, and a small table held a CD player, speakers, and an MP3 player.

"Y'all must be really into yoga and meditation. This looks more like a yoga studio than a living room."

"Thanks. It is, for us. We take classes too, but this is for our practice." Kenny led her into a spotless but aged kitchen with avocado green appliances and a cracked linoleum floor that shone as if the tenants regularly washed and waxed the ugly old surface. A window air conditioner roared, making the kitchen cool, while the yoga room was around eighty degrees. "Our rooms are so small we almost have to walk on the beds to get to the dressers," Kenny said, "so there's no place to put down your mat."

He opened the refrigerator, took out a glass pitcher, and poured a thick glob of green juice into a glass. Even from a few feet away it smelled like grass and garlic. "Want some? This is the wheat grass cleanse Muffie suggested I try this week."

"I don't think I need cleansing, thanks." The fact that Kenny took Muffie's bizarre nutritional advice surprised her. "I'd think that someone who's into yoga the way you are would hardly need it either."

Kenny took a hit of the green, made a face, and paused before drinking more of it. He took a bottle of carrot-orange juice out and poured Mae a glass, which she accepted gladly. She had been thirsty since arriving. "It's the toxins in everything else," he explained. "And from back when I wasn't so clean."

Sipping her juice, Mae thanked him and sat at the table. "Toxins?"

"Yeah, like from the water and the air, and everything I used to do. Even from your food being in plastic wrappers, did you know that? Muffie can read your toxic burden just by looking at you or touching you."

As a psychic, Mae tried not to look at anything uninvited, so she wasn't going to read Kenny for the supposed toxins unless he asked. Still, she doubted he had them. He looked incredibly fit. "I just had lunch at Dada Café. Muffie told me some things I found kind of ..." How should she say it without offending Kenny? "Hard to believe."

Kenny nodded, seeming to take this as confirmation, not argument. "I know. She's incredible, what she can see." He finished the drink, shook his head with a shuddering vocalization, rinsed the glass, and put the pitcher of pond scum back in the refrigerator. He joined Mae at the table. "Do you have a job here yet? I know your father said you're here to go to college, but if you need a job I can talk to Muffie. Frank and I both work for her, and she's really changed our lives."

Made you drink nasty slime. "That's sweet of you, but—" Mae resisted the urge to say what she really thought, and found a way to refuse and still be honest. "I'm looking for something else, teaching exercise classes or doing some personal training. And I'm leaving for Santa Fe in a few minutes, so I'll have to look for work when I get back in a week or so."

"Cool." Kenny beamed. "Santa Fe."

"I'm not so sure. I'll be cleaning a rental house."

"But it's a very spiritual place. Really high spiritual energy there. You could look up Sri Rama Kriya, Muffie's guru, there. She goes there to study with him a lot."

Mae knew she wouldn't go to this Ascended Bliss place, but didn't want to openly refuse. After all, Kenny came across as happy, and his beliefs seemed to work for him. "I'll see if I have time."

He went back into the meditation room and came back with a small glossy paperback book. "I mean, you don't have to. But if you get a chance and you're interested ..."

Mae finished the juice and looked at the book Kenny laid on the table. *The Chakra Meditations.* "I started learning about the chakras to help with my energy healing work," she said.

"You do healing? You would really love Muffie, then. You have to talk with her. She's into everything like that." Kenny sat next to Mae again and opened the book. "Muffie gave it to me when she first hired me."

The fact that Muffie had given him a gift seemed out of character. To Mae, the woman had appeared self-centered and insensitive. "That's pretty nice, for a new hire to get a present."

"I needed it." Kenny leafed through the pages. "She took a whole hour after my interview just to listen to me. I was only a few weeks out of detox, and I'd been living on the streets in Silver City, and in shelters. I was a wreck. I wanted to work at Dada because people said it was spiritual, and I wanted to stay clean."

"I'm impressed." She meant it, but was also slightly embarrassed at how much he'd told her. Kenny struck her as an excessively trusting soul. It made her like him, though. "You've really built a healthy life now."

"I don't take credit. But thanks. NA—Narcotics Anonymous—talks a lot about spirituality. I'm not a church guy, so when I met Frank at an NA meeting and he talked about Muffie and this place and her guru, it kind of spoke to me. Sorry, I just broke Frank's anonymity. I don't think he'd mind, though. We really owe a lot to Muffie for helping us get on a good path."

Mae felt guilty for provoking Muffie, now. "Have you seen her today?"

"No. Frank called and said she left during lunch and didn't come back. I work tonight—I wash dishes. I hope I see her. She always has these uplifting meetings for us before each shift. It's weird that she left. She never takes a day off. Frank said Roseanne said Muffie was going to ascend. I know she can ... but ... God, I hope not. Not yet. I'd miss her."

"She wouldn't leave you like that, if she cares that much." Hoping what she'd said was true, Mae took the book and began to look through it, expecting the wisdom that had helped Kenny with his recovery. Instead, it puzzled her. "It's mostly pictures."

"I know. The art was all I could handle. I was too rattled to read much back then. With this, I could meditate without a lot of ideas getting in the way."

Mae felt as if she'd walked into a theater where she expected to find a comedy playing, and found a drama instead. Muffie was more than a ridiculous fake. Was she spiritual after all? "She was really good to you, then."

"Saved my life. Can you imagine hiring a homeless recovering addict? She took a chance on me and took time with me." He reached over to the book and opened it to one of the first pages. "She gave me these simple instructions that worked. To spend the first week with just this page. The root chakra. "

Mae read: "*Muladhara chakra*. Root support." The words formed an arc over a picture of a red wheel, like an old wagon wheel, filled with subtle line drawings of roots that grew out though the wheel, also in the rusty red of rocks and dirt. Underneath the image were the instructions: "Chant the *bij mantra* for the chakra and contemplate the yantra, the image for that chakra. *Lam*."

"What's a *bij mantra*?" she asked.

"It's the seed mantra, the vibration of that chakra." Kenny closed his eyes and chanted "*Lam. Lam. Lam*." He had a surprisingly strong and resonant baritone. "I love it. Chanting. It clears my head."

She could see how it would. It might be like what Jangarrai's music had done for her on her trip. Mae studied the picture. It looked nothing like the mandalas or the chakra charts she'd seen at Healing Balance, and nothing like the colors typical of the Indian art displayed there, either. The fine line drawings were Western in both senses: American West, as well as non-Eastern West.

"Can you meditate on the pictures as well as the sounds?" she asked.

"I try. Muffie told me to go through one chakra a week. I still do. I'm back on the heart chakra today. I hope it helps. I'm afraid she really did ascend."

Mae turned to the heart chakra page in the book. It showed a green wheel filled with leaves and the shady spaces between them, green plants growing out of the wheel. "*Anahata chakra*. The unstruck sound. *Yam*." She liked the phrase "unstruck sound," whatever it meant.

Kenny chanted the mantra. "*Yam. Yam*."

Mae sensed that this book meant something profound to him. He was so young, and Frank looked only a couple of years older. They must have overcome some hard times to be in addiction recovery and so dedicated to their spiritual practices as part of it. Mae felt a new respect for her neighbors, and more confusion about Muffie.

"Thanks for the juice, and for helping with my boxes." Mae gave the book back to him and stood. She already had a friend in her new town. A friend who had a different view of Muffie. "The art is beautiful. Thanks for sharing this. But if it means so much to you, you won't want to be without it if she's," she felt strange saying it, the way Roseanne probably had as well, a corner of her mind doubting her own disbelief, "ascended."

Chapter Four

On the drive north to Santa Fe, Mae tried to imagine what it might be like to do what Muffie claimed she could do. How would it feel to send your soul out of your body? Did hers actually go out and travel when she did her psychic work? Did she time travel into the past and see things, or leave her body to visit lost pets where they were hiding? Though she had a natural talent as a psychic, she'd had little training or teaching. She'd always assumed she simply had extrasensory perception, but the more she thought about it, the more she realized she scarcely understood her own gifts. She wasn't qualified to judge Muffie's ascension.

Scanning through radio stations, Mae picked up Native America Calling on KUNM and caught a conversation with an Apache elder, a coherent, respectable-sounding woman, who claimed to have seen an alien. It had terrified her cat, she said. Another station featured a serious discussion between two astrologers about the Uranus-Pluto square. "Uranus energy is shocking," one said. "It's like Mercury in a higher octave." Things that were off the map in North Carolina and Virginia were on the airwaves here.

Openness to the odd fit with the character of the land: vast empty spaces of juniper-stubbled pink-beige dirt, dramatic wind-carved cliffs, narrow hoodoo towers, broad mesas, blood red arroyos, black volcanic teeth jutting from brown earth. Anything seemed possible here.

The city of Santa Fe blended into the land, with every building designed to look like adobe. As she entered the residential neighborhood where her father's rental house was located, not far from the central plaza, Mae noticed that many of the gardens had sage and lavender like she'd seen in the picture of Ascended Bliss. No grass, just dirt and rocks and flowers. The houses on the short block of Delgado Street between Palace and Alameda, her destination, had wooden bridges to their front walks, and driveways that looked like miniature drawbridges over a moat, only these crossed a dry gully, making them stand out from the rest of the buildings she'd seen.

Mae drove across one of these bridges and through an alley between two houses to reach the carport. Like the house in T or C, this one had a detached carport, a roof on poles over a short driveway, which required one to walk across the yard to get to the house. She parked beside her father's truck and stepped out into the sunset, excited to see him.

Marty came out the back door that led from the house to the garden. The sight of her father's tall, lanky frame and loping strides, his lean tanned face and sandy hair, his warm brown eyes, made Mae feel at home in the unfamiliar place. It was still strange to see him with graying hair and so many sun-lines in his face, a reminder she'd missed fourteen years of his life, but he was still Daddy, still the same laid-back, loving man.

He wrapped her in an embrace. "I've missed you, baby. Good to see you."

"It's good to see you, too."

"Thanks for doing this for us." Marty released the hug. "Come on in, but I have to warn you—it's bad."

"The outside is so pretty. I can't believe anyone would mistreat this place." Mae stopped to admire the garden that took up most of the back yard. An oval-shaped brick path surrounded a bed of sage and lavender, with a polished black stone sculpture in the center, a life-sized depiction of a graceful Native American woman wrapped in a blanket. She carried a basket and looked over her shoulder with a calm yet expectant expression. Mae found it remarkable that this sculpture could have been done by the same man who'd made the sheep from old springs and horseshoes that graced her living room in T or C. "Is that Niall's work?"

"No. That was a guy who didn't pay his rent. We only rent to artists, because of the studio space, but they aren't supposed to be the starving kind. Anyway, he left that instead of money. Niall was, as he put it, royally pissed. If there's a sculpture here he figures it should be a Niall Kerrigan, not someone imitating Alan Houser or Tim Nicola." Catching Mae's puzzled look, Marty said, "I wouldn't know their work either, if it weren't for Niall and living here, but that's what he said. He says it's 'derivative,' but it attracts renters so it stays." Marty paused, admiring the sculpture. "I like it. She's good company."

The stone woman in her smooth, curved wrap gleamed with orange highlights in the fading day.

"I like her, too." Mae took in the scent of the garden. "This smells wonderful. Maybe I'll have to sleep out here tonight." The two stone benches on the outside of the path looked long enough to lie down on, though sleeping on one would call for some padding. The adobe walls around the garden emerged from the building like soft brown arms, angling toward the carport, leaving a wide space in their embrace, but otherwise fully closed off from the street. "It feels nice and private."

"Not always. Some tenants have said tourists wander around and walk right in and look at the sculpture. Think it's public art, I guess. Come on in. I've had the windows open." His arm around Mae's shoulders, Marty led her to the back door. "Apparently our tenant was gone half the time and just had people pop in and feed Pie. Must have been a new cat sitter since no one complained before. Our rental agent here thought Ruth would be a good tenant—old New Mexico family, established artist. She was having her own place remodeled and wanted to clear out while it was torn up. Never imagined she'd be ..." He opened the door, and a stench of smoke and stale grease, like old bacon and hamburger, hit them. "Like that."

They walked into the living room first, a long room the full depth of the house. From where she stood, Mae could see the front door.

Food stains marred the coral-colored upholstered furniture, and dog hair clung in a thick mat to one chair's seat, as if the dog had slept there. On the walls hung bright abstract paintings in colors that complemented the house, and the hair had even drifted to the tops of the frames. Rings and burns marred the wooden tables, and hair and dust bunnies clung to several of Niall's smaller machine-parts sculptures. "I stocked up good on cleaning supplies, but," Marty paused, "God, I'm feeling worse about this by the second."

So was Mae, but she didn't want to rub it in for her father.

Next, he took her into the kitchen, which looked out on the back yard. Orange-yellow dog hair floated in drifts on a red tile floor, snagged in the woven frames of leather-seated basket chairs, and formed thick pads of fur at the feet of a wooden table. Mae had expected bad, but this was worse. The layer of grease and splatters coating the walls near the stove spread to the turquoise and coral cabinets and black granite countertops.

"I've mostly been dealing with the eviction and the lawyer," Marty said. "I haven't had a chance to do much else."

Mae sighed. The house in T or C had been so clean, even if simple and poor compared to this. She missed it already. "Daddy, I can't believe how bad ..."

"Sorry, babe." Marty looked down, clearly embarrassed. "I've been airing it out. Pie won't come out from under the bed. I had to feed her in the bedroom. Her litter box is in the laundry room, so I reckon she sneaks out when she feels safe. Or desperate. Poor old thing. All I've done so far is clean the litter and dump out ashtrays. Sorry."

Mae fought back the urge to complain. She'd agreed to the work. She was getting paid for it, and even if she weren't, she had a free house in T or C. Marty deserved her help. "It's still a pretty house. It'll be real sweet when I get it clean."

"It will be. This is a special place." Marty walked her to the studio, a large open room taking up half the house, with a skylight, a picture window facing the garden, and small windows that looked out the front and side, giving it extraordinary light even in the evening. "We had some good times here. Open studio nights, salons, all sorts of interesting folks coming by. Artists, musicians, poets, academics. Niall knew everybody who was anybody. We had quite the social life."

"Sounds like fun." Mae tried to imagine it without food splashes on the walls or crumbs on the floor. The studio's plain off-white walls and paint-stained cement floor looked naked. It needed someone to come in and make something in it—when it wasn't stinking or dirty. "You miss living here?"

"It was our first home together, but I'd say I'm more fond of the memories than missing it. Let's take a look at the bedroom. That's Niall's masterpiece. And you can get a look at Pie. I'm hoping you can fix her up, as well as the house."

"You want me to heal her?"

"If you can get hold of her."

They crossed back through the living room to the bedroom, at the front of the house. The walls were turquoise. The red Mexican folk art chests and chair were painted with birds and flowers in yellows and greens, and the ceiling was darker turquoise with little LED lights inset like stars. Mae flipped the switch to turn them on. "Niall did this?"

"Yeah, used to drive me crazy." Marty smiled up at the starry ceiling. "Romantic, I guess, but you can't sleep with it."

The sounds of traffic came through the open windows, distant, not annoying. The yellow curtains fluttered, and the scent of the juniper shrubs in the front yard wafted in, not quite overpowered by the smell of tobacco.

"Crouch down and you can meet Pie." Marty knelt, and then lay on his stomach, and Mae did the same. Under the bed, a small, long-haired cat with enormous eyes gazed back at them. She was what some people called a money cat, speckled like she was covered with gold coins on her dark fur. "Hey, Sweetiepie. You got a nice person with you now."

The cat cowered and drew back.

"Dog must have been awful. Poor Pie. She was always skittish, but this is sad." Marty sighed and pushed himself up to sitting on his heels. "You must be whupped. Ready for dinner and a walk?"

"I am. Especially the walk." A new concern about the house struck her as she got to her feet. "What if the tenant comes back?"

"She did." Marty stood. "We had the locks changed in the morning and she showed up this afternoon. She yelled, but she didn't have much in here, just a few clothes. I packed 'em up and met her at her hotel." That explained why he had done so little cleaning. "She wants to take us to court for breaking the lease, but we'll win. I took some pictures, and the cat sitter will testify how bad it was."

"She'll leave me alone, then?"

"Has to. Doesn't have your number, doesn't have a key, and nothing in here belongs to her. All the easels and folding tables and stuff in the studio closet come with the house. If you hear from a Ruth Smith, that's her. Don't deal with her."

"I can't believe an artist would be such a pig."

"Go figure." Marty walked to the bedroom door, turned off the lights, and Mae followed him to the front door through the living room. Taking his keys from his pocket, he slid one off the ring and handed it to Mae. "Yours. Keep it. This place is your inheritance, you know. Not that I'm kicking the bucket any time soon, but someday this is yours. Might as well get used to the idea."

They crossed the little wooden footbridge from the front walkway, took a right on Delgado, then a left on Palace, and Marty did his best to orient Mae to the city. She wanted to get to know it, and hoped to have a little free time to explore it.

He took her to the downtown Plaza, explaining there would be free concerts on weekdays at noon and in the evenings, and that the art galleries nearby were free. How well he read her mind—and knew her finances. He recommended seeing the Indian craftspeople in front of the Palace of the Governors, the former residence of Spanish Colonial governors, now a museum, and offered her a handful of twenties for groceries and for eating out until the kitchen was bearable. "There's a little extra so you can to go to a few museums, too."

Mae took the money but held onto it, not putting it away yet. "Daddy, you're already giving me a free place to live—you don't have to do all that."

"You remember how I used to spoil you?"

"I guess you did." She tucked the bills in her wallet, touched, and a little embarrassed for some reason she didn't understand. "Thanks. It's a long time ago. I'm not used to it anymore."

"Get used to it again. I may get kinda carried away at first, I'm so happy to have my girl back."

In a café upstairs over the Plaza, they dined out on a balcony, watching the people below and enjoying the cooling air. As they relaxed with dessert and coffee after a somewhat fiery meal, Marty asked, "You gonna be all right all alone here?"

"Actually, I'm looking forward to it. I've never been alone before." At eighteen, she'd gotten married, and then divorced at twenty when the husband turned out to be a drinker she couldn't save. She'd had to move back in with her mother and her stepfather. Then she'd married Hubert, and when they'd separated, she'd moved in with a friend in Norfolk. Not a single day with a place of her own. "I'm kind of excited about it."

Marty turned his cup in the saucer, his gaze on his hands. "Reckon you miss the young'uns, though."

"I do." Their eyes met, and Mae was reminded that he knew what that pain was like. "It's bad enough getting divorced again, but being a stepmother with no legal rights ..." She drank her decaf coffee, noticing how thirsty she was, as if the desert air sucked every drop of water out of her body. "Hubert says I can have them come out over Thanksgiving. Feels like forever, though."

"Try fourteen years." He half-smiled. "Somehow you live through it."

"I know. Maybe the week in this house, instead of settling right away in T or C with you and Niall there, is what I need. To kind of jump-start me being on my own. I almost feel like I don't know myself—like I've always been wrapped up in other people."

Marty leaned back in his chair and studied her. "You're not as behind as you think. Took me 'til I was a lot older than you to get a handle on knowing myself."

"But I'm not dealing with something like coming out."

He laughed. "There's other parts of ourselves we keep in a closet. Never know what you'll find. The City Different is a good place to do it."

Mae wanted to know the best outdoor places to exercise, so they walked for an hour. In a long, narrow park along a dried-out river, he said there was a good trail for short runs that would eventually come out at another park. "Trail goes down into the trees, comes back out here, then back down in. You'll see it in daylight better. Longer runs you could do the length of the park and back."

"I feel like I'm running while I'm walking right now."

"It's the altitude. Makes you spacey, too, or it did me when I first moved here. Of course I was in love, might have had something to do with it. Folks say the high desert does a number on your mind as well as your body, though. Take it easy this week, give yourself some breaks."

"I will. But I'm ready for a run, even if I'm gasping."

They reached the intersection of Alameda and Delgado. Before they turned to cross to the other side of Delgado, Marty nodded toward the bridge over the empty riverbed. "Be careful under here. You might come up on the street for that part of the trail."

"What's under there?"

"Few rocks. Kind of dark. And homeless people sometimes live in the riverbed, not so much as they used to with the new shelter that opened, but they found a kid dead under the bridge back in January. Looked like he'd been living down there."

Mae thought of Kenny, and how that could have been him. "How did he die?"

"Never was clear, looked like he'd hit his head somehow. Maybe fell off the bridge. Seems the kid was a runaway, no family around here."

Mae glanced back at the bridge. "That just breaks your heart."

"I know. Son of some friends of ours found him. His folks said it shook him up pretty bad." Marty put his arm around her shoulders. "But it's still a nice trail. Just watch your step there, that's all."

At the house on Delgado Street, Marty checked every room to make sure no one had come in, since he'd left the windows open. "It's a safe neighborhood. I'm just being your daddy. I hate to leave you, babe. But I know you'll be fine."

"You're not staying tonight?"

"Can't sleep on that nasty dog-hair sofa. Anyway, Niall needs me to help him get some stuff loaded and moved to a gallery in the morning. He's got that big show opening tomorrow. Gotta get back. Call me if you need anything."

"I will."

She walked him to his truck, watched him drive off, and then sat on a bench in the garden, gazing at the sculpture and the sky above it. The statue was a peaceful companion, as if the artist had put a spirit into it. Away from the streetlights, the stars astounded her. She'd never known their brilliance or the vast number of them that hid behind the humid air of the east.

Thinking to share the moment as a way to say goodnight to Brook and Stream, Mae took out her phone, only to remember it was too late to call them on the East Coast. The time difference would take getting used to, along with the altitude. She left Hubert a text message that she was sorry she'd missed the twins' bedtime, sparing herself the pain of talking to him.

Going inside, she locked up. The house still smelled bad, and even the sheets in the bedroom closet smelled slightly smoky. She put them on the bed anyway, showered and lay down. Odors and all, the solitude felt clear and spacious. She was truly alone, yet also safe. Someone who loved her knew where she was.

Not like that poor boy who fell off the bridge. Was he on drugs, like Kenny had been when he was homeless? It was a low bridge with a thick railing, so it didn't seem like a sober person would fall off it. There was no water in the riverbed. No one would jump off to drown himself. The only way a person would die was if he hit his head on a rock. He had to have been high or drunk to do that.

Kenny was lucky to have his job, his tiny house, a clean and sober friend like Frank, a spiritual path—and apparently, Muffie. If she was still around. If his job would survive her absence. How could Muffie simply leave him and Frank like that?

Adding to the troubling thoughts that spilled in on Mae at the edge of sleep, Sweetiepie mewed under the bed, but did not emerge.

Poor thing. Mae wanted to heal her, but she had to lay on hands to do that. What kind of person was Ruth Smith, to let her dog terrorize Pie? To trash this beautiful house and leave it half the time without even cleaning it?

The questions were exhausting. Mae couldn't stay awake to sort them out, much as they bothered her.

As she drifted off, she dropped into the psychic-vision tunnel. Sometimes the sight slipped in unwanted through objects Mae touched in a half-dream state, especially if she lay down with questions in her mind. When the tunnel turned to light, she saw a woman with narrow green-framed glasses, short dark hair spiked into yellow and red tufts, and a thick-waisted flat-chested figure clad in a sweat suit. She bent over a long table in the studio, cutting fabric. Mae felt as if she knew her, and yet she'd never seen her before.

Mae woke abruptly. Was this Ruth Smith? It had to be. She'd been saturated in Ruth's energy traces since coming into the house. No wonder the woman felt familiar. Everything, the bed included, was full of her, and Mae had been wondering about her.

Not wanting to see the slobbish tenant again, Mae reached for her purse on the nearby dresser, took out her crystals, and tucked turquoise and aventurine under the pillow to protect her sleep from intrusions. She didn't really want to know about Ruth. It had been an idle question. It was Muffie she was trying to understand. She had Jangarrai to check out, too, and Sri Rama Kriya and ascension, as well as a house to clean. That was enough.

Chapter Five

In the morning, Mae woke still tired, unable to sleep any later with the brilliant light that penetrated the closed blinds and curtains. The sun seemed twice as strong here, even indoors. She turned her phone on and walked through the living room toward the kitchen. Seven a.m., a good time to catch Brook and Stream. No, it was two hours later in North Carolina. The girls were in school. She had to remember to call on Eastern Time. Hubert wasn't having them call her—not a good sign for the way the separation would work out.

Pie, apparently on her way back from her necessary trip, dived under the couch at the sight of Mae. Not an encouraging sign here, either. Mae knelt and looked under the sofa into a pair of big staring eyes. "Come on, Sweetiepie. It's safe now." The cat cowered at the sound of Mae's soft encouragement. So this would be the feeding station today. Somehow, she was going to have to heal the cat, but she couldn't touch her yet. Strike two, and she hadn't even had breakfast yet.

Opening the refrigerator, she saw rows of soda and beer cans, and little tubs of doubtful leftovers, as well as slabs of sliming bacon and a brown, leafy blob that might once have been iceberg lettuce. She shut the door, not ready to face this sickening mess without coffee. The cabinets revealed only instant coffee with a dusty lid. There might as well not have been any. But if she didn't touch the cleaning before she went out, that would be strike three.

Mae started with a task she hoped would be easy. One room and two vacuum bags of dog hair later, she shut off the vacuum, too hungry and caffeine deprived to continue. In the sudden silence she heard her phone beeping and checked her messages. Roseanne had texted. "Still no Muffie. Good riddance. But bad for business. Will pay for search."

Bad for business. Of course. People who believed in Muffie wanted her advice, and people who didn't came to laugh behind her back. She was part of the theater of Dada Café.

Mae called back. Getting no answer, she left a message that she would give the search a try. Muffie's claim that she was ascending and her subsequent disappearance without contact made the effort ethically acceptable, not idle prying. In all likelihood, Muffie was right here in Santa Fe, with family or with her guru, not actually in a spiritual state beyond her body. Mae had packed the Sanchez and Smyth catalog in case she needed an object for tracing Muffie, but she could probably find her just by locating the Ascended Bliss Center. She'd need coffee first, whichever method she tried.

After a shower, Mae put on a short, sleeveless black dress and sun hat and sandals, slathered on a layer of sunscreen despite Muffie's advice to the contrary, and walked to a coffee shop she and Marty had passed the night before on one of the four streets leading into the Plaza. She would have time to eat and feel human again before the noon concert.

As she ordered her coffee and muffin, Mae noticed the barista's nametag said *Helix*. Real name? New name for the City Different? She had to be a kind of off-beat person.

Mae asked her, "Have you heard of a spiritual teaching center called Ascended Bliss?"

"No. But there are so many. Maybe it's new. Or out of business."

A man in line behind Mae grumbled, "Those places are a dime a dozen."

The web site Roseanne had showed her hadn't given an address or a phone number, just a tribute to Sri Rama Kriya. It didn't seem to announce a new place or introduce a new teacher, but to honor someone well established.

"I don't think it's new." Mae paid, aware of using her father's money. It was a strange feeling, being taken care of. "This lady in T or C talks it up a lot, comes up here to see her guru. Sri Rama Kriya."

"Gurus," said the man who'd been behind her, stepping up to the counter and getting his wallet out of his back pocket. "Throw a rock around here, you'll hit one." He laughed as if he'd made a good joke, and placed his order.

Mae took her breakfast to a low table with a comfy couch and a spread of local newspapers, and settled down, refreshed at being out of the smoky, hairy house.

"I can recommend some good places," Helix called across the room. "There really are a lot. What are you looking for? Buddhist? Yoga? Tibetan?"

"I'm looking for *this* place. Ascended Bliss."

"Try *The Reporter*, then." Mae started to look through the papers and found the one Helix suggested. "Look at the ads in the back. I assume you already checked the phone book, though."

"I didn't." Mae felt embarrassed. There was a phone book at the house. She must be getting spacey with the altitude at seven thousand feet. Her head did feel peculiar, as if it was full of echoes, and her thinking was slower than normal. She leafed through the paper, distracted by listings for music events—she would have to come back to that to look for Jangarrai or opportunities to find him—and then reminded herself what she was doing. She might need two coffees to get her mind focused.

The back pages featured classifieds, many for yoga classes, energy healers, massage, or personal training, ads she would be in if she lived here. There were also services like pet psychics, power animal retrieval, past life astrology, psychic surgery, and a number of other concepts odd enough to merit Muffie's approval, but no Sri Rama Kriya and no Ascended Bliss Center for Enlightenment. Of course, Mae could look in the phone book when she got back to the house.

But with so little public identity, no web site and no advertising, the odds of finding it still open and with a working phone number seemed slim. Even that negative finding was progress, though. If it didn't exist, Muffie wasn't there.

Only fifty percent spacey after her second cup, Mae left the coffee shop and walked to the Plaza. Somehow it was noon already. Half a day had flown and she'd hardly made a dent in the mess. It was silly to feel like she was wasting her time when that was why she was here, but she wanted it done already so she could be a tourist. As she walked, she could hear the musicians warming up. She might find someone who knew the missing Jangarrai.

A five-piece Celtic band including standup bass, hand drums, tin whistle, fiddle, and guitar played on a wide-roofed stage in front of an open patch of pavement that served as a dance floor. A mixed audience of all ages and walks of life sat on benches, in the grass, and on the stone wall surrounding a tall monument, or stood near the dance floor. Only one person danced, a purple-gowned woman of about sixty with questionably auburn hair and a floating purple scarf that she used as a partner. She drifted and swirled, laughing and joking occasionally about being a lonely tourist from California.

Mae found a spot on the stone wall and adjusted her hat to better shade her eyes. Toes tapping, she wished she was as uninhibited as the Californian, and wondered how likely it was that anyone in this band knew Jangarrai. His music was nothing like theirs.

Passing the dancing tourist, a lean, long-limbed black man in jeans so soft and faded they flowed like silk along his legs cut across the open space in front of the stage. Without slowing his brisk pace, he turned to face the stage, looked up at the band with a face-splitting grin, and broke into a dance so explosively alive it seemed to light up the already dazzling square. Dancing backwards, he executed a series of complex steps and turns, spinning as easily as another person might walk, tipping his straw fedora to the band. His collar-length hair, escaping from the limited control of the hat, flew out in a cloud that looked as if someone had tried to comb out a cotton ball and given up. It was ash blond, while his little tuft of a goatee was dark. He wore a thin white cotton shirt so sheer that Mae could see the warm, dark brown of his skin and the definition of the muscles in his shoulders and arms, a body as tight and toned as a wild animal's. His face was almost square, with a wide jaw and high cheekbones, a broad straight nose, and huge dark eyes. And there was a gold tooth in that blinding bright smile.

Now that was crazy. Unless she'd missed some fashion trend, no one had gold teeth any more, did they? He looked, Mae thought, like a pirate.

Breaking off his dance, he jogged away on whatever errand had taken him across the Plaza. The performance had lasted about thirty seconds, but projected more vitality than the entire band had during the song—and they were good. He stole the show.

A group of boys about eight years old began hopping and jumping to the music, and a father started dancing with a little girl on his shoulders. The purple-clad tourist floated up to Mae and said, "You could dance, too. There isn't a law against being crazy, you know."

Mae laughed. "Thanks. I'll keep that in mind."

She thought of the blond-haired black man. He hadn't been scared to dance alone. He'd left this wave of dancing in his wake, as if he'd repealed the law against being crazy. It wasn't quite enough to make Mae kick up her heels, though. Maybe Niall was right. *Stiff.*

When the band took a break, she walked over to the man at the table where their CDs were for sale and asked him if was familiar with Jangarrai.

"Sure. You just missed him."

"I did? Darn. Is he playing anywhere this week?"

"Haven't seen him have a regular gig in," he stopped and thought, "maybe four months. Seen him play on the streets now and then, and sometimes he sits in with the African drummers. I don't know. Keep your eyes peeled."

"Thanks." She bought a CD, thinking it might be fun to drive with this music. "What's the name of the African drum group?"

"There's two. Can't think of the name of the big group that plays for the dance class at the Railyard, but the trio is Afreaka. Like Africa, with 'freak' in it."

Mae thanked the man and crossed the street to look at the Indian vendors' art and jewelry. She needed to head home, though, before she forgot what she was really here for. As she browsed the jewelry, Mae tried to pierce the high-altitude brain fog, reminding herself over and over: *phone book, look up Ascended Bliss. Google Afreaka.* She couldn't believe she had just missed Jangarrai, and wondered if he had been the bleached-blond, gold-toothed, crazy dancing man. Not likely, though. He didn't look like Jangarrai's music sounded.

Back on Delgado Street, Mae stopped at the mailbox at the end of the wooden walkway and pulled out a stack of mail. She'd have to ask Marty what hotel Ruth Smith was staying in and drop off the mail at the front desk. The evicted tenant couldn't have had time to get her things forwarded.

Taking the mail inside, Mae sat on the edge of the stained and hairy coral couch to sort junk from real mail, with Pie mewing underneath her. She said a few kind words to the cat, leaned down and offered a hand, and the mewing stopped, but Pie did not come out. Sad. How could Mae heal a cat she couldn't touch?

She noticed the name on the envelopes. Not Ruth Smith. Ruth *Smyth.*

The image that had slipped into her mind in her half dream state the night before came back to her, the woman cutting fabric. Making the prototypes of the Sanchez and Smyth clothing? Vegetarian health-nut Muffie would be appalled to think she wore clothes by a bacon-eating, chain-smoking, beer-drinking designer.

Muffie. Mae got the phone book off the kitchen counter and looked for Ascended Bliss. No such place. Looked up the last name Blanchette. No such family. Muffie could stay with friends or relatives here, of course, and not have her own number, or be unlisted, but it was hard to imagine a spiritual center of some kind having no phone number. Maybe the barista who suggested it had closed had taken a good guess.

Getting her laptop from her luggage, Mae brought it out to the garden, hoping the house's wireless signal reached that far. She was in luck; she could search for Sri Rama Kriya outdoors with the scents of sage and lavender. Nothing came up online except Muffie's Sri Rama Kriya tribute web page and a book, *The Wisdom of Sri Rama Kriya.* This was getting kind of far from Muffie now. It would be more direct to do a psychic search with the Sanchez and Smyth catalog.

After checking her e-mail—a message from Deborah asking if Mae had located Jangarrai, which got an answer of "almost"—Mae took her crystals and the catalog from the house and returned to the garden. Outdoors, she was less likely to pick up Ruth's energy, more likely to get a trace of Muffie.

Mae sat facing the statue and rested one hand on the catalog, her grandmother's amethyst in her other hand. Closing her eyes, she set an intention to find where Muffie was now. The tunnel overtook her vision quickly, and the emotional input from the other end of it felt irritable and strong. When the tunnel opened, Mae didn't see Muffie, but Ruth again, talking on a telephone. She paced, cigarette in hand, and seemed to be arguing. Probably yelling at Marty or Niall. Mae withdrew from the vision.

She was going to have to look for Muffie somewhere else, and wished she had something of hers to work with that wasn't a Sanchez and Smyth catalog. It wasn't helping.

Still, holding a personal belonging someone had handled a lot had never failed before. Mae shouldn't see Ruth from the catalog, any more than she could find Jangarrai from his CDs. It was Muffie's property, so her energy should be in it. This brought up two possibilities. One, Ruth's energy was so overpowering even in the garden that it blocked Muffie's. Two, there was no energy link to Muffie anymore because she really had ascended—or because she was dead. Roseanne wouldn't care as long as she could keep the restaurant open, but Kenny would be devastated.

Hoping that more cleaning would eradicate the Ruth energy, Mae changed back into grubby work clothes, vacuumed the upholstered furniture, and cleaned it with spot remover. Maybe if she could remove Ruth, she could find Muffie, alive. Still, she needed to let Roseanne know that she hadn't succeeded so far, and called her at Dada Café. Rosanne was bound to be there. She probably wasn't getting any time off, if the owner had vanished.

Mae walked out into the garden to make her call, basking in the sweet scents, the hot sun, and the serene presence of the statue. The Dada Café hostess put her through to the office, and Roseanne answered, jumping in without small talk. "Did you find her? Or the guru?"

"No. I can't tell if it's because she doesn't exist anymore to be found, or if I'm just so swamped with energy from the tenant who was in this house. If I can find somewhere quiet to do the psychic work away from this place, I can try again. Or you could send me something else of Muffie's besides that catalog, just in case. I think the tenant was the Smyth in Sanchez and Smyth."

"I don't have any other things that were Muffie's. She cleared out. I mean, she handled everything in the restaurant a lot, but so does everybody else. Anyway, you'd have to be here to use that."

"I guess I'll try again with the catalog, then." Mae sat on a bench, watching a lizard on the bricks. It held still, its brown body almost blending with the path. "But—what if that ascension line was a suicide threat? Has anyone been to her place to see if she moved out? Or if she's lying dead in the bathtub or anything?"

"Her landlord called me, actually. He hoped she'd be at work so he could ask for more money, because her deposit won't cover hauling her furniture out. Said she left without giving notice, just dropped off the keys in his porch mailbox with a note that said 'gone.' He went in her place—no sign of anything wrong. She packed, took her clothes, all her small stuff."

"Will you be able to tell if she's cashing her paycheck or anything? Any use of her health insurance? I have no idea what a manager can find out about that stuff."

"Muffie was never on the payroll or insurance here."

"You're kidding."

"Rich. I told you. Rich and crazy. She didn't pay herself. She just did this—God only knows why. To have a place to be God or something. And if God is dead, I'm in deep doodoo, because business is down. I know it's only one day, but some people find out she's not here and they decide not to stay and eat. I hope she didn't leave with the idea of closing this place."

"I think her guru's place may have closed."

"Crap! You can't find her, you can't find him—they all drank the Kool-Aid and ascended." Roseanne sighed. She spoke to someone who seemed to enter the office, and then returned to Mae. "I wonder where her family is. They'd know."

"There aren't any Blanchettes in the phone book. If she's even from here."

"Damn. That *ascension* line, in front of the camera ... If she really could do that, we're screwed."

"But why would she pack her clothes for that? What if she's doing something else? A marketing stunt for the restaurant, getting people to think she flew off like that."

"Oh my God, what a great idea. I'll get Bryan to come up with something—that is so perfect. Yes."

The lizard began to do pushups, puffing its neck, and staring at Mae. "Wait a second," she said. "What if she's dead in some *other* way, not ascended, and you're doing a publicity gimmick about her ascension? That'd be awful."

"Not as awful as having her around. It'd be the best of both worlds, get all the business with none of the hassles."

Mae cringed at Roseanne's cynicism. "But what about the people who believe in her? Like Kenny and Frank?"

"They already miss her. Which is driving me even further up the wall. They say work was more stressful today without her leading staff meditations. I told Frank to lead it, and it was actually better, but he didn't think so." Roseanne spoke to someone else again. "Sorry. One of my servers. Their table wants aura reading guidance on what to eat and drink."

"That may seem silly to you, but Frank and Kenny are—" Mae hesitated to break their anonymity as recovering addicts. "Serious."

"So are these idiots. God! Just when I'm finally free of this wacko, I have all this pressure to keep her around. Do you know how hard it is to act like you agree with total bullshit all day? Why can't people just eat here for a vegetarian meal and good wine? Why does it have to be all this psycho drama? Why can't Kenny and Frank just go do yoga and chant and all that and not have this crackpot boss telling them this other stuff? Why can't I make money without this circus?"

Good questions. And Mae couldn't answer them. It seemed that everyone *would* be better off without Muffie, if they could only stop believing in her, though not better off if she was dead. She'd been kind to Kenny, after all, even if she gave him some strange ideas.

"I don't know if I can, but I'll keep trying to find her. You probably should do something besides ask me. Seriously. Disappearing isn't normal."

"Fine. I'll do something. And you'll look, and I'll pay you when you find her. I need to make sure she's not closing this place out from under us."

Mae wanted to say, "pay me for *trying*," but Roseanne had hung up. If Muffie was dead, there would be no finding, only trying.

Inadvertently scaring the lizard off into the lavender, Mae went back into the house. Back to the filth. She took a dust cloth from under the bag of cleaning supplies in the kitchen, but was distracted again as she got to the living room. The letters for Ruth Smyth.

She called Marty and asked for Ruth's hotel to drop off the mail.

"She's staying with her sister in Albuquerque now. Said she's got forwarding at the post office set up, so that's the last mail for her you should get. Hang on, I've got the address." He paused. "Care of Ginny Sanchez—" He gave an Albuquerque address.

Mae wrote it on the two envelopes she would need to forward. "So she really is part of Sanchez and Smyth."

"Yeah, but she's an artist, too. Painting, drawing ... Didn't think you'd've heard of Sanchez and Smyth. Kinda pricey for you."

"Niall took me to Dada Café. The owner is really into Sanchez and Smyth clothes. Have you met Muffie?"

"No. Kenny and Frank keep raving about her, but Niall hates healthy food, so we put off going there. Finally tried it about a month ago. She didn't come to our table, but we could hear her with the other patrons and it got on his nerves. Did she try to read him?"

"No. He took off to the bar."

"Smart move. He'd have bit her head off otherwise."

"I almost did. She told me I had some kind of *blockages*. Niall says health nuts and spiritual tourists are suckers, so I thought maybe she took me for a fool because I look healthy. I tried to be polite about it, but I disagreed with her. She hasn't been back there since. The manager thinks she might have come up here to see her guru. When you lived here, did you ever hear of a guru named Sri Rama Kriya? Or a place called the Center for Ascended Bliss?"

"No. But we're not into that scene. Why are you interested?"

"Kenny wanted me to go see him. And I might find out if that's where Muffie went."

"Don't waste your time on that. Kenny gets more crazy ideas from that woman. He and Frank put up some big rod, this twenty-foot pole, to attract messages from the Pleiades because Muffie told them her guru said to do that. Skip it, babe, it won't do him any good. He's got a perfectly good, sensible yoga teacher here. He doesn't need that nonsense from whoever this guru is, or Muffie."

Attracting messages from the Pleiades? That was more ridiculous than the green slime. Mae would have to look at the pole when she got back to T or C. She'd thought it was a flagpole.

"How's the house coming?" Marty asked. "You get hold of Pie yet? She come out for you?"

"Not yet." Mae felt a pang of guilt. She needed to get back to cleaning, and try again to heal the cat. "I need to check on her."

"You do that. She's a sweetie. Needs some loving care."

Mae looked under the sofa. No Pie. She checked under the bed. The eyes stared at her. She brought the food and water dishes in and lay on the floor speaking softly, but the cat only shrank further away. Giving up for the time being, Mae resumed cleaning, taking the curtains out and beating the hairs out of them, and bringing them to the laundry room along with the towels from the bathroom closet. They all smelled like smoke. She had to clean the washing machine and dryer of food spills and dog hair before she could use them. This work would take every bit of the week here. She still had all the walls to wash, floors to wash, every nook and cranny of the kitchen to clean, and more furniture to free of dust and dog hair.

With the laundry room cleaned and laundry in progress, she took another break, setting up her laptop again. Reading *The Reporter* online, she looked for music listings. Tonight, at La Villa Real Center, Afreaka was playing. Free. This was going a lot better than the Muffie search. Or the cleaning, or the cat healing. She could find people who knew Jangarrai tonight.

Chapter Six

Still reluctant to face the revolting refrigerator, Mae hadn't shopped, and would have to eat out. She dressed again in the little black dress, put on earrings and sandals, and brushed her hair, pleased with the Santa Fe version of herself in the mirror. More dressed up than she would be back home, she was looking forward to taking herself out on a date. After all her years of marriage, it was a dinner date, in a way, with a stranger.

She walked downtown and picked a small restaurant that had outdoor dining overlooking a courtyard between shops, where she could enjoy the evening breeze. While she waited for her meal, she remembered to call her stepdaughters before their bedtime on the East Coast, and made up for lost time talking with them. Long-distance connections were always bittersweet, especially the part where she had to talk with Hubert first, and hear him and his new girlfriend in the background while Brook and Stream chatted.

Reminding herself that she was better off on her own, Mae took her time over dinner after the call, letting the clear desert light and the soothing simplicity of the city's shapes and colors ease her again into her solitude.

When it was time to find the concert, she walked several blocks west of the Plaza and looked for La Villa Real Center, but it seemed invisible at first. The mall was at the end of a short side street, set back from Guadalupe Street. Mae found it only after passing it twice, and wondered how she could have missed a black 1941 Dodge truck on a pedestal, its bed full of petunias, across from the mall entrance. She hurried in to find the music already in progress.

The band was playing in the atrium in the center, in what normally served as a food court. All the seats at the first floor tables were occupied, and the upper level looked crowded as well.

Onstage, Mae saw three black men seated on tall stools, one man very dark, short and round faced, with a graying beard, another lighter brown with a long narrow face and a thin, lanky body, both playing drums as they sang, and then—the blond man from the Plaza. Two tables on either side of him displayed an array of flutes, wooden, bamboo, and metal. A drum sat on the floor behind him, and he was playing a rhythmic drone on a bamboo tube about five feet long and eight inches in diameter, painted with dotted patterns that looked like abstract aerial photography, the instrument's end resting on the floor at his feet. Those instruments. He had to be Jangarrai after all.

Elated by the music and her easy success, Mae climbed the stairs to find a seat on the upper level, noticing the effects of the high altitude on her heart during this normally effortless exercise. She had to share a table with strangers, but they smiled and didn't object.

The song built up in tempo, the short man's strong, husky voice pouring out rapid-fire words in his native tongue. He smiled while he sang, making eye contact with members of the audience, and the other drummer added harmonies on choruses, Jangarrai keeping pace on the didgeridoo as if he never stopped to breathe. The energy swelled so high Mae felt herself and the rest of the audience disappear into the wave of the rhythms, as if they and the trio all had one great heart.

At a table near the railing, two young women watched with visible excitement, often leaning into each other and talking, sometimes holding hands. They seemed to be a couple, a slightly plump black woman with short, natural hair and gold-rimmed glasses, and a graceful Asian woman wearing a short dress with an uneven hem, tall boots, and hair captured in a spray atop her head like a cockatoo's crest. The Asian woman stood several times and snapped pictures with her cell phone. She was tall, with colorful tattoos of tigers, Buddhas, moons, and suns on every willowy limb, and when she got up she partly blocked Mae's view of the band. Fortunately, her partner reminded her to sit down for the next part of the song.

The lead singer looked to Jangarrai, and he set down the huge didgeridoo and stood, picked up a small bamboo flute, and blended its ethereal, flying sounds with the African drums. The drummers picked up the tempo yet again and added another layer of rhythms. As he finished the flute solo, Jangarrai burst into an ecstatic flight of dance while the other men sang. The three of them finished on drums with a pounding finale. The two women at the table near the railing applauded loudest of anyone upstairs, and the tattooed woman jumped to her feet.

The band faced the audience with formal little bows as the applause crested, and then slowly faded. The lead singer said, "Before we take our break, let me introduce the band. We were Afreaka, but I'm sad to say Mike Donkor went home to Ghana. Sad for us, happy for him. We have a new name tonight, and a brand new permanent member. We are now Zambethalia because I am from Zambia—Mwizenge Chomba." He touched his chest lightly, and then gestured to his bandmates. "And from Ethiopia, my friend Dagmawi Molalenge on drums and vocals. And from Australia, Jangarrai, on drums, vocals, flutes, didgeridoo, and general mayhem. We'll be back with more in a few minutes. Thank you."

The band dispersed, and Mae stood to try to see where they'd gone. She needed to pin Jangarrai down. Both Deborah and the man selling CDs in the Plaza made him sound like he was hard to get hold of, and seldom seen. She could easily spot Jangarrai by his silly hat, the straw fedora with a pink-and-green band that he'd worn earlier in the day at the Plaza, and his wild, fair hair. He had to be vain, a man who dyed his hair like that. Performers were probably kind of conceited. He stood at an open coffee kiosk talking with the other men, and he and the short man looked up at her. Mwizenge clapped Jangarrai on the shoulder. The blond man nodded, smiled, and began to weave through the crowd toward the stairs.

He bounded up the steps, spilling slops of coffee, stopping to sip it hastily, wiping it off his beard with his sleeve, and then bounding up again. As if he were a child and somewhere up here was Christmas.

When he reached the second floor, he was stopped by a couple whose gushing manner suggested they were praising the music. Mae wondered if she would get a chance to ask him about Deborah ordering his CDs. The tattooed woman looked impatient to speak to him also, edging toward him, but he looked past her at Mae, flashed the gold-toothed grin at her, said something to the couple he was talking with, and crossed over to Mae.

"Hi. Um ... uh ... My mate said ... Well, no, I ... Sorry. Let me start over." He set his coffee on her table. "I'd like to give you a compliment. I looked up and saw your legs and—" He placed a hand to his heart, giving her a shy version of the shining smile. "It made my day. Or night. Or whatever this is. That's all." He was her height or an inch taller, about five eleven, but he seemed to be shrinking himself somehow as he looked into her eyes. "Sorry." A quick grin, and then he looked at his feet, his gaze snagged briefly by her breasts. He was like a kid who'd delivered a Valentine to his first-grade sweetheart, except for that pause at chest level. "You're nice to look at."

He seemed so nervous that the brief ogle didn't come across rudely like a southern boy's whoop and whistle. She found herself wanting to help him relax, the last thing she had expected in meeting such a confident performer. "Thank you," she said. "That was real sweet."

"I love your accent." He looked at her again, suddenly open and interested. "Where're you from?"

With his Australian accent charmingly strange to her, she found it funny that he was intrigued by her speech. "North Carolina." This seemed to please him. He nodded and looked hopeful. She added, "And then Virginia. I know someone there who wants me to put you in touch with her."

"Is this ... What?" He picked up his coffee, drank, and held onto it, more guarded now. "Don't follow you. Sorry. Dense, I guess."

"She wants me to talk to you about ordering your music. She could sell a lot of it if she had a way to get hold of you."

He stared past Mae, half-smiling, shook his head and looked away, the smile fading. "What does she want me to do?"

"Sell CDs. Get your web site back up. Whatever. You'll have to talk to her. I can give you her contact information."

He took a deep breath, walked over to the railing and gazed over it, squeezing his paper cup so that the liquid slopped onto his hands. "Bloody hell." He set it on the floor and looked around as if he had no idea what to do. Mae brought him a napkin from the holder on her table. He wiped his hands off, and stared at them and the napkin. "Sorry. Um. Yeah. I ... I'll see you after the show, then? I mean—can you stay? Take you out for a drink?" His huge dark eyes searched her face. "If that's all right."

She needed to talk to him for Deborah, and he seemed unnerved by the prospect. Or was it by Mae? "Sure, I can stay. I'll see you."

He grinned, started to leave, and turned back. Making a gesture toward his head as if twisting something, perhaps meant to imply his brain needed winding, he bent down and grabbed his coffee and resumed his exit.

Mae watched the musician disappear, weaving through the tightly packed tables with animal grace. So *this* was Jangarrai? Hearing the soothing, mysterious music on his recordings, she'd expected someone serene.

The tattooed woman trailed him as far as the stairs, called to him to wait, but he seemed oblivious, off in his own head. She went back to her table, spoke to her partner, and both looked at Mae.

The trio returned to the performance space, and as the Zambian lead singer started to announce a song, Jangarrai held up a hand, and pointed to the basket in front of the performing area.

He addressed the audience, "Come on now, you stingy bastards," and laughed hard, sitting back onto the tall stool as if what he'd said was so funny it knocked him down. His laugh was short and loud, a single blasting "hah" interspersed with snorts, funnier than his joke and contagious to much of the audience. "These blokes have families." He broke into the country song *I'm Busted* for a few lines, changing his voice and accent to a nasal satire of the style. "And buy some f—ing," he barely stifled a full f-word, "CDs while you're at it."

Jangarrai shot the audience a sparkling grin, stood and spun around as if he'd just finished a dance rather than a couple of sentences, and gestured to Mwizenge. The drums began again, Jangarrai blending the western flute into the eclectic mix with a jazz-classical flair.

The two young women by the railing waved to Mae to join them. They must think she knew Jangarrai, since he'd talked to her instead of them.

Wishing she'd gotten a drink on the break, Mae walked to their table and took a seat. "Thanks for the invitation."

"Thanks for joining us," the tattooed woman said. "I'm Wendy Huang, and this is my partner, Andrea Jones."

"Mae Martin-Ridley." She had to start dropping the Ridley. "Looked like you were trying to get hold of Jangarrai."

"I am. He's my next project. I'm going to discover him." Wendy sipped a tall fizzy drink. Mae didn't like soda, yet the sight of it made her even thirstier. "How well do you know him?"

"Not at all."

"Darn. I could swear he acted like he knew you."

"I'm gonna see him after the show. This lady that runs a store where I used to work wants to order his music and no one can find him or get hold of him, at least back East no one can."

"Same here so far. We just moved here from Denver, but Andrea's been trying to buy more of his music, and it's a dead end. This is the first time I've gotten close. It's like he's invisible, and he's not exactly someone you'd overlook. It's weird. Like he's hiding in plain sight."

"If you can hang around after the show, maybe I can get him to hold still for you."

Wendy glanced at Andrea, who shook her head and said, "Crack of dawn."

Andrea explained that she was a massage therapist at a spa, and she had a client who wanted a sunrise special, a massage and wrap to start the day. She and Wendy had planned to leave after Wendy caught up with Jangarrai on the break. Wendy picked up the thread from there. She had a tedious midlevel management job at a large hotel and wanted to do something more exciting with her marketing and business skills. Her project was to find musicians whose careers seemed to need help. The two women had moved to Santa Fe for Andrea's job, and Wendy, who had sold her vintage record store in Denver, was looking for a new outlet.

"I have no musical talent at all and I love music, so I come up with ways to be part of it. I'd be a real hands-on, creative manager. I'd take care of anything he needed, and steering his career. I think he could be big. I could do something for him. Considering his disappearing act, I think he needs me."

Mae asked, "Can you discover him if he already has music out?"

"Yes. He's only done these New Age things. They're great, don't get me wrong. Andrea uses that stuff a lot for massage, but some of the tracks make me think he could do something more. Doesn't his voice just blow you away? I'd have him do some songs on the other instruments at intervals, but not all that orchestration. Not with that voice at the center of it. I mean, he's an incredible composer, and he had a good producer on those CDs, but I want to showcase him in a new way. Did you know he's never toured? Never played outside Santa Fe and Albuquerque?"

"But he's with this trio now. They might already have an agent or manager."

"Performing free and taking donations? It doesn't seem that way. Anyway, they're good, but the industry has plenty of world music groups. Not that I'd say no to them if they wanted my help, but he's my *project*."

"Wendy—" Andrea glanced at her watch. "We need to go, if I'm getting eight hours sleep."

"She's an inner-peace junkie," Wendy grumbled. She finished her soda, took a brocade business card holder from a patchwork velvet purse, and gave a few cards to Mae. "Please. Get him to call me." She glanced at Andrea. "It'd be worth your sleep if I could pin him down."

"You saw him," Andrea said. "He's like a ping-pong ball. You won't pin him down even if you stay. Let Mae do it for you. It'll help her friend order his music if he works with you, so it's all covered. And," she gave Mae a playful smile, "he'd obviously rather talk to you."

Ignoring the suggestion that Jangarrai was attracted to her, Mae promised to get Wendy's card into his hands, and to explain her interest in working with him. It would, as Andrea said, help Deborah get more of his music.

"Call me. Let me know how it goes," Wendy said as she and Andrea stood to leave. "Don't let him slip away. Make him call me tonight if you can."

She'd be an aggressive manager. Wendy's pushiness reminded Mae of Roseanne at Dada Café, only nicer. "I'll do my best."

A set of African songs came to an end as the two women departed, and Mwizenge stood still, letting the applause die down. "I don't know if he knows I'm going to do this, but," he smiled at Jangarrai, "I want to turn our new man loose. We haven't had a chance to hear that voice solo." Off the mic, he spoke to the other musicians. The conference seemed to come to quick agreement, the two African men stepped back slightly, and Jangarrai came to the center mic.

"Um ... something new ..." He looked up at Mae, almost smiled, and then took the mic from its stand and closed his eyes. Taking a long pause, he seemed to disappear inside himself, to gather force until the song rose up to whip through him. A hard-driving blues filled every corner of the building with a power Mae felt all the way to her bones.

"Dark of the night in my left-alone bed,
Dark of the heart going out of my head,
I need someone to hold onto, something to lose,
Or I'm gonna drown in these left-alone blues."

His voice was like a bell, a huge bell rung hard, passionate yet seemingly effortless, with none of the rasping or straining of many rock or blues singers, every note perfectly pitched. In a second verse, he juggled the words in ways that ceased to make sense and explored the melody in variations that reached highs and lows of both sound and feeling. Eyes still closed, he almost danced, swaying, sometimes close to crouching, sometimes lifting and lengthening, only to be pulled down low again as if possessed by the song.

"Streets of the night it's the walk of the dead,
Dance of the lost going out of my head,
In the dark of my heart holding someone to lose,
Deep in the hole of the left-alone blues."

It was only when he finished that Mae realized he had sung unaccompanied. No instruments. He'd filled the song and the space with his voice alone. Mae hoped Wendy hadn't gone out the door yet. If she wanted to discover something new in Jangarrai's repertoire, this was it. The song left Mae feeling as if she'd been through an emotional catharsis, shaken clear and alive.

As the musicians divvied up the money from the basket after the concert and Mwizenge packed up the remaining Afreaka CDs, Mae came downstairs and took a seat at one of the recently vacated tables near the performers.

Jangarrai swooped in and leaned on the back of an empty chair. "Thanks for staying. This place is closing in a few minutes, so why don't we head over to the bar at Marisol's? Buy you a drink, bite to eat. Sound good?"

"I'm a tourist," she said, "so I don't know where that is." She wasn't ready to get in a car with him. "Is it close?"

"Yeah. I'll lock my instruments in the van. We can walk." Straightening up, he hesitated, fidgeted, glanced back at the other musicians, and shoved his hands in his pockets. "D'you mind carrying a few things? Or I can ask them, if you can wait a bit."

"I can carry things."

She watched him return to his bandmates. As Jangarrai began slipping his flutes into their cases, Mwizenge laid a hand on Jangarrai's arm, saying a few words, and Dagmawi smiled, adding something at which the three of them laughed. Did they think he had a date? She could swear the exchange among them had that feel, as if congratulating Jangarrai on a triumph.

She stood as the two African men carried their drums past her toward the exit and wished her a good evening with knowing smiles, like the look Andrea had given her. *Darn. He really does think this is a date.* She'd never said that. She'd clearly said she wanted to get him in touch with Deborah.

Jangarrai approached Mae with the didgeridoo. "Do the honors with the didg? I've got everything else."

He laid the long bamboo tube across her arms, and walked back to pick up his drum and a backpack containing the flutes. Mae studied the object in her arms. Listening to the CDs, she had imagined something like a bassoon. "This is different from what I thought it'd look like."

He caught the drum in one arm and felt in his pocket for keys. "Never seen a didg?"

"No. It's bigger and longer than I'd expected."

A half-swallowed laugh escaped him as he led them toward the door. The laugh turned into a snort and single *hah*. Mae didn't know him well enough to appreciate sexual innuendo from him, and stifled her urge to giggle at his laugh.

He seemed to notice her lack of response and lost his smile as he held the door for her. "Sorry. Bloody juvenile." Subdued, he led her across the parking lot to a van that looked old enough to vote. Its faded paint, possibly green at one time, wore a coat of reddish dust. "Hang on." He unlocked the driver's door, set the drum in the passenger seat, scrambled into the cargo area, and opened the back gate from the inside. "Sorry. The latch is fucked. Have to do this stupid thing with wire ..."

She walked around to the open rear gate and handed him the didgeridoo, which he gently nestled into a bed of pillows and blankets, protecting it from a bicycle, using a cardboard box to help prop the bike. Somehow she'd expected him to have better things, considering that he had some moderately successful recordings. She sensed his embarrassment as he fumbled with the latch again, muttering more apologies for the time it took, for making her carry something, and for making a stupid joke. "Off to a bloody great start."

He disappeared briefly in transit through the van. The evening air had turned cool, and Mae shivered in her sleeveless dress. The elevation had its surprises—not just lack of oxygen, but cold nights. Starting to hop from the front of the van, Jangarrai stopped, held up a finger, disappeared within, and reemerged with a sweatshirt. "Hate to cover you up, but you're cold." He offered it to her. "It's clean."

"Thank you. I'm sure it is. A gentleman would never offer a lady his dirty shirt." She pulled the shirt on, and regarded the words on it with amusement once they were displayed across her chest. *Don't Worry, Be Hopi.* The shirt was too big and didn't look like it would fit him, but it seemed old and well used. "Is it really Hopi?"

"Nah. Dunno. Maybe. Got it from a vendor at a Pueblo corn dance." As they walked, he sang a few bars of *Don't Worry, Be Happy*, complete with multi-octave vocal effects. His voice fascinated her. Who was he? There had to be quite a story to his music. How did a classically trained singer and flutist also end up playing drums and didgeridoo and singing the blues? "Don't mind me." He flashed a quick smile at her. "You put me in a good mood."

She looked away, wishing he hadn't said that. "Thank you."

"Short cut here." He led her to a paved path alongside the railroad tracks, passing bars and restaurants on one side, and several parked railway cars on the other. A cluster of couples poured out of a large brewery and pub, noisy and cheerful. "Good biking trail, if you follow it all the way. You like to ride?"

He's checking out future dates. "Not really. I'm a runner."

"Yeah, that's right." He sounded as if he knew this about her and had been reminded. How was that possible? She must have misread him. "Runner."

They crossed a parking lot behind a low brown building with a sign announcing it was Marisol's, walked around to Guadalupe Street, and he opened the door to a noisy little restaurant and bar with a neon green chile in the window above the name. The door was pink, the frame was green, its interior walls were turquoise, and the smell of food hit like a wall of warm spices.

Jangarrai took her by the elbow and steered her through the crowded room to the bar. His touch startled her. Though it was gentle and considerate, sexual energy flowed through it too, a subtle but unmistakable charge.

Not once in her years with Hubert had she had any inclination to cheat. She had come to think of other men's attraction to her as nothing more than the annoyance of a trucker's honk or a passing whistle on a street. It wasn't *real*. She still saw herself as Wife and Mama, not someone men flirted with. *Wrong on both counts.*

Chapter Seven

"Beer? Wine?" Jangarrai asked as they took seats at the bar. "What would you like?"

"Oh, I'm the one who wanted to talk to you." Mae started to open her purse. "Let me pay."

He laid his hand over hers to stop her. She felt a soft surge of his energy again. The smile, half-nervous, half-happy, flickered on and off. "You strike me as a lady who would prefer wine."

"I do."

"Go easy if you're new to the altitude, though. It'll get to you. Turn you into a two-pot screamer." He turned to the bartender, ordered a local microbrew beer for himself, and white wine and a glass of water for her, and then spun his barstool to face her again. Their knees bumped and she turned away as much as she could without being rude, aware of how unskilled she was in situations like this. With her first marriage straight out of high school and her second too close on the heels of the first, she had no experience of being a single adult going out for drinks with a man.

He watched her taste the wine. It was dry, and to her surprise, spicy, giving her a little jolt.

"Green chile wine," he explained. "I love the stuff."

"No wonder you ordered me some water."

"Do you like it?" He looked genuinely concerned that she might not.

"Actually, I do."

He smiled, and she sipped her water, avoiding his eyes. Big, long-lashed, black-brown eyes with the beginnings of smile lines crinkling the corners. If she were interested in men right now, those eyes would get to her.

"Um—I feel stupid," he took a swig of beer, exhaled, "but I didn't get your name."

"Mae Martin-Ridley."

He went from bright to gloomy halfway through her name, drank more of his beer, and stared at the bottles behind the bar. "Hyphenated. Married, then?"

Should she say she was getting divorced? Or was it better to let him think she was still married? She didn't want to lie, but she didn't want to encourage him. "Just separated a few months ago. Still married, in a way. Not done yet—and not looking."

He drank again, set the bottle down a little too hard. "Fuck. I thought that was a line, y'know? About your friend wanting my CDs. A really good one. Like me seeing your heart-stopping bum and saying, 'I've got a friend who's a photographer, you could model,' only more original. Like," his voice dropped, "like ... you *liked* me."

The way he said *liked* made her uncomfortable. It was too vulnerable. They were almost strangers. "I really do know someone who wants to sell your music. And that Asian lady with the tattoos, did you see her?"

"Yeah. Cracking onto me." He came back to his cheery, outgoing mode. "Weird. Women don't usually do that."

"She wasn't trying to hit on you. She wants to manage your music career."

"Fuck me dead. You're sure?"

"Yeah, I talked with her. And her *girlfriend*. Seriously, she's only got a professional interest in you."

"Bugger. I blew that." His mood darkened so abruptly she was taken aback. He frowned, clenched his fists and pressed them together, elbows on the bar, avoiding Mae's eyes. "So give me her card and we'll be done with it."

"I will. I wasn't sure you were even interested in selling your music. You kind of drifted off like you weren't—"

"You could have left. You could have just given me her fucking card and left."

"Don't bite my head off. I like your music." Why was she defending her decision to go out with him? She hadn't led him on. "I wanted to make sure you did something with it."

"Sorry." He relaxed in part, his body taut but his voice gentle again. Drawing lines in the cold wet sides of the beer bottle, he watched the drips from the rearranged condensation trickle, and then looked at her, his eyes soft and hopeful. "It's—it's what, then? You're into the music, you're ... what?"

The moment felt so profoundly awkward, Mae froze. At least he'd only stayed angry for about ten seconds, but now he seemed to be trying to ask her—who in the world actually asked anyone this?—if she liked him, and he so nakedly *wanted* to be liked.

"I'm here to help my daddy and his partner get their rental house ready. The manager at the Healing Balance Store in Virginia Beach asked me to try to find you while I'm here. She said your web site was down and the phone number for contacting you was gone. Then I met Wendy, who wants to handle your whole everything—you have to talk to her. So, that's what I'm doing. I like your music, and I'm helping these people sell it."

She opened her purse, got out her business card case, and set it on the bar. He'd been so disappointed that she really *meant* business, she probably should close the conversation as soon as possible, although he'd bought her a drink and been sweet in a way, before he got temperamental. Wendy's and Deborah's cards were in with her own, and she had to dump a few out to get to them.

Jangarrai picked up both of hers, one in each hand, ignoring the other cards that Mae set by his elbow.

"These are both you. Same phone number." He slid the cards together, played with them as if he were shuffling a deck of two. "You're a personal trainer and a psychic."

She nodded. "I guess that's not as weird in Santa Fe as some other places, but it worked better back home to keep it separate."

"Not here. Makes you fit right in. It'd only be weird if you did it naked with aliens, and even then, only if you added fish-slapping or something." He flashed her a smile, a sudden blast of light and warmth cracking the clouds of his moodiness. Mae started to think of it as The Smile, some patented Jangarrai mannerism calculated for effect and yet sincere at the same time. "What kind of name is Breda Outlaw?"

"Country. And family. My granma was an Outlaw."

He let out the snort laugh in mid-drink, choking on his beer, and turned away from her. "Crap, fucking beer up my nose." He grabbed a napkin, wiped his face, turned back to her, and sang in a caricature of a country western singer's voice and accent, "My granma was an outlaw, but Grampa he was the law. She stole his heart—"

"It's a *name*." She laughed. "Lots of folks are named Outlaw up in the Blue Ridge."

"It's a weird name."

"Not that weird. What kind of name is Jangarrai?"

"Not weird either. Warlpiri. It's my skin name, like a clan name, sort of like a middle name. Tells me who I could marry if I was living bush and being traditional, following the rules. Mum didn't. Obviously."

"Because you're here?"

"Nah. Because my Dad's white."

She sipped the chilled hot chile wine and the water. He looked black to her except for the hair, and that had to be dyed, a peculiar choice. She wondered why he wanted to be strange looking, when he seemed so socially awkward as it was. Maybe it was part of his performing persona, making himself memorable. Funny he'd never put his picture on his CDs if he wanted to be noticed and remembered, though. If he had, she wouldn't have missed him the first time in the Plaza, and would have been spared this awkward situation.

"You picked up the wrong cards." She nudged Wendy's card at him. "Unless you don't need a manager."

"Jeezus. All business, aren't you? Aren't you lonely here without your husband? And I bet you have kids. You seem like a mum."

"Two young'uns. Stepdaughters. I miss 'em, but—you keep changing the subject."

"You're psychic." He looked at her card again. "You know if I need a manager."

"I have to work at being psychic. I don't just sit here and know everything about you."

"That's a relief. Fuck. I'd hate to have you, y'know, *see* everything. Destroy my *aura of mystery*." Giving her a mischievous grin in the mirror, he paid as his second beer arrived. He lifted the bottle for a long swig and set it down, failing to stifle a loud belch. "Sorry." He spun the stool to face away from her for a moment. "Can't seem to drink without doing that."

"Kind of blows your aura of mystery."

"Yeah." He snort-laughed, faced the mirror again and drank more slowly, swallowing the noises. "Least I didn't blow it out the other end."

"Look, there's only two mysteries. Why are you so hard to get hold of, and why aren't you jumping on this chance to get a professional manager?"

Shrugging alternate shoulders in a kind of dance of doubt or indecision, Jangarrai picked up Wendy's card and looked at it. "How do I know she's for real? Or any good?"

"I don't know. She's done other management work, but I think you'd be her first music client."

"Is that good?"

"Talk to her. She said she'd like to do everything—guide your career, do the marketing—'hands-on' is how she put it. She thinks she could *discover* you, like you're the next big thing."

He crunched the card up in his fist and chewed on his knuckles, eyes closed, and then looked at Mae. "Fuck. Seriously?"

"Seriously."

"Jesus." Wide eyed, he fixed his gaze somewhere past her head, almost not breathing. Then, pressing his fingers to his temples, he leaned his elbows on the bar, letting the crumpled card fall beside Mae's intact ones. "Fuck."

"What's the matter?"

"Dunno what to do." The distress in his voice surprised her. What was so hard, or so alarming, about a career advancement? "Don't push me. Please."

"I didn't mean to."

He looked up and took a short, harsh breath, starting to sweat despite the air conditioning.

"Are you all right?" she asked

"Having a wobbly." His voice was tight and his eyes dazed, as if he couldn't see. "Not too bad."

What could make someone go into a state like this? Low blood sugar?

"Have you eaten?"

He shook his head, leaned it on his hands again. She picked up a menu from between a hot sauce bottle and napkin holder. "Guess you'd better get something then, sugar." Where did *that* come from? Mae never called people *sugar*. "You worked hard tonight. What do you want?"

He mumbled the word "vegan," and ran his fingers into his hair, knocking his hat onto the bar. Mae caught it from falling over onto the far side, and waved to the bartender.

"What's the best vegan thing on the menu?"

"Black bean wrap and the potatoes. His usual."

"One order of that."

Putting the menu away without looking at the price of what she'd ordered, Mae watched Jangarrai. He hadn't moved, but his breathing seemed shallow and fast. The name. Too long. That was why she'd called him *sugar*. Brook and Stream, and once upon a time Hubert, were *sweetie* and *honey,* her names for people she loved. She couldn't call him that, but she couldn't use a name like Jangarrai when she was worried about him.

"Sugar?"

He turned his head away, his hands raking his hair, his posture more contracted.

"Can you take a few slow breaths, maybe like you breathe when you sing?"

At first he seemed too far gone to respond, but after a few minutes she heard a long, shaky inhalation and exhalation, a kind of gasp, and then more normal, slow breathing as his hands relaxed. He sat up straighter, put his hat on, and pulled it over his eyes. Thus blinded, he reached over to her, and she took his hand. It was hot and damp and unsteady, and squeezed hers hard.

To Mae it felt like a long time, waiting for Jangarrai to recover, but the clock behind the bar told her it was only about five minutes. Five minutes of holding this strange man's hand.

"Thanks, love." He lifted the hat with his free hand, let go of her, and looked down, clasping his beer. "Sorry about that. Happens sometimes."

"You don't have to apologize."

"Yeah, I do. Jeezus. I meant to take you out for a nice evening and I fucking *do that*. Well, never mind the take-you-out-for-a-nice-evening part, either. Sorry. Just talk to me, keep me company, all right?"

"What do you want to talk about?"

"Doesn't matter." He shoved his hat back to its normal position. "Ask each other questions. Be nosy. What d'you want to know about me? And then I get to ask you."

She couldn't think what to ask without seeming to want to get to know him personally, which would seem like flirting, or without pressing him about his career, which seemed to upset him. Only one question popped up, and as soon as it was out she was afraid it might insult him. "Why do you dye your hair?"

"Jeezus." He sounded annoyed as he turned away from her, taking a drink of his beer, and she looked at the back of the cloud of strange hair. It wasn't curled tight like African hair, but wavy and crinkled, and she felt an urge to check out its texture to see if you could comb it. What an odd impulse. Facing her again, he put on a minor version of The Smile. "Sorry. Get sick of people asking that. It's not dyed. I'm a permanent juvenile."

He took his phone out, turned it on, and she noticed that the first thing that came up on the screen was *no service*. Like he hadn't paid his phone bill. He fumbled with the keypad, scrolled though some pictures, and handed the phone to her. "See?"

The picture displayed two boys, darker than he was, with long, wavy blond hair even lighter than his, and shy black eyes looking up into the camera. They were bare chested in shorts and sneakers, in an area of red dirt and scrubby plants.

"My nephews. Aboriginals start out blond, lots of us. My sister turned dark. Most people do. A few women don't, and even fewer men don't, but it happens. Rare and strange. I'm like a baby seal—y'know, those things people club to death—that stayed white when it grew up. Permanent juvenile. Bit of a freak for that. I used to shave my hair off and think it'd finally grow in dark, dyed it and hoped it'd take somehow ... never did. But it's not the white blood. We make blonds without 'em."

She blushed, regretting that she'd thought he was vain when he seemed resigned and not happy about his odd blondness. To cover the awkwardness, she focused on his nephews' picture. "Where was that taken? New Mexico?"

"Nah. They live in Perth, but that's in the GAFA. Sorry, Outback, Great Australian Fuck-All. Don't see 'em more than once year." He sounded sad about that as he took the phone back and closed the images, putting it away in his pocket. "Parents are there now. Not the GAFA, Australia." He pronounced it 'Straya. "Dad's on sabbatical 'til January. He studies people like us." He finished his beer, too fast by Mae's standards, and signaled to the bartender. "That's how he met Mum. Except she said, 'the only way you're studying me, anthro, is over dinner.'" In the mirror, he gave Mae a wink, and their reflected eyes locked. "I take after her."

Loud laughter erupted from a nearby table, and applause. One of the patrons rose and embraced another. Jangarrai watched with radiant delight, seeming to share the strangers' joy. The bartender brought him his food and a fresh beer, and Jangarrai drank immediately. He slid the plate of fried white and sweet potatoes toward Mae as he picked up an enormous wrap bulging with beans and dripping with a chunky green sauce.

"That's your third beer," she said. "You're not driving that van home."

"Just doing my part for the Australian stereotype." He licked a drizzle of green salsa off his wrist. "Land of rubber sidewalks and more words for getting a gutful of piss than the Eskimos have for snow." Taking another bite of the wrap, he asked, "You driving?" He talked with his mouth full, seemed to realize what he'd done, swallowed, and said, "Sorry. Gotten uncouth being single."

Better manners would help him fix the singleness, but it would be insensitive to tell him that, at least right now. "I walked." She sipped her wine and her water. "But how are you getting home?"

"Never mind me. You shouldn't walk alone this time of night." He grabbed a handful of the fried potatoes and stuffed them in his mouth. Maybe he just really enjoyed food and beer, but it looked to Mae that he ate and drank as if he were starving. "You can drive the van. That's an honor, y'know."

"So you escort me by having me drive myself in your van," she said, "and then you walk home?"

The plan sounded wrong as soon as she heard herself say it.

"Yeah, from your place." He dove into the bean wrap again, green salsa dripping onto both hands and into his beard. "Or something. I haven't figured that out yet."

Chapter Eight

When she'd found Jangarrai, Mae had thought her task so easily accomplished. Now she wasn't sure she had gotten him to agree to contact Wendy, which might be necessary for Deborah to be able to order more of his music, and somehow she'd taken on a new responsibility, to find a safe way to get him home, as well. She didn't want to get in his van with him, didn't want him to drive it, and wondered if he'd be all right going home by himself. What if he had another spell while walking, or in a cab? Delgado Street was so close she felt silly getting a taxi for herself, and the streets were busy and public enough that she'd be safe if she walked. It was him she was worried about.

A streetlight went out over their heads as they left the bar.

He seemed to think she'd agreed to drive the van, but she didn't really know who she was with, not even his whole name, let alone very much about him. She asked, "Do you have more to your name?"

"James Edward Jangarrai Ellerbee." He flashed a quick grin, and aimed their walk back toward La Villa Real Center, taking the Guadalupe Street route this time. "Mouthful, isn't it? Family calls me Jamie. Some musicians call me Jangarrai, but it's really more like, in the bush, you'd say *that* Jangarrai. I'd be one of a few blokes with that skin name. My ex thought it was good marketing to use it."

"It was. But Jamie's easier to say."

"I liked it when you called me *sugar*."

Mae avoided the flirtation implied in his tone. "I'm not sure about driving your van. How far off do you live? Walking distance?"

He frowned. "Long walks are out. My hip's fucked—well, not totally, but there's some metal in it. Don't pound the pavement if I can help it." He put on that trying-to-charm smile. "How far are you? I can get my bike out of the van and be your slow-rolling escort."

This offer struck her as avoidance of some kind. He still hadn't told her where he lived, or even how far. Was he trying to make sure he knew where *she* lived? "And leave your van?"

"Yeah. Hardly ever drive it unless I've got to carry stuff. I've left it all over town." They walked in silence for a block, and then Jamie said, "I'm not drunk, by the way. I know I drank too fast. But I'm all right. I mean, I'm not a drunk. In case you thought that's why I leave my van. Not that I don't get off my face once in a while, but—" He stopped walking. "Fuck. I'm making myself sound like I'm lying, and I'm not. What I'm trying to say—I drink sometimes, but I'm not a drunk."

"My first husband was an alcoholic." She started them moving again. "I can tell the difference."

"First husband? So you've been married *twice* already? Jesus. That's a lot to go through. Breaking up with the woman I lived with was bad enough—I can't imagine surviving a divorce. Twice." The sincerity of his compassion, the depth with which he felt her pain, disconcerted her. It was too intense for someone she'd just met. "It'd rip your heart out."

"Depends." She didn't want to talk about having her heart ripped out. "My mama's heading into marriage number three, as soon as she's divorced from number two. I don't think her heart's ripped out—she's already given it to the next man. Not that I can see doing that. I'm taking some time out."

"You've made your point." Jamie sounded annoyed. "You can stop rejecting me. I get it."

"You don't act like you do. Off and on, but you keep bouncing back."

"Can't help it. Feel like I know you."

"You couldn't."

"Yeah, I could." He stopped, lightly touching her arm to stop her with him. "Your name's Martin. Your father talks like you, right? Lives with Niall Kerrigan, the sculptor?"

"How do you know them?"

"Arts circles." He started walking again. "Mum's a poet. Back when Niall still had his studio here—I think he and your dad were as new in town as my parents were—Niall had these open studio nights every month, second Saturdays. Mum would do poetry readings and there'd be Niall's work on display, and other artists and poets and musicians would be there, and we'd be in this crazy jungle of—you've seen his stuff—"

"Not much. Just what's in the house here, and in T or C."

"It's fucking amazing, isn't it? I loved the masks. There's one he said looked like me. Had these round saw blades for eyes and a rake for a mouth, old springs on its head ..." Jamie made a face, exaggerating his large eyes and wide mouth, holding his hair stretched out to the side, and then laughed and dropped the act. "*Anyway*, I'd play didg while Mum read her stuff, very Aboriginal, y'know, exotic for the Americans—and then I'd get to hang out and watch the adults have these witty, sophisticated conversations." He slid his hands into his pockets, looking down at his feet after a quick glance at Mae. "My sister's older, and she'd float around and chat with everyone like she belonged, and I couldn't even open my mouth with kids my age, let alone with these *important artist* people, scared to death of them all. Except your dad. He didn't fit in either, but he wasn't nervous like I was. Just soaking it up and smiling. Being nice to me." A pause. "He showed me your picture. Talked about you a lot. You ran track, played softball. I remember that."

So he really had recognized that she was a runner. Her father had told him, way back when Marty had first disappeared from her life. Mae felt a pang of jealousy, irrational as it was. Jamie had been there for the part of her father's life she'd missed. Then she pictured Marty, missing her, talking about her to a gawky teenage Jamie while the artists had their wine and clever conversation. The jealousy melted into a kind of kinship, as if he was a brother.

At the parking lot, they found the van alone under a light. Jamie unlocked it, moved his drum out of the passenger seat. "Is it the house on Delgado that you're cleaning? That's one fucking gorgeous house. I loved that place."

"Yeah, but you wouldn't love it right now. It's all smoked in and dog-hairy—the lady that rented it was a pig. Grease, and spills—it's disgusting."

"Jesus. You're living in it in that shape?"

"I have to."

"No, you don't. Hop in. We'll give it a burl, see if we can get the whole thing done tonight. How's that sound? Can't have that hanging over your whole time here."

"Jamie—that's what I'm here for."

"Nah, you're here to find me." He jumped into the passenger seat and tossed her his keys. "For that lady in Virginia." A quick smile. "Or Wendy Huang."

Get the whole thing done tonight. It was tempting, but it would mean bringing him in, not just riding with him. "Hang on a second." She took her cell phone out and called Marty. He might be asleep, but he might not.

"Marty's phone, he's sleeping. Niall speaking."

"Hey, this is Mae—"

"I know who you are."

"I'm sorry to bother you—"

"Cut the Southern courtesy crap. Get to the point. We're old men, we get tired."

"Okay. You weren't an old man yesterday, now you are." Was Niall always this abrupt? Maybe he was just being Northern. She walked a few steps away from the van and lowered her voice. "I met

Jamie Ellerbee and I want to know if it's okay to trust him. Is he all right?"

"Is he there?"

"Uh-huh."

"Let me talk to him."

Puzzled, Mae returned to the van and passed Jamie the phone. He looked quizzical as he took it, listened for a moment, and smiled. Apparently Niall hadn't been as disagreeable to him. "Jeezus ... No, I'm not ... Fuck, no—no ..." He grew serious and looked a little sad while Niall talked for a while. "Nah, I'm all right. Yeah? ... Of course. Too right." He smiled again. "Yeah. Catcha." He handed the phone back to Mae.

"Hey, I'm back," she said.

Niall snapped, "Of course he's safe. Have fun. Good night."

She wondered what Niall had said to Jamie. They seemed to get along well. Putting her phone back in her purse, she got into the driver's seat and looked around. The van was a mess, the desert's red-pink grit thick on the floor, paperback books and papers crammed into the side pockets. The glove box hung open, apparently broken, spewing crunched old maps. As she turned the key, the engine coughed, and she tried again. The van started this time, but the check engine light came on.

What would Hubert think of this vehicle? The reflex to think of her mechanic husband struck her, a guerilla grief attack. She pushed it down. Still, this van was the most neglected thing she'd ever seen on four wheels. Hubert would be bothered by it. He didn't like to see cars mistreated.

"You need to get this van to a mechanic."

"Nah, still runs. Might put some tape over the light." Jamie tipped his seat back, stretching. "Nice to talk to Niall," he said wistfully. "He sounds the same. The cranky Yankee."

"So that's normal?"

"Yeah. Grows on you. He remembered at lot about me. Wanted to know if I was singing at the Met yet." A sad laugh. "Not bloody likely, but, y'know, he thought to ask. Even if he knows I'm not."

Mae started the van out of the parking lot. "This street is two way, isn't it?"

"Yeah."

"Did you train for opera?"

"Yeah. Caught the train. Missed the boat. Or something. Whoop—missed the street— Chuck a yewy— Nah, never mind, take your next left. You can't get lost. It'll all get you there." He tipped the seat a little further back. "Bloody hell, I ate too much. Beer and beans. Hope I don't fart."

"I hope not, too. I'm trying to air the place out."

Jamie cracked up, as if this were much funnier than it was. "Fuck." He caught his breath. "When you first get to know someone, d'you ever worry about that crap? Like, what if I fart, or what if I have things stuck in my teeth or hanging out of my nose, or what if I stink up the bathroom or whatever, and it's bound to happen, y'know, sooner or later, and I fucking *die* of it, get terrified, paralyzed. Like I'll be disgusting and she'll hate me—fuck, you just have to *do it*, y'know?"

Having never worried about these things, Mae wondered what to say. He had just listed his fears and embarrassments with a candor somewhere between neurotic and funny. Did he want a laugh, or compassion?

Jamie seemed to take her silence as a comment. "All right, just shoot me. Shut me up. Shoot me." He pulled his hat over his face. "Jesus. I'm such an idiot."

It was going to be a long, long night. Mae hoped she could get through it still liking him. He had the potential to either entertain her or get on her nerves, and it was fifty-fifty which way things would go.

When they parked, he crawled into the back of the van and came back with a toothbrush that wore a little plastic cap. "Not moving in, don't worry, just anxious. Y'know. The teeth."

In the house, he made sick noises about the smell, apologized for his adolescent humor, and excused himself to brush his teeth. When he returned, toothbrush sticking out of his pocket, he seemed calmer. "Ahh. Minty fresh." He beamed The Smile.

While they scrubbed the nicotine stains and food splashes off walls, and the bacon grease off the stove, he claimed his turn to ask nosy questions, and inquired about her work as a psychic and in fitness, about the place she grew up, her favorite music, favorite foods, if she liked to dance, what she liked to read, and what she would study in college. Normally reserved, Mae found that Jamie's clumsy honesty combined with his strange off-and-on shyness made him easy to talk to. So far, he was more fun than aggravating, and seemed to have moved past flirting. To her relief he showed no signs of another spell like he'd had in the bar. His moods didn't seem as erratic any more. Maybe eating had made him more steady, and that was all that had been wrong with him. A whole day without food could make anyone moody and light-headed.

They cleaned the refrigerator, dumping out the nauseating remnants from the plastic tubs, and he sang a lower-volume version of his blues song, hips and feet dancing as he worked.

"She's like something gone bad in the back of my fridge.
My memory gags on the things that she did,
But I'm throwing her out, cooking up something new,
'Cause I can't stand the smell of these left-over blues."

Time flew. Somewhere in her muscles and bones, Mae knew she was tired and that the effort of the work was wearing on her, but Jamie's randomness and silliness distracted her from the difficulty of even such repellent tasks as getting dog hair out of the freezer.

"All right, not even light out yet. We just need to air the furniture and we're done." He clapped his hands together overhead, looked at Mae. "Ready? You can lift as much as I can, I bet."

"What, take it outside?"

"Yeah, blow the stink off."

"What if it rains?"

"Not 'til tomorrow afternoon. Monsoons hit at two or three, usually. Night sometimes, but there're no clouds. I'll help you put it back in, rock up around two or so." He squatted and began to lift one end of the couch. Pie ran out and dashed into the bedroom with a terrified squawk, and Jamie set the couch down with a look of shock and worry. "Fuck. Poor thing. That's that same cat. Sweetiepie. Must be a hundred years old now. Is she all right?"

"No. I think the dog must have scared her a lot. She's kind of traumatized."

"You're a healer, though, right? You said you do that stuff. You can help her."

"I can't get hold of her."

"Sure you can. Got some cat food?"

He walked into the kitchen, opened cabinets until he found the cans, and then dug through drawers. "Place needs better cooking stuff. Bodgy knives and things." Flourishing a can opener, he closed the drawer and sang under his breath as he opened the cat food. "Love cats, hate cat food. Smell that dead fish."

He dipped his fingers in the stuff nonetheless and walked to the bedroom. In slow motion, he lay on the floor near the bed and even more slowly, seeming to take ten minutes or more, extended his arm under the bed, cat-food fingers reaching toward Pie.

"Now don't make me laugh, all right?" Jamie whispered. "I've got enough bloody methane built up to melt the polar ice caps. Don't want to scare poor old Pie."

Mae sat in the big green-and-yellow wooden chair beside the bed, kept back a laugh and said nothing. Fart jokes again, and she thought it was funny. She was punchy from lack of sleep and physical exhaustion as well as the altitude. And she was starting to like him, crudeness, cussing, bad manners and all, the way she might feel if she'd had a brother. Smiling, she watched him, waited for Pie.

Nothing happened.

How could he be so patient and kind, and yet so moody and erratic? What a puzzling person. As Jamie held still and made no sound, Mae began to feel drained and sleepy. Her eyes dropped shut. It was what—three in the morning?

In seconds she was in the psychic tunnel and then plunged through it, coming out on a beach. Two boys walked hand in hand, a white boy about twelve or thirteen with a stocky build and red face, and a chubby dark brown boy of about three, with thick ash blond hair. The older boy had the air of a martyr as the little one clung to him, and he shook the toddler off. "I'm taking a dip. It's too bloody hot and I'm sick of you, all right? Stay put."

"But the jellyfish. Mum said jellyfish."

"I'm not scared of jellyfish." The older boy splashed out into the waves, and the young one stared after him, digging his toes into the sand. The scene blurred, and now the older boy lay in the shallow surf, his eyes wide open, his once red face now blue, the little boy again holding his hand, whispering, "Come on, Pat, come back. Pat? Pat?" A lifeguard stood behind them, talking on a radio, and Mae could make out the words "sea wasp." The older boy made a sound, a gasping rattle, and the little boy, gazing into Pat's open eyes, seemed to hold his own breath as the other's stopped.

"Mae, she's licking my fingers," Jamie whispered. She opened her eyes. What had she just seen? It looked like his friend or babysitter had died before his eyes when he was little. Did he remember it? Could he have understood what happened? Witnessing death, at such an age. And why had she seen this? Her mind jumped to the kid who'd died under the bridge. *Son of some friends of ours found him. His folks said it shook him up pretty bad.*

"Love that little funny cat tongue. Yeah, good girl, Pie, that's it. You're safe, love." Still in slow motion, Jamie extended his other arm under the bed, no faster than his first reach. Then, bending his knees so he could use his feet to drag himself on his back along the floor, he brought the thin, old cat out from under the bed. He drew her to his chest and held her. "Got you, Pie. You'll be all right. No more dog."

I could have done that. Mae hadn't even thought of it. "You're good with her."

"Fear. Y'know? I get it. I'm a fucking fear machine and a trauma magnet." He stroked Pie's thick fur and smiled. "Could you take her, love? Let's feed her in the kitchen, let her feel all loved and taken care of." His voice was so tender, Mae wondered if he'd be a good father—if he were more stable. Mae took the cat to let Jamie get up, and carried Pie to the kitchen. The old cat felt as if she weighed only about three pounds.

Jamie followed. He put a little blob of cat food in a bowl, set a bowl of water beside it, and sat on the floor beside Pie, talking nonsense in a soothing voice. When Pie looked around nervously, he held still, and then reached his hand slowly toward her. She sniffed it, and let him touch her. He petted her, and she turned back to her food. When she seemed calm, he rubbed her back, massaging her bony shoulders.

"You can heal her now, love." He looked at Mae. "All yours."

"I think you already did."

"Nah, just tamed her. The crap doesn't go out of your head that fast."

"It doesn't with energy healing, either. It's just a start. Like what you did. Maybe you'd be a good healer."

"Nah. Too bloody fucked up." He glanced down at Pie, and then stood. "But thanks. Let's move some furniture. After I—" He ran from the kitchen through the living room and out the back door, letting it slam. After a moment, the snort-laugh. "Jeeezus. Hope I didn't kill the plants." He came back in, twitched a corner of a smile. "Sorry. Just shoot me."

They carried the kitchen chairs, the living room chairs, the sofa, and even the mattress and box spring into the garden, leaning the bed parts against the adobe wall and setting the rest of the furniture along the path. Mae collapsed onto the couch and looked up at the blazing stars. She wanted to go to bed, but was too tired to get back up, and too grateful to Jamie to evict him quite yet. "I don't think I can move."

"You don't have to." He held up a hand, signaling her to wait, jogged into the house, and returned with two beers. Ruth's beer supply was the only thing they hadn't thrown out from the refrigerator. He opened both, handed one to Mae. "Washed the tops off, hate to think what was on 'em. Cheers, then. Fucking cheap piss, but it's the champagne of the moment. We're done."

Remaining where she had flopped back, Mae clicked her beer can to his. "To your kindness, sugar. You helped me and Pie more than I can say."

"My pleasure. It was fun. Anyway, I hated to think of this lovely place all vile and stinking." He slouched beside her, stretched his legs out, drank his beer, and belched as loudly as an opera singer could project his voice. "Sorry. Forgot. Thanks for putting up with me."

What a funny thing to say. Putting up with him? He'd done half her work for her and tamed the traumatized cat, and he thought she'd had to tolerate him. She had expected it would be hard, but his lapses of grace and manners had already stopped bothering her. She looked over to him in the starlight, and he was smiling at her, the gold tooth glinting. A lot was strange about him, and that tooth had to be one of the oddest things. In her fatigue, she didn't filter the question, though it sounded rude as soon as it was out. "Why do you have a gold tooth?"

"Good onya. Still asking nosy questions. I broke it. Sped into a pothole on my bike and smashed my mouth on the road in India when I was thirteen. Village dentist didn't do porcelain. Old-fashioned. He said gold was 'very good.' " Jamie imitated a strong India accent. "That gold had some kind of signature, like it was good for you, your luck, your energy, something."

"That kinda makes sense. Minerals having some vibrations or effects. I work with crystals as a healer. Did the gold work?"

"Maybe. Didn't have another trauma for," he looked thoughtful, "five years. But that's not why I kept it. Having it done was so bloody awful I didn't want to go through replacing it with a white tooth. So there you have it. My souvenir of our year in India. A gold tooth and my fear of the dentist, fear number five hundred and nine." He lifted the beer, gestured a toast and took a long swallow. "You finally asked me a question." He grinned. "First one since we left the bar."

"You asked me so many, I didn't get a chance."

"Nah, you're not nosy like I am. Keep to yourself, mind your own bizzo. Am I right?"

It was what mountain people were like. Appalachian normal. "Kind of. I try, anyway."

"So try not to. Ask me something else."

So many things she could ask. What had happened to him in the bar, why did he call himself a trauma magnet, why had his family been in India for a year ... But she hadn't ever gotten a firm answer to her first question of the night.

"Are you gonna call Wendy?"

He closed his eyes. "Fuck. Dunno."

She remembered the out-of-service message on his phone. He hadn't paid his phone bill, had he? Did that mean he couldn't call her? No, he probably had a land line at home. He spent money, ate out—the bartender had identified that meal as "his usual." He didn't act poor, although his van looked neglected. More likely he was chaotic and didn't get around to things. That explanation fit with the way his mind bounced around.

"Why not? You need a manager."

Squeezing his eyes shut tighter Jamie shook his head, and then sat up and looked at the statue. He drank from his beer and set it down. "I guess I should go. Let you rest." He swallowed hard, nodded to the statue. Some unspilled emotion roughened his voice. "She'll keep you company. Pie will, too."

"Jamie? What's the matter?"

"Nothing, love." He stood. "Why don't you bring Pie out here to sleep with you? It'll do her good. All right? Hold her." He smiled down at her tenderly, then more brightly, as a thought seemed to flash into his mind. "Don't move."

He dashed into the house, came back at a slower pace with a blanket and the cat, tucked the blanket over Mae's legs, and settled Pie onto her lap. "There you go." He stroked Pie, straightened up. "See you tomorrow. We'll move the furniture in. Sweet dreams, both of you." He tipped his hat to her and walked out the back of the garden, his steps as silent as a cat's.

Mae wanted to think about what had happened, all of it, to figure him out. How much trauma had he had? Was finding the dead homeless kid part of it? Why wouldn't he call Wendy? What was wrong with him—having that spell in the bar? Her tired brain wouldn't hold on to the thoughts, and the last thing she noticed was the van's double cough before it started, followed by its rumbling, unhealthy departure. She fell into a state like sleep with Pie purring in her lap. It wasn't sleep, but she was too exhausted to notice the difference or control it as the tunnel that signaled a psychic journey opened yet again.

Chapter Nine

As the tunnel pulled her in, she felt a bright splash of emotion spread over her body, soaking into her arms and chest, and then she saw Jamie. The event had to be in the past. He had slightly shorter hair and was fifteen or twenty pounds heavier, fit and healthy. Climbing the outdoor stairway in an apartment complex, carrying a plastic bag from a department store, he sang aloud, something cheerful and operatic. He let himself into an apartment with frilled curtains and pink and blue cushions on a blue sofa. In the kitchen, he opened the package and took out a wooden box of chef's knives, washed each one by hand, dried them, and left two out on the counter. He put the others back in their slots.

Singing more softly now, he began to prepare a meal, starting rice in a rice cooker, pressing the water out of a block of tofu with a plate, and peeling garlic and onions.

A gray tabby cat pattered in and began to rub around Jamie's ankles. He reached down and petted the cat, talking to it, washed his hands, and resumed chopping. The sound of the living room door made him turn and call out, "Hello, love. How are you?"

A blonde woman with an oval face, narrow shoulders, and surprisingly curvy hips for her delicate frame, came into the kitchen. "I'm good." She stood beside Jamie as he bent down to give her a kiss. "Students did all right on their presentations." She glanced at what he was doing, and looked up at him. "Why are you home already? Don't you have a rehearsal?"

"Cancelled it. They're driving me crazy, and it's a short drive. Have to ... dunno ... *do* something. It feels like—adversarial, y'know? Bunch of teenage coyotes waiting to pounce."

"Avoiding them won't fix it."

"I know. But it feels like going to fucking school all over again."

"So you cook." She shook her head. "That's not going to help. You're spending too much time in the kitchen."

"What? Am I fat?" His eyes darkened, his voice sounded hurt. "Fuck. I'm trying not to be."

"I didn't say you were fat. You look fine. Chill. But you're wasting time and money." She looked at his hands, chopping garlic, and then at the new wooden box of knives. "You bought *knives?*"

"I got the small set, not the big two thousand dollar thing. This was only eight hundred. No meat knives."

"I asked you not to."

"Yeah, but don't you want me to cook for you?" Sliding the garlic aside, he brought a head of cabbage to the cutting board. "I'm sick of those little cheap dull knives. You can't even slice a fucking tomato."

The woman sighed, leaning against the counter. "It's not just the money. You know that."

"So I have to work with fucking kindergarten scissors for the rest of my life?"

"I don't see you handling stress so well."

"Or money, or my job, or fuck-all anything." He rammed the knife into the cabbage and shoved the entire half-prepared meal aside, spilling garlic and tofu along the counter and into the sink with unwashed dishes and soapy water. "I'm not going to do some bloody stupid thing with a knife."

"Really?" His girlfriend pulled the knife out of the cabbage with obvious effort—he seemed to have stuck it all the way into the cutting board—and washed the knife, as well as the smaller one he'd used for the garlic. Turning off the rice cooker, she wiped the knives down and put them back in the box, checked the bag for the receipt, and then placed the knife set in the bag. "I'm taking them back. *Now.* I think you just proved my point."

"Lisa." He glared at her. "I just want to fucking *cook*. You don't get it." Jamie walked to the door, caught himself in the doorway with both arms, his voice tight with pain. "You don't get *me*."

"I look at those scars every day. I get *that*."

He strode out through the living room and out the door, leaving it wide open, and ran down the outdoor staircase. At the bottom, he leaned against the adobe wall in the streetlight semi-darkness, closed his eyes, and slid into a huddle on his knees. Head against the wall, fists against his chest, he seemed to struggle for breath. Lisa followed him, her steps small and slow. After a frozen moment she came up behind him, sat on the gravel, and laid a hand in his shoulder.

He clasped her hand and whispered, "Please. Please, just let me feel like a normal human being."

Too distant to be comforting, too close to be cold, her eyes sad and tired, she said nothing, letting him cling to her hand.

Mae woke up in a sweat, feeling suffocated. Was the sensation something left over from being in Jamie's mind? She pulled off his sweatshirt and dropped it on the ground. The night air chilled her damp skin. She drew the blanket up. The stars looked even wilder and brighter now. Pie crept under the blanket and cuddled close. Mae wanted to think it out, to understand, but exhaustion took her once more, this time into a heavy, dreamless sleep.

Where was she? Somewhere hot, stifled, and dark. Mae flung the cover off her face and found she was in the garden, on the couch. She must have sheltered from the sun under the blanket. Getting up, she slung it over her shoulder, propped the pillows against the side of the couch to air and carried Pie inside.

In the kitchen, Mae drank two glasses of water, overwhelmed by the desert air, and put the blanket away in the bedroom closet. She remembered the beer in the garden and went back for it, not wanting to have a new mess as a result of cleaning the old one. Jamie's *Don't Worry Be Hopi* sweatshirt lay on the bricks beside the open cans of warm beer. The images flooded back to her.

Twice, she'd fallen into psychic visions and seen his life. First the death on the beach, then the argument about knives. She'd been wearing his shirt, wrapped in his energy. What was wrong with him, the self-described trauma magnet, the man who called himself *too fucked up*? He'd said that after the gold tooth he didn't have another trauma for five years, as if this gap was a record. Pat's death must have been the first, but there had been others, more serious than painful dentistry.

What scars had Lisa been talking about? Were they hers or his? What had he done with a knife? The ferocity with which he had stabbed the cabbage, even though it had only been a vegetable, was troubling. He got angry with a knife in his hand and struck out with it.

Mae looked around at the furniture in the garden, the hard work Jamie had helped her accomplish. She returned to the spotless kitchen, dumped the remainder of the beer down the sink, dropped the cans in the recycling bin, and fed the now friendly cat. Jamie had done all that work, and tamed Pie. It seemed so unlikely, and yet, was it possible he could be dangerous? He had a short fuse and a hot temper. Niall had said to trust him. But something bad had happened, and Marty and Niall might have been gone from Santa Fe by then. Would they know what it was?

Marty didn't answer his cell phone, and Mae remembered he was running a week-long softball camp for middle school girls. She tried the landline, and Niall answered with a disgruntled, "What?" as if he didn't think phones should ring.

"Hey, Niall." Mae tried to sound cheerful in the face of his attitude. As she talked, she finally began to unpack, keeping a set of running clothes out. "How'd your opening go?"

"Adequate. One sale. One commission. Rather sell what's already there, but it's work."

She didn't know whether to commiserate or congratulate, so she did a little of both, and skipped to the reason for her call. "I've got kind of a tough question. I know you said to trust him, but how well do you know Jamie Ellerbee?"

"Known him since he was fourteen. I already told you that."

"But have you seen him lately?"

"No." A clatter and a sigh. "Get to the point. I almost didn't pick up. I'm in the middle of something."

"Sorry. He helped me clean the house, completely, all night. He was really helpful, and he's coming back to help me move the furniture we put out to air."

"So? Is that a *problem* that he's nice to you?"

"I haven't gotten to the problem yet. I met someone that's a music manager who wants to work with him. I want to put her in touch with him if he'll just agree to it and give me some way to do it. But he kept avoiding it. And he had this ... *spell*. So, before I see him again today, I wanted to know ... Is there ..." She didn't want to bring up the psychic material, but she had to hint at what it implied. "Is there something wrong with him?"

"Christ. I said you can trust him. That means you can trust him."

"You didn't answer my question."

"Look. I haven't seen Jamie for years, but his mother is one of my best friends. What she tells me is none of your business. Anything you want to know about Jamie, you ask Jamie, and if he doesn't tell you, you don't have to know. Just pay him for the cleaning. We're paying you."

She had forgotten all about that. Of course she should share the pay. "I think I have enough to cover half of it when he gets here."

"Good. If that agent or manager is any good, make sure he signs with her. He needs that."

"So he doesn't have anyone."

"You heard me. Trust him, pay him, and get him a manager. He could no more manage his own career than I could run a marathon. Now, I'm welding the legs on a pig. I'm done talking."

The cranky Yankee. Jamie had sounded so fond of Niall when he called him that. She wished their friendship didn't make Niall so protective about Jamie. It sounded as if there was some troubling secret, and Niall wasn't going to break a confidence about it.

She needed to clear her head better to think this through, but there was still no food or coffee in the house. A run first, and then she would go out to eat, and afterwards shop for groceries. The clock on the stove read eleven. She had lost what felt like half a day, though it had been necessary to get enough sleep.

As she slapped on a layer of sunscreen, it made her think of Muffie's bad advice about the sun, and reminded her to try later to search out Muffie again. Leaving the back windows open a crack to finish airing the house, Mae locked the front windows and dressed for running. Time to finally wear the pink-and-orange five-toed barefoot shoes. Her birthday gift from Hubert, back in April.

Mae had never taken the shoes out of the box, but kept on wearing her old, worn-out standard shoes, though she knew a more natural foot strike would be better for her. The last-straw fight that led to the end of their marriage had started on her birthday.

There was a little note inside one shoe. She took it out. She'd never even read this.

Honey, I hope you'll think of me with every step. These will keep your knees healthy so we can still run together when we're eighty. Romantic aren't I? Thinking of your orthopedic health. Take it real easy getting used to them or your legs will get sore. Sorry they're so pink but Brook and Stream helped me shop, and they liked these better than the blue ones. Love, Hubert.

And she'd thought he was inconsiderate, getting something this color, but he'd been shopping with the twins. The marriage that was ending had not been all bad.

Mae wriggled her toes into the little toe pockets of the shoes and remembered making fun of Hubert's black shoes like this, saying they looked like gorilla feet ... Pictured him running alone—or with his new girlfriend—on those farm roads where he'd run with Mae. Somehow, after all their disagreements, she could still miss Hubert.

Enough. Mae was alone and liked it. She was in Santa Fe, ready to run the memories out of her body and make some new ones.

She walked the block to Alameda Street, crossed the bridge to the other section of Delgado, and picked up the trail Marty had showed her that ran parallel to Alameda and the river. The thought of the young man who had fallen and died there made her glance back at the dark cave of the bridge's shadow—but she didn't need more sadness. She looked ahead and started running. The soft dirt felt good under the barefoot shoes, the gait more natural and freer than when she was wearing her old shoes. As the trail took her into a cluster of tall, sweet-earthy smelling sage plants, her head cleared, and she felt better already.

Although the river held barely a trickle of thin brown water, the banks were thick with trees and occasional wildflowers. Sometimes she had to duck under branches to run, and sometimes the trail became so narrow that she jogged down into the riverbed and back up. Running at seven thousand feet above sea level in strange shoes was a humbling experience. After what felt like only half a mile, she was winded and her calf muscles ached. Slowing to a walk, she caught her breath and resumed her run at a pace so slow she felt ridiculous. This must be how her out-of-shape beginner clients felt.

The trail ended at a park, where Mae did a few laps of run-walk intervals, and then turned back to follow the river. The return trip drained her, and she wanted water desperately. Maybe she was pushing herself too hard to try to feel normal after only two days at high altitude. *Feel normal.*

The image of Jamie from her vision came back. It was not her business to know this about him, but why didn't he feel like a normal human being? No matter what Niall said, should she trust Jamie? She couldn't bring the furniture back in on her own, and she didn't know anyone else in the city yet. As she'd left for her run, she'd caught a glimpse of the neighbors on their way to their car. They were elderly and frail. They couldn't help, even if she asked them. The clouds over the mountains promised rain in the afternoon as Jamie had predicted, and she didn't want to ruin the bed.

Approaching the bridge at Delgado and Alameda, she heard a flute playing a melancholy but beautiful tune. Jamie, still in last night's clothes, was sitting on a bench under a tree near the place where she had picked up the trail. He set the flute down, scribbled something in a notebook, played a variation on the melody and wrote again. What was he doing hanging out here? Why hadn't he gone home and changed? And if he'd found the body, why would he want to be so near the spot?

Mae slowed down. This was public enough to be safe. What a thought. How could she suddenly doubt him when he'd been so kind and companionable last night? She knew both too much and too little.

A flash of the sun-sized smile vanished as quickly as it shone. He ducked his head and fidgeted his hands along his flute. "You shouldn't be chasing me." He made shy eye contact and forced a return of the smile. "Especially in those ugly shoes."

"My husband gave 'em to me." She stopped, but jogged in place so her pounding heart wouldn't have to cool down too suddenly. "They're not ugly."

"Pig's arse. If I were me—fuck—I am me. I mean, if I were him, I'd give you flowers." His voice went soft, as did his huge black long-lashed eyes. "Furniture at two?"

She couldn't say no. She had to move it. Then she'd be done with him. "See you then."

Running off, Mae crossed the street and then cooled down to a walk. What was he doing on the river trail in the middle of the day, like he had no job, nothing to do? Near the bridge. Marty had said not to go under the bridges, because homeless people lived there. Was Jamie homeless?

No, that was ridiculous. He was clean, and there had been other keys on the key ring when he had her drive the van, keys that looked like house keys. He wouldn't have those if he didn't live somewhere. So what had he done? Hung out near her house all night? Stalked her? Ridiculous. Of course not. He'd left on his own the night before. Musicians had different schedules and lifestyles. If she hadn't had that vision about the knife, she wouldn't be thinking like this. Or would she? Maybe this was how single women living alone thought when strange men took an interest in them. The shadow side of her freedom.

The brighter side came back. She still had the sense of taking herself out on a date when she went out in Santa Fe. The beauty of the place made her feel like dressing up, caring how she looked, so she put on a sunny yellow knit dress and flat sandals to walk to the coffee shop off the Plaza.

Settled with her brunch and her laptop at the same table as the day before, she tried writing an e-mail explanation to Wendy. It was hard. Jamie made too little sense. She gave up writing, looked up the number on Wendy's card and called her. The memory of Jamie crumpling the card and dropping it on the bar came back. He hadn't kept it, had he? Had he kept Mae's?

Wendy's youthful voice answered, apparently trying to sound older. "Wendy Huang Management. Speaking."

"Hey, it's Mae. I talked with Jangarrai."

Wendy dropped the cool, mature act. "Awesome. What's he like?"

Whatever his troubles and quirks might be, musically he was what Wendy was looking for, probably exceeding her expectations. "He doesn't have any agent or manager, but he left your card on a bar and freaked out."

"What?"

"He's weird. Kind of nervous, but then he'll be funny and friendly. I have no idea what's with him." Mae hesitated to mention the depth of her concern, not knowing what it meant yet. It wouldn't be fair to make wild guesses. She could safely say something about his mood swings, though. "He might be a little high maintenance."

"I'm not planning to marry him. I want to manage his career. Sounds like he needs it."

"That's what an old friend of his family said. I'll see him later today and I'll try again. I have to warn you, though, you're not getting into normal here."

As soon she said it, Mae felt guilty. Jamie wanted so badly to be liked and feel like he was normal.

"He can be as weird as he wants. Have you got his number?"

Mae couldn't bring herself to mention the out-of-service phone. It might embarrass Jamie. "Not yet."

"See if you can get him to send me a sound file, some of his solo stuff. Does this band take up all his time now or what?"

"I don't know." Sitting on a bench composing music, he didn't look like he was tied up with the band. Or much of anything. "I don't think so."

"If this works out, I'll pay you, like a finder's fee or something. Keep after him."

What if he wasn't ready for this? Mae didn't like the idea of being paid to pressure Jamie to do something that seemed to frighten him. "I'll ask him when I see him. But if he doesn't agree to get in touch with you this time, I'm going to get his contact information and turn it over to you. Don't pay me for it. I don't want to keep hanging out with him."

"But I'm tired of chasing his shadow. Seriously, if you could set up a chance for me to meet him, I'd pay you."

After Wendy said goodbye, the words *I'd pay you* echoed in Mae's mind. She owed Jamie for his share of the cleaning work. As soon as they moved the furniture back in, she'd give him the money, get his contact information for Wendy, and say goodbye. Then Mae could squeeze in one more attempt to find Muffie, and head back to T or C tonight. She'd have to forget about being a Santa Fe tourist, even though the house was done and she had the time. Much as she wanted to trust Jamie, she wasn't sure she should. He was so sweet, and yet he was unstable in some way. And he knew where she lived.

Chapter Ten

Bringing the Sanchez and Smyth catalog and her crystals, Mae walked back to the river trail. It was close by, and the only suitable spot she knew of in the middle of the city. She needed a quiet place away from Ruth Smyth's energy to pick up Muffie's. Jamie, she hoped, couldn't still be there.

He wasn't. She sat on the bench he'd used earlier and leaned back against the tree. Enough people used this bench that she shouldn't be inundated with his energy like she had been when sleeping in his old sweatshirt, and it was private compared to the park. She hadn't seen any signs of homeless people camping down here so far.

Setting the intention to see Muffie, Mae closed her eyes and let the energy from the catalog and the crystals enter her, her mind clearing to open the tunnel. The image that appeared at the end of the tunnel was Muffie. Finally. She was alive after all, walking around a white-walled room, examining a series of prints hung on the wall. An art gallery. Mae tried to see the art in case she could locate the gallery by the type of work or the artist's name, and was startled to recognize the heart chakra drawing from Kenny's book, in a green metallic frame.

This had to be the original. As Muffie walked along the gallery, Mae discovered that the exhibit consisted of the whole series from the book, the fine line drawings in the rainbow spectrum of colors that followed the chakras. Muffie turned and struck a pose, and a young man with a camera crossed the room, knelt, and took a shot at an upward angle. Why was she having her picture taken in this gallery? Was it in Santa Fe? If it was in T or C, Roseanne should have known, and Kenny and Frank for sure would have known. So would Niall. It was a small town. Muffie couldn't be there and not be seen.

Muffie walked to a sloping rack that held books displayed face out, plucked one of the *Chakra Meditations* books, and posed with it. She did the same with Sri Rama Kriya's wisdom book, holding the black-and-white cover photo of the smiling, bald Indian man beside her own smiling face. Maybe this gallery was at his Ascended Bliss Center. In the past or the present?

A rumble of thunder distracted Mae, and she lost the vision and opened her eyes. A strong, cool wind flowed up the riverbed, fat blue-gray clouds and flashes of lightning riding its distant tail. A curtain of rain brushed the mountains like a woman's long gray hair being combed along their peaks.

Not knowing how severe a storm to expect, but impressed with the size of the clouds, she put her crystals away and started home. Her calf muscles felt tight from her first barefoot-style run. Hubert's note had reminded her to be careful about easing into those shoes at first, and she knew it was good advice, but she'd kept pushing herself.

It was exactly two o'clock when she got home, and she found Jamie, hatless, in a long-sleeved gray T-shirt and a slightly less faded pair of jeans, standing on the little bridge, leaning on the railing with a sad and anxious look. His bicycle was propped against the house, and his hair was soft and fluffy with no signs of helmet head.

As she approached, his face brightened. "G'day." He straightened up. "Thought you'd stood me up."

"You were early."

"Oh. Sorry. Didn't know." Half a smile, uncertain. "Um, so ... Shall we?"

"Move the furniture? I think we're just in time. Looks like a bad storm."

"No such thing as a bad storm here. Rain, you go out and dance in it. Dance *for* it, like on the Pueblos." He danced a few small steps as he followed her to the door. She set the catalog on the floor when they stepped inside. "What are you doing with that stuff?" he asked. "Sanchez and Smyth. Bloody expensive."

"Psychic work." She went to the kitchen, and Jamie came with her while she looked in the cabinets. "That's right. No salt." They'd thrown it out the night before, the container had been so coated with grease.

"Salt?"

"I use the crystals and something the person touched, something connected with them, to find them. Then I need either salt or sunlight to clean the crystals."

"Sun'll be back in an hour or less." He opened another cupboard. "Fuck, your shelves are empty." He opened the refrigerator, shut it, and looked at her with bewilderment. "You haven't shopped yet? Jesus. Got this nice clean kitchen—you've got to be dying to cook in it."

"Not really. I don't like to cook. But I do need some food. Come on, let's grab the furniture."

He trailed her into the garden. The wind slammed the door shut behind them, and he took a landscaping stone from the herb beds to prop it open. Grit blew into the living room.

"We just cleaned that," Mae said.

"But it's *clean* dirt. Part of life here. The earth comes in. So, who were you trying to find?"

They piled cushions back onto the sofa and carried it in. "Muffie Blanchette."

"Fuck. You don't need to be psychic for that. I can take you to see her."

Jamie had lived in Santa Fe a long time. He was vegan. If Muffie was involved in a restaurant venue here, they might have met, but the coincidence still startled Mae. "Seriously?"

"Yeah." He let the couch down and rubbed his left hip. "I'm surprised you're into Muffie, not being from here."

They returned to the garden for the next load of furniture. "I'm not exactly into her, but my neighbors are. Where are you gonna take me to see her?"

"Ruth Smyth's opening, of course, where else? Thursday night. Is that why you had the catalog, then?"

Not a restaurant. A gallery. Mae wondered if her vision had been Muffie at Ruth Smyth's exhibit. It would mean Ruth did the art for the books, and they knew each other, though they made an unlikely pair. "Yeah. Muffie is all over Sanchez and Smyth."

"That she is." Jamie sounded amused. "From her cowgirl hat to her batik bum to her million dollar boots."

They carried a heavy upholstered chair in and went back for the next. A few drops of rain began to fall as the sky blackened rapidly. "Ruth Smyth was the tenant here that Daddy and Niall kicked out."

"She was the pig? Never know what people are like offstage, do you? Tough that they kicked her out, but—nah—Ruth could swing it. Probably doesn't even care."

"I guess she makes some good money off those clothes."

"And her family. And her art. Which is pretty good, even if a pig made it. So ... Thursday night. I'll take you."

Mae wanted to protest being taken somewhere, or staying that long, but she did want to locate Muffie. Two more days would be worth it if she could accomplish that, though preferably without Jamie. "You sure she'll be there?"

"There hasn't been a Ruth Smyth show without Muffie for ages. So, how'd you discover Muffie?"

"My neighbors in T or C work in her restaurant. She up and left. Everybody's worried what's gonna happen to it."

"She really has a *Muffie* restaurant? I thought that was all a story, y'know? Part of her act. Fuck me dead. She actually did it."

"What act—like being a psychic?"

"Yeah." He grinned. "Reading your food aura, all that."

A crack of thunder made them both jump, and they hastened with their load, setting the second chair down carelessly and going back out for the bed. As they carried the box spring, Mae felt her calf muscles starting to cramp again, but she couldn't stop. By the time they had brought the mattress in, dropped it on the floor, and returned for the last things, loud splats of rain struck on the leather seats of the kitchen chairs.

Mae and Jamie each carried one, and then dashed back for to the other two. As soon as they were in the living room, he shoved the rock aside and let the wind close the door. Rain pelted the garden, washing the statue, making it glint as lightning flashed.

"Best rain of the summer. Lovely." Jamie remained at the back door watching the storm through the window while Mae stretched her legs. "River'll have a little water in it. Hope this lasts."

If it did, she'd have to keep him in the house. She couldn't send him out in a thunderstorm on a bicycle. He turned to her with a radiant smile, as if he had thought the same thing.

Uncomfortable, Mae put him to work. "We need to get the mattress and spring onto the bed frame. Put the chairs in place."

"You looked a little ... off ... or something. What's the matter?"

"Nothing."

She started for the bedroom. She didn't want to say, *because you looked so happy to get stuck here.* As soon as the storm was over, she'd pay him for his share of the work, get him to call Wendy, and somehow explain that he needed to leave her alone. She could go to Ruth Smyth's opening without him. Even though he'd been kind enough to help her. All night. And right now.

Feeling guilty for imagining he wasn't safe, but unable to totally dismiss the idea, she got her phone from her purse and carried it with her into the bedroom. Right now her only choice was to kick a seemingly kind and helpful man out into the rain, or keep a possible stalker in the house.

"Spider." Jamie dropped his end of the box spring, sprang back, and scrambled up onto the wooden chair, where he crouched in a deep squat, arms wrapped around his shins. Mae wanted to laugh, a grown man climbing on the furniture to get away from a spider, but his wild-eyed terror was no joke.

"I'll take care of it," she said, and took a tissue from the box on the dresser. "It must have come in from the garden."

"Don't kill it."

"But you're scared to death of it."

"Catch it in a cup and put it out. You can't kill it for being ugly."

"Fine. I'll catch it." She went to the kitchen for a glass and piece of junk mail from the recycling bin, captured the spider, and carried it out into the storm. Popcorn hail was falling now, balls of ice. The liberated spider scurried under a cedar shrub.

Mae found Jamie slumped in the chair rather than crouched in a ball. "It's out," she said.

"You didn't get any of its legs stuck, did you? Under the edge of the glass? I hate it when that happens."

"No. It went under a bush, all eight legs."

With a long sigh, he closed his eyes. "Sorry to make you do that. They scare the crap out of me, anything with too many legs."

"But you don't want to hurt its legs."

He shook his head. "Can't stand to hurt anything." He opened his eyes, exhaled a little laugh. "Mum thought it'd be great to make me and Haley—my sister—get some Aboriginal culture since we're city kids. Had us spend a season in the bush with her relatives. Learn to eat bush tucker, be part of it all." He pushed himself up straighter in the chair. "The men killed a goanna—"

"A what?"

"It's a big lizard." He held his arms out, measuring about two and half feet. "I cried. Couldn't stand it. Cutting that poor thing up and cooking it. Supposed to get my hunter-gatherer cred, and I went ve-jjo instead."

"How old were you?"

"Twelve. Yeah, I know, you'd think I was five, wouldn't you?"

"No. Twelve-year-olds can cry." The story was sweet, in a way. He'd been a sensitive kid, and had quite a few unusual experiences. Maybe if she found out more of his history, she could get at what was wrong with him. "You've moved a lot. You said you were in India when you were thirteen."

"We were. Twelve was one of our on years for Oz." He stood and helped Mae lift the box spring onto the frame. "We were all over the place for Dad's studies, home for a year or two and gone again some-where else. Japan, India, Bali, Korea. I didn't really have any sense of my culture, other than the didg. Didn't fit. Anywhere, actually."

They put the mattress on the bed. "Do you fit here? Santa Fe?"

"Y'know—I do." He looked surprised, as if he'd never realized it. "Yeah." He smiled. "It's nice here."

Mae took the sheets from the top of the dresser, and Jamie helped her make the bed. Somehow his spider terror had made her trust him more. He couldn't stand the thought of a spider's leg break-ing when he also couldn't stand the sight of a spider. He'd cried over the death of a big lizard. It made her doubt he could be violent or dangerous. What had he done with a knife, though? She still didn't understand him. The more she learned, the more she realized she didn't know.

"Why'd you move to Santa Fe?" she asked, leading him out of the bedroom.

Jamie helped her move one of the upholstered chairs back to its original spot. "Dad's from here. Born and raised. He ... they ..." Jamie looked at the second chair, walked over to it, and Mae wondered at his pause in what ought to be a simple story. They moved the chair. Jamie, still delaying, drifted to one of the kitchen chairs, started to lift it, and then set it down, rubbing a hand along its rough basket weave frame. "Dad took a job at the tribal college, the Eight Northern Pueblos College. Their token Anglo. Time to settle."

He lifted the chair again and Mae carried another to the kitchen. Sensing an incompleteness or evasion in the story, she asked, "Why then?"

At first, Jamie didn't answer. They took the other two chairs in and set them at the table, and he leaned on the back of one and sighed. "All right, they did it for me, mostly. I wasn't handling things well, all the moves. They thought I needed," he looked around the room, "stability. Funny. This house is part of that. And your dad and Niall. First few years here. Living somewhere steady and safe." He patted the chair's back. "I liked it."

"So you've lived here ever since you were fourteen?"

"We'd go back to Perth summers. Well, winter there. And I went to UNM in Albuquerque. But I've been here, yeah. It's home now." He walked to the window. "Love the weather here. Is that a work of art or what? Look at that. Perfectly round and white and in the middle of bloody hot August."

Mae looked at the hail. It was, if you stopped to pay attention, a remarkable thing. Jamie seemed to feel everything at triple intensity—beauty, fear, joy, affection, humor. What else? Anger? Time to start winding down with him. She went to the living room, got her wallet from her purse. Marty had given her a lot of cash for living expenses. Guessing at a probable fee, she took half of it and Wendy's card to Jamie in the kitchen. He still stood at the window, drinking a glass of water, humming between sips and micro-dancing to the music in his head.

"Jamie."

"Hm?"

"I'm gonna give you Wendy's card again. She really wants to talk with you, and she wants a sound file." He set his water down as he turned, and stopped short of taking the card, frowning at the handful of cash. Mae held it out to him. "This is your share for helping me clean the place."

"Bloody hell. *Money?*" His jaw clenched, and he looked at her with wounded eyes. "What the fuck d'you think I'm— What? *Money?* Jeezus."

"It's not fair if I don't—"

He strode past her through the house and out the front door into the storm. Hail pelted him as he grabbed his bicycle. Dropping the money, Mae ran after him. He jumped on his bike and rode skidding over the walkway. The ice balls piling up in the dirt of the yard and melting on the pavement were slick, and he had no helmet.

"Jamie—it's not safe—"

Lightning cracked as he turned onto the street in front of an approaching car and rode blindly into its front bumper. The car braked and slid as Jamie fell to the pavement. Heart racing, Mae dashed across the hail-slicked walkway, while the driver got out and Jamie picked himself up off the street.

"I didn't see you," said the driver, a tourist-looking type in shorts and a T-shirt, speaking with a New York accent. "You came out so fast. Christ. Are you all right?"

"Yeah, if your bumper is. Sorry. My fault." Jamie walked over to the car and stroked the bumper. "Little dent. Fuck, sorry. I ..." He looked at the driver. "I can't pay." His voice faded. "I'm sorry."

"Just watch where you're going." The man shook his head, got back in his car, and pressed an electric window button. Through the rolled-down window, he said, "Lunatic." And drove off, rolling the window back up.

Jamie stood in the street, holding his bicycle. Its front wheel was bent under. He knelt and touched it, sounding as if his heart would break. "Oh, fuck, hell, no, my *bike*."

"Let's get out of this," Mae said. He didn't move, so she took his arm and led him, startled by how ropy hard his arm felt, no give or softness at all, as if all the fat had been melted out of his body. Must be only two or three percent body fat. Way too low. When he'd been at a healthier weight, he used to worry about being fat. Strange. He knelt by his bike again at the door, and checked its damage with gentle prods as if it were a wounded animal.

"Come on in, Jamie, your bike won't get cold. But we will."

"I wrecked it, though."

She opened the door. "I'm more worried about your head."

"Jesus." A flash of anger. "Do you think there's something wrong with my head?"

"Did you hit it?"

"Yeah." He softened, looking down. Barely any voice at all now. "Maybe." He stepped inside, shaking hail off his hair like a wet dog. Mae scooped the ice balls, threw them out, and closed the door.

"Fucking idiot," he said. "I'm so sorry. I'm so sorry." He sank to the floor cross-legged and rested his elbows on his thighs, head in his hands.

"How hard?"

"Not hard enough."

Had he done it on purpose? "Jamie?"

"To knock sense into me. It was a joke." He looked up, but there was no laughter in the black wells of his eyes. "Sorry. I just ... The money ... Why the fuck did you try to give me money? I helped you from my heart. It was a gift. I thought we were friends, and that I could make you happy. And that you wouldn't be lonely, doing this awful crappy work all by yourself. And then—fuck, did you think I wanted *money*? What d'you take me for?"

"I didn't mean anything like that, sugar." She sat beside him, and caught herself about to push the wet hair from his face. *Don't.* She wanted to mother him. He would take it wrong. "I'm getting paid to clean the place, and it wasn't fair not to share it if you did half the work, that's all."

He nodded slowly, and lay face down on the floor.

Mae placed the handful of money she had dropped on her way out the door close beside him, and then went into the kitchen to get him some water. When she came back, Pie was walking on Jamie's back, purring. He hadn't moved. He might have a concussion. She couldn't send him off even when the storm cleared.

She set the glass of water beside him and watched the cat massage his back. When Jamie still didn't reach around to pet Pie, much as he seemed fond of her, Mae asked, "Does your head hurt?"

"A little."

She thought back to when she had knocked heads with another girl in a softball game and gotten concussed. She'd felt nauseous, seen double, had headaches. Had she been dizzy? She couldn't remember other than that she'd felt bad for quite a few days. "Can you sit up and see if you feel all right? I want to know if I need to take you to a hospital."

"No hospital." He sat slowly, and caught up Pie with a graceful reach behind his back to gather her to his heart and hold her like a baby. Pie lay on her back, and Jamie rubbed her belly, stroked her legs as if pulling them longer. Mae had never seen anyone handle a cat that way. It seemed odd, yet Pie purred even louder. "I'll be fine."

"Are you light-headed?"

"Little." He sipped the water. "Thanks. But I didn't eat. Yet."

"All day?"

"Been busy. Lot to do." He glanced up. "We should shop. Soon as it's clear. I'll cook you dinner. Love to cook, and you don't." He offered a tentative version of The Smile. "How's that sound?"

"What do you do all day that you don't have time to eat?"

He scratched Pie under her chin, rubbed her cheeks with one finger, and her eyes closed in bliss. "Went outside and did some mu-

sic practice. Went for a swim, did some dance practice." His speech
picked up speed and energy, accelerating as he went on. "You should
see the Chavez center, you're a fitness person. We've got a great community fitness place here. I love the pool, and they let me use the aer-
obics studio when there are no classes, so I can dance—part of my
show, y'know, being a dancer. Come with me tomorrow—"

He struck her as running from one or all of her questions, the
way he shifted the subject away from why he didn't eat all day and
turned it into a plan to spend more time with her.

"I can't go everywhere with you," Mae said. "You're acting as if
you're dating me or something."

"Nah, I know, you're still sort of married. Not ready, all that. Just
don't want you to be lonely here, that's all. I'll be your tour guide,
your chef, y'know? Make the time pass."

The last thing she wanted was a tour guide or a chef. She wanted
to be alone, not swamped with attention. But he had made the cleaning fly. When he wasn't acting crazy, Jamie was good company. Last
night, she'd even felt like he was a brother. It was the vision of him
with his girlfriend that had thrown her off him, and his lingering in
the neighborhood, still in the same clothes. The more she saw of him,
the more she wondered about his well-being. He didn't seem to want
to tell her how he was.

"Why don't you want to go the hospital? If you hit your head
and you feel dizzy—"

"I owe them money for my hip." He stood, putting Pie on his
shoulder, and walked to the window. "No more hail. We should get a
rainbow in a bit."

"Don't you have health insurance?"

"Full-time musician."

"But when you're young and healthy, it's not that expensive. I had
to get my own when my first husband was out of work and I was

working a bunch of part-time jobs. It was worth it, in case of accidents."

He shook his head, carried Pie to the couch and sat down. She jumped free, and he watched her walk off. "I'm not insurable 'til the new law kicks in. Just hanging in there for 2014, y'know? I have a history." He looked at Mae. "Long story. But I've been in a hospital six times in the past ten years."

"Six times?"

"Last one was the hip. Femoral neck fracture."

"What happened?"

"There's this thing you can do rock climbing, called bouldering, where you free climb, no harness or anything. Ideally you don't go more than twenty feet, and you have this crash pad, but I ... fuck, I dunno. Bad judgment. Something. Went too high, missed the pad, bounced off a ledge, kept going. Broke the ball off in the socket."

She cringed at the thought. That was a bad break. "And no insurance."

"Well, I had insurance when I started climbing. I don't mean that climb, not like they cancelled me up on the rock." He shot her a quick grin. "I mean when I took it up. But I fell a couple of times, stupid stuff. Smashed up my left arm and collarbone, then a right tib-fib break a few years later." He pulled up his jeans, showed her a long dark line on his lower leg. "I scar bad. It's not pretty." He lowered the pants leg. "Sorry. Shouldn't show you stuff like that."

"I'm not squeamish." Mae sensed he'd detoured again. "But you still haven't told me why you can't get insurance. Falling off a rock isn't a pre-existing condition. Being accident prone isn't a disease."

"For me it is." He jumped to his feet, beaming and sparkling, and opened the front door as if nothing had ever been wrong, no raging departure to crash into a car, no lying face down on the floor. Like the weather, his sun was back out in full force. "Let's look for the rainbow."

Mae followed Jamie onto the walkway, and he turned, his eyes wide with delight, and pointed to the sky behind the house. "Look."

A brilliant double rainbow arched over the mountains beyond the city. The mist of rain faded into a clear, dry heat, nothing left of the storm but its glowing echoes over the peaks. They gazed in silence for a while, and then Jamie said, "Can I tell you how happy I am?"

Mae turned to see his outstretched arms, too late to say *yes* or *no* to a hug as he squeezed her and practically lifted her off her feet. If she'd been a smaller woman, he probably would have.

He released her, the smile stopping short of full fearless abandon and beginning to fade. "I hope—sorry. I mean that—if that was—too—" His face now serious, he hugged himself, hands nervously massaging his forearms, his eyes wider and darker. "Too much?"

"Kind of." She didn't want to hurt him or alienate him, but she didn't want to encourage him, either. "You're like five pounds of sugar in a two-pound sack. Too much, but sweet."

He seemed on the verge of another explosion of some sort, but managed to contain it, or else it was so strong he couldn't even get it out. With a flicker of The Smile, he ducked his head, his hands on the railing, and gave himself a little liftoff. When he landed again, he faced her and said, "Shopping? I'm so hungry I could eat the arse end out of a low-flying duck."

Chapter Eleven

Mae needed food, and Jamie hadn't eaten all day—again. She still had to get him to contact Wendy, and needed to keep an eye on the health of his road-smacked head. It looked like she was committed to more time with him.

"We'll go if you take the money." Mae led the way back indoors, picked up the cash one more time, and handed it to Jamie with Wendy's card. The way he'd told the driver he couldn't pay for the bumper—as if a cyclist hit by a car should have to—made her think he was as short on cash as on survival instinct. He was too accident prone for a normal person, and he had to be up to his ears in medical debt, with the surgery on his hip. To her relief, he put the money in his pocket without protest. "You can use it to fix your bike."

"Yeah. Reckon." He followed her through the house, out the back door, and through the garden to the driveway. "But I'll put a little into dinner. I'm not broke, y'know. Don't want you to think that, just because I don't have insurance."

They got into the car. "I didn't say that." She suspected a borderline lie. "But if you're cooking, I'm buying. Give me directions. Where am I going?"

As they started out of the driveway, he asked, "You want the big Whole Foods or the little Whole Foods? I like the little one. Get lost in the other."

"There's two?"

"We're healthy here, what can I say? Well, I'm not exactly a health nut, but y'know, in general, we are. I could live on chiles and chocolate, beer and beans. The four major food groups." He gave her The Smile. "You want some spicy food? I can do some real New Mexican something for you. Don't have my cookbooks, but I can riff."

"We can stop by your place and get a cookbook."

"Waste of time—most of 'em are in storage. Only got one with me. Had to move twice, put a load of crap in my parents' attic, and they've got the place rented out to a bloke who's on *his* sabbatical doing research here." He looked out the window, told her where to turn. "Hate going in there and bothering him and his family."

"Is that where your helmet is?"

"Yeah."

"You should go bother him. You could get hurt."

He tapped the glass, pointing out a bareheaded young woman cycling past. "Lots of people don't wear 'em."

"That doesn't mean you shouldn't."

He continued to watch the street, and all she could see was the back of his head, his hair now tangled and knotted. "Van's not fond of going to Tesuque," he said.

"Where's that?"

"North on 285. Not that far, but—you heard the van."

"I need to go to a Ford place." She couldn't believe she was about to propose doing something with Jamie, but since Hubert was partial to Ford products, she knew something about them, and had noticed that Jamie's ancient van was a Ford Aerostar. "Your check engine light is on, and I need an oil change after that drive from Virginia. You could show me the way and get the van checked up at the same time. *It* doesn't need health insurance to go to the hospital."

"Nah. Scared they'll tell me it's terminal."

"You know if you keep putting things off, they don't go away. You need a manager. You need your helmet. You need to get the van fixed. You need to eat before noon or midnight or whatever you're doing these days. What's the matter with you?"

"My check engine light is on." He cracked himself up, several loud bursts of hah-snort-hah, and then slumped, fidgeting with the seatbelt. "My whole fucking life. Check engine."

Jamie directed Mae to the smaller of the two Whole Foods stores. While she shopped for what she wanted, he made suggestions for their dinner, chattering happily about favorite recipes.

A bouncy sixties pop song played on the store's music system, its lyrics ranging from *oowah ditty* to *happy every day*, a silly love song if one had ever been sung. Mae noticed movement beside her as she started to pick up a package of whole wheat tortillas from the refrigerator case. Jamie was dancing. Not toe-tapping, but full-out dancing. Embarrassed, she turned to suggest he stop, but he grabbed her hands, making her drop the tortillas, and led her, cuing the steps. "Triple step, triple step, rock back, yeah, you got it, just keep that going, even when I turn you—" He spun her and pulled her back to him. "Perfect, love, you're fucking brilliant. A natural."

It was her first time dancing with a man who could lead, unlike the freestyle get-up-and-boogie dancing she was used to, but Jamie guided her so effortlessly she couldn't tell where his touch ended and her own movement started. It was both fascinating and disorienting.

He sang along louder than the store's speakers as they danced beside the coolers in the wide aisle at the back of the store, and other shoppers genially gave them space. A store associate in a Whole Foods apron, passing with a product in hand, called, "Go, dude!"

No one apparently minded, but it was hard for Mae to let go of her reserve and fully enjoy herself. Dancing in a grocery store with a peculiar man she'd known for two days was off the map. To do it she had to shift gears into a part of her personality she hadn't met before.

As the song ended, several shoppers applauded. Mae, slightly breathless from exertion at high altitude, began to giggle. They had actually *done* this. Niall would be pleased. She had cut loose.

Jamie hugged her, and she felt the full frontal heat of him so suddenly she could neither resist nor return the embrace. He said, "You're a quick learner, love. We'll have to dance again." He let her go and turned back to the refrigerated case. "Where were we? Tortillas?"

"Yeah." At a loss, she pulled back into her known self and known space. Something had happened that she wasn't ready for. She didn't even want to know what it was. "Why don't you pick up everything for dinner and I'll get what I need for the rest of the week and meet you up front?"

"What? Was the dancing wrong? Should I not do that? I mean, we were having fun, I thought, y'know, and now you— I'm sorry." He crashed. "You want to go off separate."

She did. She wanted time out from him in a big way. He didn't seem concussed after all, and she regretted agreeing to shop with him and letting him cook. She still needed to understand more about what his problems were, to spend that much time with him.

"We need to talk."

"Now?" A hint of fear tightened the muscles under his eyes. "I mean, if you want to, I can ... Look, I'm really sorry. I like to dance."

"I'm not mad at you for dancing." She sighed. "We'll talk while we shop. But you have to stay focused, all right? Don't run off on some tangent. I seriously need to ask you some questions."

But as they walked along, picking up food, wine, and spices, Mae had to keep interrupting Jamie's raptures about some particular brand of dark chocolate or organic coffee, to initiate her serious questions. She got two words out each time before he cut in with a distraction, placing things under her nose for her to smell, or going into ecstasy over free samples of green chile guacamole.

A clerk behind the deli counter called out, "What? Cooking? No take-out?"

"Got someone to cook for," Jamie answered, beaming.

He talked to strangers, too, chatting about the joke on someone's T-shirt or admiring a hat, leaving a swath of smiles around him. Did she really want to ask him something to find out if he was dangerous? It seemed unlikely now. Or poor? The questions were shifting. A poor person hardly shopped at Whole Foods so much the employees knew him, or had a fitness center membership. He made less sense by the minute.

When they got to the produce area, she watched him select garlic and onions and hot peppers. The image of his hands sweeping his chopped vegetables aside, the knife slammed into the cabbage, came back. It was hardly full-scale violence, and yet it was destructive and out of control.

Mae needed either to do a psychic search and see the whole story soon, or ask him. She had an aversion to looking in on people without their willingness, though, and disliked it when it happened by accident. People had a right to be left alone, not intruded on by her visions. Hubert had held that against her once he knew the sight was real, and so had her mother. If her own safety was at stake, though ... A foolish thought. Jamie had been in the garden last night and tucked a blanket around her and left. Then today he'd aimed his bike right into that car. If he was likely to hurt anyone, it was himself.

His thin arms in the long sleeves caught her eyes. He was so lean she could see every subtle movement of the flexors and extensors in his forearms showing through the soft cloth as he handled peppers, examined them, put one back, chose another. Hot weather and long sleeves. Might be sun protection, but he didn't even wear sunglasses, and his usual hat had too little brim to be anything but a way to control his hair. He might be a cutter. Sad, but more in keeping with his personality than violence against another.

"Hope you like hot," he said, spinning the plastic produce bag with peppers in it, and tying the top. The Smile. "In New Mexico, pain is a flavor."

Pain is a flavor. Maybe it was a regional joke, but maybe it fit with the shape of his mind. "Not too hot," she said. "I don't like to hurt myself."

"Wish I didn't." He steered the cart toward the checkout, and she laid a hand on his arm, stopping him, trying to voice the question. It wouldn't come out. "What are you looking at?" he asked. "What'd you think I meant?"

"I'd been wondering about you ..." She let him go, and they joined a line, framed by racks of health and spirituality magazines. She said so softly only he could hear, "Have you ever done something to hurt yourself?"

"Bloody hell. Is that—is that what you thought I meant? Fuck. All I meant was like, y'know, eating a whole pan of brownies or something. Hurt myself." He placed his hands against his belly with a weak smile, and then turned away from her. As they waited in silence behind a long slow order, he curled over on the handle of the cart, his face disappearing behind his cloud of hair. As his hair fell forward, Mae saw an ugly scar high on the back of his neck, toward his right ear. It couldn't be self-inflicted, could it? Not unless he'd had a Van Gogh moment. "Jesus." His voice sounded tight, short of breath.

"Are you all right, sugar? Is it your head?"

He said nothing. He might be concussed after all.

"Jamie, are you dizzy? Do you feel sick?"

Pushing past the other people in the line, he rushed from the store, barely missing a display of melons. He collapsed at a table, head on his hands. To Mae's relief, a store employee who'd been putting carts away stopped and sat with him. It was like the episode in the bar. What he'd called having a wobbly. How often did he feel this way? And what had he done to hurt himself? It had to have been something worse than pigging out on a pan of brownies to trigger this reaction.

Mae finished her purchases, keeping an eye on Jamie through the window.

She parked the grocery cart next to his table and thanked the store employee who had sat with him. The woman left, and Mae took her seat. Jamie looked up. "Minor wobbly. Nothing serious. My head's all right. Sorry I scared you." The smile seemed intended to reassure her. "Shall we cook, then?"

"Not yet."

"It's hot. The veggies will wilt."

"Jamie. You're taking over my life, and I need to know what's the matter with you. You worry me. All I meant to do was get you in touch with Wendy, and get you to sell your music to Deborah. I wasn't trying to take you home with me, and here we are shopping, and—"

"I thought you liked me."

"I do, sugar. I do. But ..." It hit her what was happening, and it troubled her. "I'm starting to rescue you."

He broke into a sixties Motown song, *Rescue Me*, dancing to it in his chair, and she laid a hand on his arm, quieting him. She was getting the hang of his avoidance mechanisms now, and not letting them distract her as much.

"Let me explain. When I was eighteen, I married a smart, funny boy who wanted to be a writer. My first husband. He drank too much, he couldn't be faithful, but all I could see was this mess I could clean up and rescue, this great artist I knew was in there somewhere. I think there's a word for it—codependent. People like me who get wrapped up in taking care of messed-up people. I'm afraid you're kind of a mess, and I'm getting all tied up in trying to help you."

"I'll be stuffed. You're fucking kidding. I was trying to help *you*."

"What?"

"Seriously. To clean the house. To show you around Santa Fe. To cook for you. To keep you company so you're not lonely all by yourself here. Why'd you think *I* need help? I mean, I hit my head, all right, fucking stupid, but—but I'm all right. Basically. I mean, I'm not like your ex-husband."

He sounded so rational, it took her by surprise. She'd expected a more emotional overreaction. "I didn't say you were." Since he was being rational, she felt it was safe to ask. "But you seem a little self-destructive." She didn't want to admit to the psychic intrusion. It made people uneasy, even angry, if they knew she had seen some private part of their lives. "When I asked if you'd ever hurt yourself ... Like, what's that scar on your neck?"

"I didn't try to cut my fucking ear off." He grinned. "I'm a trauma magnet, I told you. We were in Bali, and they have all these dogs that eat the offerings to the gods in the streets. I was about four, five, not sure—can't keep track of my childhood. Anyway, Haley and I went outside for like ten minutes without Mum and Dad, and I picked up this puppy. I thought it looked sick and I wanted to take care of it."

"You picked up a rabid puppy?"

"Yeah. Stupid. Scared of dogs now, but I wasn't then. Haley was screaming at me, 'Don't touch it,' and it went for me. At least it was only a puppy. Dog could have killed me. Still, fucked things up for the family for weeks. Taking me for those shots—fuck, that was bad. Had to have plastic surgery on my ear, too. So we ended up back in Perth early. Cut Dad's research short. Thanks to me."

He blamed himself, as if he had done something bad.

"You've had a hard life, haven't you, sugar?" He shook his head, looking away. "A lot of accidents," Mae went on. "But have you ever, on purpose—"

"You don't give up, do you?" He met her eyes, bordering on angry. "All right. Yeah, I did. Once. *Once.* I had a bad spell in college. It's been seven or eight years. Come on. I don't want to talk about it, it's past and over. Let's cook." He stood, shifted to a softer tone and a half-smile. "Don't want to blight your trip with my old miseries. You leave when?"

She rose also, and they started for her car with the cart. "After I catch up with Muffie."

"We should dance tomorrow, then, and go to Ruth's opening Thursday. And I can take you round some of the galleries then, too, if you like. Won't take over your life, though, I promise. Not unless you want me to, of course."

Mae ignored Jamie's broad, suggestive smile and wink, and opened her car's trunk. That was cartoon flirting. It wasn't serious. "You're sure we'll see Muffie at Ruth's opening?"

"Fuck, yeah. She's as big an attraction as the art." He placed a bag in the trunk, straightened up, and looked suddenly blank. "Bloody hell." He sat on the bumper. "Get a thing, I don't care what ..."

"You light-headed, sugar? You need food?"

"Yeah. Sorry." She reached into a bag and grabbed a pear, handed it to him. "I think that's all," he said. "Don't think my head's cracked. Sorry." He bit into the pear, eyes closed, and fell silent, eating.

"Better?"

He nodded, slurped at the ripe pear, and opened his eyes, wiping a drizzle of pear juice out of his beard with his free hand. "Yeah. It's fucking perfect. Like, the best thing I ever ate."

This spell was different from the one in the store. No panic. Making sure he didn't get dizzy again, Mae watched him walk to the passenger door and get in, and then finished loading the groceries and returned the cart. When she got into the car, Jamie had eaten the pear down to the skeletal core, which he dropped out the window with the word "biodegradable."

He tipped the seat back and closed his eyes. Within seconds of the car starting to move, he fell asleep.

Something told her not to let him sleep with a possible concussion, though she wasn't sure where she got the idea. Anyway, in the car she had him captive and could try again to get him to contact Wendy. To wake him gently she reached to turn on the radio, and remembered Jamie's music was in the CD player. She turned that on instead, and he stirred.

"Bloody hell, you listen to *me*." Dreamy, dazed, he smiled. "You didn't tell me that."

"Deborah gave these to me. It's beautiful music. Healing."

"Thanks. It's meant to be." He sat straighter. "I used to volunteer with the music in medicine program at UNM hospital—they have singers and musicians do concerts, or sing or play next to someone's bed, help them feel better. I knew what it was like to be the bloke with the pain, y'know, so I wanted to help make it go away. But most people who don't feel good don't have someone show up and sing to them." He looked out the window, running a finger back and forth over the rim of the door. "So this was for them."

"It helped me on my trip. Leaving my young'uns and all." She paused. Time to ask. "You're so good at what you do. Why did you stop recording?"

Gripping his elbows as if he were cold, he didn't answer.

As she made the left turn off Alameda onto Delgado, away from the bridge, Mae couldn't help thinking about what had happened under it. What if Jamie had been the one who found the body? It seemed all too likely. She thought of her first accidental vision, of Jamie as a child holding the older boy's hand while he died. Had the homeless youth been still alive and dying when Jamie found him?

"Did something bad happen to you?" she asked softly. "Is that why you stopped?"

He turned wide, frightened eyes to her and froze, still not speaking. She pulled into the driveway and cut off the engine. "I'm sorry I mentioned it, sugar. That's none of my business. I just want you to call Wendy, get your music going again."

He made her think of Pie hiding under the bed, and she wanted to reach to him the way he'd tamed the terrified cat. She offered her hand slowly. He didn't take it. Maybe Niall was right about leaving Jamie's troubles private. Urging him to talk seemed to make him feel worse.

Jamie opened the car door, a forced cheerfulness in his voice. "Your chef has work to do."

As they unloaded and put away groceries in silence, Mae wondered how to undo the damage of her questions. The answer was obviously *yes*, something bad had happened to him. She wished she knew what it was, to understand whether or not she should still nudge him to get on with his career or not, but there didn't seem to be a way to get an answer.

He took pots and pans out, set a rice cooker on the counter, and finally spoke as he opened the bag of rice they'd bought. "Thanks for letting me cook for you." His voice was weighted with emotion. "It means a lot to me."

Mae felt embarrassed. He sounded like this was such a big deal. He had to be reading too much into it. "It's just cooking—"

He turned to her, his voice passionate and urgent. "It's important," he said, and immediately looked embarrassed. An attempt at The Smile made it halfway. "Give me a hug, love. I need it."

He reached out, the uncertain smile hovering. To refuse would be unkind, especially after he'd turned down her open hand in the car. She gave him what she meant to be a quick squeeze, but he prolonged it with a powerful hold and a loud exhalation.

When he let go, he reached up like someone waking up in the morning, beamed a true sunshine smile at her, and did a little pulsing, rippling dance. With a burst of energy, he returned to the counter and opened drawers, getting utensils out, including the "bodgy" knives, and began to sing a ballad that might have come from an operetta, his voice sweet and floating as he washed vegetables.

"Need any help?" Mae asked

"Nah, you hate to cook. Keep me company if you like, though."

"I need to call my young'uns."

"Oh." He stopped singing and looked around at her with concern. "Yeah. Your stepdaughters. You miss them. Will you be all right?"

She nodded. "I'll be fine." Truth was, though, it always hurt.

She closed herself in the bedroom and set up her laptop for her Skype date with the girls. She needed to call Roseanne, too. Jamie had kept her so preoccupied she hadn't yet told Roseanne about Muffie, and it was important news. She could do that after dinner. Hopefully right after she finally drove Jamie and his wrecked bicycle home. Then she needed to talk to Marty, ask him about Jamie. He might tell her more than Niall had.

Hubert answered on Skype, and Mae felt the usual pang at the sight of his long, strong gentle face, and was grateful that he kept the greeting short and hollered for the girls to come talk to Mama. The thunder of their feet carried over the microphone, and then they bounced onto the couch beside Hubert. He rose, with an affectionate mussing of their lank, dark hair, and left them to talk with Mae.

"Y'all look so good right now, I could kiss you right though this camera," Mae said "I miss you, sweeties."

"We miss you, Mama," Stream said

"We got a new toy box," Brook added.

"Good, you can put all your little cars and trucks in it."

"That's why." Stream giggled. "Daddy says no more fire truck in the foot in the middle of the night."

Suddenly longing for the sounds of her family around her, Mae pictured Hubert getting up to bring one of the girls a glass of water, muttering some clean expletive suitable for children as he stepped on a sharp little toy, and coming back to bed with her, lying against her the way he always did, back to back. "Right now I even miss stepping on toys, I miss y'all so much."

They told her about their day, shared their new first-grader type jokes, and Mae laughed at their pleasure if not their wit. She told them about things they would like, such as the hailstorm and the rainbow, until Hubert came back.

"Hey, little wildcats, tell your mama goodnight. I'm gonna talk boring grown-up stuff with her, okay?"

They waved and blew kisses. "'Night, Mama!"

When they'd gone, Hubert settled alone on the living room couch. What did he want? A crazy hope of the impossible crossed her heart, and her mind pushed it down. She could almost feel herself next to him, what it would be like to slip her arm around him. His solid, broad-shouldered body still drew her, even with all their distance and disagreements.

After some hesitation, he asked, "How's it going in Santa Fe?"

"It's pretty." No way she could explain how it was going. She stuck to small talk. "I ran in my pink paws today. I like 'em."

"Great." Hubert's smile was warm, affectionate. "Take your time with 'em, though." He talked on a while about running, about his work—about everything they didn't fight about. He was being a Southerner, easing into the hard stuff.

While she listened, the floral-papered walls of their old home behind him began to look gloomy to her, as if she could see the dampness and the cracked plaster behind those flowers, and all the work that would need to be done on that place for the rest of their lives. No—his life, not *theirs* any more. She felt the small town around the house, like a slow, heavy, choking snake. She might miss him at times, and miss the girls so bad it hurt, but she couldn't live in a town that thought she was a misfit, a witchy-woman, for being psychic.

He finally got to his point. "I'm going to the Outer Banks with Jen for a few days. Just letting you know to call at the folks' place Saturday and Sunday to talk to the girls."

They had only separated in April. Four months felt so fast to her. "You're spending a weekend with Jen already?"

"Already?" He frowned. "It's a third of a year. But don't worry, she never spends the night here. I don't want the girls seeing her as a mother yet."

"Yet?" Mae's heart dropped. "As a mother *yet*?"

"Take it easy. You raised 'em. She won't replace you even if it does come to that."

"I hope not." She forced herself to add, "Thanks for telling me about the weekend." But she didn't feel grateful at all.

They said goodbye. Change was coming. Change she didn't want. *I'm not over him yet.* Looking up at the starry ceiling, Mae wanted to sit in the bedroom and take time to think, to listen to her own heart and mind. She craved the time alone she'd hoped for here. Instead, she heard singing and clattering in the kitchen.

Jamie seemed to have no need to be alone, and he took up space out of proportion to his words or actions, even sitting and saying nothing. If he was happy, he lit up the world. When she took care of him, he blanketed her with a warm, fuzzy cloud. When he worried, he sent out little tendrils of neediness. When he flirted, he seemed to pollinate—to send out sexuality into the air like a male tree, recklessly open to the winds. At least he had stopped doing that, but now he was fixing dinner for her as if it was the most important thing he'd done in his life. Doing his best to keep her from being lonely, when that was exactly what she wanted to be.

Chapter Twelve

Returning to the kitchen, Mae found that Jamie had set the table with candles and poured glasses of wine. *No.* He'd gone romantic again. The longer she waited to put a stop to it, the worse it would get. She had to wrap this up and send him home. Somehow. Without hurting him.

Jamie carried Pie on his shoulder, rubbing his cheek against her fur, while with his free hand he spooned a spicy-smelling concoction of beans, rice, and vegetables onto plates, laying hot tortillas neatly folded beside each serving. "Sorry about the white rice, but it's quick. I do brown and wild mix, normally."

"You don't have to apologize. It looks wonderful."

"Hope so. Kind of winging it." As if they were on a date in a five-star restaurant, he pulled her chair out for her, and she sat. "Never got the next part, like, is the man supposed to *shove* the woman in at the table then or what? But manners aren't my strong point. Not that you'd ever notice." With a quick, self-deprecating grin, he sat down across from her. "Yell at me if I need civilizing."

He set Pie down one paw at a time, so no impact affected her small, old bones, and stroked her a few times as if to ease her transition to the floor. "Did you heal her yet?"

"I don't think she needs it. She's good now."

"Nah. I'm not a healer. After dinner, give her a treatment. She'll like it." He raised his glass. "To another beautiful day in Santa Fe. And to two more."

"To two more."

As soon as she said it, Mae regretted it. Today had hardly been a beautiful day. Jamie'd had two or three episodes of strange and troubled behavior, and he didn't seem to realize it. Maybe all he saw was the rainbow, not his own storm clouds. Worse, her toast might have sounded like she'd committed to spending two days with him. Yes, she needed to go to Ruth Smyth's opening, and it looked like she'd be going with him, but a day without him in between would be good. Except she might have talked him into getting his van fixed while she got her oil changed tomorrow.

She needed to have at least half days free of him. Telling him felt awkward, but he would never think of it on his own. "We said two days, but I hope you'll understand that I need part of those days to myself."

"Jesus." Jamie's eyes darkened. "I just fixed you dinner and you're shoving me off already. Can't that wait? At least eat the fucking meal before you push me out."

His anger startled her. They weren't in some sort of close relationship where he could expect to spend every hour with her, and they had enough plans for the next two days that she thought it should be clear that she wasn't rejecting him. She started to defend herself, but he looked so nakedly hurt that she stopped. "I'm not pushing you out."

He stabbed a forkful of food. "Yeah, you are."

Mae sighed and ate, at a loss what to do with him. He'd worked hard to please her. The food was as good as Dada Café's, with extraordinarily complex and unexpected tastes. "This is great, sugar."

He brightened, and asked with his mouth full, "Really? You like it?"

"Yes, I do." She smiled. "Manners."

He swallowed, sipped wine. "Sorry. Fucking pig. Don't eat 'em, but I am one." He took another taste of wine. "So tell me more about what you do as a healer. If you fix up Pie, will she be all new and shiny inside, or what?"

"Only ever tried to heal one cat, and he couldn't talk."

Jamie's soft smile at her little joke was too tender, as if she were utterly wonderful and brilliant. Uncomfortable, Mae continued, "People say they feel like they can make better decisions, have more insight into why they do what they do. I don't think they're all new inside."

"Do you see what's in people's heads? Kitties' heads?"

"Not really. Sometimes I pick up emotions or energy, but I don't read minds. I can see the past, though, if I need to get to the root for healing something. Why'd you ask?"

"Nosy, that's all. Are you ... well, y'know, like a shrink? You can't, like—have relationships with your clients?"

Was he asking if she would heal him? Or get involved with him? Both? "Of course not. It'd be all wrong."

"I thought that. Like ... yeah ... I get it. Like with teachers." He shoveled beans and rice into a tortilla and took a bite, seeming to make a conscious effort to avoid spilling, and to chew and swallow before he spoke. She could sense words bubbling around under the surface, see him almost talking and then stopping himself. "I fell in love with my voice teacher when I was eighteen. Of course, she had the sense to turn me down. Or the taste." He glanced at her with a flicker of attempted humor. "I was funny looking. Anyway, she fired me as a student once I bared my sorry little soul."

"I reckon she had to. Y'all would have been so awkward after that." The story touched her, but Mae wanted to get off the subject of romance. "So ... you studied opera."

"Mind if we don't talk about that?"

"No, you don't have to, of course." She'd thought it was safe small talk. What *was* safe, with him? "I'm curious about your music, though. You're so ... diverse. And so good."

"You really like that music? The albums?"

"I told you, it really helped me feel better. You could sell a lot more of it, but no one can order it. I'm trying to get you in touch with Wendy Huang and you won't call her." He gave her the one-two shrug, drank wine. She persisted. "I don't see how you're gonna sell your work if you don't get a manager. Unless Zambethalia is gonna take off."

"Fuck, no. Mwizenge's got a business here. Dagmawi's a nurse. The blokes have families, careers, lives. Just play for fun, music's a sideline."

"But they record."

"Yeah. They did, as Afreaka. Mwizenge's got all that crap down. I don't. Don't get on well with—computers, fuck, the whole making and selling and bloody fine print and—" He stared across the room, a lost and frightened look in his eyes.

"What is it?"

"All that—that *stuff.* Self-promotion—tech—I don't fucking *know.*" He held his hands up as if to prevent the avalanche of stressors he'd listed from falling on his head. "Please. New subject."

"I can't talk about opera *or* about selling your new music? Why?"

Jamie picked up some spilled beans from the table, ate them, and licked his fingers, eyes downcast.

"Unless you're changing careers, you can't keep avoiding this. Wendy wants a sound file of some of your solo work, not your healing music, but something live. Like that blues song. I want you to send it to her. You can get Mwizenge to help you do it." From what she'd seen, Mwizenge acted sort of fatherly toward Jamie. He'd probably help. "Can you tell me you'll do that?"

"I want to. I really do." Running a hand over his hair, leaving a little streak of sauce, Jamie took a deep breath. "I'm scared."

"Of technology? Success? Failure? Something else?"

He pressed his lips together and gripped his fork as if to choke it.

Mae said, "Take your time. I'm sorry if I'm pressuring you." She had to move carefully if she didn't want to trigger another of his wobblies. Giving him a moment, she ate, sipped her wine, and let Jamie do the same. He didn't have a working phone. Was that his fear? Admitting a money problem? "If I call Wendy for you and I sit here while you talk to her, would that be better?"

Jamie rolled his right shoulder, focused on eating.

"You'll feel better once you've talked to her." Mae had done a lot of self-promotion as a freelance trainer and fitness instructor. It hadn't bothered her, but she could see that it wouldn't be easy for someone like Jamie, and the music business had to be more complicated. "Sounds like you're not good at business, sales, that end of things."

He nodded. "My girlfriend did all that for me. She was supposed to teach me when we broke up, but ... I wasn't in good shape for a while ..."

Jamie poked his food around, and then ate as if he'd suddenly realized he was starving, spilling beans and rice onto the table and his clothes.

"Manners, sugar. Slow down. You're getting messy."

"Thanks. Jesus, I'm an awful person to have dinner with. I get so fucking nervous. Candlelight and slob." He belched in spite of an attempt not to, and put his hands over his face. "Fuck. Sorry. Shoot me."

"You'll be all right. Relax. Your manners would be better if you just slowed everything down." Jamie dropped his hands, and Mae met his anxious look with a smile she hoped was reassuring. "It'll all turn out fine. You can use my phone to talk to Wendy. We have to do it right after dinner, so I can make another call, though."

"No hurry." Lifting his wine glass, he brightened. "No worries. Make your call first. Gives me plenty of time to clean up for you."

"No. I shouldn't have mentioned it. I'd be leaving you alone to do all the work twice. You don't have to clean. I'll do it later, when you go home."

He shook his head. "I'm here to help you, remember? Make your call. I'm doing the dishes."

I've really stepped in it. Somehow she'd committed to keeping him in her house even longer. Mae went back to the bedroom to make her call in relative quiet, closing the door to muffle Jamie's singing. When she got through to Dada Café, the hostess put her on hold to wait for Roseanne, and Mae listened to Jamie. The song was brisk and bright, operetta again.

"Mae." Roseanne came on after a few minutes, breathless. "You gave us the best idea. We've got a good crowd."

"What happened? People don't miss her any more already? Wait—what idea?"

"A publicity stunt about her ascension. I know that wasn't what you meant when you said it, but we did it. Bryan put up a web site. We spread the word. Look it up. 'Ascended Muffie: the Word from Beyond the Beyond.'"

Mae turned her laptop back on. The web page, which claimed to be "maintained by an earth-walking friend in contact with our ascended teacher," showed Muffie with big blue seabird feet instead of her legs, and a collage of various vegetables for arms and fingers. Hindu deities with smilies masking their normal countenances hovered around her. The god with many arms still danced over a snake, but with a silly yellow disk for a face. Underneath Muffie's big blue bird feet was a menu of topics in a font that resembled the restaurant's menu. Ascendance. Aura cleansing. Avocados. Bathing in light. Broccoli overrated. Colon health and your aura. Cows. Destiny revealed. *Dharma pitta padha* and Little Feat. Ecology of economy of eating. The alphabet went on through Rutabaga skin scrub and Sri Rama Kriya Says to Zucchini Detox Bath.

The collage Muffie character spouted speech balloons. One said, "I am here and there. There is not up. Ascendance is but is not ascendance. The work goes on." Another: "Dada Café staff. Stay on your toes. Stay on the path. Serve the message with a smile. Rotating cleanse." The third said, "To Kenny and Frank, special thanks for supporting and assisting my extraordinary transition. Olive oil, garlic, and black pepper. Hot foot baths."

Two links in the side bar menu invited communication: Report Sightings, and Ask the Masters.

Although the art kept the Dada spirit, it made fun of Muffie. Worse, Bryan mocked Kenny and Frank.

"So what do you think?" Roseanne asked. "Are you looking at it?"

"I am. It's mean."

"It is not. And it worked. It's started a buzz. We had to do something to get by without her until we know something. We're in limbo as long as she is."

"Well, you can take it down. She's alive and in Santa Fe. I did a psychic journey and I finally saw her. She was in some art gallery with the originals for the art in this chakra meditation book she gave Kenny, and she had Sri Rama Kriya's books and was posing with the art. I think she must be planning some kind of publicity herself, or she wouldn't be doing that."

"I hope it's publicity for the restaurant. How do you know that was in Santa Fe?"

"A friend here." Jamie's glorious tenor voice penetrated the closed door with even more vigor, and Mae realized she had just identified him as a friend. "He said she's bound to be at this artist's gallery opening. Ruth Smyth, the designer who does Sanchez and Smyth clothing."

"God. She would, wouldn't she? Her organic cotton heroine. So you can go there and pin her down and find out what she's doing? She still doesn't answer. I have to renew the lease in a week, and I can't make that decision without her."

"I'll try. I hope she'll talk to me. I made her pretty mad."

"Bryan loved it for his movie, though."

"Pardon my saying it, but Bryan doesn't seem to care about people as much as his art. Like it's okay with him to upset people." Mae clicked on the link to Sri Rama Kriya says. "What's this gonna look like to people who follow this guru? Bryan's put his words right in the middle of this satire."

"Like it isn't a joke already?"

"I don't think so." Mae read the quotation aloud. "'As you incinerate accumulated karma in the chakras, you acquire the light of its flame. As you become luminous, you illuminate. As you illuminate, you eliminate samskaras. You will not be reborn.' I don't get it, but some folks take it seriously."

"But it's so preposterous."

"Is it? I don't know any Eastern philosophy."

"I don't, either. It's just really bad prose. Incinerate, accumulate, illuminate, eliminate ... it'd only be good if it was a joke."

Jamie was into a new song now, something with a rapid patter of words, still operatic but comic. It reminded her of what Roseanne had just said about the Sri Rama Kriya quote, although Jamie's song was something about the model of a modern major general. Luminous, illuminate, eliminate ... She imagined the guru's words to this silly song. They didn't quite fit the rhythm, but the ring was similar. Taken out of context, the quote did sound like nonsense. "The web site is a joke, though, not the guru."

"But it's a great joke, don't you think? It's totally like Muffie."

"Not to people who believed her."

"No, it's exactly like her."

"Please." As Jamie stopped singing, Mae lowered her voice, realizing she'd turned up her own volume to hear herself over him. "Kenny is really grateful to her, and he doesn't deserve to be made fun of. At least take the message to him and Frank down. They'll know it's not from her."

"We have to take the whole damned thing down eventually any-way. Some lawyer called Bryan about intellectual property rights. Can you believe that?"

"What? For being Dada?"

"I don't think so. It's a style, not a property. Probably for quoting Sri Rama Kriya, that's all I can think of. I can't afford a legal battle. Bryan agreed to take it down, but we're putting it off. He's mad. He worked hard on that."

"I can't even find Sri Rama Kriya, and he can send a lawyer after you for quoting his book? That's crazy."

"It might have been his publisher. I don't know. Bryan talked to the lawyer, not me. How much do I owe you for finding out Muffie's alive?"

Mae thought of her failed effort as well as her successful one. Less than an hour's work. She named her fee. "But if you take that site down right away—"

"No. One more day. I'd rather pay you. We'll make more money while it's up."

"Have you talked to Frank and Kenny? Are you telling them it's really Muffie?"

"We're saying we don't know, that it's a mystery who's communi-cating with her. But I asked them what they think and they say they like it."

"Because you're their boss and you like it, and they need their jobs. Don't ruin the place for them. They think the restaurant is spir-itual."

"It's a business. Kenny and Frank are spiritual. Come on, you met Muffie, she isn't—" Roseanne stopped to attend to an interruption, someone asking her a question. "I've got to go. Let me know what the green goddess says when you see her."

As they ended the call, Mae rose from the wooden chair. Her calf muscles were even sorer than they had been earlier. Dancing in the store hadn't helped. She stretched. Jamie must be done with the dishes. Time to call Wendy.

But first she should call Kenny. He had to be either insulted or fooled by the pseudo-ascension web site. She should let him know she would see Muffie in a few days and ask if he had any message for her. He might be relieved to know she hadn't ascended, but he might also be let down that she had lied.

Mae sat back down with her laptop and checked what readers had posted on the Ascended Muffie site. Maybe someone else had already undermined the ascension, or Kenny might have logged in to take it all seriously. To her surprise, some readers had actually asked the ascended masters questions. Under Report Sightings, someone claimed a vision of Muffie at the T or C farmer's market, floating above it like an angel blessing the food. More satire, or a deluded follower? No wonder it was keeping the customers coming in. Bryan had done the right thing, in a way—except for mocking her neighbors.

It was a good sign that Kenny and Frank hadn't posted anything. Maybe they could handle the travesty, and Mae's call. They lived a coherent, disciplined lifestyle, after all, even if Muffie was part of the reason they did. As long as the restaurant survived, they would be all right. It was really Dada Café's future, not Muffie's pretended ascension, that Mae needed to find out about. If the business had been abandoned for some reason, a lot of livelihoods were at stake.

She called Kenny, but had to leave the news as a message. Of course he didn't pick up. He would be at the restaurant, washing dishes as a spiritual practice—the only thing he might be qualified to do.

When Mae emerged, she found the living room quiet, the kitchen empty. She looked through the open door to the studio. No one there, or in the bathroom. Had Jamie left? Why? They still had to make his call to Wendy. Did it scare him that much?

The arrangement of the living room furniture, the sofa with its back to the bedroom door, created a kind of walkway to the kitchen, and on a second look Mae saw that Jamie lay on the sofa, shoes off, eyes closed, holding Pie to his chest. The old cat's head rested cheek to cheek beside his, and one of her front legs lay across his throat. He hadn't walked out, he was just tired. They looked sweet together, both of them still and peaceful finally. Mae felt guilty for having to wake him.

Pie flicked an ear, tossing off a drop of water. He wasn't sleeping. Silent tears slid down Jamie's cheeks, dripping onto his companion.

Chapter Thirteen

A surge of worry tugging at her heart, Mae dropped to her knees beside him and touched his shoulder. "Jamie, what's wrong?"

He sat up, wiping his tears on his sleeve, letting the cat slip onto the cushion. He petted her as she landed, sniffed, and pressed his hands to his eyes. "Sorry."

"Don't apologize, sugar. What is it?"

He took a deep breath and leaned his elbows on his thighs, his face hidden by his hair. "I'm just sad."

Mae sat beside him on the couch. "About what?"

"My cat died."

"I'm so sorry." It had to be recent, to upset him like this. "When?"

He said something unintelligible, a fist jammed against his mouth, and turned away from her. Heat radiated off him as if he had a fever. Concerned, she laid a hand on his back, and met his ribs through a ropy layer of muscle. He didn't seem to be breathing.

As she gently rubbed his back, something in him came unmoored. He shuddered and broke down in deep, gasping sobs. Sweating and trembling, he curled up, but seemed unable to hold still, rocking, twisting, and grabbing the back of the couch, and then clutching a cushion as if literally struggling to stay afloat. With a long, agonized inhalation, he let go of the cushion and convulsed into a tight ball again.

At the first pause in his thrashing, Mae wrapped her arms around him from behind. Her dress was quickly dampened by the sweat soaking through his shirt, her body shaken by his crying. Frightened and aching for Jamie, she held him until his storm faded to an exhausted quiver. He turned to her, leaned his head on her shoulder, and she stroked his damp hair. She had never before seen anyone in this kind of emotional distress. This had to be about more than the death of his cat. "Can you talk, sugar?"

Sniffing loudly, he sat up. "Fuck. Snot. Hope it didn't get on your nice dress."

He got up and went to the bedroom for the box of tissues and a waste basket, and sat back down, blowing his nose several times. "Sorry. Sweat. Snot. Disgusting." An uneven laugh. "The sensitive man is a bloody mess."

Mae tucked her feet up under her, leaned into the arm of the couch, and studied him. He still hadn't looked at her. "I know there are things you don't like to share ... but maybe you could try. You might not feel so bad."

He held a sofa seat cushion against his chest, leaning his chin on its top. "It's hard."

"That's okay. Take your time."

"It'd take a year. Jesus. It'd take a fucking year ..." He looked around. "Where'd Pie go?"

"Don't worry about her. She's fine."

"Kind of wanted to hold onto her. Calms me down. Having a cat. I'm ... It's been ... it's been a bad year. No, not that. Not all bad. I mean—it's just hard, that's all."

"What's been hard?"

He looked into her eyes. "I ... I've been living—Christ this is so bloody stupid—living alone for the first time in my life. At twenty-eight. Can you believe that?"

"I can. So am I. Twenty-seven, first time all alone."

"But you like it—you keep wanting to be alone." He knotted his hands together and watched them. "I fucking hate it. No ... Jeezus." He glanced at her, forced a smile. "That sounded pathetic. I'm doing all right, really. Well, for me I am. For me, I'm doing great." He leaned onto the cushion again. "Yeah, right. Fucking great. I'm lying."

"It's hard being alone. You broke up with your girlfriend, your cat died ..."

"Fuck. I wish I wasn't telling you this. I'd rather be telling you some heroic crap about climbing a mountain or singing at the Met, things to make you ... But, Jeezus, it's no use, y'know? I'm fucked up." He met her eyes for a second, and then ducked her gaze, folding his arms over the top of the cushion, fists stacked, chewing on a thumb knuckle. "I'll come around all right, though. It's a rough patch right now, that's all. Don't want you to think I'm always throwing a wobbly."

"I don't think that, sugar." She reached over and patted his arm. "But I do think your check engine light is on."

"That it is." The joke seemed to relax him. He stood, smiled down at her. "Can I get you a beer? Still got that cheap piss in your fridge? Or wine?"

"Water. Thanks."

He went to the kitchen, returned with a glass of water for her, a beer for himself. "Nice to have you here," Jamie said as he sat again. His voice was soft. "I mean, in Santa Fe. It really is. Makes it less lonely."

"Thank you, but ..." She could hardly be his only friend. "What about your friends? Your family? Are you really alone?"

"Yeah, I am. Can't even have a fucking cat where I live now." He took a deep breath, looked into Mae's eyes. "And that's hard. I can't sleep alone. *Really* can't sleep."

"What do you do, then?"

"Sing, write music. Stay up all night. Hit a bar. I don't mean, y'know, *always*, not every night. Some are ... manageable."

"You pick up women at the bars, do you?" she teased, trying to lighten his mood.

He exhaled a sort of laugh. "Never had a fucking anxiety problem, have you? Pick up women. Christ. You've seen me. Not exactly
the smooth operator."

"You are when you dance." From his crooked smile and unsteady
sigh, Mae could tell this hadn't been the right thing to say. She'd
meant to reassure him, but he'd read another meaning into her
words. "Sorry. That came out wrong."

"Nah, it's true." He took a swig of beer and looked into the can
as if there were something important in the hole. "If I could just sing
and dance instead of having to talk and do anything else, I'd get on
all right."

"You want to tell me what's wrong with you, sugar? Do you have
a diagnosis?"

"Jeeeezus." He thudded the beer can onto the coffee table. "I'm
having a chat, relaxing, getting myself back in gear, what does she
ask?" He stood up, pitched a sofa pillow at the wall. "My fucking *diagnosis.*"

Without thinking, Mae snapped at him the way she would at a
child having a tantrum. "Stop yelling."

To her surprise, it worked. He picked up the pillow, put it back
on the couch. "Sorry. I'm so tired, I fly off. I'm not like this. Not really."

"But right now you are. And I'm trying to understand you.
Maybe I didn't ask it right. You told me you're 'fucked up.' That
you're a 'trauma magnet.' And I want you to explain it better."

"Right, then. I'll serve it all up, see if you run, see if you kick me
out." He paced to the bedroom door and framed himself there, his
back to her, hands on either side of the door as if holding himself
from falling through. After a pause, he said, "One: panic. Two: anxiety. Three: phobias. Four ..." He pushed back off the doorframe and
tapped one hand against it. "This last one's over, y'know. It's my success story, all right?"

Mae waited. Jamie seemed to have frozen. When he thawed, his hands drew into clenched fists that fidgeted as if he had something alive in them.

"Can I help, sugar?"

He shook his head, and came back to the couch and picked up his beer as he sat again. "Sorry. Panic's bad lately. Four was depression. Don't like to talk about it. Makes me panic." He flashed her The Smile and took a long drink of beer. "You're supposed to laugh. That was a good joke."

"Depression's not funny."

"But I'm not depressed now. Crying like that, it was just ... Fixing dinner and cleaning up, lying down to relax with the cat, hearing your voice through the door, someone else nearby ... it was all so much like ... like having a real life again. It got to me. I'm sensitive, that's all. I cry easy. But I'm not depressed."

"I won't judge you if you are. My stepfather was depressed when he was out of work. He didn't even cry. Just ate and slept. Kind of a ghost of himself."

"Yeah." Jamie nodded. "You know, then." His eyes searched hers. "I'm scared of ever falling there again. Terrified. Fear number five out of three hundred and ten." He chugged the beer again, tried to stifle the belch. "Wish I was afraid of doing that." A sudden laugh attack. Mae wondered if his spells of hilarity were a symptom of his exhaustion, like his short temper and his tears. "Fuck. At least I *am* scared of farting in bed."

"Is that a joke or a real fear? You keep putting these big numbers up."

"Want the list? Fear of spiders, scorpions, octopuses, jellyfish, anything with tentacles or extra legs. Fear of the dentist, and of having crap in my teeth." He flashed the gold tooth with a corner of a smile. "Fear of getting depressed again, fear of farting in bed with a woman and all that other embarrassing crap. Fear of fat, fear of num-

bers, legal documents, reading directions, getting lost, fear of aban-
donment, fear of rejection—shall I keep going?"

"No, I get the picture. Some of it. You're so friendly, though. You don't act scared of rejection."

"I don't?" He looked genuinely surprised. "Guess I put myself in the way of it anyway." He paused, turned his beer can without drinking. "Yeah. More scared of not trying than of rejection, I guess. Scared of both. Being alone, being rejected. Bad paradox."

No wonder she couldn't get rid of him. He was afraid to leave. She thought of the fear list, sipped her water, and took a moment to piece together how the other fears fit his behavior. Fear of being fat. Did he have an eating disorder? He was skinny and went without meals, but when he ate, he ate like a ravenously hungry person, not like an anorexic. And he'd been honest about his other diagnoses and worries, except that his fear of numbers, legal documents, and read-ing directions suggested he might have learning disabilities on top of everything else.

"Do you panic when you have to deal with a lot of things for your career?"

"Yeah. Lisa handled all of it. Contracts, marketing, booking recording studios, performances. I'm bad at all that. Something in me just shakes and runs when I see a bunch of little dense words on a screen or piece of paper, and I'm not stupid, I can read, but I get scared of that stuff ... Bad at math to the point that it frightens me."

This might explain some of his failure to establish a career on his own, but it didn't explain his aversion and fear over getting in touch with Wendy. "So you should be really glad to get a professional man-ager."

He did the fifty-fifty shrug. "If she doesn't *reject* me."

"She won't." Of course, if she got to know him, she really might think twice, but Mae had to hope Wendy would find him worth the challenges. "She wants to work with you. You look like you're feeling better. Can we call her now?"

Jamie shook his head, retreating into the corner of the couch. "Not ready," he said. "Tomorrow."

"Why do you have to put it off? I'm here to help you. You don't have to be scared."

Drawing his legs up, he wrapped into a condensed, protective huddle and shook his head again.

Mae sighed. "I'm trying, sugar, but I still don't understand you."

For some reason this appeared to strike Jamie as funny, and he laughed, unfolded, and reached for his beer. "Bloody hell, neither do I." He drank, emptying the can. "I had therapy way back when, but it's like cleaning up fucking Chernobyl."

"And you can't get therapy now, uninsured."

"Not unless I could pay a fortune. And I already owe for my hip."

"Can I just say that rock climbing is a crazy hobby for a man with a panic disorder and no health insurance?"

"It seemed like a good idea at the time." Jamie leaned back and grinned at her. "I'm not scared of heights."

Just as he seemed to be reviving, Mae felt drained. What were the chances he'd stay upbeat long enough to go home intact and safe? He was scared of sleeping alone. She wished he hadn't told her that. But if he wasn't going to call Wendy, it was best to get him moving now, while his mood was brightening.

He rose, took the beer can to the recycling bin in the kitchen, and started toward the bathroom. "Got a spare toothbrush? I'm getting a little anxious about the teeth."

There was such a moving-in, weirdly intimate thing about this request, she didn't want to answer it, though she had a spare toothbrush. "I'm taking you home now. You can wait."

"Nah. Can't. Seriously."

She could hear him taking a piss with the door open. Either he felt too much at home, or it wasn't just his table manners that needed civilizing. "Look in the cabinet under the sink."

"Thanks, love."

She got her purse, took her keys out, and made sure she was standing by the door putting shoes on when Jamie emerged.

His face lit up. "Where are we going?"

"I'm kind of tired, sugar. I just told you a minute ago, I'm gonna take you home."

"Oh." He shoved his hands into his pockets. "Sorry. I was getting on a roll. Sort of ... refreshed, y'know? Got all that out of me. Not pissing, I mean, y'know, crying. Telling you about me."

"Then that's a good time to go home. While you feel good."

He shook his head. "I need to ..." He mimed juggling, his eyes following the imaginary balls in the air, and looked at her as if she should understand. She didn't, and shook her head, holding up her keys. Jamie dropped the invisible balls and let them roll away, watching them, and then joined her at the door and slipped into his sandals. "All right. I'm on my bike."

"You need a ride. Your bike's messed up."

"Meant, like, 'Strayan for go away, rack off. *Onya bike.* The van's just a mile off, actually. Not a bad hike."

"Let me drive you." She opened the door and stepped out. "You've got a bad hip, a wrecked bike, a van that makes noises—"

"Jeezus." Following her, Jamie took his bike from its place against the house and began to wheel it toward the street. "You make me sound like a fucking orphan."

Mae locked the door. "You won't be once you get the bike fixed. And the van." Suspecting the depth of his attachment to his bike, she caught up with him, put her hand to the handlebar and began to steer it around the corner toward the alley and the carport. He wouldn't fight her if she was holding his bike. "We're going to the Ford place tomorrow, remember?"

"That's right, yeah. We've got to get your car in tomorrow." Why did he sound so happy? Like he thought this was a *date*? For an oil change? Jamie took his hands off the bike, letting her steer. "And it's Latin music tomorrow night in the Plaza, I've got to teach you salsa and rumba." He executed a hip-leading dance step, turning as if he had a partner is his arms. "And when are you ever going to get *that* chance again? And—d'you want to go the Geneveva with me?"

"The what?"

"The Geneveva Chavez Center, the community fitness place. It's fucking incredible. The pool is gorgeous—but you'd want the weight room, I suppose. I mean, you must want to do your thing, whatever you normally do."

It would feel good to go there. She hadn't done her strength workout for a while, and it was something that the altitude wouldn't compromise. After all, she'd urged him to get the van fixed while she got her oil changed. "All right. We'll do that in the morning. But here's the deal. While we wait at the Ford place, we're on the phone to Wendy. No more delays."

They reached her car, she opened the trunk, and Jamie lifted the bike in. In its deformed shape, it almost fit, and he regarded it sadly, spinning the airborne front wheel. "Yeah, I'll be all peaceful after my swim." He looked at her, his eyes unguarded. "You're sure it's all right? I mean, you're sending me home, and I—I told you how crazy I am. And I cried. Jesus. I like you so much, and—maybe you—"

"Don't take it personally. I'm tired, that's all."

It wasn't all, but what else could she say? *I like you so much.* What kind of adult man said things like that? For someone afraid of rejection, he sure did set himself up for it, those baby seal eyes waiting for the hit, a kick-me sign right on his heart.

As they got in her car, Mae asked, pushing through her guilt, "Are you gonna be all right if I take you home?"

"You're taking me to the van." Jamie reached up with both hands and began to work on a knot in his hair. "Fuck. Don't have a comb, do you?"

"In the outside pocket of my purse."

"Thanks."

While she backed the car out, turned around in the end of the neighbor's parking spot, and took the alley to Delgado, Jamie began to comb his hair, wincing at knots, stopping to untangle them with small groans as if it were far more painful than it could actually be. "Ow! Fuck!" Jamie dropped the comb in his lap and ran his fingers through his hair. "Bloody hell. I didn't wear my hat. I wanted to be *pretty*. Fucking imbecile."

"Stop complaining. You could do a ponytail."

"Scar shows." Growling, he aimed a snapping-jaws hand at his right ear, and resumed combing. "When we stop, could you groom me? I like to have someone do my hair. Better with a brush, but you could comb it."

"No, I am not grooming you." What a bizarre request, and yet he didn't even seem embarrassed to ask it. "Where's your van?"

"De Vargas Mall."

"I don't know where that is."

He attended to a tangle, saying in a small voice, "Better if you do it."

"Sugar, what's bothering you? You said you'd be all right, but this is kind of neurotic, with the hair."

"Nah. Makes me calm. It'd help me sleep. I told you, sleep is hard."

As they passed the bridge, she wondered if there was more to his insomnia, some other trauma he hadn't shared yet. She kept her voice gentle. "Did you find him? That kid that died down there?"

His eyes widened. "Who told you?"

"Daddy. He didn't say it was you, but he said it was the son of some friends. I thought it might have got to you pretty bad if you saw this kid die."

"Fuck." Jamie stopped working on the tangle, the comb hanging from his hair. "Nobody knows that. That he wasn't dead yet."

Mae realized she'd made that assumption after her vision of Jamie's early trauma, witnessing a death. "I didn't know, sugar. I guessed."

Jamie yanked the comb out and leaned back, folded his arms across his stomach and fidgeted, the comb falling into the space between his thighs. Finally, he gave directions. "Turn here. Left at the light. You'll see the van up near the road."

This seemed like a signal not to pry. As much as he'd bared his heart and soul, this last trauma might still be more than he could handle talking about. Following his directions, Mae located the mall with ease, pulled into the entrance, and drove up to the van where it sat like a lone, aging dinosaur after the others had all died, its faded skin dull with dirt. She cut off the engine.

"We're here."

Jamie nodded, but didn't stir. After a moment he opened his eyes, picked up the comb, and gestured to her and then toward his hair with it, eyebrows lifted. She shook her head, and he tucked her comb back into her purse. *What a strange man.*

As she watched him get out of the car, she felt unnaturally aware of his body, the shape of his bones and muscles though his shirt and jeans, as if she could feel him, his physicality suddenly hyper real and tangible. Dispelling the odd feeling, she got out and helped him lift his bike from the trunk. He leaned it against his van and unlocked the ancient vehicle.

While he scrambled through it to unlock the back with the jerry-rigged wire latch, she wondered if he would be all right alone. What would he do when he got home? Stay up until dawn writing music? Pace, panic, cry? What was it like to be him?

The back of the van popped open, and Mae rolled the bike around to the gate and lifted it to Jamie.

"Thanks, love." With tender care, he nestled it into a spot between cardboard boxes, away from the pillows and blankets that protected the didgeridoo. "I'll take it in for a fix-up soon."

While he closed the gate and fiddled with the wire, Mae walked around to the driver's side to wait for Jamie to crawl through and settle into the seat. Once he was ready to drive, he rolled the window down and reached out to her. She took his hand.

"Are you sure you'll be all right?" she asked.

"Might roll up to the park by the Zen place, play flutes for a while under the stars. You could come with me."

The pastime seemed healing enough that she trusted he'd get through the night, even if he didn't sleep. If she weren't so tired, it would even be an appealing invitation. "I need to rest."

Jamie rubbed her thumb, then let go of her hand and leaned across the passenger seat to rummage through the clutter jammed into the open glove box. "Here. You told me how you work, while we were cleaning." He handed her a small speckled feather. "Don't like to talk about the dead. But ... think it's been long enough that I can say his name ... This was Dusty's. He gave it to me."

"You *knew* him?"

"Tried to."

"Are you asking me to use the sight?"

He nodded. She didn't want to see what Jamie couldn't talk about, though. If it was that distressing, it was too private. "I don't understand. You sure you want me to look? I have clear visions, sugar, I see everything."

He closed her fingers around the feather. "Find out why he died."

Mae looked down at their hands, Jamie's long brown fingers wrapped gently around hers. "I thought he fell."

He let go. "Yeah, but *why*? The kid was fucking agile, he wouldn't fall." Jamie leaned back and gazed ahead through the windshield. "Sorry. You don't have to."

Mae wondered what she would find, if anything. "I'll try. But more likely I'll see you, since you've kept this feather. I don't see dead people. I can't get hold of 'em. It's not as if they leave ghosts."

"Jesus, love, every culture's got ghosts. Hungry ghosts in Japan, Navajo *chindi* ..." He frowned, clearly puzzled. "Can't believe you don't believe in 'em."

"I never had any reason to. I mean, as a psychic I can't get any energy from dead people's things. Like there's nothing left."

"But if they don't die well or need to finish something, they stay around. He didn't die right or he'd be gone."

"What? You mean you *see* him?"

"Yeah. Down where ... Sorry. That's fucking gloomy." Jamie shook his head, gave her an incongruous smile, and grasped the steering wheel. "So ... Jeezus. Dunno how to say goodnight. I'd just sit here for hours yabbering at you, and you need to sleep. What time tomorrow?"

"Not too early. Do you sleep once it's light out?"

"Might." The smile brightened. "No worries. Nine? Ten?"

Later might let him sleep more. "Ten."

"Hooroo, then. Catcha." He started the van and Mae walked back to her car, holding the feather. The van hesitated, jerked, and then crawled out of the mall lot into the street.

She'd gotten more than she asked for. Jamie had not only told her his troubles, he'd given her his ghost.

Chapter Fourteen

After parking in the carport, Mae paused in the garden before going inside. The little speckled feather bothered her, and she didn't want it in the house, didn't want to take a ghost's unanswered questions to bed with her. She had never dealt with the unrestful dead before, and she didn't feel easy with it. Would the feather really bring her in contact with the dead boy? If ghosts were as real as Jamie believed, they might have energy traces, unlike the peaceful dead. If so, would she get too close to a troubled spirit?

She picked some stalks of sage and bundled them together, remembering the way an American Indian mentor back in Norfolk had used sage and cedar to clear out bad spirits and to make a sacred space. She didn't have matches to light it and make a smudge stick, but the ceremony of gathering the plants and the calming effect of their scent gave her time to think.

Why am I doing this? She kept saying yes to Jamie. It was one thing to keep an eye on him after he got himself hit by a car, but looking into a death? Her first reaction when her father had told her about the boy under the bridge had been pity for someone alone with nowhere to go, dying without family around. Someone like Kenny when he'd been homeless, before Muffie gave him his job. Now she knew that the boy hadn't been alone at his last moment and that Jamie had tried to be a friend to him, had known him well enough to say *the kid was fucking agile, he wouldn't fall.*

What if he'd been pushed? Was she looking for a murder? The idea was so frightening, it cleared her doubts about the psychic work. The truth was important.

Mae sat on the bench, took the velvet pouch of stones from her purse, and chose crystals for the journey. For strong protection—turquoise and aventurine. For clairvoyance—charoite and amethyst.

Setting the intention to see the story of what happened to Dusty, she closed her eyes and slowed her breath, tuning into the energy from the feather. As her mind began to shift into its altered state, the fear of seeing someone die rose in Mae's chest, but the tunnel took her.

The scene that opened wasn't the river bed under the bridge, but a street downtown near the Plaza, outside a restaurant at night. People walking past wore coats or sweaters. Jamie, on crutches and heavier than in her first view of his past, up around two hundred pounds or more, came out of the restaurant with Lisa, the elegant blonde girlfriend from that earlier vision. She was dressed up, in a sleek blue dress, high heels, and a soft shawl, while he wore jeans and a sweater. They didn't hold hands or look at each other. She carried her purse in one hand and a paper box, the remains of a restaurant meal, in her other hand.

For a couple on a date, they seemed distant. Not speaking. Mae wondered about Jamie's weight. From being disabled by the hip surgery, or from depression? Probably both. The relationship looked to be in its last stages, the broken togetherness Mae knew all too well. She guessed they were still trying to save it, trying to have a romantic evening, and not succeeding.

An ululating war whoop sounded, and a thin, pale youth of about fifteen, with flying dark curls under a black Western hat, zigzagged at Olympic-sprint speed from across the street, snatched the leftovers from Lisa's hand, and dashed away with another whoop. She gasped, looked at her purse, and felt Jamie's back pocket for his wallet.

"You think you're bloody Geronimo?" Jamie shouted after the thief, and the boy let out one more whoop as he turned the corner. Other pedestrians glanced around at Jamie, not at the running boy. It had happened so fast, no one else detected that the boy had even taken anything.

"Jeezus. You all right?" Jamie asked Lisa. "Sorry I can't run after him."

"It's only leftovers."

"Yeah. Just the male urges, y'know? Illusion of protecting you, that crap."

They moved off in the opposite direction from the thief's escape. "Did you smell him?" Lisa asked. "He's probably homeless."

"Fucked-up way of getting food, though." Jamie frowned, thoughtful, and then laughed, like he had almost forgotten how, not the loud snort-laugh Mae was used to. "Fucking brilliant. Wish I hadn't finished mine—I'd like to have seen him steal two. He bloody well needed it more than I do."

Withdrawing halfway from her trance, Mae felt like she'd missed, taken a wrong turn in time. Sometimes the sight showed her what she needed to know, even when it didn't answer her question, but she asked again, being more specific this time. *What happened to Dusty? How did Jamie find him dying?*

She slipped through the tunnel once more, and it pulled her to the river trail, a thin layer of snow along the sides, the dirt dry and clear, the cottonwoods bare. Jamie, still heavy but no longer on crutches, rode his bicycle slowly along the path, wearing a soft mouse-brown fedora, no helmet. So was that a lie about having it in storage? He just didn't wear one. Mae silenced her judgment, focused on the vision.

Approaching the dark place under the bridge, Jamie dismounted and said to the shadows, "So this is where you swag out."

He rolled the bike under the bridge and propped it against the tunnel wall behind some large rocks. Seated on a single dirty pink-and-white fuzzy blanket was the boy who had stolen the leftovers. He wore too little clothing for the weather, and his fair skin was almost blue with cold. He said nothing to Jamie, who nodded at the blanket.

"Got lice, or is it safe if I sit? I hate fucking bugs."

Dusty scratched, and Jamie grinned, sat on a rock.

"Listen, mate, I think you're new in town. Am I right?" No answer. Jamie continued. "The river's not the place any more. There's a good shelter, d'you know about it? On Cerrillos, right near a bus stop." He reached in his pocket, brought out a bus pass and offered it to the boy. "Place with dinosaurs on the roof, used to be a pet store, can't miss it. You could come in, get warm, get a meal."

"I'm a free man." Dusty solemnly placed a fist to his chest. He had a Southern accent not unlike Mae's, the twang of Appalachia. "I'm not going in."

"Jeezus. It's only food. You like to swag out in the cold, do it. Just an offer, y'know?"

"If you were a white man, I'd kill you."

Jamie let out the full-volume hah-and-snort laugh. "Bloody hell, you do think you're Geronimo. I'll bet you've never killed a white man in your life. You *are* a white man."

Dusty shook his head. "I'm an Indian."

"And I'm a bloody Chinese." Jamie stood, shifted his hips as if sore and stiff, and sat back down. "What's your blood quantum? What's your tribe? One sixty-fourth Cherokee?"

The boy sounded contemptuous. "I'm a full-blood Apache."

"Fuck. No wonder you won't go in. You think you'll get committed." Jamie sighed. "Not on any meds, are you?"

Dusty stood, raised his arms toward the roof of his bridge cave, and chanted in nonsense syllables. Chest thrust out, facing Jamie, the boy dropped his arms and fell silent. He touched his beads, and then the feathers in his hat. "I have hawk medicine."

"Right. Keeps you safe on your raids. You can see from the sky, fly in on your prey."

The boy stared at Jamie, and with a slow dawning of trust, smiled and nodded.

"Beats being locked up and drugged," Jamie said softly. "I get it. But it's cold. You need a better swag." The boy frowned. "Camp. Gear. That's your swag. And you need warmer clothes, something."

Dusty sat on his blanket again, back stiff, lips pressed together.

"Yeah, you do." Jamie pulled his sweater over his head and handed it to the boy, and then unbuttoned his flannel shirt and gave it to him as well, leaving himself in just a T-shirt. He looked partially in shape, thick around the belly but strong in the shoulders and arms. Compared to the boy, he looked healthy. "Can I bring you food? Or do you only like to raid, *free man*?"

Briefly taking off his feathered hat, the boy slipped the shirt and sweater on. In the too-large clothing, his wiry frame looked even thinner. He lay on his side and curled up, the hat falling over the side of his face.

"What's your name?" Jamie asked

"Dust and Wind."

"Jangarrai." Silence. "It's Aboriginal." More silence. "I'd give you my *gadia* name but you might kill me."

"You don't think I really can kill people."

"Dunno. Can you? You got a knife or gun or something?"

"I have *this!*" The boy spun on his blanket, sitting up so fast he seemed electrified, and flung one arm out, two fingers pointing at Jamie, not like a child playing at guns, but with the palm down, and a wild light in his small blue eyes. "That could have killed you."

"Felt a little something, yeah. Kind of a spark, right? I get it. The Aboriginal law men, they can do that to you. You need to die, done something bad, they can point a bone at you. Kangaroo bone. And you're dead. Might take days, but you're done." Jamie rose and did the hip shift side to side again. "Hope you didn't use it full out on me, mate, because I thought I'd bring you dinner if you're hungry."

The boy looked intrigued. "Point a bone?"

"Yeah, but not some old bone you get from a dumpster. Don't try it. You'll turn someone into a chicken. You want food that's not somebody's garbage or not?"

"I hunt. I forage. I'm a free man."

"I'm a good cook."

"You look it," Dusty sneered.

"Bloody hell." Jamie walked with a slight limp to take his bike from its parking place. Finding a small heap of trash at his feet, he shook his head. "Clean this up, mate. Us *indigenous people* love the earth, y'know? And you never know when you'll have guests. Some fat bloke might show up with some tucker. Catcha." He wheeled the bike out from under the bridge, mounted again, and rode off.

The tunnel pulled Mae abruptly to a new vision, the sun shining on the bridge above Dusty's camp. It was still winter. The snow on the ground was thicker, and a thin trickle of ice-edged water ran though the center of the riverbed. Jamie and a middle-aged, heavy-set, brown-skinned woman half-slid down the trail's steep bank and paused at the edge of the shadow under the bridge. Although she wore jeans and sneakers, the woman also wore a name badge that suggested she might be with a social services agency, and she carried a large woven bag with the top of a clipboard sticking out of it. Jamie called, "You in here, mate? Brought you a friend. Indian lady wants to talk to you."

Dusty snatched a backpack, bolted out the other end of the bridge cave, and dashed up the slippery trail and onto the sidewalk at a speed neither of them could hope to match. Jamie, limping, led the social worker into the makeshift camp. "Sorry. Thought he might trust you. But anyway, this is his swag. He might not trust me any more after this."

"I'll try again. If he doesn't move out."

"Make sure you act like you think he's Indian. And powerful, like he's this big shaman."

"I'll do what I can to communicate with him." She looked around. There was nothing under the bridge but the neatly folded blanket. "He keeps it clean, at least."

They started back out, and Jamie paused. "Stupid question, but—I had this weird conflict, asking you to meet him. I'd be fucking miserable if I didn't bathe and if I was stealing food and eating out of dumpsters and crap like that, but ... can he be *happy*? I mean, what if he likes it? He says he's a free man."

"You did the right thing. Don't feel bad about it. When you're that delusional, you're not really free."

The tunnel spun through again, and the image shifted to the garden of the house on Delgado Street. Ruth, smoking, sketched at an easel. She was wearing a heavy sweater and a battered broad-brimmed leather hat. Dusty appeared at the wall. He could barely peer over it, only his head showing.

"This is a private garden, asshole, quit gawking," Ruth snapped. "How many times do I have to tell you that?"

Ruth knew Dusty? The image was so startling Mae almost lost her focus and made an effort to return her mind to its quiet state. She couldn't afford to lose the momentum. A rapid flow of energy took her back into the garden, this time at night. The plants were leaf-less, dry stalks. The homeless boy side-stepped in a shuffling dance, arms outstretched, palms up as if he might think he was in an Indian ceremony, circling the statue. Ruth opened the back door and sent her dog out. Dusty darted to the carport and into the alley, the dog rushing after him, barking and growling, stopping at the edge of the property. Then the scene shifted to another night, with snow on the ground, Dusty dancing in the garden, chanting under his breath. Ruth stepped out in a nightgown and sneaked up behind him. Grabbing his wrist, she said, "I've called the cops this time. You won't get away."

Dusty yanked his arm free and pointed two fingers at her, palm down, as he ran for the wall—a quicker exit than the carport—but she grabbed a large stone and threw it at him. With an athlete's reflex he caught it. Inside the house, the dog barked as Dusty bolted to the wall, dropped the stone, and used it as a step to vault over, giving a war whoop. It was an amazingly quick and coordinated series of moves, but he landed with a stumble and a cry of pain. Favoring one foot as if he'd twisted his ankle, Dusty scrambled upright and sprinted down the alley like a rocket in spite of his uneven gait.

As Dusty reached the bridge, a single car's lights appeared, several blocks up Alameda. He swung onto the railing, stood unsteadily on his injured foot, spread his arms, eyes to the sky, whooped like he had when he'd stolen the food—and jumped. As if he had wings. On the snow-slicked rocks, his ankle instantly collapsed. Without a second on his feet to break the impact of the fall, Dusty struck his head on a rock as hard as if he'd been thrown on it. Incredibly, he managed to crawl under the bridge.

While the car's headlights passed, turning left on Delgado, Dusty lay on his blanket, gasping for breath, and let out a sound like a hawk's cry.

No pursuit. No flashing lights. Stillness.

Sunrise touched the shadow of Dusty's camp, and Jamie appeared at the edge of the bridge, wearing a heavy denim jacket, a small backpack, and his brown fedora, walking his bicycle to the riverbank. "G'day, mate. Wake up. I've been up all fucking night. Share the joy."

No answer.

"I can see you in there. Sorry about the social worker, all right? You're a free man. I'm sorry. Brought you some—"

A small wave ran through Dusty, and Jamie leaned his bike against the abutment of the bridge. "Come on. Wake up. It's a bad dream."

The jerking continued, spasms from the center of Dusty's body, and Jamie limped closer. "Oh, fuck." He pulled his phone from his coat pocket and made a call. "I'm under the bridge. Delgado and Alameda—there's this homeless kid lives there—" Jamie dropped to his knees, let go of the phone and grabbed Dusty's hand. "Oh, Jeezus, mate. No—"

Dusty, his forehead gashed, fluids running from his nose and mouth, jerked again and stopped moving. Jamie's breathing became rapid and shallow and he froze, still holding the boy's hand, staring blindly while the voice of the 911 operator called to him, "Sir? We're sending an ambulance. Are you still there? Can you tell me his condition?"

Mae closed the vision and lay back on the bench, shaken, gazing up into the stars. No wonder she had seen so much. To answer her question, she had to know of Dusty's delusion. It was what had killed him. He thought he had hawk power. Thought he could fly.

Did Jamie blame himself for not saving the boy? For panicking at the sight of his condition? Maybe it would help him to know no one had pushed Dusty, but it wouldn't erase the trauma.

And what about Ruth? She hadn't killed him, but when she threw that rock she might have wanted to. What did she think when she heard the news? She had to have connected the dead body with her trespasser.

The police must have been a far greater threat to Dusty than a social worker. If only he hadn't been so fast, so scared that he could run right through his pain. He might have feared the police, but maybe if he'd been slower they would have caught him. It would have saved his life.

Haunted, compelled, yet unable to explain to herself the need to do this, Mae locked the house and took the feather to the rail of the bridge. She imagined Dusty's confused, mad soul as a hawk, taking flight. Then, in a dim, half-formed way, Mae actually saw him with her own wide-open eyes, Dusty, looking back at her with his sharp little eyes. The longer they looked at each other, the more she sensed the ghost was somehow telling her something, though he didn't speak.

"What is it? What did you need to finish?"

His face seemed to be turning into the beaked face of a bird of prey, his shoulders growing feathers and wings.

"Is that it?"

The form became fainter and more birdlike, and this felt like an answer.

Holding the crystals, Mae blew the feather out on the night breeze and watched it fly. Goodbye to the real boy. Then goodbye to the ghost. "You're a free man now, Dust and Wind. I'll tell your friend Jangarrai that you flew."

The hawk-man shadow rose and disappeared.

Chapter Fifteen

What had happened? In a daze of awe and bewilderment, Mae left the bridge and walked back across Alameda and up Delgado. *A ghost.* She had actually seen one—and sent it on to finish its passage. There was more to the spirit world than she'd realized. Until now, she'd only touched the edges of a universe vaster and more mysterious than she had imagined. All her visions, remarkable as her psychic gift could be, were of ordinary life, like time travel to the past. Now a hole had opened in the ordinary, and another reality waited beyond it, like the street outside a movie theater.

Letting herself into the house, she heard every small sound, the click of the latch, the thunk of her shoes landing on the doormat, the slap of her bare feet on the hardwood floor, as if she had just discovered her sense of hearing.

How many spirits clung to this house and the land it stood on? She brewed a cup of herbal tea. As she sat and drank it, she gazed around the clean, brightly colored kitchen. *Ghosts are real.* The house didn't feel haunted—but then, neither had the river or the bridge. The whole world was probably haunted, if a person had the gift—or curse—to be able to see it. Or if the spirit wanted to be seen.

For the moment, she was glad Jamie didn't have a working phone, or she would probably have called him, tired as she was, and told him more than he could handle. Ruth calling the police, and Dusty's jump. The hawk-man-ghost-boy. And her views of the past winter's Jamie.

Could he explain to her how much he had changed? Except for his humor surfacing at times, Jamie in her visions of Dusty was a different man, and not just physically. He was not as loud or as fidgety, and didn't flip moods into wild highs, snapping temper, and crashing lows. She liked this other Jamie. Maybe that was what depression looked like on him, though, a quiet solidity. Or maybe that was what health looked like, when he ate and slept. She couldn't tell which weight or state of mind was his natural set point, or if he even had one.

Dusty's death, however, might have been the tipping point. Not just the death itself, but the way, after all he'd done for the boy, Jamie had panicked at the last chance to help. The 911 operator could have talked him through some steps that might have made a difference. If it had been too late and there was nothing he could have done, Jamie still could have tried—if he'd kept his head—and then he'd know he'd done his best. Having a panic disorder wasn't a failure, of course, it was an illness, but Jamie had a way of blaming himself when things were not his fault.

Pie came into the room and sat at Mae's feet, looking up at her and mewing.

"Come on up, Sweetiepie," she said.

The ancient cat didn't jump up at the invitation, but still sat and mewed. Of course, poor thing. She didn't have that much spring left in her old legs. Mae lifted her, surprised again by Pie's delicacy, her weightlessness, nothing but fur and bones. Could Jamie have been right that Pie still needed further healing? She seemed to have forgotten the trauma of Ruth Smyth's dog, but maybe it was still stuck in the back of her little mind somehow. Jamie certainly knew more about trauma than Mae did. He'd been in a hospital six times in the past ten years or so.

And he'd only mentioned three broken bones. The numbers didn't match. She still didn't have his whole story. Three major chapters missing, though she could guess at their nature.

Carrying the cat, Mae got a quartz point from her pouch of crystals. She sat with Pie in her lap and stroked her with the crystal, letting it rest in places that seemed to need attention. An image of Ruth's orangey-brown Chow dog, barking snappishly, face down near its front paws, as seen from under a chair or sofa, hovered briefly and faintly in Mae's mind, then faded. Pie stretched and purred. Either trauma didn't cling as deep in the feline brain as in the human, or Jamie had, in his loving attention, been a healer. Though the better Mae knew him, the less that seemed possible.

What would she see if she tried to heal Jamie? Probably more than she could handle. He needed a psychologist, not an energy healer. For that he needed money. She had to get him signed up with Wendy; he was clearly incapable of managing his own career. Even Niall, who wouldn't talk about him, had said that much.

Pie began punching contentedly with her claws, nesting on Mae's thigh. It was annoying but she didn't want to reject the recently healed, de-traumatized cat. "Stop it, Pie." Mae shifted gently, and Pie clung.

Mae carried her as she went to the laundry room and put Jamie's sweatshirt in with her clothes that needed washing, so she could give it back to him the next morning. That shirt would fit the "fat bloke" post-injury Jamie she had seen in her visions. Who literally gave Dusty the shirt off his back.

She shook the thought off. Time out from him. He wasn't in the house, finally. Could she get him out of her head, too? As she started the load of laundry, she imagined dropping her brain into it and washing out Jamie.

Although her legs still felt the effects of the barefoot shoes the next morning, a short run-walk along the trail exploring the river in the opposite direction from the day before appealed to Mae. She'd had almost no tourist time. Maybe she could fit in the museums this afternoon, after the workout and the car appointment. Jamie had threatened—no, offered—to be her guide to go to galleries before Ruth's opening. Not that she needed a guide. Maybe she could put him off on that.

The section of trail she took led along the river through a park with tables where people played backgammon or checkers, and then to a bigger, hilly park where the river plunged into a deep ravine thick with trees—and litter. Mae left the trail and ran on the grass. Sadly, the treed area looked like another homeless camp.

After she passed a skateboard park, she found herself faced with too much traffic and pavement to keep running. Her short workout came to an end near a set of impressive, institutional-looking buildings and a four-way intersection. Out of curiosity, she crossed the street and found herself at a church with a statue of the Lady of Guadalupe. Hoping it wasn't irreverent, Mae took time to stretch while admiring the statue, its golden corona, full-body halo and blue cape full of stars. She didn't believe in any religion, but the feel of the place was spiritual. The adobe building's subtle curves, the Lady's kind face and radiant colors, and the scent of roses in a nearby garden made her wonder if what she felt here was like what Dusty had felt in her garden. A healing presence, a kind of maternal divinity.

Since her calf muscles objected to more barefoot running, Mae walked back toward the park. Hearing faint traces of music, she detoured toward it, crossing the street and following the sound two blocks in to the Plaza. It was not time for a concert, but a small crowd of about eight or ten had gathered. Around Jamie.

He was on the green, not the stage, and had a drum and several flutes. As he ended a lively song accompanied by drum that had his listeners swaying and clapping, he took off his straw fedora. In one graceful swoop he set it down as part of a bow, and picked up the bamboo flute. A few people dropped money into his hat. Smooth, how he'd made it look like he was getting a new instrument, with a kind of choreographed plan so he didn't openly ask for the money. He began a sweet, haunting tune that contrasted with the pounding excitement of the one before. Most of his audience was now sitting down on benches or the grass. One couple leaned into a close embrace and started to kiss.

Mae watched from a distance. How much did he make doing this? Did the city encourage it, or was he doing something he might get arrested for? After the flute song, he picked up the drum again, slinging its strap over his shoulder, and asked people to sing, teaching the audience parts to an old song, *The Lion Sleeps Tonight*. With the low "weem-awuh" parts, the high, almost howling parts, and the main melody sung by members of the little crowd, Jamie switched around among all the parts while playing the drum.

Was he just having fun, or was this how he made his living? What a fall-off from aspiring to a career in opera, from his extraordinary albums, or even from being a teacher, much as he'd disliked that job. He might be embarrassed if he knew Mae had seen him.

She resumed her run in spite of the altitude and the objections of her soleus muscles. Jamie's voice followed her. Even in a silly song like this, he sang with a power and purity and passion that seemed to vibrate right through her body to her soul. At times he seemed like he could hardly function enough to handle the basics of survival, but the man could sing. Far too well to be collecting dollars in his hat.

Mae cooled down to a walk as she reached Delgado Street and went to the garden to stretch and collect her crystals. Inexplicably, her heart felt full, and as sore as her legs. She lingered through another long, slow stretch, bewildered by her feelings, and then went inside to put the crystals away. What was happening to her? It had to be the altitude, too much strangeness, and too little time alone. And now it was time for more of Jamie.

She would have to tell him how Dusty had died. But could he handle it? She'd need to be careful. Her number-one goal was still to get Jamie to talk to Wendy, the first step toward getting his life together. Off Mae's hands and into better ones.

Jamie arrived at the front door almost on time. Mae heard his knock, but no gasping of the van's sickly engine. He hadn't brought it. Carrying his drum and a backpack, he flashed his best smile when she opened the door, and stepped in with a hesitation that Mae sensed as a conscious effort to stop himself from hugging her.

"G'day, love. Ready for the next adventure? Mind if I leave the drum here?"

He seemed so lively, she hated to break the bubble by telling him about Dusty's leap from the bridge. She'd have to find the right moment. "Where's the van?"

"Can't part with it while the bike's being fixed. Need some sort of wheels."

"But you didn't use it."

"Don't need two cars for this trip. Save the planet, right?"

He walked to center of the room, sat on the floor at the coffee table, unpacked his flutes from his backpack, and laid them out on the table, along with a laminated City of Santa Fe business license. At least he was legal. Why was he unpacking it all here?

"What are you doing, sugar?"

"Don't want to take all this into the locker room. Too valuable. Got the shakuhachi in Japan when I was little. Hardly knew what I was doing, but I loved it. Wherever we went I picked up a little something. Started the Native flute when we moved here." He caressed a wooden flute, and stood. "Got into drums in India." Closing his eyes, he hummed an Eastern-sounding tune and played air drum. "Didg in Australia, of course. Family heirloom, that. Sorry. I get drifty. Shall we? Fill your water bottle. Don't leave home without it. Ever." Jamie hoisted a huge steel bottle from his pack, making his point, and then put it back in. "You'll dry up like dead dingo's donger."

Mae sensed a high level of evasion in his chattiness and good cheer. What was he crowding out? Dusty's death? His reason for not bringing the van? Both?

Approaching the car, she noticed he had a subtle hint of a limp, limiting the range of motion in his left hip joint. He'd walked too much on pavement, which meant he wasn't using the van while the bike was in the shop. Why had he lied? "You got a hitch in your git-up."

"Swim'll fix it." He put on The Smile again. "No worries. Did you have a good run this morning?"

"I didn't think you saw me."

"You can't disappear in a crowd, love, any more than I can."

She unlocked the car, they got in, and she backed out of the parking spot. "You sing in the Plaza a lot? Is that most of your work?"

"Mm. Yeah—nah—maybe. Stuff coming up with Zambethalia. I'm not a beggar, y'know. I have a business license."

"I saw that." He must have displayed it to her on purpose. "Give me directions. This city confuses me."

He recited a series of simple directions, leaned the seat back and closed his eyes. "Wake me up when we get to Rodeo."

Sleeping again as soon as he was in the car. Avoidance or exhaustion? Mae sighed. She couldn't tell him about her vision of Dusty if he was asleep, but it gave her a kind of time-out from him. When Brook and Stream were little, they slept in the car easily. Maybe Jamie felt safe, like being a child again, in this contained place with someone beside him.

The drive through an adobe version of every city's strip, slowed down by construction and lights, took her past the shelter Jamie had recommended to Dusty. With its pair of green dinosaurs on the roof, the building was unmistakable, though there was no sign other than a thankful farewell from the former pet store.

It was a long way from downtown. When Jamie had brought Dusty the bus pass, he had to have planned ahead. Or did Jamie live out this way, and give away his own bus pass? No, he seemed to live closer to downtown, since she'd seen him hanging out on the river trail. Did he take this trip for his swim in that unreliable van every day? She hoped he took the bus instead. Depending where he lived, riding his bike to the fitness center could be enough of a workout in itself. He'd hardly need the swim. Eating one meal a day and getting that much exercise, he'd be running on empty. He must have lost as much as forty pounds since the winter, as well as part of his mind.

He was not only not eating, but getting how little sleep, to nap so abruptly as soon as the car was moving?

Jamie seemed to drop into a dream, making small, distressed sounds. Should she wake him up? Was he dreaming about finding Dusty? Reliving earlier traumas? All of it? But at least he was sleeping, which he needed badly.

When she made the left onto Rodeo at the big four-way intersection, Jamie woke with a start before she could say anything.

"Fuck." He adjusted the seat upright. "I made noises, didn't I?"

"Little ones."

"Sorry. Lisa used to say I whimpered."

"That's what I'd call it, yeah."

"Drove her up a wall. Can't help it, though—I'm asleep, y'know? I don't do it on purpose. Dunno why I do it." Staring out the window, he sank into himself. "What are my chances, really?"

"For what?"

"Sorry. Inner question."

"You have nightmares?"

"Yeah." He rubbed his eyes, dragged his hands through his hair. "Jeezus. Fucking crap in my head. It never ends."

"Would it help to know what happened to Dusty?"

Jamie looked at her, tension around his eyes. "Is it bad? Did somebody kill him?"

"No. Had you thought that?"

"Maybe. Police did. No one was ever arrested or anything, but—Jeezus. His head was fucking smashed—that wasn't from just slipping on the ice." Squirming, Jamie turned to the window again. "Thought that was why he was haunting me."

"No. He jumped. He thought he had those hawk powers. He was—like he was excited, like it was a superpower sort of jump. Ruth caught him trespassing. He had some obsession with our Indian statue. She was really mad and he jumped the wall, if you can believe that—"

"Yeah, I can. Come on. Don't drag me through all this. How'd he die?"

"When he got to the bridge, he thought he could fly. I think he wanted you to know that." Mae's tension released. *There. I said it. He can have some peace.* "No one pushed him."

Nodding his head slowly, Jamie closed his eyes. "And no one saved him."

Maybe it had been too late and Dusty's injury too severe, left untreated all night. Maybe not. The rescue squad had to have arrived within minutes of Jamie's call. Santa Fe was a small city, and there was not much traffic at the crack of dawn, but those minutes without oxygen could have been the difference between life and death. How long did it take? Four minutes? Ten minutes? Jamie had panicked those minutes away.

"You tried." She knew he had fallen apart, but what could she say? She couldn't tell him that she'd seen this. "You did your best."

"Not really."

Eyes open and staring now, he turned his head away just enough to avoid her, but she could still see his face. The ghost might be gone, but Jamie remained haunted.

The workout felt good, the best exercise she'd had since being in Santa Fe. The sound of weights clanging into racks and the occasional grunts of other exercisers made her feel both at home and homesick for the steadiness and sense of competence she got from her work. After she showered and dressed, Mae went to the lobby. No Jamie. She looked at the clock. This was when they'd agreed to meet. She found the pool and entered the deck area, to see if Jamie was still swimming. He'd been distressed. Maybe he needed an extra-long swim to feel better.

His hair tied back in a little round wad of ponytail revealing the scar on his neck, Jamie slashed through the water, making smooth rolling turns at the end of each lap. As he flipped over to do a back-stroke, Mae noticed another scar, this one on his left shoulder, all the way down to his elbow. That explained the long sleeves. It must have been an agonizing fall, tearing skin, not just breaking bones. She could see the scar on his right shin, too, but his trunks covered whatever had been done to his upper thigh and hip.

Then she noticed more scars. Three short, thick scars on his belly. What in the world had happened there? She watched him through another few laps of backstroke. No one would fall on their belly from a rock, people curled up instinctively, didn't they? And it seemed that gravity would make a heavy bone mass, like a hip or shoulder or head, strike first. A man might try to land on his feet and break his lower leg—Jamie had done that once. These scars on Jamie's belly didn't look like the thin, clean lines of surgical scars or the jagged tearing of rocks and branches and gravel. More like a knife—no.

No one could do that. He must have gotten into a fight, made someone that angry with him. He had a hot temper, he threw things, and snapped quickly. It would be traumatic to be attacked like that, even if he had provoked it. No—Lisa had wanted to keep him away from knives. He said he'd hurt himself once, and there were no marks on his arms like a typical cutter, or on his wrists like a suicide attempt. But *stab wounds?* How could anyone turn on himself that way? The thought made her shudder, worse than the idea of a fight.

She walked to the end of his lane and knelt to meet him when he arrived. He stopped, coiled, feet and hands on the wall, hiding the scars with his thighs tucked up against his belly. "Bloody hell, you scared me. Am I running late? What are you doing in here? I said the lobby."

"Too late." She glanced down toward the hidden scars. "You've had a long swim. Let's go make some phone calls."

Mae returned to the lobby. Jamie kept her waiting, taking more time than a man should in the shower, so that she began to wonder if he'd had a panic attack and passed out. It seemed that facing anything stressful, including dealing with his career, could trigger panic. If he'd wanted to hide his body from her, her seeing him in the pool could have upset him. She was on the verge of asking a man from the front desk to go check on Jamie when he finally appeared, his hair fluffing out from under his hat. He wore clean clothes, a bright pink shirt of thin, crinkly cotton that matched the pink stripe in his hatband, and old, soft black jeans.

"Sorry. Had to shave, beard trim, all that," he said, surprisingly cheerful. "Did you have a good workout?"

"I did."

As they walked out to her car, he avoided her eyes, but seemed full of a secret bubbliness, and said remarkably little once they got in, other than to give her directions to the Ford dealership down Cerrillos Road. Facing the window, he sang to himself, dancing a little in his seat.

Once her Focus was in for its oil change, Mae put on her visor hat and sunglasses, and suggested a walk. Jamie might be more relaxed outdoors, and they couldn't make a phone call with the TV running in the waiting room.

"Can't walk much. My hip's bad. There's a good place to go sit outside, though," he said. "I'll show you. Out at the back of the lot."

He led her past the new cars, the used cars, and the offices to a chain-link fence around a small lot with some older vehicles in it, perhaps employees' cars and trucks, and through that to an unpaved lot bordering on a patch of pink dirt desert speckled with cacti and scrub juniper. In this final lot sat a tire-less truck bed detached from its cab, and five or six camper shells, some propped up on bricks or cinderblocks, others tipped against each other, making a kind of tent. As Mae and Jamie approached, cats scattered.

"Hold still," he said. "They'll come back."

Mae did as he asked. On an old wooden pallet under a tent-like pair of leaning shells someone had put water and food dishes. The longer she looked, the more dishes Mae discovered as well as blankets and cushions in each little house-like contraption. It was a cat village.

One by one, cats of all ages, sizes, and colors crept back. Cautious at first, they came in slow motion, freezing in mid-step to gaze at the intruders. Some sat and stared, while others went into the shelters. Gradually, they resumed their lives, older cats eating, sleeping, and bathing, kittens wrestling.

Mae sensed a strange tenderness in the way Jamie felt about the odd scene. "You like this," she said.

"I do. It's sweet." He leaned on the detached truck bed. "Safe place for the little wild ones. Food and shelter. I like how they made it with the camper shells, like they're all just camping." He let out a sigh. "That gray one looks like William. My late cat."

She suspected the feral colony brought up thoughts of the homeless Dusty as well, and Jamie's attempts to get him food and shelter. To make the wild one safe. "Don't go getting all sad on me, sugar. We have a deal. You're gonna call Wendy, and you're gonna call Mwizenge about recording so she can hear your solo act."

"But—" He stood straighter, gripping the metal rim with both hands. "You've *told* her about me, haven't you?" His voice grew tight and his speech sped up. "She won't want to work with me—I'm fucked. I can't—"

"I didn't tell her your diagnoses or anything. Worst I said was that you're high maintenance, and she didn't care." In retrospect, that description seemed like an understatement. "I think you should tell her everything, though, when you get started working with her." Mae paused. This next step needed to be handled carefully. "Tell her your whole story. Even what you haven't told me."

"Jeezus." He sighed. "More diagnoses."

This wasn't what she'd expected. "You have more?"

"Maybe. ADHD, LD, I think. Not bad, though. I mean, someone said so, some school in one place we lived. I'm not sure. We moved too much, different teachers."

Hard to believe he didn't know for sure. She had already figured this out just observing him. "But you were here all through high school. You'd know."

"Yeah, fuck. All right, I know. But I don't—I don't *believe* in it, y'know? I can handle it, it's not like I need special treatment or anything. I don't like being *learning disabled*."

Pride. He couldn't see it was more disabling than admitting a need. "You should tell her about it, though. When you meet her, if you get that far, bring someone you trust with you. If you have trouble understanding a contract, that could matter a lot."

He tensed, pushing some unseen thing away, as if she had handed him a dense legal document that overwhelmed him. "Fuck. I can't sign a contract. I'll need to pay her. And I'll have to drive on some fucking tour, I'll have to go all over the fucking place by myself—" He paced away, arms clasped to his body again, massaging his forearms. "Jesus. I can't do it."

"Slow down, sugar, breathe, before you get yourself in a wobbly, whatever you call it."

He walked back to her, leaned on the truck bed again, looking down into it. "Wish I could catch one of those cats."

"What for?"

"Hold onto him while I talk. Jesus, I miss William. Y'know? I could *hold* him."

"Listen to me, before you get all scared about this call." She didn't want to make this offer, but if it would get the mission accomplished, it was worth it. "If you'll feel better you can hold onto me, hold my hand while you talk." It was hard to tell if his lack of response meant she'd insulted him or if his mind was simply in too much of a knot for her words to penetrate. "Let's call her, sugar. If this works out, you can make a real living. You'll be able to eat better, and sleep better, and move somewhere where you can have a cat. You might even make enough money to get therapy again. I don't know. Maybe even get insurance."

"But I can't *pay* her."

This, then, had been the big stumbling block. He sounded close to tears. When she'd guessed he was poor, she had guessed right.

"Maybe her fees are like—" Mae took a guess, based on sharing percentages of her training fees with gyms, "a percentage, not something you have pay up front. You'd have to make money for her to make money." If this wasn't true, Wendy would correct him soon. "Remember, she's new to this business. She can't charge too much. And I think you'll like her."

"Might. I like most people." A shaky inhalation. He looked at her with a hint of The Smile and stood straighter. "You'll hold my hand?" He reached out, almost laughing at himself. Then the laughter vanished, and his eyes became dark, deep pools that swallowed her. "Jeezus. You're the most fucking decent human being I've ever met. D'you know that?"

"I'm about average." Mae looked away and took her phone from her purse. "But thanks for the compliment."

"I mean it." There was passion in his appreciation, a kind of urgency. "If I let people see what a bloody mess I am—it's like the blond hair, the gold tooth. People don't see my face, they see the weird stuff. Find out I'm fucked, and no one sees where I'm all right. You act like I'm all right." He squeezed her hand in both of his. "Like you can see my face."

Mae felt embarrassed. She'd asked him about the hair and the tooth, first thing when she met him. She was like everyone else—and she hadn't for a minute thought of him as being all right.

But she did see his face. Hopeful, open, anxious, and strangely beautiful.

Chapter Sixteen

They sat on the ground on the shady side of the truck bed. Not far away, the dirt swarmed with fat red ants piling up pink pebbles at the mouth of their underground city. Mae dialed Wendy's number and handed Jamie the phone. "You can do this, sugar. It's your new life."

He moved the phone to his left hand, took Mae's hand in his right, and listened, lips pressed together, shoulders hunched in. A startled look then came over him, as if he hadn't really expected Wendy to answer. "Uh, yeah ... G'day. This is Jamie Ellerbee. Jangarrai." He listened, and seemed to tense all over like an animal braced for flight, still squeezing Mae's hand. In spite of the parched air, his was as wet as if he'd dipped it in water.

Mae wondered if he would tell Wendy the truth about his problems, and if it would get in the way of his career. He faced a double bind. It would be a long time before he'd make the money he'd need to get therapy, and he'd have to be stable enough to earn it.

Before she fully realized she was making this decision, Mae's free hand reached for the crystals in her purse. She felt the familiar shapes of the stones without looking, without showing what she was doing. Turquoise for protection, Apache tear for healing old grief, tree agate for trauma, and amethyst for clairvoyance. She folded her fingers over them. In a way, it went against her principles as a psychic and healer, to do this. What would be worse? To help him without his asking, or leave him so anxious and unstable he might not even finish this conversation? He needed to be grounded enough to commit to a manager and communicate with her, and to focus on the work that would follow.

Mae wished she had seen the need for this sooner. Under the circumstances, it was impossible to do the full preparation she normally did as a healer, to raise her own energies and target the healing, but there wasn't time to do it later. Jamie had to make the connection and decision now, and be ready to move on with it.

While he talked, Mae closed her eyes and focused on reaching the seed moment of his career troubles, feeling the trembling, bright energy from Jamie meeting the power from the crystals. The healing needed to reach the root. She fell through the tunnel and emerged in a small, cluttered office.

A robust, fair-skinned woman with erect posture and gray hair swept up in a twist typed at her computer, while a tall heavyset young black man with short dark hair looked on, seated in a chair at the far end of her L-shaped desk. The woman brought up a chart and said, "Look at your grades. This is your fourth year. You're going to have to do a fifth. It's not that you're not capable musically, you're more gifted than any student I've seen in this program in ten years, but you've missed classes, and you've missed rehearsals. I know it's been ... *medical*, but—I don't know how to put this—I think you need to change your major to music education, not performance." *Medical* had clearly been an uncomfortable euphemism. "Just focus on your studies, not the stage. I don't think it's wise for you to," she turned to face him, "to take the risks of a performing career. You need security, predictability. Health insurance."

"But ... I'd get work. Fuck. I can *sing*. I got into the Santa Fe Opera apprentice program when I was only eighteen." Mae hardly recognized this boy as Jamie. He'd dyed his hair to look normal. He was seriously overweight and out of shape. Only the eyes, the voice and accent, and the f-word, told her this was him.

"But you didn't perform, did you?"

He wriggled his shoulders, clasped his hands, elbows on his thighs, and looked down. "My parents were away. My sister had left for Australia. It was ... it was different. I was a kid." He raised his face again, eyes huge and desperate. "Fuck, I *hate* fucking schools. I don't want to teach."

"It's music, though. Think about it, Jamie. What else would you do? If you needed to work?"

"Nothing. I mean—no. Yeah. It's all I can do. Music. That's it."

"I want you to talk to Dr. Lawson and to academic advising about switching to education. You'll need certain courses to be able to teach. We have to be realistic. You have the talent, Jamie, but I don't think you have the toughness it would take to compete and survive. A performing career is not for everyone. I did it, but I find teaching just as rewarding."

"Yeah, because you succeeded first. You didn't get shuffled off into the bloody failure wagon before you'd even started." He stood and strode out of the office, hands in his pockets. His advisor rose and called after him from her office door, but he kept going.

Was this his deep wound, then? Had this professor's advice destroyed his confidence? Unsure if she'd reached the seed moment, Mae hesitated to send the healing yet. The tunnel moved her vision through to another setting, a darkened bedroom. Rock music, loud voices, laughter, and an occasional thud suggested a party in other rooms. In the bedroom, two figures moved under a sheet.

A young woman's exasperated voice whined, "Not like that, come on, what is the *matter* with you? Haven't you ever done this before?"

"No. Sorry." The breathless partner under the sheets was Jamie. "What do you want me to do?"

"You idiot." She sounded raucously drunk. "I want you to ram your dick in me and fuck me."

The sheets changed shape in the dark, as he knelt over her. Silence. "Bloody hell. Oh, Jesus, I'm sorry. Give me a minute."

"Are you kidding? I'm sick of waiting." A brown-skinned young woman with long, disheveled hair swung her legs out of the bed and sat up. She still wore a black lace bra, and a pair of tiny black panties clung to one ankle. After yanking the panties over her other foot, she lost her balance when she stood to pull them all the way up, and sat back on the bed. "I must be drunk. I can't believe I got into bed with the fat guy. And then he's a virgin. A *virgin!* Can't even get the—"

"Don't yell it, please. I'm ... I never drank before. Not supposed to. These meds I'm on, and—it's that, it's not you, it's not your body, you're sexy, you're beautiful. I want you, it's just—"

"You're damned right it's not me." Standing unsteadily, she grabbed a dress off the chair near the bed and pulled it over her head. "It's you. You're hopeless."

"Oh, fuck." He got out the other side of the bed, staggered, and pulled on a pair of jeans, while she fished under the bed for her shoes and struggled to fit her toes into them, as if she couldn't aim her feet properly. "It's over," he groaned. "Fucking over. Every bloody fucking thing is over."

Stumbling past the girl, Jamie crossed through a living room full of loud, dancing people, some in couples, others standing on the sofa clapping and singing along with the music on the stereo. A young man with spiky reddish hair, bouncing among the couch-dancers, called, "Ellerbee must have *done it*! Coming out of his cave!"

Jamie ignored the cheery shout, his urgent, unsteady steps taking him into the kitchen. Dishes lay in the sink, and he reached into the heap as if he knew what he would find, coming up with a short, sharp knife. Closing his eyes, he grasped the handle with both hands, and thrust hard into his own belly, falling to his knees with a groan. Blood flooded over his hands and onto the floor as he stabbed again, and again.

The spiky-haired boy ran into the kitchen, grabbing Jamie's arms from behind and hauling them up over his head. "Somebody call 911. He's lost it." The boy was smaller than Jamie, but seemed stronger, and slightly less intoxicated. He managed to force Jamie's arms apart so he lost his two handed grip on the knife. From there, the red-haired boy knocked Jamie face down and sat on him, while

Jamie still clutched the knife in one hand, stabbing at the floor over his head. "You stupid ass." The friend's tone was tender as well as angry. "I can't believe you did that. God, you're crazy." He rested a hand on the back of Jamie's head, where the hair was light at the roots over the scar on his neck. "You are one fucked-up dude."

Jamie stopped struggling as other people crowded into the kitchen doorway, one of them talking on a phone. The vision went dark.

He must have gotten drunk after his professor had crushed his hopes, and tried to prove himself at something by bedding this girl—only to fail there as well. Mae felt profoundly uncomfortable that her vision had shown her this, but maybe it was the bottom of the hole where the healing needed to reach. *Fear of rejection.*

She took a deep breath, opened the energy channels in her heart and hands, and visualized a soft light, something pale blue and delicate, moving from her hand into Jamie. She knew she couldn't fully heal him, could only take the edge off his pain and traumas, but it was better than nothing. To her surprise, he drew his hand away, and turned from his talk with Wendy to say softly, "No love, you mustn't do that."

"You could feel that?"

"I'm a sensitive man." He took her hand again, brought it to his lips for a kiss, and gave her an unexpectedly radiant smile. "I'm your friend, not your patient." He placed his arm over her shoulders, resuming his talk with Wendy, laughing, happy, excited. Then, giving Mae a quick side-hug, he stood up and began to sing over the phone, belting out a song Mae had never heard before.

"*I feel so good, I feel so good.*" The word *feel* stretched out, rose and fell, as the melody rolled through his extraordinary range. "*I feel so good that I——can't stand it.*"

Handing Mae the phone, he drummed a rhythm on the truck bed, sang another verse, and took the phone back, laughing. She wished Wendy could see this performance. Mae had never seen Jamie so exalted, and wondered if she had touched a note of healing before he stopped her. Or if all it took was courage and hope.

In his subsequent call to Mwizenge, Jamie was almost unable to get the words out, startling and scattering the cats as he executed half turns and occasional low jumps, as if he literally couldn't keep his feet on the ground.

When he hung up and handed Mae her phone he said, "Jeezus, I'm going to *do* this! I'm going to make it! I'm— Fuck, I can't—I'm—" His inarticulate ecstasy exploded in a hug that lifted Mae an inch off the ground, and he sang his feel-good song on the way back to the office. If they hadn't been so close in height and weight, she suspected he might have swung her up to the sky.

With Jamie in that ebullient mood, she found it easy to drop him at Mwizenge's house in a neighborhood between and Rodeo and Cerrillos, behind the malls and hotels. Mwizenge had a home-based graphic design business and had agreed to take some time out to help. He didn't have a professional recording studio, but he had enough technical expertise to get a song onto a computer file and sent, which was more than Jamie had.

As he got out of Mae's car at the adobe ranch house, Jamie said, "See you at the Plaza at six. I'll bring a picnic. Wear your dancing shoes," and jogged up the walk before she could say *No, I need time off from you.*

She'd been too deep into Jamie's life and feelings. She was glad he was happy, but even then, he was somehow disruptive to be around. At the house on Delgado, she went into the garden to put out her crystals for cleansing in the sun, and then decided to use them on herself, the way she did after working with healing or psychic clients. Something inside her felt off balance.

Closing her eyes, Mae used her grandmother's unpolished ruby, a piece of the North Carolina mountains, for balancing and restoring herself, brushing the air around her with it. Her mind went quiet and she stood still, feeling the steadiness of the ruby's vibration, the earth's pull, the strong New Mexico sun, and something from the statue, like the spirit of both the art and the rock it was made from. The disturbance she'd been carrying faded. It didn't leave, but it diminished enough that she felt more like herself.

Relieved, Mae laid the ruby with all the crystals she had used since the night before on the bench to be cleansed by the sun. Between her vision of the hawk ghost and this immersion in Jamie, it would take more than this to fully relieve her. At least she had the afternoon alone. Time out from everything.

After visiting the museum in the Palace of the Governors, Mae strolled along the arcade outside, admiring the pottery and jewelry of the Indian vendors, and then stopped to sit on the wall around the monument in the center of the Plaza to rest her sore legs before walking home. The tourist activities had helped clear her mind, though they hadn't helped her legs much. She had perspective now, a realization that all this stuff with Jamie, while intense, would be over soon.

She'd done what she needed to as far he was concerned. He'd talked with a manager, taken that step toward recording again. Deborah would be able to order his music. That was the mission, and it was accomplished. Hard to believe it had taken so long or been so difficult. It amazed and puzzled her, when Jamie wasn't around, how she kept getting swept up into more plans with him. She was done with him. And yet she wasn't. She was dancing with him tonight, something she wouldn't have agreed to if he'd held still long enough for her to say no, or he'd had a working phone. She couldn't very well have hollered her refusal, could she? And she was going to Ruth's opening with him, which she also should have refused. *How does he talk me into all this?*

With a moment's thought, she halfway understood how she'd ended up with the plan to see Ruth. It had been the shock of finding out Jamie knew Muffie and where to find her. This reminded her of the other business she hadn't quite finished, with Roseanne and that awful web site, and Kenny and Frank. She'd gotten too wrapped up in Jamie's business, let him take over so much of her time and energy that she still hadn't talked to Kenny since leaving the message that she would see Muffie.

Putting her feet up on the wall and massaging her calf muscles, she called him. He should be between shifts about now.

While she waited for Kenny to answer, she remembered the woman in purple she'd seen here her first day, dancing around alone, and Jamie, flashing through like a shooting star. Mae hadn't danced, though she'd wanted to. *There isn't a law against being crazy.* The woman had meant her own kind of crazy, free-spirited and eccentric, not dysfunctional crazy. Jamie seemed to be a little—or a lot—of both.

Kenny's voice broke in on her thoughts. "Namaste."

"Um— Hey, Kenny, this is Mae. What did you just say?"

"Namaste. It's Sanskrit, hello or goodbye. It means like, my spirit honors your spirit. How are you?"

"I'm good. I like Santa Fe."

"Cool. I knew you would. Your message was weird."

"Sorry. I guess I should have explained how I'm gonna see Muffie, if she said she was ascending. A friend here says he's sure she'll be at this artist's gallery opening tomorrow. That she never misses this woman's shows. I got the feeling she might even be involved in the catering or something, if I remember what he said. Maybe not. But anyway, he's taking me to meet her."

"That's so strange." Kenny sounded confused. "I read Sri Rama Kriya on ascendance, and he doesn't say anything about it misfiring. Did you find his place?"

"No. It's closed. Or never existed."

"Are you sure? It has to be open. She goes there."

Mae doubted the place would turn out to be any more substantial than Muffie's psychic insights were. "I'll ask about it when I see her. Is there anything you'd like me to tell her or ask her?"

"Yeah. I'd like to know about that Ascended Muffie web site. It's so Dada, it could be her, but she'd have to be communicating with someone physical. Or ..." A hint of worry crept in. "That stuff on the site about ascending not being what we think it is makes me wonder if she had to back off from it. Can you ask her what happened?"

"I'll try." Mae marveled at what a follower could come up with to explain his mentor abandoning him. She'd been sure Frank and Kenny would think the site was satire and be insulted. "Do you have a guess?"

"I think that quote from Sri Rama Kriya, about incinerating karma stored in chakras so you can eliminate your samskaras, might be saying she hadn't quite eliminated all of them. She wasn't illuminated." The tongue-twister nature of the quote, now that Roseanne had pointed it out, sounded funny to Mae even paraphrased. "So she couldn't ascend. She had to be reborn right here, and walk back in."

"What are samskaras?"

"Stuff from this life or a past life that left a mark on you, so you keep reacting to it. It makes you accumulate new karma. Makes you act certain ways. Maybe she still had some left and couldn't walk out."

"Thanks. I think I get samskaras." *I think I have some.* Codependence. Taking care of messed-up people. "I don't get walking out and walking in, though."

"Sri Rama Kriya says there are walk-ins and crawl-ins. This is really esoteric, sort of a secret teaching; it's not what most of the yoga books or teachers will share with you. He says people who are born in this body are crawl-ins, and people who come and go, who use a body for a while and go in and out of a higher plane, are walk-ins. Muffie's a walk-in, and she might have been ready to walk out."

"Wow." Mae had an image of a soul stepping partway through the skin of a body and stopping, saying, *oops, forgot my keys*. She was more impressed with Kenny's gullibility than the strange idea, but she let her *wow* pass for shared awe. "So, I'll ask her about the web site. And about her samskaras. Why she didn't walk out." Of her body. She'd certainly walked out on her restaurant. "And I guess you hope she'll come back, since she didn't ascend."

"I don't know. We miss her, but Frank and I were talking about it, and we kind of think she wouldn't have left if she didn't believe we were ready to be without her. She cared too much about me to leave if she didn't think I could handle it. Like Frank said, 'When the student is ready, the teacher will disappear.'"

"I like that." Mae's relief at the young men's humorous coping lasted only a second, vanishing behind the real problem with Muffie's absence. "But I don't see how the business was ready for the owner to disappear."

During Kenny's silence, Mae looked around at the crowd in the Plaza. Many were watching a belly dancer in gold spangles who entertained for donations the way Jamie had earlier in the day. Mae's attention was drawn to a young couple in dusty clothes carrying large backpacks. As they passed her, she caught a whiff of how badly unwashed they were. They weren't on a hiking trip. They had holes in their canvas shoes, and the woman's socks below a sagging skirt were so grimy they had no color other than the red dirt of the city.

Homelessness showed up everywhere now that she'd been sensitized to it. She had lost her home suddenly with the end of her marriage, but she'd had friends to turn to, and now her father. Kenny must have had no one, no family, or maybe everyone had cut him off when he'd been on drugs. Muffie couldn't leave him unemployed, knowing that, could she?

Kenny's voice came back, full of forced confidence. "We're trying really hard to trust the universe on that."

"Forget the universe. I'm gonna make sure you can trust Muffie."

Chapter Seventeen

On her walk back to Delgado Street, Mae wondered what had made her tell Kenny that she would make Muffie do right by him. The woman had been angry and insulted the last time Mae spoke to her. *Samskaras.* She had a rut in her karma. It was one thing to agree to find missing people, but something else altogether to think she could fix everything and rescue everyone. Yet she couldn't seem to stop herself.

A small shop full of Zuni fetishes caught her attention. After browsing the tiny carvings, many no larger than half her thumb, she bought an inexpensive corn mother carved from deer antler. The salesperson said the image of a woman emerging from an ear of corn was supposed to represent the nurturance of the earth and the sacredness of the life cycle and food. No wonder Mae was drawn to it, being a mothering kind of person.

When she got back to the house, she set the corn mother on the coffee table and did as the Zuni shop employee had suggested, sprinkling the fetish with a little of the blue cornmeal and chips of turquoise that came with it, to feed it and bring its spirit to life. *I'm going to be careful and wise with this mama urge I've got.*

As she finished the ritual with the tiny carving, she noticed Jamie's flutes on the table. His drum was still here, too. She couldn't carry his instruments to the Plaza that evening and leave them lying around. She would have to bring him back here after the concert to get them. Had he done this on purpose?

No, it had to be an oversight. Jamie seemed capable of many things, but a coherent plan wasn't one of them. Leaving his things here said he didn't have to plan. He trusted her to take care of his valuables, and him.

It was five o'clock in North Carolina and time to call Brook and Stream. Missing them was surely part of why she was taking care of Kenny and Jamie. Talking to the girls wasn't the same as mothering them, and she missed having children need her.

She called, but Hubert didn't answer, and the twins weren't at her in-laws' place when she called there. Disappointed, Mae reminded herself it was only one day. It wasn't the end of her relationship with them. Hubert had even made sure she'd know where to reach them when he took that trip with Jen on the weekend. Still, not reaching them today rubbed it in—changes were taking place in the twins' lives without her.

Her father could help her cope with all of this, help her figure herself out. She called him, taking her phone out to her favorite spot, the bench by the statue.

When she asked how he'd handled having to leave her behind, his mellow voice grew very quiet. "Talked about you a lot. Reckon I drove folks crazy. Even Niall said I had to ease off on it. I think I was trying to feel like I still had you."

His words touched her, and she wished she could hug him. If she talked to him that much about Brook and Stream, he would listen and understand. It might help.

Marty continued, with a new current of energy and warmth. "The one person who could listen forever was Jamie. Soon as I said I had a girl near his age and showed him your picture, he—I wonder if he remembers this—he fell in love with you."

"With my picture?" Mae tried to remember her thirteen-year-old self in the pictures Marty would have had back then. "I was gawky. I was taller than all the boys. And I had braces."

"But you were still pretty. And I may have made my baby girl sound perfect, missing you and running on about you."

"What was Jamie like then?"

"Kinda chubby, baby-faced. Too much going on in him, like he didn't have room for himself. Funny. Gifted. All over the place ... Good kid, though. Good heart. So sincere it kind of embarrassed you sometimes." Marty paused. "Niall said you met him. That he helped you with the house. You two getting on good?"

"I can't seem to make him go away."

A low chuckle. "So he latched onto you."

"It's not funny, Daddy. He's sweet, but I feel like he's always hiding something, holding something back, no matter how much I learn about him."

"Huh. Sounds like he's changed some." A long pause. "But he's had a rough year. I haven't talked to him, but we hear the news from his folks. He quit his job end of last school year—he'd been teaching music—to go into performing full time. Then he had a bad rock-climbing accident. And then his fiancée broke up with him. And then he found that homeless kid that died that I told you about. He might have a few things he's not up for telling you. He could be a little stressed out trying to handle it all."

"That's like saying a hurricane is a little breezy."

"I know. His mama used to call him Typhoon Jamie." Marty chuckled again. "Speaking of stressed out, how's Pie? You got her out from under things? Can you pet her yet?"

"Jamie got her to come out. She seems all right now."

"Good. Why don't you stick around a few days longer and make sure she's okay? I'd just as soon she transitioned to the new tenants in good shape. Can you wait 'til they get there Tuesday?"

She was eager to get back to her own house and to look for work. "I'd planned to leave Friday morning. Seeing as the house is done and all. Especially since I can't unglue Jamie. He could look in on Pie for you, he's real good with her, but I need to get some space from him."

"I can think of worse people to have stuck to you. But if you don't want him around, baby, send him off. Just be kind about it."

Marty had said more than Niall had, but Mae could hear that same protectiveness coming in. "He's sensitive."

"I'll try. I explained about not even being divorced yet, and I think he gets it, he's just clingy. I'm not giving him any encouragement."

"You sure?"

"Daddy, that's ridiculous. No, I'm—" The idea of Jamie as a candidate for a romantic relationship, even if she was interested or available for one, was out in left field. "I'm not into him."

"All right." She could swear Marty was disappointed. "Be friends with him if you can, though. His folks would like that, our young'uns getting along. So would I."

As she walked back downtown to the Plaza at six, Mae thought of the balancing act she had to manage tonight. It could be fun, and she and Jamie could be friends like their families wanted if she handled it well, but handling him well was difficult.

Past a cluster of hula-hooping young people in tie-dyed clothing, Mae easily spotted him in his pink shirt, his wild hair flying out from under the straw fedora. Pacing, scanning the crowd, he seemed not to have seen her yet, and she had a moment to watch his anxious eagerness. He reminded her of some delicate yet strong wildcat, like a Florida panther.

When he found her and met her eyes, his face lit up. With a flourish he bowed to reach into a paper bag at his feet, drew out a white cloth which he whipped out like a matador's cape, then stuffed back into the bag with embarrassed haste. Mae slowed down. God, he looked so excited, with that bright, face-splitting smile. Like he'd never been happier in his life.

The realization hit like a train-crossing signal dropped in front of her. Jamie wasn't just flirting, or reliving some remnant of his teenage fantasy. Not just being needy, or trying to help her and keep her company. He was in love with her.

Dazed, unsure what to say or how to act, she walked over to join him, and he met her with a light hug, followed by a pause in which she sensed the energy of an intended but held-back impulse to a kiss. As he led her to a spot on the grass near the monument, the discomfort of her realization was like white noise in her head, and she only half heard his greeting. Jamie looked hurt by her lack of response.

"I'm sorry. I was ... daydreaming. What'd you say?"

"Said you look beautiful. Nice dancing clothes, pretty." She was wearing a full skirt with a floral print. A few of its flowers accidentally matched his shirt. "I hope you like the music." Jamie spread out the white cloth, an old sheet, on the grass. On the bandstand, musicians in bright shirts and dark pants tuned stringed instruments, talked, and played a few notes on horns. "I love Latin night."

"I've never heard much Latin music." She helped him smooth out the cloth. "But I think I'll enjoy it."

He sat too close to her, and began to unpack a picnic, starting with a bottle of sparkling cider and two plastic champagne glasses. When he'd filled their glasses, he signaled a toast. His eyes met hers as their glasses touched. "To a soul as beautiful as her face and body."

Mae blushed and looked away. How was she going to get through this? His words overwhelmed her with a kind of guilty sweetness. To be so admired, and yet so unready to love him back. She drank and set her glass down carefully on a flat spot, while Jamie slugged his drink down and dropped the glass on the cloth.

"And now I undo all this elegance, and present," he set out paper plates and sandwiches, "things you can spill on your pretty clothes."

The toast still bothered her. "I'll try not to."

"Yeah, but the tomatoes always fall out. *Always.*" To the spread he added a plate of cherries and grapes. She could see something else still in the bag—it looked like a chocolate cake in a plastic container.

A whole cake? He'd gotten carried away. Too much effort to please her.

"You didn't bake the bread, did you?" she asked.

"Actually, I do bake bread, but this isn't mine. I'm fucking domestic, what can I say?" He flashed The Smile. "Green chile hummus and red chile hummus, by yours truly."

"You didn't have to do homemade."

"Sorry. I just like to, y'know?" He fidgeted with the picnic things, adjusting the placement of dishes on the cloth. "Jesus. The first night I moved into my place when I split with Lisa and I saw that crappy little kitchen and no one to cook for, it broke my heart. I felt so useless. I like ..." He looked down, picked up a cherry, and pulled the stem off in a twist. His voice almost vanished. "I like having someone to take care of."

"You'll find someone."

He ate the cherry and spat the pit. "Right. Thanks for the bloody platitude." His angry tone took her aback. After a moment, he said, with a quick glance at her. "Sorry."

For once, he'd apologized for his temper right away and not made a scene. "It's all right." She unwrapped and tasted a sandwich, catching a slippery tomato that almost landed on her skirt. "Good but messy."

Jamie put on a small smile and unwrapped a sandwich for himself. "Warned you about that."

He ate leaning over his plate, dropping tomatoes and recovering them. In the silence the air between them felt dense with expectations and disappointment. Mae steered toward the safest, most productive topic. "Did you get your sound file to Wendy?"

"I did," he said with his mouth full, and then chewed and swallowed, making impatient gestures that kept time with the process. "Sorry. Manners. You can dress me up, but you can't take me out."

She hadn't complimented him on dressing up, if that's what to-day's outfit was. Did he want her to? She hoped not. Liking his crinkly pink shirt was too much to ask, and she didn't want to seem to flirt. "Does Wendy have a way to get hold of you?"

"Yeah, I've got an e-mail address. Fuck—you know my phone's off, don't you?" He looked up at the bandstand. "Guess it was obvious."

"Kind of. It says *no service* when you turn it on. Like you just carry it around for the pictures."

He nodded. "Can't lose the pictures." His voice sounded rough, emotional. Mae didn't want to see him drop off into a mood, but didn't know how to pull him back. "Makes me look like a regular bloke, too, y'know? Pull out a phone, do something with it. Act like I have a life."

"Sugar, you have a life."

"Nah. I'm busy as a cat burying shit, but I don't have a life. Oh, bloody hell, stop me. Fucking dismal. Sorry. Just shoot me if I get like that." He forced a smile. "Sorry."

Mae wondered what to say or do. Was there any end to his troubles? They ate in an uneasy silence again. As Jamie bit into his sandwich, a blob of hummus fell out along with a tomato, landing on the cloth, just missing his folded legs as well as missing his plate. "Watch me sit in that. Fuck. Don't let me."

"Didn't you bring napkins?"

"No."

Mae wiggled tomato-messy fingers at him, teasing, but he didn't seem to take it lightly.

"I forgot." He bit his thumb knuckle. "Sorry. Lick your fingers. Use the cloth. Jesus, I'm fucking incompetent."

"You're not." To him, a little mistake like forgetting napkins might feel like a failure out of proportion to its significance. "And you've had a good day. You got a start on your career again. First step."

"Yeah. Think I did." He ate a few cherries, spat the pits off the far edge of the cloth, while twisting the stems into a little rope. "Got a little ... a little ... maybe it's hope ..." Jamie dropped the rope of cherry stems. "Lot of hoops still to jump through, though."

"You can do it. One hoop at a time. Wendy will help you. That's her job."

Jamie drew into himself, legs pulled up, arms around his shins. "She wants me to travel. Says it's the only way musicians really make money anymore." He took a breath, removed his hat and shook his hair out, began turning the hat over in his hands. "Touring. Scares me."

Which of his fears did it trigger? Being alone? Being rejected? "What about it scares you?"

"Directions ..." He began to roll the brim of his hat tightly. "Getting lost."

That was silly. One fear too many. Mae took the hat away from him to stop him before he damaged it. "You could get a GPS thing. They don't cost that much if you get a refurbished one. You have to download maps and learn to use it but ..." She stopped. This was technology and other directions to follow, and she could see it only added another layer of irrational stress for him. She sighed. "You don't have to worry about that right now."

"Fuck." He folded his arms on his knees and laid his head down. "I can't help it. It's all closing in on me."

Nothing worked. She'd tried to keep things upbeat and friendly, but he was having some kind of upset anyway.

Looking at his bowed head, Mae noticed that he had done the strangest thing with his hair, plaiting some of the sun-bleached top hairs into five tiny braids, bright little ropes over the thick, unruly underlayer. What had made him think of doing this? It was probably what had taken forever at the fitness center and made him come out so silly-happy. He'd been making himself look good for her.

She pictured him all worried and desperate to be liked, bobbing back and forth between excitement and anxiety, picking out the crinkly pink shirt, baking a cake, and doing this hairstyle. It was all so—goofy. Sweet and goofy. If it had been directed at some other woman, it would be endearing. It still was. But it was for her. She ached to hug him, yet held back. How could she show she cared, and yet not act like his girlfriend?

When he stayed in his contracted position too long, the nurturing urge won out. She tugged on one of the little braids, and then rubbed her hand in his hair. He felt hot. The sign of something emotional brewing. Why? Over his fear of touring? Mae wondered if he even knew what overwhelmed him.

Trying to reassure him, with no idea what she meant or what she was promising, she said, "You'll be all right, sugar. It'll all work out." No response. She played with another little braid. "I like your hair-do."

He turned his head, still in his curled position, looked at her through his half-spilled hair and smiled. "Thanks."

She pushed the rest of his hair out of his face, and he sat straight again, smiling at her, not the nervous trying-to-charm smile, but nakedly vulnerable and trusting, like a child, like a lover in the morning. She shouldn't have touched him.

The bandleader came to the front of the bandstand, introduced his group, and welcomed the audience. Jamie rose and drew her to her feet. "May I?" As he stepped back to lead her to the dance floor, he slipped in his spilled hummus, catching his balance with her help. "Bugger." He snort-laughed. "That was supposed to be fucking elegant." Still laughing, leading her by the hand, he walked backwards toward the open space in front of the band. "But this'll make up for it."

She slowed down. "Wait, I can't—"

"Yeah, you can. I can lead. Like we did in the store. You'll do great."

"It's not that—it's—" *It's the way you looked at me.* "It's not a good idea."

"Bloody hell. You need a chaperone? Jesus. We're just *dancing.*"

"Sorry." Maybe she had been too careful. She was trying to keep him for a friend, after all. People danced with partners they didn't have romantic feelings for all the time. Danced for the sake of going out dancing. She opened her arms to him. "Let's dance."

Holding her hand and her upper back, sending subtle signals with his touch, Jamie talked her through the basic foot pattern and rhythm for salsa. Mae looked down to make sure she had it right, and noticed how he moved his hips with every step, almost touching hers in a snaky, sensual rhythm. This wasn't what she'd expected when she'd agreed to dance. The movement would have been seductive if he weren't Jamie.

"Don't look at your feet, love. Look at your partner."

Bringing her gaze back up, she said, "I got the feet. I was checking out the hips." That came out wrong. As if she'd been thinking about him being sexy. She had to fix it. Ask for instruction, something. "How do you *do* that?"

He drew her closer and smiled. "What? You thought I couldn't, with three big screws in one of 'em?"

"No, I meant, teach me how."

"Don't think about it. Just feel it. Your hips'll swing on their own if you set 'em free."

She had to stop thinking about more than the movement. Stop thinking about him flirting. Or about how she liked him so much but wasn't in love. It was a summer night in Santa Fe. All around them people were celebrating, and she longed to let go and be part of it. In her small-town life in North Carolina, there had never been anything like this. The music delighted her and she *wanted* to dance to it. Jamie led with such a skillful touch that if she stopped all the clatter in her head and followed, she *could* feel the music move her hips, like a force field below the waist, when she let go into it.

Much as she didn't want to encourage Jamie, the dance itself took her over. Her resistance dissolved into the flash of the horns, the beat of the drums, and she let herself flow with his lead. It felt wonderful and free, as if she had slipped halfway out of her skin.

As Jamie guided her in a playful hand exchange pattern while their feet and hips kept the beat, she said, "You're amazing."

There was fire in his eyes now, a blaze of uninhibited joy. "Am I?" He drew her in and spun her out. "Guess I am." Pulling her back in, he caught her hip to hip, before releasing her into an open position. "Nah—correction. *We* are amazing."

Her dancing vision became a kaleidoscope—the band's sparkling costumes, the green of the grass, the bare blue sky with its low golden blast of sun, the first hint of the moon, other dancers spinning—each turn of the dizzying wheel coming back to Jamie's eyes. Full of passion, joy, and love. A deep black pool of *what have I done* in the middle of her whirl of joy.

The first band finished, and the second one began to set up. A man came to the microphone and made announcements about the final concerts of the season. Mae felt relieved in some strange way, as if she had escaped something, though she didn't know what.

She and Jamie sat on the white cloth again. He opened the picnic basket, lifted out a cake, removed its plastic cover, and took a knife and forks from the basket. "We've earned dessert."

In the center of the thick chocolate frosting, fresh velvety raspberries formed a heart with an arrow.

Mae's heart tumbled through too many feelings—guilt, amazement, worry, sadness—as well as the thought that he'd be a gem for some patient woman who could understand him. But he'd done this for *her*, a woman in the middle of a divorce who would be leaving in two days. The sense of having escaped collapsed. "Oh, Jamie, what am I going to do with you?"

He cut big squares from the undecorated end of the cake and slid them onto paper plates. "Dance and eat chocolate?"

Evasion, his usual refuge. "You know what I mean."

"Yeah, I do." Dropping the knife onto the cloth, he served the gooey slabs of cake, and lifted out a thermos from the bag. "Share the cup? I brought coffee and forgot cups." Unscrewing the lid, he filled its cup cap and offered Mae the first sip. "I'll try not to spit crumbs in it or anything."

"Sugar, the cake is good, and you're the sweetest thing on earth, but—"

"Jeezus, all right, I get it, so shut up and eat it. I'm sorry. I took a risk." He grabbed the knife and stabbed it into the raspberry heart. "I fucked up."

Alarmed, Mae set the coffee down slowly. "I don't like that drama."

"Yeah. You're right." Yanking the knife out, he tossed it into the bag and took hold of her forearm. "I should have done *this*." He shoved her hand into the middle of the cake, crushing the heart.

Stunned, Mae looked down at her hand, wrist deep in cake and frosting. She could feel the berries smushing under her hand at the bottom of the pan. All his hard work and romance destroyed. Torn between outrage and sadness, she lifted her hand out. "What is *wrong* with you?"

As soon as she said it, she wanted to take it back. Of all the things to say to Jamie. She watched his eyes for the pain, the anger. Instead, the light came back. First a hint of smile lines around his eyes, then a huge grin and the snort-laugh. "Jeeezus." Laughter, almost out of control. "You still have to ask?"

He lay back and held her cake-covered hand, examining the mess. And began to lick it clean.

At first, the unexpected gesture made her laugh with him in relief. She'd thought he was going to panic, or walk off. Instead, he was like a cat licking a kitten.

But in seconds, as his tongue stroked her palm and the inside of her wrist, it felt so intensely erotic that she hardly could move. *Stop him. This is awful.* Her body fought her mind, craving sexuality suddenly the way she had craved water on getting to the desert. It had been so long since a man had touched her like this. Eyes closed, Jamie might as well have been in bed with her, licking chocolate off her breasts. She pulled away.

Angry with herself, swamped with lingering longing and with regret, Mae wiped the remaining chocolate on the cloth. She should have stopped him even sooner. For a few seconds of feeling desired and aroused, for a fraction of a fantasy in her prolonged celibacy, she'd let him love her.

Still in a blissful state, Jamie tugged a corner of the cloth over his face and wiped himself clean.

"You shouldn't have done that," Mae said.

"No worries." Jamie opened his eyes and smiled at her. "No calories in food licked off another person. Any frosting in my beard?"

"No. And I should have said, *I* shouldn't have done that."

She sipped the coffee and passed it to him. Still twinkling and happy, he propped up on his elbow to drink. As the second band's leader introduced their first song, Jamie said with a grin, "Fuck. It was harmless fun. Come on, ya gotta be a little wicked once in a while."

"I still think we made a mistake here, sugar. I shouldn't have let you."

"No worries. Just play." He sat up, refilled the coffee cup, and drank more. "Forget I did that."

She took a bite of cake. Hard to believe someone as intense as Jamie could take what bordered on foreplay so lightly. "Are you sure?"

The music began. He rose, reached out his hand to her. "I know you're a married woman. Sort of. Halfway. Not done yet. Whatever you said about it. I'm not delusional. But," dancing a few steps, still reaching out to her, "if I were going to die tomorrow, this is how I'd spend today."

If her time were that short, would she do the same? She looked at his outstretched hand, not taking it. Too much had happened. She'd let herself slip, get carried away. Not a good move, with him.

"Come on, love. Let's have fun. I'm sorry about the cake and the—the," he seemed to teeter between ascent to joy and descent to sadness, "the scene. I'm sorry. Please. Forget the crap. Forget everything." He held out both hands. "Please. Let's dance."

Not sure if she should, not sure what would happen if she did or she didn't, Mae took his hands, and Jamie pulled her to her feet with a sunburst of a smile. Joy triumphed.

"I'm making a big mistake," she said. "You know that."

"No, you're not." He drew her in, leading her into a soft turn and spinning her to face him again. "Fuck. We're *alive*. This is *it*."

Chapter Eighteen

The Plaza felt strangely quiet in the twilight after the concert, even with all the people still sitting, strolling, talking. Tiny lights sparkled in the trees. Jamie put his hat on and packed the cloth into the bag. "Best night I've had in months, love. Maybe in a year." He looked into Mae's eyes, and then hugged her with a crushing enthusiasm, cheek to cheek, chest to chest. "Thanks for that."

His best night in a year included a near panic, a cake-stabbing, and a heart-smashing. Mae regretted that his glorious dancing was marred with moments like that. She pushed away gently, not wanting to seem cold in such a warm embrace. It would be easier on him if she could say goodnight and send him home now, but they had to prolong the evening a little more.

"You left your flutes and drum at my place. I reckon you want them."

"Was that today? Yeah, guess it was. Feels like it was yesterday. I have to get the van. Walk to it with me? Then I'll—no. Maybe ..." He froze, and when he resumed, his energy was subdued. "Sorry. My hip's done for. Dancing on cement. Van's a bit of a hike. Your place is closer. Could you give me and my things a lift to it?"

"Sounds like a plan."

In the silence as they started up Palace Street, Mae began to notice her legs. She had been so swept up in the music, the dancing, the conflicted and yet joyous surrender to the moment, that she had tuned out the pain. Dancing asked more of the same muscles that were already sore from barefoot running. The subtle stretch from the uphill slope of the street was the only thing keeping her calves from going into knots. Like the way she'd played hurt in softball games in high school and not even noticed an injury until the ninth inning was over, she'd overridden this pain and the gasping intensity of breath and heartbeat at high altitude. Now the endorphins faded and the intensity of her discomfort came on full blast.

She stopped and dropped a heel over the curb, stretching. "Hang on. My legs are cramping."

"Yeah, dancing does that." Jamie took her elbow to help her balance. "When I first started ballroom, it did a number on me. But I was out of shape. Thought you'd be all right."

"Mmm. Not on top of running in my foot gloves. I think I did too much." She held a stretch on each leg for about a minute, hoped for the best, and resumed walking. "I feel like this place makes me kind of flaky. Like I don't think as clearly as I do at home. I'd normally know better than to do all that in the same day."

"Maybe the place frees you up, y'know? Floats your lid off, and you go for it, pain and all."

Did she have a tight lid on? She didn't think of herself that way, although Niall did, and she had certainly done a few things lately that she wouldn't normally do.

As they turned the corner to Delgado and started to cross, both Mae's legs seized up with pain like spikes being driven deep into her calf muscles. She had to stop in the middle of the street to try to stretch again, but the knot was so strong, even her arch was cramping and she couldn't stand. Leaning on Jamie, she wanted to laugh at the absurdity of it, but it hurt so much she could only make *ouch* and *ow* sounds.

"Want me to massage you?" he offered.

"No. I need you to hold my foot—"

"What? And you walk on my hands?"

"No, you press from the top and I push back—ow—with opposing muscles and you—" The pain cut her off as Jamie squatted obediently at her feet, tenderly stroking the tops of them, looking up at her with worry and bewilderment. Either he didn't understand her directions, or was too concerned about her to even listen. "It's a way to stop a cramp—"

"Nah. Trust me. Don't need it. Massage is best." Before Mae could stop him, he wrapped his arms around her hips and lifted with a loud grunt. Within a few steps he was groaning and staggering, but he delivered her to the sidewalk. "Jeeeezus. You're like a bloody load of bricks." He nearly fell as he set her down. "Sorry. I mean, you're lovely, but fuck—" He laughed so hard he couldn't finish.

Mae braced her arms on a neighbor's adobe garden wall and attempted to stretch again. Her leg resisted. "Ow. Yeah, I probably weigh as much as you do."

"You think?" He sat on the sidewalk and began to massage one of her legs. "Might. I've kind of shrunk lately." He stroked her calf, not forcing the knot, but easing through from the surface, as if taming her muscles the way he'd tamed Pie. "Is this all right? If we go inside I could do both at once."

"I can't walk yet. I'm gonna sit right here." She lowered herself to the sidewalk. "Let me explain this PNF thing again, sugar. You give me resistance and—"

"Relax. You don't have to do all that." Jamie moved her legs into his lap, quietly determined. Mae wondered if he really didn't understand what she meant, or if he didn't want to. "Let me take care of you."

Let him be a man. Not just a mess. She couldn't refuse. Her legs needed something urgently, and this was the way he wanted to show he could help. "Thank you, sugar." She felt silly and awkward, but at least for the moment the residential street was quiet, with no witnesses to their preposterous position. "I'll try not to holler again."

"I know. Hurts like bloody hell. I've danced myself sore before." Jamie worked on both her legs at once for a while, and then switched to a deeper two-handed exploration of one leg, his fingers slowly penetrating to the knots, sometimes making her start a little, but effectively reaching the painful place. "Got it. Jesus, it's like a fucking ball of cement in there." He rocked the ball of cement gently. "All right? Not too rough? Don't want to hurt you."

"You're doing fine. Thank you."

A man on a bicycle appeared, on his way toward Alameda from Palace. "Honeymoon?"

"First date," Jamie called back. "She won't let me kiss her."

With a wave and a starlit grin, the cyclist vanished, tires whooshing in the quiet night as he crossed Alameda and then the bridge.

"You know him?"

"Nah." Jamie began to roll her lower leg in both his hands, easing the cramp more fully. "People here talk to you."

Mae stared down the street at the bridge. Pictured Dusty jumping, crawling under. The police never coming. It was so close, Ruth would have heard him running. He would have been louder than the bicycle for sure, meaning she would have known which way to direct the cops. She'd wanted him arrested. What had happened?

Jamie's run-on chatter shook her out of her thoughts. "You need to drink a ton more water, love. This place, seriously, you can't let yourself dry out. Got orange juice in the house? Potassium. Good for you. Yeah, we bought juice the other day. We'll get you in, get you some juice, rub you down some more." He took the other leg and gave it the same treatment. "Arnica, too. Homeopathy. You use that? I can run out and get you some."

He sounded eager to do it, as if hoping to be chosen for an honor. "That's okay, sugar. Just help me inside. That'll be enough. Thank you. You've already helped a lot."

Slowly, Mae and Jamie stood and made their way down the sidewalk and over the footbridge, stopping for her to stretch several times, and got in the door before her legs cramped again. She could feel her big toe muscle all the way through her arch to where it attached in the calf, as well as the deeper calf muscle layer again, and fell into a chair as soon as she could limp to it. Propping an ankle on her thigh, she began to massage herself, but the knot fought back.

Jamie took the bag with the remains of the cake and the food-stained cloth into the kitchen, and returned with a tall glass of orange juice, a bottle of olive oil, a dish towel and some red chile powder. "Better service coming."

"You cooking my leg?"

He handed her the juice. "Hot peppers for pain relief. Oil for the massage. Then I can lick it off—joke, love. Joke. I'll keep my tongue in my head." Sitting cross-legged at her feet, he put the towel on his shoulder and laid her ankle on it, and then poured a puddle of oil into his hand. After rubbing it around, he added some red pepper to it, and began to repeat with even greater care the slow, gentle process he had done earlier, the sleeves of his crinkly pink shirt coming close to the oil as his stroked the length of her calf.

"Is that your best shirt, sugar?"

A hopeful smile and eager eyes turned up to her. "You like it?"

Her turn for evasion. "I don't want you to ruin it."

"No worries. Thrift shop. More where it came from. I lost so much weight, I had to do some crash shopping." He rolled his sleeves up to the elbow, and resumed the massage. "Pants were falling off. Showing my grundies."

Was he trying to tell her something, or leaking information he didn't mean to let out? It was the second time he'd mentioned it.

"I hope you weren't trying to get that skinny."

He frowned with a hint of anxiety. "Do I look bad?"

She couldn't say he did. He would look better a little more filled out, but his body was, in a bare way, graceful and strong. "No. Just skinny."

"Yeah." He went back to massaging her leg, apparently relieved. "I'm normally a bigger bloke. Feels funny not to carry much weight. Like, if I've got my head on straight, I'm about one seventy-five—fighting off one ninety." A short laugh. "Back then, I could have lifted you, lovely big girl that you are."

"Hard to keep weight on if you only eat once a day."

He kept his eyes on her leg, added another sprinkling of the red pepper to the oil. The heat felt better than she'd expected. "Twice, today. Had lunch with Mwizenge. He's got a nice kitchen. Nice home. Two little kids running about. And his wife works with him." Jamie went on, too long in Mae's opinion, about his friend's business and family and house. A digression, a distraction. He'd brought up a problem, and then run from it.

She drank the juice and listened until his ramblings ran down. "Is it money? Is that why you don't eat?"

He avoided her eyes, attending to her foot now, finding the ridge along the medial arch that felt tight. "I've got enough."

"Your phone's cut off, you skip meals, you don't fix your van—"

"I said, I've got enough. All right?" There was a kind of ferocity in his tone. "Anything I want you to know about me, I'll tell you."

"Sorry." She thought about her vision of his self-harming with a touch of guilt. He hadn't told her that. "I'm not being nosy. I want to make sure you're all right."

"Fuck. I don't need someone to make sure I'm all right. I'm not a bloody cripple. I'm taking care of myself." In silence, he finished with her right leg and foot, and picked up the left. As he applied the peppered oil in long strokes, he finally spoke again. "Sorry I bit your head off, love. Hate people worrying about me, that's all."

"Means they like you. Friends, family. It's only natural."

Wiping the oil from his hands on the towel, he took his hat off, shook his hair, the little braids wagging, and resumed the massage. "But I've made people worry too much, y'know? I'm tired of it."

Mae wanted to say something, but she could think of nothing useful. Would his friends and family have less to worry about because he was tired of making them do it? In just a few days he'd given her plenty of cause for concern. Yet he wanted to be the one taking care of her, not being taken care of.

As he oiled his hands again and began to work on her arch, bringing her foot down from his shoulder, he accidentally drew a long streak of oil and pepper along his shirt. "Fuck. I like this shirt."

"I can put some spot remover on it."

He seemed to jerk back from a threat. "I'm not taking my shirt off." Then he caught himself, gave her The Smile. "Bashful."

"You don't have to be." She watched for a panic or anger impulse in him, but he kept rubbing her foot, his thumb working out the tightness with expert care. He must have given his ex-girlfriend a lot of massages. "I already saw your scars." Still no reaction. Was it safe to keep talking about it? "In the pool. The scars on your belly. Not just your arm."

"That." He glanced up at her, and then back at her foot. "Not as bad as it looks, really."

"It does look bad. You told me you hurt yourself once."

"Yeah, but it was a little fucking paring knife, y'know? And I was heavy, like, two-twenty-five. Didn't hit anything but fat." He stretched her big toe back, and then the rest of her toes one by one. Finished, he kissed the top of her foot, set it down and began the toe stretches on the other one. "It was ... meds, mostly. The black box warning labels? They finally figured that out after a few people like me."

Did that mean he could still go off the deep end like that? "Are you on any meds now?"

He stood, stretched, and walked over to the bedroom door, flipped on the starry ceiling switch. "Love this thing. Used to leave the parties and the adults and come lie on the floor and look at it."

"Jamie. I asked—"

"Nah, haven't been on meds for years. Got a new therapist when I got my first job, learned some ways to handle myself without 'em.

You've got fifty fucking diagnoses, Jeezus, try medicating that. You end up in the fucking Guinness Book of World Records for side effects. One drug fixes one thing and fucks up the next, so you fix that, and it fucks with the other problem. My shrink in Albuquerque when I was in college was all about pharmacy, though. And my parents, poor souls, they had no idea, they were scared out of their minds. Trusted her. Anything to save me."

"From what?"

He did the alternate shoulder shrug, drifted to the couch and lay back, examining his stained shirt. "Being me, I suppose. I mean, I was always—Mum used to call me Typhoon Jamie. Storm blowing through. But I wasn't crazy. I was all right, in a way, just didn't handle stuff ... the opera, or college, being on my own kind of. Y'know—the stuff that happens." He fidgeted with the buttons on his shirt. "I only did the thing with the knife once. It was with my meds the other times."

"You overdosed?"

"Tried."

"And you ended up in the hospital?"

"Fucking nuthouse, love. Three times. Twice for the drugs, once for the knife." He sighed. "I was a walking dead man for like five years. Jeezus, I'm done with that, y'know? Don't want that crap. I want to live. Dance, cook, eat, drink, sing—*live*." He sat up, gave her The Smile. "So there's nothing to worry about. You see?"

She wasn't sure of the logic in that. He was no longer suicidal, so there was nothing to worry about? It was irrational optimism, but at least it *was* optimism, and she didn't want to undermine it. "I'm glad you're better."

"Fuck, yeah." He grinned. "I feel great, like ten times a day. Really happy. A little wobbly here and there, but that's nothing. Nah, I'm bloody great. How are your legs?"

"Better." She tested standing up. So far, no cramps. And he did seem to be feeling good, even if his assessment of his own mental health struck her as either dishonest or self-deluding. "Might be able to drive you to your van now."

"Don't you want to wash my shirt first?" Before she could say anything, he had it off. The sight of his uncovered torso this time, unlike the view in the pool, didn't draw her to the scars. She saw, rather, his nakedness. His dark brown skin and long, corded muscles, his ribs and collarbones, a hard yet vulnerable body, bared to her. She felt her heart jolt, and took the shirt to the laundry room, sprayed spot remover on the stain, and noticed the warmth of his body still in the cloth.

Was she, could she be—*attracted* to him? Now, who was crazy? It had to be a passing impulse, a reflex after his licking her hand and four months without sex.

His sweatshirt sat on top of the dryer in the rumpled heap of her earlier load of clean laundry. It would be a waste of water to wash this one shirt. She needed to be a good desert dweller. *Distractions, thinking about water and laundry.* She went to the kitchen and got the chocolate-smeared cloth from the bag, brought it to the laundry, started the load, and walked back to the living room with Jamie's old, forty-pounds-ago sweatshirt.

He lay with Pie on the couch, holding her above him, her legs dangling. Somehow she didn't mind, but seemed peaceful. He set the cat on his bare chest and stroked her. "Poor old Pie. Wonder how long she'll last."

"That's morbid."

"She's fucking old, love. She'll go."

Mae held out the sweatshirt. "You can wear this. So I don't send you home shirtless."

"So that's the plan, is it? Time to go?"

Pie's tail switched over his flat, hard belly, and Mae imagined the sensation. Stroking his skin. Or was she imagining being him, feeling fur on flesh? She stopped the thought. "That was the plan when we walked here, yeah. I give you a ride to the van and you go home. Come on, sugar, you said ... you said you get it, that I'm not through with my divorce, that you're not ... delusional."

"I'm not. But it doesn't mean I want to go." He sat up, set Pie aside, and gestured with both hands for Mae to join him. She didn't move. "Come here, love. Sit with me. Talk."

"About what?"

"Jeezus. Just sit, will you? I'm leaving my fucking pants on, all right?"

Handing him the sweatshirt, which he laid on the back of the couch without even looking at it, she sat on the farthest cushion away from him.

"You like me, right?" he asked.

"Of course I do."

"And you're leaving Friday morning. We've got one more day. Two more nights. You don't get it back. You throw it away, it's gone. But it's like, you're—dunno—*hiding*. You were so free that night we cleaned this place. I loved that. I made you laugh. It was fucking great, y'know?" He reached toward her, but she didn't return the gesture. He let his hands drop and picked up Pie again, placing her in his lap. The cat squirmed a little at the disturbance, and he spoke softly to her, stroking her head, her front legs, even gently pulling her tail. Mysteriously, she seemed soothed by this.

Jamie looked at Mae again. "You told me all about you, and I loved hearing you talk. Your Bible-totin' two-timin' Mama, your dreary little town, your husband, your step-kids, your roommate in Norfolk, your jobs ... I got a sense of you, y'know? What makes you *you*. And the more I see you, I think—All right, step on me if I'm rude, but I think—you're not happy, love."

"Me?" The idea stunned her.

"Listen. I know happy, and I know bloody fucking miserable. And you're not happy."

"You don't know that."

"Yeah, I do. I see your—I see your face. I don't need to hear the words. How bloody hard was it to make you dance? Jesus. And when you talk about your husband, you shut down. Bet you haven't been happy for years."

"That's not true. I loved him. I kind of still do. I'm ... getting over him."

"Lights are out, love." Jamie shook his head, and then flung his hair back and grinned. He spread his arms out wide, no fear or shame now, his thin, scarred body open to her. "But *I* light you up."

When? It wasn't possible. She'd been so bogged down in her concern for him, how could she have lit up like that? He *was* delusional.

When she didn't move or speak, he let his arms drop again and resumed toying with Pie, twirling her fur around a finger. "I know you can't see it yet, but you're my soul mate." His eyes grew soft, even darker and deeper, and his voice faded out, rough and overwhelmed. "We're a match, love. Meant to be."

Mae stood and walked to the empty studio. If it had come from anyone but Jamie, she'd have thought it a pick-up line. But she knew him too well already. He wasn't like that. From what he'd told her, and from what she'd learned in that vision, he might have had only one girlfriend in his whole life. When he said something like this, he meant it. She'd seen that look when she arrived in the Plaza. As a kid he'd even been in love with her picture and Marty's stories about her. *Now what?* She walked into the middle of the huge, dark room.

This mess was her fault. She should have seen it coming, but instead she'd let it happen. Never sent him away. He got to her all right, but she didn't light up with love like a girlfriend. She worried like a mother. There was always some crisis, some need he had to be rescued and cared for. Or he'd make some sweet suggestion of things they should do, with those big eyes looking at her so open and vulnerable, so hard to hurt. It was like she was trapped up to her knees in syrup, and he wanted her to fall down and get covered in it.

His voice broke into her thoughts. "I'm sorry."

She looked around to see Jamie, wearing the oversized sweatshirt, in the doorway of the studio with his hands against each side of it, his head tilted to the side, observing her. He pushed himself off the doorframe, walked to her, and took both her hands in his, lifted them and kissed them. "I'll go. I can catch the bus."

He turned and left the room. At a loss, struggling to speak, Mae watched him let himself out the back door. He looked fragile in that huge shirt that used to fit him, and she wanted to go after him, hold him, stop him. Make sure he was all right.

But then she would never get him to go home. He'd done it on his own. It was what she wanted. He'd left. Leaving behind his drum and his flutes again, and now his hat and his silly pink shirt. He'd be back. And that, too, was what she wanted.

Chapter Nineteen

How could she feel this—whatever it was? A linear feeling, like a cord stretching from her to Jamie, dragged her toward him. At the same time something else, like an airbag popping open, resisted him. Mae wished she had someone she could talk to. It was late to call her father. When she'd called at night previously, he'd already been asleep. She might call her old roommate in Norfolk. Randi was a night owl—but it was two hours later in Virginia. Anyway, she'd given Mae those romance audio books, not a good sign for wisdom.

Standing in the dark, empty studio, Mae wondered what she would say if she did call someone. *I just felt attracted to this really sweet disaster.* After failing at two marriages back to back, men were out. She needed to go into some kind of recovery plan. Ask Kenny and Frank how they kicked drugs. Maybe she was addicted to bad choices and train wrecks.

No. Hubert hadn't been a bad choice like Mack, her alcoholic first husband. Hubert was stable and reliable. Even though they'd grown apart, if she listed his virtues he had plenty, and his faults were few. Jamie, on the other hand, was a mess. He had a kind heart within all that chaos, but that was hardly a sign he was her soul mate. *Someone* should love him, someone who had room for all the scattered pieces of him, but that wasn't her.

So what was her problem? Why was she feeling around for some decision, when there wasn't even one to make?

Going to the kitchen for water, Mae saw the paper bag on the counter. She had to clean up after that picnic. Reaching into the bag, she brought out a sandwich and put it in the refrigerator along with the remaining grapes and cherries. The cake was troubling, though. Keep it? Throw it away? She set the container on the counter and took the lid off. There sat her handprint, a knife slash plunging between the fingers, in the remains of the raspberry heart. The sight of it made her sad and she wanted to toss it, to erase the thought of Jamie making so much effort for her. But she couldn't quite do it. Instead, she cut the edible edges off the cake, sliding the crushed heart from its center into the trash. *Sorry, sugar.* The sight was unexpectedly distressing, like she had dumped *his* heart.

The next day being trash pick-up day, Mae took the bag out back to the outdoor garbage can and wheeled it through the garden. It was faster to reach the street through the house, but she wanted to protect its cleanliness, not roll the garbage through.

As she walked up the alley, she remembered Dusty's final flight, and imagined what it must have been like to run on that twisted ankle. The boy had been tough, with that crazed mind driving his body.

An idea from earlier in the night came back as she parked the trash can. Its wheels were loud enough she was sure the neighbors could hear them, with their windows open. They would have heard Dusty, too, unless it had happened later at night. Maybe only Ruth had been up, awakened by her dog's bark or growl. Mae stood at the curb, stretching her calves again, the muscles tightened slightly by the short walk. She didn't want to undo all of Jamie's good work, and should go to bed and rest, but the puzzle held her in place.

If Ruth had been standing here, the view of the bridge was clear. If she'd still been in the garden the view down Delgado to either side would be blocked by other houses even if she'd hauled herself up to see over the wall, but she would have been able to tell by sound which way he'd turned. If she were trying to make sure Dusty was caught, which seemed almost certain—calling the cops before she even confronted him, and grabbing his wrist to make him stay—wouldn't she have tried to notice which way he went?

Everything about Dusty said *mentally ill homeless person.* Ruth had seen his strange behavior and had to have smelled him when she grabbed his wrist. Also, she had to have known he'd hurt himself when he leaped over her wall—and then off the bridge, if she'd seen that. Surely she'd want him found for those reasons as well as his tres-passing. If the police had picked Dusty up shortly after Ruth called, he probably would have lived. Might even have gotten treatment for more than his injuries. They hadn't come to his shelter under the bridge, though, the most likely place to look for a homeless person. Why not? What had happened?

Going back in the house through the front door, Mae locked it, wondering if she still had anything of Ruth's with which to do a psy-chic search. No. They had cleaned out every trace, drunk her beer and thrown out her trash, aired the furniture, washed the linens, and scrubbed walls. Ruth was eradicated. The only way to find out any-thing would be to ask her in person.

Except, she could hardly be expected to talk to a total stranger about something that stranger shouldn't even know. It might be easi-er to get some small object Ruth had handled tomorrow at her open-ing.

As she showered and readied for bed, Mae sorted through all the other ways she could find out why the police had not gone to the bridge. She could look in the archives of the local paper. There had to be articles, if she knew what week in the past winter this had taken place. Would the details she needed be there?

Mae picked up Pie to place her on the bed. Why was she clinging to this mystery? What would it accomplish if she solved it? It wouldn't save Dusty, or spare Jamie the trauma of having found him, or the guilt over failing to save him. Still, more information might help Jamie move some of the blame from himself to Ruth or the po-lice. It wouldn't make things right, just a tiny bit better. In the shape he was in, even the smallest relief could matter. That would be one last thing she could do for him.

She turned on the starry ceiling and lay down, resting one hand on Pie's bony back, feeling the small ribs expand and contract. Time passing with each breath. The old cat probably was on the cusp, like Jamie had said. Jamie thought too much about death.

But he also lived, intensely. Was she half-living her days, unfulfilled? Mae honestly didn't know. What did he see in her that made him think that? What was she missing?

To Jamie, being happy ten times a day in the midst of his struggles was enough. He didn't expect to be healed, or to be normal. Just to have good moments, and someone to take care of.

Motor noises outside stirred her briefly in the morning, but it had been so hard to fall asleep she drifted back into a half-dream state and lingered in bed. Smelling coffee. How nice. Hubert must have gotten up early and made breakfast. She rolled over, expecting to see the bedroom of their house in Tylerton, the old brown nightstand and the rumpled pillows, the pale blue wallpaper with the tiny flowers in it. Instead she saw the turquoise walls, the Mexican painted chest and chair, and remembered where she was. It hurt to have drifted back into her marriage. The dream was so lifelike she could still smell the coffee.

No, the aroma was real. How could it be? Had she programmed the coffeemaker? She didn't remember doing that. Or turning off the starry ceiling. Another odd thing—Pie had left the bed. It was a hard jump for the old cat. She usually waited to be handed down onto the floor, like a little old lady being helped across a street. Mae rose and pulled on her bathrobe. She'd left windows open and the house had cooled overnight. *Coffee smell must be from outside somehow.*

Walking out into the living room, she noticed that the crystals she had left in the garden were now arranged on the coffee table like a rock garden around the corn maiden fetish, with a few stalks of sage and lavender like an offering at a shrine. She hadn't done that. No.

He couldn't—yes, he could have. She hadn't locked the back door after she took out the trash. *Jamie.*

She hurried into the kitchen. He stood at the stove, singing softly, stirring something with a spatula, Pie rubbing around his ankles. His hair was damp, as if he'd just gotten back from a swim, and the little braids had come partially undone. The nerve of him, walking in and ... fixing breakfast. Trying to prove yet again that he could take care of her. He was making it harder and harder to get rid of him, and more important that she should.

The urge to scold him died away into a soft heap of pain. On weekend mornings, Hubert had cooked breakfast for her and the girls, and the memory of being a family barged in on top of her conflicts about Jamie. Her voice came out sounding sadder than she'd meant to. "You should have knocked, sugar."

He turned with a start. "Fuck—sorry. You scared me. Didn't think you were up. I was going to bring it to you in bed." He held his free hand up, made an erasing gesture across his face. "I mean, breakfast. Came out wrong. Sorry." He flashed a grin. "Let's start over. G'day, love. Sleep well? You sound a little down. You doing all right?"

"Well enough, I reckon." She didn't want to talk with him about missing Hubert. His concern was as uncomfortably intimate as his presence in her kitchen. "Heard something earlier. Was that your van?"

"Yeah. Sorry. It does its Elvis impersonation for like ten minutes after I cut it off." He imitated a cross between the engine and the "uh-huh-huh" section of Elvis's *All Shook Up*, and then sang a few lines of the song in a low motor-ish voice. "Ought to take the old clunker to Vegas."

She sat at the table, laughing in spite of her objection to his being there, and he brought her a mug of coffee.

"You take it black?" he asked. "I like it that way. Taste the beans, y'know?"

She nodded, inhaled the scent of coffee before drinking. "Yeah, thanks."

"Aromatherapy. Best kind. Doesn't it just," he took a dramatic breath, did a little wriggly, sizzling dance, "do something to your spine?" Returning to the stove, he slurped his coffee loudly, "Fuck. Manners. Sorry," and picked up the spatula again. "Making scrambled tofu with green chile. Muffins in the oven. Almost ready."

"I was gonna be mad at you for walking in without knocking."

"But you're not?"

"I kind of still am. I mean, I didn't invite you for breakfast." Pie weaved around his legs. She would have mewed to be lifted and set down before she would have jumped from the bed on her own. Jamie might have come into the bedroom. Turned off the stars, collected the cat. He didn't make a sound when he walked, just glided around like those long-legged bugs that walked on water. Easily, he could have intruded far worse than cooking without an invitation. "And I sure as heck didn't want you in my bedroom. Did you do that?"

"Fuck. I didn't molest you. I—"

"I know. You got Pie and you turned off the star lights. Like you live here. Like you have some right to walk in while I'm sleeping. You don't."

"Sorry." His voice faded, and he stared down at the stove. "Thought I was being kind. Y'know? I'd bring you this feast and you'd wake up and smile and it'd be nice, not waking up alone."

With a sigh, Mae sipped her coffee while Jamie opened the oven and slid a pan of muffins out, setting it on hot pads on the counter, and poked at the tofu again with the spatula. She noticed he had peeled oranges and arranged the sections along the edges of plates. *Damn.* He'd probably been so excited while he did it. Happy-anxious, and afraid of rejection.

"I mean, you were married, you're used to having someone." Jamie served the scrambled-egg-like concoction and a muffin onto each plate and brought them to the table. "Got to be hard every morning, y'know? Wake up, no one there."

"I'm trying to get good with not having him. For me, that means I *need* to be alone."

"Fuck." Jamie froze, about to sit down. "Jeezus." He closed his eyes, squeezed the back of his chair. Mae sensed he was stifling one of his tantrums. He probably wanted to dramatize the rejection. If he threw anything or stuck a knife in something, he'd be out on his ear. After a tense moment, he yanked his chair out and dropped into it. "I'm a fucking idiot."

"Not an idiot, Jamie. But I think you did what *you* needed. You're lonely, so you think I am. You meant well. But ask—"

"I don't think I asked you to do whatever the fuck you did with those crystals yesterday." Attacking his food, he slid tofu off his plate as well as shoving it into his mouth. Mae wanted to say something about manners, but maybe it wasn't the time. "So we're even."

"I shouldn't have done that." Mae picked up a muffin, but couldn't eat, and set it back down. "You're right. I should have asked."

"Really, because I think you—*did* something, y'know? I tried to stop you, but there was this little buzz. And—fuck, now it's like 'Reject me, I dare you.' I'm hanging myself up like a fucking piñata for you to whack at." He continued eating as if someone were going to steal his plate, talking with his mouth full. "What in bloody hell were you trying to *heal*?"

Your manners. No, don't say that. What had she aimed at? She'd been looking for the roots of his career problems, but she'd found more. She should have stopped the process when he left his advisor's office, and sent the healing then. Softly, watching his eyes for further signs of anger or fear, she said, "The things that make you scared about your work."

"You don't even know what those are. You could have messed with fuck-all—*anything*." Dropping his fork, he pushed away from the table and paced across the room. "Jesus. I told you not to do that. I don't want to be your patient, your sick person. I want you to like me. To love me. Not to fucking rescue me."

Mae felt ashamed of her invasion into his life. He'd finally told her about the knife, but not what led up to it. He wouldn't want her to know all that. She stood and approached him with an ache of regret. What she'd done was far worse than his walking into her bedroom. If she felt intruded on, how did he feel? "I'm sorry, sugar." She tried to put her hands on his shoulders from behind, but he dodged her. "Jamie?"

"Jesus. Can't believe I'm saying this—but," he faced her, leaning his back against the wall beside the doorway, "I don't want you to touch me. I think you're going to—read my mind or something. Look in my past. And, fuck, my past, my life—" He shook his head, seeming to try to get free of something.

What would he think if he knew she *had* done this? "I'm sorry, sugar, really. I won't do anything like that again."

"Promise?"

"I do."

"*I do.*" He grinned and hugged her, holding tight. "Like the sound of that."

Mae stepped back from his embrace, hoping he was joking about the *I do.* "One minute you don't trust me, and the next minute you want to marry me? I hope you know that's hard to figure out."

"Nah, not if you get to know me." Giving her a quick flash of the gold-toothed grin, he walked to the counter and refilled his coffee. "Typhoon Jamie, blowing through."

To Mae's amazement, Jamie sat back down to breakfast in good spirits, and urged her to do the same. His small talk ranged from silly to interesting, bouncing around art and music and cooking and local lore and jokes, so the meal passed pleasantly, with no requirement for Mae to say much at all until they were done.

"Thanks for breakfast, even if you did barge in. Why don't you come back a little before we need to leave for Ruth Smyth's opening—"

"But this is your art day."

"I can do that on my own."

"Nah, I'm your tour guide. Tour guide and chef. I've got a whole list of galleries for you to see. It'll take all day, and we still won't have seen everything. You can tell me if I pick the right places, like, how I do with your taste in art." He closed the last cabinet and hung up the dish towel. "Anyway, it's our last day. You don't want to send me off, do you?"

Our last day? Like they were a couple? Mae searched for an answer, and realized her silence had answered already.

Jamie looked at his feet. "Fuck. I'm begging. Or insisting. Something. Sorry." He unrolled his sleeves slowly, watching his hands. "But ... I saw your little corn maiden and I thought you'd like certain galleries, maybe, y'know, Native artists, so I planned those ... I won't whine again." He met her eyes, turned on fifty percent luminosity of The Smile. "All sunshine, I promise."

She surrendered. What else could she do? She wanted to see more galleries, she did like Native American art, and Jamie knew where to go. On top of that, she felt as if she owed him something, some kind of atonement for her secret intrusions into his past. For the hurt she could not avoid giving him, whether it came tonight or tomorrow, now or later. "All right, be my guide. But—"

"Got it. You don't need to hammer me with it."

"You know what I was gonna say?"

Keeping his eyes locked with hers, he mimed taking his heart from his chest and putting it in his mouth, and then stopped and put it back. Like a kid caught about to sneak a cookie. He raised his eyebrows and dropped his chin, giving her a funny but pointed look.

No words needed. Ironically, his manner of accepting of her rejection made her want to hug him.

As soon as they were halfway out the front door, he signaled a stop. "Sorry. Have to get something out of the van. Leave the house open." They went back through the house and garden to the carport. Jamie unlocked the van and clambered through from the front seats into its cargo area, muttering a longer than usual string of cuss words.

"You all right?" Mae asked.

"Bloody backpack spilled, I'll be fossicking around under everything for a year. Fuck. Need my toothbrush. Wish I'd left that spare I used in your bathroom. Idiot. Took it with me ..."

She was rather glad he wasn't keeping a toothbrush in her bathroom, but he was taking a long time looking for one. "Do you have to do that right now?"

"Come on, you're at home, you got to brush *your* teeth. Imagine if you couldn't. Fucking tofu sticks. You wouldn't think that, but it does. Looks like tartar from hell. I told you my fears, remember? The dentist, and stuff in my teeth. Real fears, love. Real fears."

More amused than annoyed, she stepped into the van's open front door and watched him. His vehicle had looked bad at night, but seen in daylight, it was like someone's worst closet. Cardboard boxes. Books. The bike, still bent, not in the shop to be fixed. A laundry basket with neatly folded clean clothes, a bottle of detergent. A Whole Foods paper bag full of something—she couldn't see into it. The didgeridoo, mostly hidden by a blanket. A lightweight sleeping bag and what looked like a small ultra-light tent folded up. A one-eared faded stuffed toy kangaroo, possibly red once, threadbare with a lifetime of use, perched in the passenger seat as if it was going for a ride.

Mae picked it up. "This your driving buddy?"

Jamie glanced around from his digging and searching. "My roo?" He smiled. "Yeah. Goes everywhere with me. You like him? Had him since I was three."

Mae was embarrassed, though Jamie wasn't. She set the toy down, trying to not picture him giving the roo a little squeeze for comfort as he drove along, while the van coughed and stalled and begged him to check its engine.

Reaching between a box and the laundry basket, he came up with a toothbrush that wore a plastic cap, and floss and toothpaste. Then, scattered along the van and slipped into spaces between larger objects, he located shampoo, hair conditioner, razors, and deodorant. He repacked his backpack, double-checked its fastening and set it down. "Must not have buckled it right. Sorry. Back in a flash."

Mae got out, and Jamie followed, jogging back into the house with his dental care items. While he attended to his fears and hygiene, she sat in the garden, massaging her tight calf muscles in preparation for a day of walking and standing. She could almost think Jamie lived out of the van, except he hardly ever drove it. He had those keys, too, and he'd baked a cake. But to look at what he carried—no, he'd been to the fitness center for a swim, of course he had his personal care things, and he was frankly neurotic about teeth, so he'd carry a toothbrush everywhere. He might be stressed for money, but he wasn't living in his van. Yet. She wondered how close to the brink he was and if Wendy would have work for him in time to spare him that fate.

Chapter Twenty

Jamie took her first to a gallery featuring the work of Native glass sculptors. Mae was fascinated by the modern versions of traditional masks, glowing with color and light. "How'd I do?" he asked, hovering a little too close. "This the sort of stuff you like?"

"I love it, it's beautiful."

She walked on to another display, making some space between them. He was being so sweet and thoughtful and yet so exhaustingly attentive, she didn't know how to handle him. Or herself. If only she could put him on hold for a year and then see how she felt.

"If you were staying longer, I'd take you out to Museum Hill. Pretty place, has the Indian art, the folk art. You'd like that."

She let the suggestion fade away. Staying longer was out of the question.

"Doing all right?" Jamie asked. "How are your legs?"

"Sore, but if I stop and stretch a lot I'm all right."

He came closer than she wanted again. "Need a massage?"

"No, thank you. You did a wonderful job last night, but not now." They were in an art gallery. What was he thinking? He gave her a wounded look as if he'd really meant to sit her down and rub her legs again, repeating his great success in taking care of her. "Come on, sugar. Don't look at me like that." She felt guilty. He'd meant well, even if his sense of appropriate behavior was a little off. "How's your hip?"

"Full of metal. Fucked up. Hurts like a bastard." He folded his arms and scuffed irritably at the floor. "Bloody hell, I live with it, y'know?" He laughed softly. "Couple of old farts. Listen to us." Shrinking his posture to suggest old age, he put on a squinty expression and a creaky voice. "How are your aches and pains, dear?" Grinning, he let out the snort-laugh. "I bet you'll still be beautiful when you're old." He tilted his head and studied Mae with a wistful look. "Hair'll turn sort of pink, get the white in with the red ..."

Was he fantasizing growing old together? She couldn't even figure if she wanted to grow old with anyone, let alone him. Once again at a loss what to say to him, Mae knelt to get eye to eye with a glass killer whale face. Its intense yet emotionless expression, an essence of some life force, stared back at her.

"Speaking of old," Jamie seemed incapable of not talking, "wait 'til you see the next gallery. Great pictures of old people. Amazing what this bloke does with hair. Like it's sacred, old Indians' white hair."

He offered Mae his hand. She hesitated to take it, aware of how ridiculously stuck she was. His soul mate declaration of the night before had put her into a kind of wall-less, disorienting space in which she didn't know how to move. Every word or touch felt like it could be misunderstood. Was this a romantic gesture or not?

"Jeezus." Jamie flung both hands out. "I didn't hand you my fucking donger." His outrage turned into a laugh, and he shook his head, regarding her as if she were the strangest person on earth. "Don't be such a wowser."

"I'm sorry." She stood. "I'm scared to say or do things to hurt you, but I'm scared to make you think I'm more than a friend. I reckon everything is gonna come out wrong until we're on the same page with that. I thought you understood."

He said nothing, but Mae could see the tension in his body as they left the gallery. Outdoors in the blazing blue light, he spun a half turn as if to meet her in a dance, but instead walked backwards toward wherever he was taking her next. "I'm *it*. You won't let yourself see it. I'm your soul mate."

"Please. You said I didn't need to hammer it to you."

"Changed my mind. I'm the one that needs to hammer it to you. If you turn me down, you'll—dunno—have to be born back again as someone who'll love me next time, and I'll have to come back as the person who'll love you next time—or *something.* We can't get out of this."

"Where'd you get that idea?"

His hands flew up in a flustered grasp at the air, and he stopped with a little jump. "Fuck, I made it up. Where d'you think? Jeezus." Another small hop. "I'm trying to get your attention." She looked away, hiding a smile, not sure if he'd meant to be funny, and resumed walking. He fell in step beside her, shoulder to shoulder, barely an inch away, and added, "And it's true—even if I lied."

A hard point to argue, since it made no sense.

In the next gallery, which included the portraits of Native elders that Jamie had praised, Mae attempted to focus on the art, but was also aware of Jamie, restlessly moving to look from varied angles and distances, almost speaking to her, and then silencing himself.

He moved off and began to chat with the gallery staff in another room. In his absence, Mae felt the bubble of tension around her skin ease into a relief that let her breathe. But it also felt like a kind of ordinariness, as if an energy essence had been subtracted.

As she stood transfixed by the sculpture of a bronze shamanic creature, half-deer, half-human, she felt the return of tightness and vibration in the air, the sense of Jamie looking at her, and turned to him. His eyes were full of a strange light.

Intense and awed, he said, "You get it."

The sense of the extraordinary, the merging of the natural with the supernatural—yes, she got it. Very few people she'd known fully grasped how entirely she could move into another world, how reality was not what it seemed. After her encounter with Dusty's ghost, that other reality was even stranger and deeper. This artist might understand. She nodded and looked back at the sculpture.

Jamie stepped closer, looking up at the deer-headed being's raised arms, its human hands holding a circle and a moon. "Lisa—my fiancée—never liked this kind of thing. She's a scientist."

"Seems like a scientist could still like it as art."

"Nah. She hated it when people got all mystical, especially about quantum physics. Didn't believe in mysteries or spirits."

"But you do."

Jamie fidgeted with the ends of his sleeves, tugging them toward his wrists with opposite hands. He inhaled, stopped, looked at Mae, at the sculpture, and at his feet. "Grew up with that stuff, y'know? Dad's an anthropologist, studied shamans around the world. Healers, magic, music, dancing, visions ..." He seemed to struggle for words. Mae wondered if he was talking about a spiritual experience, or if it was more about the connection he was trying to establish with her. "I've been to a lot of ceremonies, and ..." He stopped, sighed, reaching toward her as if handing her some large, invisible offering. "This is hard to explain."

"Is it something that happened with a shaman, or about—" She didn't want to say *us*. "About what you think we have in common?"

"Kind of both. Maybe. If you get the gift, it's who you are." He looked up at the deer-man sculpture. "A shaman."

A woman behind them said to her companion, "That statue looks like Bullwinkle."

Jamie startled out of his reverie. Fizzing with stifled laughter, he rushed from the gallery. His ear-blasting hah-snort-hah exploded as soon as he reached the sidewalk. Mae followed him, breaking into a fit of giggles on top of her lingering curiosity over where their conversation might have led.

While Jamie laughed so hard that passersby stared at him, some bordering on catching the hilarity themselves, Mae looked at the outdoor version of the same sculptural theme, another towering deer shaman. This one held an arrow. A raven perched on his other upstretched hand. It was so powerful. Like Dusty's hawk form, in a way. Half-deer, half-human. Who could see that as *Bullwinkle*?

"Jesus, that's almost as good as sex, y'know? Having a good laugh." Jamie pulled himself together, taking his hat off, shaking his hair, and put the hat back on. He nodded in the direction of the next gallery, and they started walking. "We'll try again."

"Try again at what?"

He answered with the one-two shrug and mimed juggling balls.

They crossed the street, walked another block, and Jamie held the door of the chosen gallery open for her. Inside, Mae let her mind and senses adjust to the images: intricately carved and painted pottery, more glass art, and huge canvases with spirit beings in vivid colors. Jamie had again chosen well. "You're a good tour guide," she said.

A weak bit of praise, considering how much more he wanted, but he accepted it with a smile. "Thanks."

They walked around the perimeter of the room first, silently absorbed in the paintings, and then came to the center display of works in glass. The most striking among them showed a small, birdlike human in pale blue opaque glass emerging from the crown of a man's split-open head.

"You have stuff like this happen to you?" Jamie asked as they stood in front it.

"Not usually." Only once. Dusty's ghost.

"Yeah, you're pretty down-to-earth for a healer type. Like a traditional shaman. Keeps you from getting lost in the spirit world."

One of her first mentors in healing and psychic work had said something similar, and the insight surprised her, coming from Jamie. "Sometimes I see more than I want to, but it's not spirits or anything. It's more like stuff about people's lives."

"Crap." Jamie stared at the spirit bird. "How much of my past did you see?"

The question made her deeply uncomfortable. "A lot."

"Like?"

"Are you sure you want to know?"

"Yeah. See what I can still lie about." A brief flash of The Smile, followed by a return to shadows. "Nah. Just trying to figure out," he did his right-left shoulder, truth-dodging dance, "how well you know me."

"Better than I've got a right to, and I'm sorry."

"Jesus." His eyes grew wide. "That much?"

"Sometimes I have visions I can't control. I might fall asleep touching something that someone else used a lot, and if I've been wondering about that person, I'll see something about them. I don't mean to, but if I'm really tired I can't help it."

"So what was it?"

She owed him the truth, but in case he became emotional or panicked, she didn't want to be in the gallery. "Let's go outside."

The nearest place to sit was the wall around a street corner garden that grew a few stalks of corn. It made Mae think of her corn mother fetish. Maybe this was meant to be a sacred garden, symbolic of the same things. Traffic poked along in front of them, and music floated from a passing car, while crowds of pedestrians passed at varying speeds.

Jamie's voice held an edge of anxiety under forced humor. "Making me sit down for it—fuck, how bad is this? You sure it was my life?"

With growing unease, Mae told him about falling asleep in his sweatshirt and seeing the fight with Lisa over buying knives, and his early trauma with the older boy's death. Jamie kept his gaze fixed on the rooftops across the street, yet she could feel his attention. His only words when she finished were, "What else?"

"You sure you want to know?"

"I have to. Yeah. Everything."

She shared what she'd seen of the events leading up to his suicide attempt, and his whole history with Dusty, including his panic at the boy's death. Jamie watched passing feet on the sidewalk, his expression inward and foggy, and stayed silent when she was done.

"I'm sorry, sugar. Really. I don't know what I'm doing sometimes."

His eyes met hers, and for a second she sensed all the past Jamies from her visions, their eyes on her as well. He sighed and looked out into the street, hugging himself, rubbing his forearms.

Mae listened to make sure his breath stayed steady, no sounds of panic. After what felt like an eternity, he placed his hot moist hand over hers on the stucco wall, his fingers worming back and forth. He took a deep breath. "I see things I don't mean to, too."

The surprise was too much to process, and she felt her reaction trailing behind her words. "You do?"

"I see souls."

He closed his eyes and tilted his face to the sky. "Yours is ..." He swayed, picking her hand up and rubbing it with both of his. "I can't describe it ... Beautiful."

Was this possible? Or was he crazier than she'd ever realized? He seemed far from sane at the moment. Unsure whether she should ask for more, she waited.

His hands tightened on hers, and he squeezed his eyes shut tighter. "I ... I *feel* it first. Like, this ... terror."

"When you see a soul?"

He shook his head with a confused urgency. Mae sensed that he couldn't quite come out of his inner world to answer her. "Like you've never been so frightened in your life, like—" He looked at her, suddenly normal. "Jeezus, that was stupid. Of course you've never been so frightened in your life, it's your fucking *death*." He dropped his gaze to their hands and spoke just over a whisper. "It's huge, y'know? Blinding. Bigger than God."

She began to follow him. That was *his* vision she'd picked up at the bridge—Dusty as hawk-man. No wonder it had been so alien and mysterious to her. Jamie saw souls, and he saw them leave. "You see death?"

"It stops. The light stops." He let go of her and slowly pressed his hands into a prayer position in front of his eyes, like closing an aperture. "Then something leaves. Jesus, it fucking explodes, like something under pressure, y'know? And what's left, it's like," he parted his hands, and then cupped them and brought his wrists together like a hinge slowly closing its two sides, "it's like the inside of a little marry-me jewelry box. Dark. Black. Velvet. Without the ring."

Jamie shuddered, let the box dissolve, and leaned against Mae, his head on her shoulder, his hat falling back into the corn. He was hot, but still breathing steadily. No longer worried that he might misread her touch, she wrapped an arm around him and held him. This was too much for him to contain. He needed her.

"When they're scared," he reached out into the empty space in front of him, "this *thing* tries to push out of me, this ... this ..." He extended his fingers, and his hand shook as if a kind of frustrated force were trying to reach through him. "This power I don't have. Like that little buzz you sent into me. I'm blinded with them, in that fucking light that's bigger than God. And then they die."

He let his arm drop and rested against her, drained and still.

"You saw all this when you were a little kid? When that older boy died?"

Jamie sat up, reached back for his hat and put it on. "Yeah."

"That's a lot for a kid to see. I didn't start to have visions 'til I was thirteen. And then I shut it off again until I was twenty-six."

"Yeah, well, you're called as healer, y'know? The gift waits for you to be ready. Fuck, I'm the opposite of a healer. I'm called ... I dunno ... to see death."

"But you've seen my soul, too, and I'm alive."

Jamie fidgeted, kicked the wall a few times with his heels, let out a long, loud vocalized breath. "Yeah. Dunno what's with that. Go for hours, sometimes days without it and then—Jesus. I have to hide. Can't look at people. It's like ... like ..." He turned to her, took her sunglasses off her face. She squinted in the blazing light. He fitted the glasses back on her, brushed her hair back behind her ears. "Like that."

"Too bright?"

"Some people. Yeah. Some are too dark. Got *shapes* to 'em ..." He stared into space, holding his breath. "Can't believe I told you all that. Jeezus. That took it out of me, y'know?" Another few kicks of the wall, another noisy sigh. "I could use some chocolate. And coffee." Bouncing to his feet, he gave her The Smile. "Got any of that cake left?"

As they headed back toward her house, Mae thought of the bird-emergence sculpture. Had Jamie planned the whole art-tour sequence to build to this revelation?

The pain in his hip made his graceful, silent walk uneven, but so subtly a person would have to know him to notice and realize he was hiding something. Did he give any such signs of his secret inner life? Was there some way to tell when he was seeing souls? The first time she saw him, when he'd danced across the Plaza, coiled intensity in every muscle and a wild radiance in his smile, she'd sensed power in him. Zigzagging and misdirected, but a deep power. There was more to Jamie than she'd realized, and she didn't know what to do with the discovery.

Had he always seen souls and spirits? He made it sound unbearable, but he couldn't have always been so fractured and erratic. He'd composed and recorded that extraordinary music. Held a job, and had a relationship that lasted a long time. Between his suicidal breakdowns in college and the state he was in today, he had to have had some fairly functional years. The man who had helped Dusty, while somewhat depressed, had been functional. Not wholly well, but not like this, not panicking every day, not mood-swinging every minute. Even little things like his language and his manners had to have been better before something slipped or snapped. What had done it? Was it one trauma, or the cumulative stresses of a hard year in his life? Or was it the burden of seeing souls? Had a gift become a curse?

Seemingly unaware of her, Jamie started singing a song in Italian, tragic and yet transcendent. He didn't take notice when drivers with open windows waved, or pedestrians slowed down and listened. The music flowed as if he couldn't hold it in, swelled out in a voice so pure, strong, and sweet it was hard to believe he had room for it in him.

Mae knew in her heart this singing was his truth, an answer to something about him, but she couldn't explain it to herself. Something drove his music, something psychological or spiritual that was his like his bones—both damaged and strong, the bones of his soul, holding him together under the surface. This peculiar and complicated man was someone other than she had thought he was, someone she was still only starting to know.

Chapter Twenty-One

At the end of the song, Jamie slipped his arm around Mae's waist and walked hip to hip with her in silence. No flirtation, no anxious chatter. It was like the way he'd leaned on her after telling her about seeing death, an anchoring. She could feel that without his having to say so, and let him hold on.

When they reached the house, he left his shoes at the door and collapsed on the couch with Pie, setting her on his belly, one hand resting on the cat. Mae thought he looked like he could fall asleep, so she didn't remind him he had come in search of chocolate and coffee.

She stretched her legs, expecting Jamie to drift off. He blinked as if fighting sleep, fidgeted, and petted the cat. As she finished her third set of calf stretches, Mae said, "You need a nap, sugar."

"Nah. I'll sleep when you're gone. Don't want to miss a minute." His voice was drowsy, his speech mumbly. "Unless you'd lie down next to me."

"That's a little too much, sorry. You know I can't do that."

"Fuck." Still half-asleep. "You mean you *won't*. You bloody well *can*." He turned on his side. Tipping Pie onto the cushions, he rubbed her and kissed the tip of her ear, and then reached out to hold an imaginary partner. "Just a cuddle. Innocent. Like those tiny little monkeys that sleep in heaps in trees."

"Like what?"

"Pygmy marmosets. See 'em in zoos." In his fatigue, he was beginning to sound drunk. "All piled up together. Sweet."

Mae sat on the floor near the couch. "How much sleep did you get last night?"

"None."

"Were you seeing spirits?"

"Nah. Not last night. Little aurora on you now, though." He stroked the air around her as if she wore rays of light like the Virgin of Guadalupe. "Why'd you ask?"

"I wondered if they kept you up at night."

He shook his head. "I'm alone. At night." His eyes searched hers. "Did anything keep *you* up?"

"Yeah, for a while." She looked away. Best not to tell him one cause of her wakefulness—not when she didn't understand it or know what to do with it. "I was thinking about the police not finding Dusty. It doesn't make sense. It could have saved him if they'd gone right to him."

"Were they looking for him?" Jamie snapped awake, and Mae regretted bringing up the topic. She should have waited and let him take a nap. Would she ever get the hang of choreographing the emotional steps of communicating with Jamie? "They didn't tell me that."

"Ruth called them when he got into the garden. At least she told him she had, and I saw someone driving up Alameda, but I couldn't tell if it was a police car. I don't think they could see him. Then the car turned like it was coming here. But my vision was with him, not Ruth."

"Maybe she changed her mind, since he ran off."

"She was angry, though. I saw her three times, and it was like she hated him, or at least like he really bothered her. I can't believe she'd drop it. Was there anything about him in the papers? There had to be."

Jamie sat up, stroked Pie. "Yeah. Something. Not much." He stood and went into the kitchen. "I need coffee. You want some?"

"You need sleep."

"Coffee. We have more galleries to see. Canyon Road."

"My legs need a break, and so does your hip. Let's wait an hour or so. I want to look this up, see if there's anything in the papers. When did it happen?"

Silence, then the coffee grinder. Was she pushing too hard? He'd already shared the worst of it, though, talking about seeing death.

A death that might have been prevented if the police had gone that one block from this house to the bridge.

Mae got up, followed Jamie to the kitchen, and unfolded her laptop on the table. She repeated her question. Jamie poured water into the coffeemaker. "Jesus. I didn't write it on my fucking calendar, did I? Find dead boy."

"Sorry. But—it was winter. When?"

"January. I know that much." Jamie got mugs from a cabinet. "Getting my own place when I should have been on my fucking honeymoon."

"That must have been hard." Mae brought up the web page for *The New Mexican*. A whole month would still be too much to sort through. "Can you give me a week, maybe?"

"Yeah. Got off crutches around Christmas, so Lisa was finally free to get rid of me. You get your hip pinned, you spend a week in the hospital and then six to eight more on crutches. Had to stretch out the breakup an extra two months until I could walk." Jamie opened the cake box, cut a large piece of cake and offered it to Mae. She shook her head, and Jamie bit into the gooey chocolate and talked through it, crumbs falling on the floor. "I started looking to help him out as soon as I could ride my bike. Sorry." He swallowed. "Fuck, I could still hardly walk when I moved. Skipped PT—insurance, y'know?"

He seemed determined to talk about his injury instead of Dusty. Mae tried to make use of his detour. "That trail isn't much good for bicycling—it's so narrow and overgrown and short."

"I know. I was looking for him."

"Why?"

Jamie shrugged, ate cake. "Dunno. I liked him." He licked his fingers. "The way he stole Lisa's dinner. Impressed me." A half-smile, a single shoulder lifting. "There I was, all heavy, gloomy sort of crazy, and there he was, crazy like a rocket, y'know?"

Leave it to Jamie to think other people could be crazy better than he could. "You were depressed."

"Didn't tell you that."

"Sorry. Were you?"

"Maybe. Yeah. But gray depression." He rubbed crumbs out of his beard. "Not the black hole, y'know? Just medium to foggy."

"Dusty might have been schizophrenic or manic or something. How long did you know him?"

"Couple of weeks. Must have been ... second week of January, when he died."

Mae clicked on the police reports, but found they only went back two weeks on the web site. She tried the archives, but she would have to pay for anything as far back as January. It would have to be a feature article, and she would need more information to search for it, even if she wanted to pay.

"Clean up your crumbs, sugar. Get a plate." Unoffended, Jamie obeyed. "Do you remember what it said in the paper? I can't get anything."

The coffeemaker made comforting gurgling noises. Jamie, standing with his back to it, now eating off a small plate, leaned on the counter. "They thought someone had killed him. Healthy young bloke, no drugs, no alcohol, wouldn't fall off a bridge like that. And you don't jump into two inches of ice to drown yourself."

"Did the police keep looking?"

"Dunno. Never found anyone if they did. Fuck—of course. Because he jumped."

"Did they find out anything about him?"

"Yeah." Jamie poured coffee, his hands covered with frosting, and stopped to wipe the mess off the carafe handle. "Paper said he was Dustyn Dwayne Gobble. Jesus, can you picture living with a name like that? From some little place in West Virginia. Ran away in the middle of December after his parents asked him to go into a mental hospital. He'd got these obsessions with Indian lore and begun to identify himself as Apache, said they weren't really his parents. Family had no Indian ancestry." He carried their coffee mugs to the table and went back for his cake. "That's really all they said. Nothing about Ruth or trespassing. More about what someone here or there said about him back home, what sports he'd done in high school, or some evidence of his being strange ..."

Dusty's parents wanted him to go into a mental hospital. Jamie had given a kind of doubting respect to the boy's delusions, and had sympathy for his fear of going to an institution. She looked up at Jamie, and he immediately turned to the counter and cut another piece of cake. Hiding from her.

"What happened to you after that? Were you—" She thought of how Marty had put it, that Jamie had been shaken up pretty bad. "Did you have some kind of breakdown?"

"I didn't go into a hospital, if that's what you mean." He came back to the table and slurped his coffee. "Fuck. Sorry. Bloody annoying." Then through a mouthful of cake, "Don't let me do that." He swallowed. "Or that."

She let the manners pass without comment. He wasn't panicking, which was amazing, given what they were talking about. Maybe eating cake helped. Maybe eating at all, like having breakfast, made him more stable. "Can you tell me what happened?"

The one-two shrug dance. "Couldn't afford therapy or anything, but I did all the things that worked, y'know, exercised, ate healthy, slept with my cat, did a lot of music. Called my parents a lot. I pulled out of it, mostly—having panic attacks still but otherwise, y'know, not bad—"

"What about the visions, sugar? Are you sure you really got better?"

"Fuck. I even *looked* good. Got back down to perfect one seventy-five, the magic number." He drank his coffee without noises, sniffed it, and sighed. "Jeezus, that's nice. They should give you this in the hospital instead of that weak fucking crap they have. Instead of drugs. This'd cure what ails you."

Evasion. He'd coped with the topic well, but hadn't touched her last questions. "You're a lot less than perfect-one-seventy-five now." From what she'd seen of his history and how he ate, he wasn't one of nature's thin people, and he'd just implied that he'd worked hard to get down to that ideal weight. "You want to explain that?"

"Nah, I'm healthy. No worries. Just busy. Drink your coffee. We have art to enjoy."

As they walked toward Canyon Road, their route was the one Dusty had taken in his final run. Still working on the puzzle of Ruth's trespass complaint, Mae stopped as they were about to cross Alameda and looked back at her house. "Last night, when you were massaging my legs in the street, I could see and hear that guy on the bike all the way to the bridge. You'd think Ruth could see or hear Dusty. I don't get it."

"Can you let go of that, love? I'm on my lovely last day with you. Look at the sky, look at me, come on, not at this death crap."

She looked at the sky, brilliant blue with tall, fat clouds gathering, and into Jamie's deep black eyes, and hesitated. "But if Ruth tried to get him arrested, he shouldn't have died. I have to figure this out."

Jamie sighed, pulled his hat lower on his head. "Jeeezus. All right, then. Look, can you see the garden wall from here?"

"No."

"So she couldn't see him from there. End of story."

"No, it's not. What would you do if you'd called the cops? And the person you wanted arrested had run away?"

"I'd try to see—fuck, you're right. She'd hear him run up the alley, make a mad dash though the house to see where he went—"

"And tell the police she saw him jump."

Jamie glanced to the bridge. "He was a fast runner, love. Lightning. She might not have seen."

"He'd hurt his ankle. He was still fast, but he had to be slower than usual."

"You want to know? Let's get this over with, then. Go back and do it."

"What do you mean?"

"Act it out. I start from where he went over the wall, and you run through the house as fast as you think she would, maybe she has to grab her phone again, trip on the dog, I dunno, but give or take a few seconds, say, make it the long version of—"

"It's a good idea, but you can't run."

"It hurts, but I can. I'd run like a bloke with one limb fucked up—perfect. I'm in shape, just damaged."

"If we're gonna do that, I should run."

He shook his head. "Both your legs hurt. You'll cramp up again."

He was right. If she ran now she risked her calves knotting up again. "Are you sure you want to do this? It's more death stuff."

"You're going to hang onto it like a fucking dog if we don't, and I want it out of your head so we can have a good day."

"You'll hurt yourself, and you'll feel sick after all that cake."

"I already have, and I already do. And I'm about to hurt myself more walking all day. Anyway, running one block isn't going to break my hip. Or if it does I can get a refund and I won't owe all that money."

He turned back toward the house. Mae sensed there was something wrong with the plan. The sound of a car behind her—of course.

Traffic. Dusty had run in the middle of the empty night. She could use the stopwatch on her phone to time how long Jamie paused if he had to and still know if the time it took to rush through the house explained Ruth missing or seeing Dusty. It wasn't perfectly accurate, but close enough, and it would, as Jamie had said, get it out of her head.

She unlocked the house so she could go through from the back to the front. In the garden she showed Jamie where to start. He walked around through the carport and down the alley to the place where Dusty had landed, and Mae took the spot where she had last seen Ruth in her vision of that night. Setting her phone to its stopwatch function, Mae said, "Ready, don't hurt yourself, set, go."

As Jamie took off, she hurried into the house, imagined and mimed having to hastily close an excited dog into the bedroom, and rushed out the front door in time to see Jamie plunge into traffic. Her heart jumped. Not stopping to look, he forced cars to slow down for him, brakes squealing. He sprinted onto the bridge, and then sat on the railing and waved to Mae.

She felt herself breathe, and realized how long she had suspended that function. A shaken anger rose inside her as her fear faded. After hastily locking the house again, she walked the block of Delgado, stopped to let a car pass, and then crossed Alameda and planted herself in front of him. "I can't believe you ran in front of cars."

"Twenty-five zone." He put on a little smile. "No worries."

"You could have killed yourself."

Jamie let out a roar-and-snort of laughter.

"Sugar, that isn't funny."

"It bloody well is. Jesus. *You could have killed yourself.*" Still laughing, he stood and hugged her, holding on until he settled down and caught his breath. As he let go, he turned to look over the railing, intense and serious now. "Could she have seen him?"

"Did you to stop at all before you played chicken with the cars?"

"Nah, took off like he would."

"Then she would have seen him, if she came out front."

"Means she let him die." Jamie removed his hat and leaned his elbows on the railing. "On purpose."

He dropped the hat and watched it fall.

Chapter Twenty-Two

Mae checked the time. Only twelve minutes had passed since she'd started timing their reenactment of Dusty's and Ruth's movements. If the car coming up Alameda in her vision of that night had been the police, it might not have taken that long to reach Ruth. Maybe five minutes, and then a minute to get to Dusty.

Ruth had to have known where he'd gone. While Mae was outdoors, she had heard the normally soundless Jamie running, landing harder on one foot to spare the painful joint, like Dusty would have run. Jamie's steps had faded into the sounds of traffic, but at night there would have been nothing to drown out Dusty. The only way Ruth wouldn't have heard the boy was if she had gone indoors and not come back out. "She might have stayed in the house—I don't know why. We can't think of her letting him die like that if we don't know for sure."

Jamie stood up straight, walked to the edge of the bridge, and started down the riverbank. Mae followed. Ever since he'd finally started talking about Dusty's death, he seemed less frightened by it, an angry gloom replacing his anxiety.

In the shadow under the bridge, Jamie stood still. His hat lay in the dirt of the empty riverbed. Walking further into the cave-like space, he sat on a large rock and stared at the place that had been Dusty's bed.

Mae picked up his hat and brought it to him. "Are you sure you want to be under here? We did what I needed to do—"

"And you don't fucking believe what you found out. Ruth let him die."

"Maybe. You can't know that. She had to know he was hurt from a jump like that, but not that he hit his head. She couldn't see that."

"Right." He stared into his hat, holding it in both hands. "But you can."

"I already did."

"Nah. I mean, see what she did. Did she watch him jump and say, 'Fuck it, good riddance'? Send the cops off?"

"We got rid of all her stuff, every trace of it. Unless I can pick up something she's handled a lot at her opening tonight, I can't do anything as a psychic." The light outside the bridge's dark shelter dimmed, and the air cooled. Clouds. A reason to get moving. "Let's go before it rains."

Jamie sniffed the wind. "Rain won't come for a while." He stood and paced to the edge of the shadow. "I want to drag Ruth under here and make her see where he died. Wish his ghost was still around to haunt her."

He walked over to the cluster of rocks where Dusty had landed, touched the projecting edge of the largest rock. "This where he hit?"

"Yes. Please, you don't need to dwell on this."

Looking up to the bridge, and then back at the rocks, Jamie said, "In the dark, with ice ... Jesus. Bet he didn't even look. Probably war-whooped and just took off."

"He did." Mae had forgotten that whoop. How could Ruth *not* have known where he was unless she had suddenly started ignoring him? The shout was loud. "And when he crawled in and lay down here he did this hawk scream."

"Yeah? Doesn't surprise me. He was a tough kind of lunatic, y'know? Fearless. Like a hawk." Jamie jammed his hat on. "I'm a fucking rabbit."

"You are not. It took courage for you to come under here and try to help a mentally ill homeless person. And he was afraid of some things, like the social worker taking him someplace."

"Nah. He had fun running from her. Probably made his fucking day. Gave him a chance to be a wild Apache." Jamie rubbed a foot along the rock where Dusty had taken the death blow. "I was just feeding my ego, feeding him. He'd rather steal and forage. He could hang from his knee pits upside down into a dumpster and grab the decent food out of a pile of stinking garbage. Like a monkey hanging by its tail picking fruit."

"You went with him?"

"Not *into* the dumpster. Jesus." Pausing, Jamie seemed to watch something in his mind and gave a small shudder. "I couldn't eat that crap. Fuck, if I was *starving*, I couldn't." He stared at the rock. "Dusty was strong, though. He would have eaten the lizard."

It took Mae a moment to connect this to Jamie's story of his exposure to the Aboriginal diet, how he'd been overcome at the death of the goanna.

"Jamie, being sensitive isn't being weak." It sounded like a cliché as soon as she said it, and she could tell by the twist of a half-smile and the one-up one-down eyebrows, Jamie heard it that way too. "Okay, it sounds corny, but I mean it. You've finally talked about all this—that took strength. Now let's get out from under here. I've had enough." She thought he'd had all he could handle, but it was better to put the need for a break on herself. She felt guilty now for putting him through the reenactment. It had been foolish to think that she could lighten his load a little by proving that someone else should have saved Dusty. Instead, she'd added another burden. "Be my tour guide again. You've done great so far. You wanted to enjoy the day."

He nodded, and they walked back up the riverbank to Delgado. "Yeah. I want you to enjoy it, too, love. Sorry I've been so—Jesus, whatever I've been. The Death Man."

"It's not your fault. I'm the one who wanted to figure this thing out."

"Still, I owe you a good time, y'know? I'll get the old charm back up."

But he didn't launch the random chatter that she expected as his charm. They walked to Canyon Road in silence, and Mae stopped to stretch again in front of a gallery displaying silently whirling metal sculptures on poles. It reminded her of Frank and Kenny's pole in their back yard. Aiming to lighten the mood, she said, "Muffie might think those could contact aliens from the Pleiades."

Jamie watched them turn, and frowned. "*Muffie*. Jeezus. Fucking ruined the evening, haven't we? I'll be looking at Ruth all night and thinking *killer*."

"We still don't know. Wait 'til I find out before you judge her."

In the center of a sculpture garden, a huge red stone woman emerging from the pink earth brought them to a standstill, deepening and changing the silence between them into a moment of shared mystery. The figure was thick and strong, head tilted back, long hair merging with the dirt, knees, breasts, shoulders and hands above the surface, perhaps rising from the earth, or sinking into it like a bath. Mae felt it as the essence of birth or creation, but she wondered if to Jamie it was more like death.

In the darkening sky, the afternoon's monsoon had crossed the mountains, a tower of black clouds promising ten minutes of delicate rain, or an hour of a crashing, roaring storm. Jamie stood gazing at the sculpture with his hands in his pockets, shoulders hunched in, the wind rippling his clothes against his body. As the rain started, slow, heavy drops patterned the stone carvings and the dry earth, spotting their clothes and touching their skin with fingers of sudden cold. Mae shivered, but he seemed impervious.

Thunder rolled closer, and the rain fell harder. Another explosion of thunder, closer this time, and with lightning. Mae touched Jamie on the arm. "We might get struck—better get indoors."

"Been out in worse. I like it." He turned his face up to the rain. "Go rain crazy. Out camping with my climbing group, they dive in their tents, and I take off my clothes and run around like a wild man."

"In a thunderstorm?" He was afraid of spiders and dentists, but not of things that could actually hurt him. "God. And you think you're some frightened rabbit."

His face lit up, and he reached to her, suddenly and inexplicably joyful. For a split second his eyes and his smile knocked her off guard. He took both her hands. "I have my moments."

Lightning cracked, and Mae pulled back from his attempt to draw her in closer. He shook his head as if he wanted to scold her for the refusal. Turning toward the gallery that stood at the entrance to the sculpture garden, he wrapped a sheltering arm around her shoulders. "Let's get you in, you're cold."

She slid out of his hold with a guilty feeling. No matter what she said or did, he wouldn't give up. The longer they were together, the more she liked him and the harder it got not to let him misunderstand her.

As they hurried to the building, the storm began to dump heavy sheets of rain and the rising wind snatched his hat. It flew over the adobe wall. Mae started to run after it, but Jamie stopped her. "It's gone. It's all right."

They ducked inside the gallery, greeted by a trim woman with over-groomed hair, who exchanged cheerful praise of the rain with Jamie. A series of small, constrained abstracts in big frames filled all four walls. Mae and Jamie walked past the displays to a window, pretending brief interest in the unappealing works. He spoke softly so the gallery attendant couldn't hear. "You're not following your heart. You should fly with it, like you went for my hat."

"You don't know my heart. You can't say if I'm following it or not."

"Pig's arse. It's you that doesn't know."

A bewildering possibility occurred to her. "Can you see my soul right now? Is that why you said that?"

He shook his head, looked down, and fidgeted his hands together. "Nah."

"So you can't know my heart."

"I do, though. I just ... *know*."

She watched rain slash the sky and wash the street. Her chest felt full, her heart too big to hold. "I shouldn't have let you talk me into spending the whole day together."

"Yeah, I'm like a fucking fly, aren't I? Buzzing 'round your head."

She looked at him to see if he was joking. He was smiling but bordering on sad.

"Kind of," she said softly. "But I'd never put it that way."

"It's all right. I get it. I'll behave myself. And if I don't," he took her hand and tapped it against his cheek in a mock slap, the depths of his eyes contrasting with his playful gesture, "you can swat me."

Mae didn't want to swat him. She withdrew her hand and turned away. A little wall seemed to rise between them, but not very high. They watched the storm again. Something light and bright bobbed down the street. Jamie's straw fedora. He perked up, excited. "Look—it's alive."

He jogged to the door and sprinted out into the storm. A car braked hard as he dashed in front of it, and Mae's strange, full heart skipped a beat. He couldn't get himself hit by a car *again*. It missed him by less than a foot as he grabbed his hat and placed a hand to his chest, flashing The Smile at the driver and making an apologetic bow. Rain-soaked, he ran back toward the gallery, grinning and waving the rescued fedora at Mae.

As the sun returned through a rainbow, Mae and Jamie walked back to Delgado Street. Her calf muscles felt sore still, and he was moving like the old man he'd joked about being earlier. He held up his hat, which was already half-dry, and studied it. "Has more character now, y'think? After the battering?"

"That silly hat couldn't have more character."

"Silly? *Suave*." He placed it on his head at a jaunty angle and danced a few jazzy steps. "It's fucking *suave*."

"Whatever it is, it's not worth diving in front of a car for. Why do you *do* stuff like that?"

"Dunno."

"You have to."

"Nah, I really don't." The two-part shrug. He tossed and caught his hat a few times, and paused to hip-shift, as if trying unsuccessfully to put something back in place. "Just happens."

"You need to get off that hip joint, sugar. I'd like you to rest while I talk with my family." After missing them yesterday Mae needed to Skype with the girls. "I'm gonna need some extra time. My husband didn't pick up yesterday. I don't know what's going on. He's supposed to make sure the girls get to talk with me. You might as well take a nap while we sort it out."

"Nah, I'll fix you lunch. You haven't eaten yet and it's late. Nice lunch'll brighten you up again after your lights go out."

Mae felt her patience begin to fray. Something about this cheery offer was a last straw. She knew it shouldn't have been, but his car encounter had pushed her Jamie endurance to the edge. "My lights don't go out, and will you please stop cooking for me? It's getting on my nerves."

"Just trying to help you, love. Jeezus. You *yelled* at me."

"I did *not* yell." She let out a frustrated sigh. "And you said I could swat you."

"Fair. I won't cook." He winked at her and grinned. "I'll just make a salad."

"Sugar—"

"It'll keep me out of the way while you chat with your warden."

"I don't think that's funny."

"Neither do I. I've been committed, y'know, and I know what it feels like."

"We *were* committed. That's why it's so hard."

"Nah, I meant in the nuthouse. Couldn't sign myself out. Locked up." He put his hat on, matching her strides in spite of his limp. "You're not involuntary, though. You could get out."

They crossed Alameda onto the final block of Delgado. "I'm not locked up, and Hubert's hardly my *warden*."

"Yeah? You act like you're in a bloody straitjacket." Jamie stopped walking and looked into Mae's eyes as she stopped with him. He became serious, curious. "What's he like?" Then before she could answer he half laughed, scrunching his face as if he'd seen something awful. "Fuck. Don't tell me. You look up normal in the dictionary, you find his picture."

"Kind of." She resumed walking. "Cross between a good ol' boy mechanic and an organic farmer."

Jamie caught up with her. "That's what he *does*. What's he *like*?"

"Smart. Works hard. Good father ... Good looking."

"Bloody shopping list."

"Will you lay off?" The pain of losing Hubert shot through her suddenly, as if talking about him had ripped the stitches out of a healing wound. "We were good together."

"Bored shitless, you mean."

When she started to snap back, Jamie made a buzzing noise and mimed watching a circling fly. He smacked the imaginary pest between his hands and offered it to her, slowly opening his palms with a wide-eyed, don't-be-mad-at me look.

Anger softened, Mae said, "Keep your thoughts on my marriage to yourself."

"It's not a marriage, love. It's a divorce."

Chapter Twenty-Three

Leaving Jamie in the kitchen, Mae set up her laptop in the garden. The quiet was soothing. It seemed like a year ago when she'd brought him here to help her clean, yet it had been only a few days. She'd never thought he would keep coming back like this. He meant well, but he was so persistent. *Bzzzz* ... She swatted the image away. He probably had no idea what a healthy relationship looked like. She did, and she missed it. The call was bound to make it hurt more.

It was a little after five o'clock in North Carolina. Hubert, still in his blue coveralls from the garage, came on Skype, looking hot and tired.

"Hey," Mae said cautiously, "I missed the young'uns yesterday. What happened?"

"Talk to them first." He took off his ball cap and let his hair down, the long, thick dark ponytail tumbling in a wave along his back. "Let me get cleaned up. We got things to talk about. Brook? Stream? Come on and talk to your mama."

The twins bounced onto the sofa behind the coffee table where he'd set up the computer, and he left.

Mae and the girls chatted a while about the things they'd been doing, more to hear each other's voices and see each other's faces than from any need to say the words, stretching the conversation until they ran out of things to say, still wanting to look at each other. Into the silence, Stream said in a small uncertain voice, "Granma Sallie and Grampa Jim say *hey*."

Mae hadn't stayed in touch with her in-laws. A greeting through the children was awkward and sad. It reminded Mae of the whole process of her marriage falling apart.

"Speaking of grandparents," she tried to make the talk cheerful again, "you young'uns have to meet my daddy sometime. I'll have to Skype you with him when I get back to his town."

"But," Brook squirmed closer to Stream, "will he be our grampa if you're not our mama anymore?"

Mae's heart seemed to stop. "Not your mama? Where'd you get that idea?"

"If Daddy marries Miss Jen," Brook said, and Stream nodded. "Will she be our mama?"

Hubert came in, as if he'd been listening not far off. "All right, girls. Don't you be worrying about that. She's always your mama. Blow her a big kiss. We gotta talk about some grown-up stuff now." The twins, reassured, said goodbye with kissy-face gestures that made them giggle and ran off. "Hey—y'all wait up." The thundering little feet stopped. "You can go out in the back yard, but don't get where I can't hear you holler."

A good father. Mae ached when she saw Hubert in that role, one of the things she had loved about him. He'd changed into shorts and a T-shirt, and the sight of him, that perfectly proportioned, well-muscled body—another thing she'd loved about him—made her think of what he'd look like while he changed, the way his tan lines stopped at his sleeves, the little patch of curly hair in the middle of his chest ... She pulled back into the present. Why was she going there?

Hubert rubbed his hands along his thighs, and planted them there. "All right, might as well get into it."

"Are we gonna fight about something?"

"Could. I hope not, but here's why I didn't answer yesterday. We were over at Jen's house. All of us." Mae knew her hurt look must have shown from the way Hubert sighed and leaned back. "I ... Look, hon, I'm trying to build a relationship there."

"You're already going off together for the weekend. Isn't that enough?"

He straightened up again, leaned toward the screen. "I'm talking about Jen and the girls. If you call every day and they don't get any time with just her and me, it's not gonna work. They need to get over you."

"Get over me? I raised them from when they were one year old. I'm the only mama they know."

"But you're gone. You won't always be the *only* mama they know."

"We're not even divorced yet, and you're planning on marrying Jen?"

"I didn't say that. I never said that."

"Brook said it."

"Come on, Mae—you know her imagination. But we're getting along good, and Jen really likes the girls, and it'll help them heal if they have a woman in their lives here. You calling every day, it doesn't help. I want them to still love you and know you, but—you can't pretend it's like you're still here. You're not."

"And Jen is."

"You know her, Mae. You can't say she's not a good person, or that she isn't good for them."

"I never said any of that. I just don't want her to be their mama."

"Sooner or later, somebody else will be. Couple of years, it might be her. I think it could. We're taking it slow, but ... I'm happy with her. You and me gotta move on. So do Brook and Stream."

Mae fought back tears. "So how often can I call?"

"Let's cut back a little. How about you don't call on weekends, except this one while we're away? So Jen and the girls get some good times together. And maybe ... let me think about it. Jen's off Wednesday nights, how about you don't call on Wednesdays either. Can you handle that?"

"Does she spend the night?"

"No, not yet. I said we're taking it slow. But if and when we get there—it's gonna be none of your business."

"Fine." Mae heard her own voice as sulky and petulant. She didn't want to be that way, and tried to sound more adult. "Four calls a week. I can handle it."

The call ended with silent gazes across the distance. No more "I love you." He said that to someone else now. The distance from Hubert was bigger than ever, and he was dragging Brook and Stream over that gap with him. It hurt like a piece of her heart being pulled out. Mae turned off the laptop and set it on the ground, lay back on the bench and closed her eyes. Even with sunglasses, the sky seemed too bright. Too much light coming in. More than she could handle.

They're my girls. Tears burned her eyes, and her throat tightened. *We should have stayed together. We should have worked this out.*

A soft touch tickled against the arm dangling at her side. Pie's tail. Then Pie's head rubbed under her hand. Mae stroked the cat blindly, and let herself weep. She wanted to hold her stepdaughters, to wrap them in her arms, because she knew, deeply and certainly, that she was losing them along with her husband. That someday she wouldn't be their mama.

A shadow came over her face, and she felt hot, strong hands along her temples, long fingers reaching around to touch away her tears. Jamie had to be kneeling in the sage and lavender and the rocks. He'd arrived as silently as the cat.

While she cried, he gently pressed his hands onto the fronts of her shoulders, holding her heart open so she couldn't run from the pain or his witness to it. Somehow this helped her to purge the grief. When she stopped sobbing, he stroked the tops of her ears with the feathery touch of a single finger, then rubbed the base of her skull as if scooping it off her neck. These odd movements reminded her of the strange things he did to Pie, even as they softened the torn places in her soul. Jamie held her head in his hands, still and silent, and Mae felt him drawing her pain out, letting it soak into him like he was a porous stone in a rainstorm, leaving her drained but soothed.

After this moment of stillness, Jamie rested his forehead on hers and sniffed loudly. "Fuck. Sorry. Can't help it. Anybody cries I—" He started laughing. "What a fucking mess." The laughter crashed to a halt. "Jesus, bloody *hell,* what a fucking mess."

Mae took off her sunglasses and opened her eyes, and Jamie raised his head from hers enough for their eyes to meet, upside down to each other. "Yeah, it sure is, sugar."

She sat up, and he stood, raising his face to the sky, rubbing his eyes, and then dragging his hands back through his hair. He made a sound halfway between a growl and a groan.

"Thanks for being with me," Mae said. "You're sweet. You helped."

He glanced at her with too much hope, and she shook her head.

"I'm not ready," she said. "You can see that. Nowhere near ready."

Jamie nodded, and sat beside her with his hands interlaced and arms locked, making a kind of dagger shape that he clasped with his knees. His shoulders drew forward, forming a sheltering cave around his heart, and he looked at the ground. "Why?"

"I feel like Hubert and me shouldn't have split. Shouldn't have let our stuff take me away from the girls."

"But you had to, or you wouldn't have done it." Still in his concave and braced position, Jamie raised his head a few inches. "I mean, I know. Kids—you want to stay." Rocking, silent. A deep breath. "But you're all right, y'know? And your parents split."

"But Daddy being gay, that was no ordinary fight. They had some big issues."

"And *you're* all right." He turned to her, freeing his arms, hands crawling over each other. "Your dad's all right."

"I didn't see him for fourteen years."

"But look at you. Look at him. You're good. You're *well.* Nobody died of it. Jesus—picture if he'd stayed. Did you think they were happy?"

"No."

With a one-shoulder shrug, Jamie looked away, rubbing one hand along the other arm. "My mum and dad—love story. Passionate. Still are. But Mum had Haley from some bloke she fooled around with before Dad, and Haley's fucking brilliant, sane, feet on the ground, head on straight. Had a single Mum 'til she was four. Me? Product of the perfect union, and look at me." He looked to the sky again, rocking. "Bloody disaster. And it's nobody's fault."

"You're not a disaster. You're brilliant, too." Even if he didn't have his feet on the ground or his head on straight.

"I wasn't asking for that." Jamie faced her, no longer fidgeting. "That wasn't the point."

She got his point. It was the same as Hubert's.

Mae felt relieved when Jamie left after lunch, taking a few of his instruments and his business license to go make money in the Plaza. He had been kind and thoughtful and healing, yet even on his best behavior he wasn't restful to be around. She took a couple of issues of *IDEA Fitness Journal* from her suitcase and lay on the bed, looking for escape into work. Her future. Her normal life. Some time alone.

Almost alone. Pie mewed to be brought up onto the bed, and Mae couldn't refuse her. She picked her up and lay back to read again. Articles about exercise programming should make her think about what she would study in school, but instead she found herself remembering her old job, the one at the wellness center in Cauwetska, North Carolina. Where Jen had been her boss.

She dropped the journal onto the bed and sat up to look through the few books that sat on the bedroom bookshelf. There were guides to local sights for the visiting artist who was the typical tenant, and several novels by local authors. The largest book stuck out an inch from the shelf as if it had been put away carelessly, and had a torn piece of a junk-mail coupon flyer stuck in one of the front pages as a bookmark, like a big red tongue hanging out. *Old Roots, New Branches: Indigenous Shamanism in Urban Cultures, Vol. I, Asia,* by Stanley Ellerbee.

Intrigued, Mae opened it and found it was inscribed "To Niall and Marty. Are you sure you wanted to read this? Sleep well, and don't let it fall on you. Stan."

His humility and humor made her smile, but maybe the book would be sleep-inducing. The table of contents suggested a scholarly book, and not light reading in either the literal sense of its bulk or its subject matter. Nonetheless, Mae was curious to give a book by Jamie's father a try, and lay back down with the heavy volume. She doubted that Niall or Marty, or whatever tenant had attempted the book, had gotten far. The bookmark was at the very beginning.

Preface

I grew up in a middle-class Anglo family in Santa Fe New, Mexico, aware of my otherness, surrounded as I was by Hispanic, Pueblo, Navajo, and Apache cultures. My interest in how other people saw the world began at my first Pueblo corn dance and grew to take me around the world. I did my doctoral dissertation on the survival of traditional Aboriginal culture in urban settings in Australia, where I had the good fortune to meet my future wife, a Warlpiri woman who refused to be studied except over dinner.

When our son was born, a traditional healer held my infant boy over a smoking pile of konkerberry leaves to cleanse and purify him and start his ceremonial life. At the time, all I could think about was him breathing smoke. I was humoring my wife. Though I respected this ritual, I didn't believe in it. The healer wanted to smoke me, too (as a "whitefella" with no ancient culture of my own, she thought I needed it), and I let her, for the same reason.

To my surprise, I felt better in some inexplicable way. Not very scientific, a feeling, but it happened. That brief, silent immersion in the sweet smelling smoke was the beginning of a change of heart. Of questioning not only how other people saw the world, but how I did.

When our son was three, he witnessed the accidental death of a friend's son who was babysitting him. Our boy seemed strange afterwards, halfway in another world, but we thought he was too young to understand death and would be all right if we loved him. He wasn't. We finally had the sense to take him to a psychologist, a woman considered the best in her field with young children, but he was afraid of her because she "had a bad spot." (I still don't know what that was—her appearance was entirely pleasant and normal, but it was something he saw.)

The next year when we went to Korea for my research into the practices of traditional mudangs, *my key informant invited me to bring my whole family to a* kut, *a healing and divination ceremony. I agreed, since I knew it involved music and dance and colorful costumes, which my children loved. Sometimes the music was shrill or cacophonous, but the dancing was powerful and entrancing. My normally distractible son never lost interest, often trying to dance with the shamans. We had to sit him down. When they invoked the spirits of the cardinal directions, he seemed to watch things fly in. Even when the music became too intense for my daughter and she covered her ears, my son grew excited. He was afraid of many things, but not this. Not the shamans.*

When we left for a break for lunch, I was advised not to bring the children back into the main hall for some time afterwards. It was good advice.

An animal offering, the skinned carcass of a cow, was brought in for the second half of the kut, *and one of the younger* mudangs *bit raw severed bovine testicles and liver to impress the spirits with her courage and strength. I watched this violent segment without my family. When the bloody-faced shaman had left the room and the raw meat had been tak-*

en to the kitchen, Addie brought the children back in for more music, dancing, bright clothing, banners waving, and bursts of divination.

At the end of the kut we were invited outside to a yard with carvings much like totem poles, and one of the mudangs, Ms. Kim, the one who'd bitten the bull testicles, showed her powers by walking barefoot on enormous sharp blades, and other acts to frighten away evil spirits with her superior strength. Had I been one, I would have run from her. She drew a sharp knife across her tongue and remained unharmed, though I was close enough to see that it should have drawn blood. I wished I'd been warned of this to spare my children the sight.

After the ceremony, Ms. Kim approached me. I had an interview scheduled with her teacher, the elder shaman who had conducted central parts of the kut, so I didn't expect more than goodbye, but she said she wanted to see my son.

I had him in my arms. He was four years old and in need of a nap, so cranky and miserable that I felt like the worst father in the world for bringing him, even though he'd loved it. It was too long and too strange.

He looked at Ms. Kim suddenly with wide, wild eyes, as if he was seeing something even more extraordinary than her dancing or her feats with knives. In her stilted English, she said, "Too soon. Close off," and placed her hand on top of his head. He looked puzzled and even sad for a moment, and then rested his head against me to fall asleep. "Watch out for him," the mudang said. "The spirits want him."

"Which spirits?"

"Good, bad. All of them."

I don't know what she did. She declined an interview. I don't know what he saw, but after that he no longer appeared to see it. His musical gifts emerged soon after, as if the spirits had found a new route through him. He is twelve years old at the time of this writing, and he says that sometimes he can't remember what he used to see before the mudang touched his head, and that other times it's so strange he feels like he must have made it up.

The scientist and the skeptic say that people believe in spirits, they don't actually see them, and that shamanism works with expectation and emotion. The magic is the magic of the placebo. I can only say that this episode, which belongs not to me but to my son, opened my mind's window and let something in which will not leave. I have tried to write this book as an unbiased observer, and I hope that as an anthropologist I have succeeded. As a father, though, I will always wonder. I hope that as a reader of the studies in this book, you will open up and wonder as well. How do other people see the world? What is out there that we might be missing?

Stanley Ellerbee, Perth, Western Australia.

Chapter Twenty-Four

Mae set the book down and stared at the ceiling and its unlit star lights. Jamie hadn't spent his whole life seeing souls and spirits. Witnessing death when Dusty died must have broken the barrier between the worlds again. For all the years in between, the shaman had sealed it off.

But she hadn't *healed* him. The trauma of seeing death was still in him; every trauma of his life was still in him. He had been raised with love, blessed at birth, and yet he'd tried repeatedly to kill himself. He'd been in mental hospitals. He'd had therapy again when he got his first job, but he was still troubled. Was he too broken to ever fully recover? Or was this somehow a sign of his calling? When she'd fought her psychic gift to keep peace in her family, Mae had been struck with bad luck. It had ceased when she accepted the spirit world's call. The scope of her bad luck had been nothing compared to Jamie's, though. Did that mean he had a stronger calling?

Mae rose and closed the bedroom door. Jamie could come back in the house, but she needed more time alone before she talked to him. She lay back down beside his father's book.

Since the spirit vision came and went, she might not have seen Jamie under its full influence, unless that was part of what had struck him in Marisol's, the restaurant where he'd taken her that first evening. Could someone as emotionally unstable as he was live with seeing souls? He seemed no more ready than when he'd been four years old, but ready or not, the spirits wanted him.

She thought of the effects of Jamie's touch when he'd held her head and stroked her ears. It wasn't the same as simply being comforted. It was literally as if he'd taken her pain and soaked it up into him, almost the opposite of the way she worked as a healer. She sent something into people, moving energies and giving stuck places a nudge. Mae looked at Pie, curled and peaceful against her leg. If

Jamie's healing of the cat had been like his healing of her, he'd soaked up fear and trauma the way he'd taken her grief. How many people had he done this for? What did he do with it when he took in the pain? He already had no room for his own.

Mae scarcely had any teaching in how to work as a psychic and healer. Jamie, although he'd been around shamans his whole life, had no training at all. No preparation. The gift had been buried beneath the surface for twenty-four years. He didn't seem happy to have it re-emerge. He'd called himself the Death Man, and said he sometimes had to hide from the blinding brightness and frightening darkness of what he saw. He had enough to do to get his music career on track and take care of his mental and financial health, both of which looked precarious.

Was there anything Mae could do for him? She'd thought that getting him in touch with Wendy was enough. But if he had fallen off the edge emotionally and professionally because of an unbearable spiritual experience, a manager for his career wouldn't fix that.

Other than opening and closing the front door, Jamie made no sound when he entered the house. Unready to face him, still gnawing at her questions, Mae sat up and tried to think more, but Jamie's prolonged silence became its own kind of noise, making her wonder what he was doing.

She came out into the living room and met him coming from the laundry room, buttoning up his pink shirt, probably imagining himself well dressed, though he looked disarrayed, his hair even wilder than usual, windblown and tangled, topped off with the disintegrating braids. She'd need to remind him to get himself looking right before they went to the opening. *No. It's not my job to make him presentable.*

"Get a good audience?" she asked.

A few twisting and twirling gestures of his hands, a crooked half-smile, and he sat on the floor near the coffee table, rearranging his flutes on it, lining them up and gently touching them as if putting them to bed.

Mae sat on the couch. "Did you play? Did you make any money?"

"Fuck. I don't want to talk about it, all right? It was bad."

Had he had a panic attack? Seen someone with a bad spot, whatever that was?

"Sometimes things get better when you talk about them."

Sulky, bordering on pouting, he rolled the bamboo flute back and forth. "You should have come with me."

"I was reading some of my fitness journals. I need to keep up for my work—"

"But I couldn't *play*." He ran a finger along a flute case, leaned his elbows on the coffee table, and rubbed his eyes. "Fuck. I'm fucking brain-dead."

He reminded Mae of the cranky and miserable four-year-old in his father's preface, the child who'd missed his nap and been seeing spirits. Jamie had been awake for over twenty-four hours, and from the way he described his challenges living alone, he probably hadn't had adequate sleep for months. For what felt like the tenth time that day, she said, "You need to take a nap."

He shook his head. "Leaving for the bloody Ruth Smyth thing soon."

"We've got two hours, sugar. You can sleep." No response. Only his curled-over back and the chaos of his hair. She waited. No panic, just fidgeting. "Your head looks like a hoo-rah's nest. You need to either redo or undo your braids."

"Scares me. Been putting it off." He reached up and pulled off the threads that tied the ends of the braids, wincing, and began to unbraid. "Ow! Fuck, it hurts."

"It can't be that painful."

"It is. I've got bad hair." This sounded like another diagnosis, the way he said it. With an anxious frown, he made another attempt, yanking the braid apart and letting go abruptly, smacking the table with his fists. "I need some scissors."

"Stop that. You can't have a tantrum over your *hair*."

"Sorry." He sighed and lay back on the floor. "It's better if someone grooms me. I get mad and start tearing at it. Cut the braids off once and had little nubs on my head." His eyes met hers, strangely unashamed of his childish behavior. She realized he trusted her so fully now he would share every bit of his weirdness, every neurotic eccentricity, with an open heart. It was touching—and troubling. "Haven't done myself up for a year after that. Two. Dunno. Scared I'd cut 'em off again."

After a minute under his soft yet unrelenting gaze, Mae surrendered and fetched a brush from the bedroom.

"Sit in a chair, sugar."

With sudden, silly eagerness, he obeyed, and Mae began the slow process of undoing each minute plait, grateful that he hadn't done more than five of them and that most of his hair still hung free, though it was badly knotted. Jamie wriggled happily against the back of the chair and closed his eyes.

"You could learn to calm down, do it yourself without tearing at it," she said. "My young'uns are learning that much, and they're six." The thought of brushing the girls' lank dark hair mixed with the sensation of touching Jamie's thick mane. Little things like this, taking care of them as a mother, would be so hard to lose. She pushed the sadness down. "You just want me to baby you."

"Nah. Not babying. We take care of each other. Haven't I taken good care of you?"

"You have. You've been real sweet." His heart was in the right place, but his mind wasn't. As she eased the brush though his hair, pausing to untangle knots, she couldn't help thinking that the outside of his head reflected the inside, and wondered how much of the inner mess was mental health, and how much the intrusion of other layers of reality. Touching the crown of his head as she brushed, she imagined the *mudang* touching him, and wondered again about closing that door, the opening to other worlds. "Can I talk about something I read?"

"If it's not about weight lifting. I hate fucking weight lifting."

"No. I looked at some of the books Daddy and Niall keep here. I read a little in one of your father's books, long title—starts with *Old Roots, New Branches*."

"Jesus. Almost as boring as weight lifting."

"I don't think so. Do you remember a Korean woman in a fancy costume, a shaman, laying her hand on your head, when you were little?"

"That's an old edition. He took that out of the new ones. I didn't want it out there anymore, y'know? Didn't care when I was twelve, but it embarrassed me later."

"I asked if you remember, though. Do you remember her? And what happened?"

His head moved in a rapid, tight-necked nod beneath her hands. Seeing the hint of distress, she slowed down her work on his hair and found a smooth area she could brush a while. It worked. Jamie sighed and wriggled again.

Mae kept brushing gently. "I'm gonna tell you what I think happened, and you tell me if I'm wrong. I won't make you talk about it, but can you listen to me and just give me a yes or no?"

Another affirmative head movement, and his hand slid up to briefly clasp hers.

"When you were real young and saw your friend Pat die, some kind of door opened, like he didn't close it behind him when he went out. You spent a whole year seeing things, like your family's souls, your psychologist's soul, and any spirits that were running around. You saw the spirits those Korean shamans brought into this ceremony. This shaman lady could tell, and she thought you were too little to be seeing that stuff, and she closed the door. Then when Dusty died, the door got stuck open again."

Jamie's hand reached up to hers again and gripped her.

"Do you need me to stop talking?"

He shook his head. "Just do my hair."

Mae undid a knot, and brushed until he seemed steadier. "I was wondering—do you want to learn to work with it, or do you want it closed again? I think I might be able to help."

A layer of his energy softened. "That's why I marked that page."

The level of planning surprised her. He might have noticed the book while they were cleaning and come back to mark the page with a scrap from the recycling when he sneaked in to get Pie in the morning. He wasn't a hundred percent chaotic. There were lines of strategizing going on within the crossed wires and jumbled jigsaw puzzles of his mind. "You could have just told me. What if I didn't read it?"

"Then ... it'd mean I'm supposed to keep the ..." He made a gesture across his eyes with taut, spread hands, a substitute for saying some unnamable thing. Mae realized he hadn't been so much strategizing as superstitious. He said, "I don't know if I can, though. You have to tell me."

"Sugar, you could have a calling. This is big. I can't decide that for you."

"You *have* to. You can think straight. I can't."

"You should talk to your folks. Your daddy knows a lot about this stuff. And your mama's people must have—"

"Old people out in the bush who'd teach me? Fuck. Can you picture that?"

In a way she could, but not really. He wasn't ready for that kind of immersion as a shaman. "But your folks could give you some guidance."

"If I told them, they'd be back here in a heartbeat taking care of me. Had to talk 'em out of coming back when I broke my hip, and then when I split with Lisa, Mum was ready to get on a plane and come sleep on my couch. After I found Dusty—Jesus. They got so worried, I had to stop telling them my fucked-up-ed-ness or I'd have ruined Dad's sabbatical. Mum's chance to be home for a whole year."

"But you can't put it all on me, sugar. You can't ask me to decide. If someone sneaked up on me and took away the sight, I'd be—I don't know what. I'd be mad, I'd be—like I'd been robbed. And you didn't like it when I tried to heal you without asking."

He made an exasperated sound. "You're expecting me to make sense."

She brushed his hair and thought. Could she make sense of him, when he couldn't do it himself? The spiritual perception seemed to burden him, but he'd said, *If you get the gift, it's who you are.* He accepted that her gift was her destiny. What about his own? "I think you might be a healer, sugar. You did something for me today, when I was crying after I talked to my family. Felt like you healed me."

"Nah. Loved you, that's all."

"It felt like more."

"Love."

Was his love that powerful? She didn't want to think about that. Love she couldn't return the way he wanted her to.

What if what he called love was more like a healing power? "Do you feel like you can love people differently, or stronger, when this door is open?"

"Maybe ... But I was a little kid. Can't remember."

"I mean, this time."

"Dunno. I've been alone a lot. Maybe something's different, but—I've always loved strong. Four talents. That's it. Sing, dance, cook, love ya. No good at anything else."

"Well, you're real good at all of that. If I closed this door for you, if I can, could you love the same way? You wouldn't feel like you missed anything?"

He tipped his head back far enough that he could look into her eyes. "I'd miss a lot."

"So I shouldn't try to do this."

He let his head relax again, squirmed his shoulders, and resettled. Mae resumed brushing his hair, letting him gather himself. Jamie exhaled and seemed not to inhale for a long time. "I'd miss seeing your soul, love, it's beautiful ... But," he glanced up at her with an unexpected twinkle, "I could still see your bum. It's almost as nice."

"Sugar, I'm taking my bum back to T or C tomorrow. What about your life? Are you better off if I try to close the door, or leave it open?"

"I can't think." He slouched, and then pushed himself back up where she could reach his hair better. "I can't decide."

In silence, waiting for him to calm down and become capable of thought, she kept grooming until the former mass of knots and braids was fluffy and soft. As she finished, she felt him go slack. He'd fallen asleep.

Though he'd made no decision, it was good to see him truly peaceful. Resting her hand on the crown of his head, she wondered again if she could do what the *mudang* had done. Wondered if she should. Maybe Jamie would be capable of deciding after he'd slept. No. He'd marked the book and waited for a sign. That *was* his decision.

She let go and closed herself in the bedroom again, and put on her yellow dress and gold jewelry. Although she'd deliberately not dressed up in the morning, trying not to look like they were on a date, she needed to look more formal for this evening's event. She dressed slowly. Ten minutes without Jamie felt like the air after the storm, clean and clear over ground still damp from what had passed. Did he ever get that kind of relief from himself?

Mae returned to the living room and sat in the other chair, watching over him. He leaned against the wing of the chair's back, his normally hyper-vigilant body softened. Yet even now something crossed his face, a shift into a frown, a tightening of the jaw. What was it like to be him? He looked so odd and different, a cross between bizarre and beautiful. He came from so far away, and had lived such a disrupted life with a troubled mind. He said he was happy ten times a day, but how long did those moments last? They seemed deep, like the glorious view of a vast canyon or forest clearing, but the stretches of chaos, pain, fear, anxiety, and confusion seemed to crowd them out. Was there room for visions? Did he have the strength to endure a spiritual opening? Would closing it off be the stroke that undid him completely, or the first step on a climb to wholeness?

Mae searched for any indication that his gift would help him survive, but she didn't see it. Without it, he'd been through hell but at least partially recovered. Now, he'd had a year of hard times, and when his visions re-emerged he'd fallen further. Though he strung little threads of strategies around her, he spent more time in a tumult of emotion than in coherent thought. His career had tanked, and he couldn't handle the simplest things. He couldn't think straight, and he knew it.

Still, how could he put this decision on her? If only there were someone she trusted to guide her now, the way he trusted her. She wished she knew his parents and could ask them—but he didn't want their advice or he would have asked them. He wanted Mae to decide. Another person with a strange gift.

It was like being a surgeon. *Should I operate?* No, that was ridiculous, this wasn't life or death—or maybe it was. Without his gift he'd been suicidal, and when he was supposedly well later, he had crashed off cliffs and rocks while climbing. Even as a child, bitten by a rabid puppy, or breaking a tooth in a bike crash, he'd been accident prone beyond what any normal person could fit into one life.

Was he still suicidal at some level now, or was his risk-taking with cars his version of the shaman walking on knives and biting bulls' balls to show her strength to the spirits? No telling what he was doing, dancing with death the way he did. He didn't seem to understand it himself.

With logical analysis getting her nowhere, Mae turned to her crystals. They were lying on the coffee table with Jamie's flutes and the corn mother, and the now-dried sage and lavender Jamie had offered to the fetish. She would have to let the spirit world guide her. Let the spirits advise her.

Mae chose a clear quartz point. Tree agate and Apache tear, for healing trauma and grief, she left on the table. He didn't want her to try to change him, fix him, heal him. Didn't want to be her "patient," as he'd put it, didn't want her to see him as sick. She would only approach the spirit door—if she could—and see if anything from his visionary world spoke to her and helped her.

Hoping Jamie stayed asleep, she stood behind him and rested her hand on his head again. She wished she could bring in the power of that shaman who had done this before. The *mudang* had made such a clear decision, and known why and how. Mae closed her eyes, concentrating on the energy of the crystal and what she felt coming through Jamie.

It was like a white fire. Was this his gift, or his normal energy? Or was that the doorway itself? Silencing her questioning mind, she tuned into the white fire again. She had to let the rational thinking part of her mind go, and let the needs of the person she sought to help guide her, to draw what was needed through her and through the crystals. Stilling her thoughts, she waited.

Something seemed to jolt and shift, as if she had fallen through the tunnel that brought her visions so fast she missed it. When her energy steadied again, she saw an Asian woman in a long, bright, multi-layered dress with three-quarter sleeves and a strange crown-like hat. From four-year-old Jamie's view, carried on his father's shoulder, Mae glimpsed Stan Ellerbee as an ear, dark curly hair and the edge of his beard and neck. He towered over the shaman. The woman's eyes gazed up, fierce and brilliant in her round, girlish face. She reached up to Jamie and touched his head. *Too soon. Close off.* Mae sensed a heavy pull through her hand that touched Jamie, and a quieting of the fire. The vision vanished.

Jamie stirred, eyes still closed, ran a hand over his soft cloud of hair, and smiled. "Thanks, love. That felt wonderful."

Chapter Twenty-Five

What had she done? Second-guessing her decision to trust the spirit world, Mae feared she had done something irreversible, something Jamie might regret. Then again, it was also possible she'd helped him—or affected nothing. She might have only had a vision of his past. What would he see now? Would he be disappointed? Relieved? Unchanged?

Hearing Pie mewing in the bedroom—Mae had forgotten to take her off the bed—she briefly left Jamie to fetch the elderly cat and carry her back to the living room.

Jamie curled up tighter in the chair, half-stretching, half-contracting. "Jeezus, I could lie here for a hundred years. How long did I sleep?"

"Not long." Mae lowered Pie into the chair with him, and the cat rubbed her head against Jamie's hip and then walked on his thighs, purring as he petted her. "You didn't miss much of your grooming."

"Good. Hate to miss that." He uncurled, lifting Pie to his chest and rubbing his face in her fur. As he looked up at Mae, his soft smile and dreamy eyes reassured her. But then he kept looking at her, as if discovering something, and narrowed his eyes with a slowly deepening frown. He glanced down at Pie, back up at Mae, and let out a sharp breath, his look changing to awe. "Fuck me dead. You did it."

"Did I?"

"Yeah, yeah." He looked her over again. "It's all right. Fuck, I can see you *better*, like—your face, your body. It's ... it's nice."

She thought he sounded like someone getting used to a new haircut on a woman. "I hope I did the right thing, sugar."

"You did. I like that dress on you ... Yeah. Seeing just you, y'know?"

"But you said the visions come and go, that you get days or hours without 'em. Are you sure I really did anything?"

"Yeah. Even when it's off there's always a little," he gestured a rapid vibration, "hummingbird sort of thing. Hard to describe." He looked down at Pie again, stroking her very slowly, lifting her tail to complete the long sweeping line all the way to its tip. "Jesus." He let Pie's tail drop. "It's really gone."

Was he soul-checking the cat? Mae had just closed off an extraordinary spiritual facet of his being. Maybe she'd saved him from drowning in it, but she couldn't tell if he was entirely relieved, or of some part of him felt regretful.

"Are you happy? Are you mad at me? Is it okay that I did it?"

"Dunno." Avoiding Mae's eyes, Jamie slid Pie off his lap and drifted out to the kitchen. She heard the refrigerator open. "Jesus, we're out of grog. Didn't we get beer?"

"No, we drank Ruth's stuff. You did." Rattling and rummaging sounds, as if he could force beer to come out of hiding. "We should talk about what I did for you. This was big."

"Nah. It's done."

"Please—"

"I want a beer."

"Not now, sugar. We need to get going soon."

"Right." He reappeared in the kitchen doorway, dazed and sulky. "Go watch Muffie pretend she can see people's souls." Hands in his pockets, he looked at the back door, the front door, and then at Mae. He shook his head as if shaking off water. "Fuck. I'm still asleep."

"No. You're awake. You just went to look for a beer."

"Yeah, yeah ... Hard to come back, that's all."

His comment about Muffie's fake aura reading worried Mae. "Because of what I did?"

"Nah. Just tired." He looked down, dropping inward. "Really fucking tired."

Mae's heart sank. He said she'd done the right thing, but she felt like she'd done wrong.

With Jamie giving directions, Mae drove down Canyon Road and parked at a long, low-slung pink-brown adobe building with apricot trees shedding fruit onto the graveled parking lot. The lot was almost full, and more people, some in suits and dresses, others attired in a style reminiscent of Sanchez and Smyth, arrived on foot.

"This is big," Mae said. She hoped she would be able to find Muffie and talk to her in such a crowd. It might be hard to get something from Ruth for a psychic search, too. "Ruth Smyth is really someone, then?"

Jamie stopped and collected a few small apricots off the ground, popped one whole into his mouth, and spat out the pit. "Best ones are off the street sometimes. Yeah, Ruth is kind of a celebrity. For the clothes and the Muffie bit as much as her art." He ate another apricot, offered the remaining one to Mae. It was unwashed and overripe and she didn't move to accept it. "Sorry. You don't eat off dirt—what am I thinking? There'll be good food here. She really caters, y'know, does the Muffie menu."

"They're that tight? I wouldn't have thought that, looking at the junk Ruth ate."

"What are you talking about? I thought you knew her act. Kind of an in-joke here, but you were on to it."

He ate the third apricot, spat the pit a good six feet, and opened the door for Mae. She stopped and stared at the sign near the door. Framed in turquoise metal, it read: *Ruth Smyth: Life as Satire: the Further Adventures of Muffie Blanchette.*

"Fuck," Jamie said with a frown, "You look like something's wrong. Isn't this what you wanted to see?"

"I thought ... Oh my God." Roseanne had said the guru's words would only be good if they were a joke. It *was* a joke. Bryan had been told to take down the Muffie web site over intellectual property rights. Muffie *herself* was the intellectual property. "Jamie. You have no idea what she's done."

"After what she did to your house and to Pie, I'd believe anything. And what she probably did to Dusty—fuck. Can't think about that." He nodded toward the interior of the gallery. "Tell me later."

Mae stepped inside, still stunned, and Jamie pulled the door shut behind them.

This was the gallery from her vision, with the elaborately detailed chakra imagery hanging on the walls. Visitors talked and laughed as they examined the drawings, carrying drinks and snacks from a large table tended by two servers and a bartender. Mae glanced through the doorway into a second room and saw a large flat screen TV mounted on the wall, and chairs and tables set up like a cocktail lounge or comedy club. At the far end of that room, near the screen, Ruth Smyth, unmistakable with her spiky multi-colored hair and little green glasses, wearing an unflattering skin-tight camisole and Lycra pants on her sausage-shaped body, talked with a tall, thin man. He had his back to Mae, but his hair looked familiar. Sandy brown hair in a ponytail of fat dreadlocks. Bryan.

Recovering from the shock and distraction, Mae noticed Jamie completing the purchase of tickets at a small table directly inside the door they'd come through. It wasn't a free event like all the other galleries. Her heart sank with dismay. He shouldn't be spending money on her, like a date. She wanted to argue with him over it, but they were in a crowd, some of whom he seemed to know. Jamie waved and called greetings as he stuffed a few bills back in his pocket.

Taking Mae by the arm, Jamie approached a short, stocky Native American man with thick eyebrows, a gentle face, and grey streaks in his long black hair.

"Mae, this is Alan Pacheco. He teaches art, same college where my dad works. He knows Niall of course. Alan, this is Mae Martin-Ridley, Marty's daughter."

Alan smiled, shook Mae's hand. "A loss to Santa Fe when they left. Nice to meet you." He asked Mae about Niall and Marty, and after some small talk with her, turned back to Jamie. "Do you hear from your parents?"

"E-mail every day."

"Good. I'm sure they like to hear from you." A hint of parental concern in his own voice, Alan seemed to approve of Jamie staying in touch with his parents. "How's life treating them down under?"

"Not bad. He's working, she's playing. Y'know. Being a happy grannie."

"You doing all right?" Alan looked at him with a worried expression. "You've lost a lot of weight."

"Triathlete. Swim, bike, dance." The two-part shrug. "So, does Ruth get a good review, or what?"

"For the drawings, yes. That's what I'm most interested in. But since Muffie is at center stage tonight, I'll cover her as well. Should be interesting." The art professor went on at some length about Ruth's integration of southwestern imagery into the chakra symbolism from India, and how perfectly the combination captured the current spirit of Santa Fe, even if she'd done it as part of a satire. "Ruth calls the state of things here 'the New Age spiritualization of formerly intact cultures,'" he explained to Mae. "And I get it. I've got nothing against yoga, of course, I'm dating a woman who does it, but there *is* a Muffie element in the city. Preppy white girl gone mystically overboard."

A gallery employee took Alan aside, and Jamie turned to introduce Mae to more friends of his parents, a couple who stood at the cash table purchasing a Sri Rama Kriya book from the rack Mae had seen in her vision. This couple also remembered Mae's father and Niall and seemed happy to make the connection.

After some light chat, the woman, graceful but sunbaked and past the age to be naturally blonde, opened the little book to a random page and read aloud.

"If worldly pollution dilutes *purusha*, pursuit of truth will push your future into the present and through again." She stared wide eyed at her husband, and then both burst out laughing. "It doesn't mean a thing!"

"Meditate on it until it does," her husband said in an imitation East Indian accent, and laughed again. "Mae, I'm surprised someone from out of town even gets the Muffie joke."

"Virginia Beach has some of the same stuff." Mae had worked at Healing Balance long enough to see plenty of fringe spirituality. "But Muffie played it straight in T or C—like it wasn't a joke."

Although the couple looked interested, just then the lights in the gallery gave a double blink and began to dim, drawing their attention away. They said quick goodbyes and moved off into the theater. Other guests skimming through the books and laughing at them finished their purchases. The more serious attendees left off contemplation of the drawings. No one in the crowd migrating into the theater seemed to have any idea what Ruth had done in T or C.

"What's going on with you?" Jamie asked, as he and Mae walked to a table with a good view of the screen. "I thought you liked her stuff. You said you were looking for her. This was supposed to be, y'know, like a treat. Fun. Even if Ruth's bloody heartless, Muffie's a good laugh." He looked at the floor. "Or was. Dunno. Thought we'd try to enjoy her still."

"It's not your fault, sugar. We had our wires crossed." They'd hardly talked about Muffie, and not at all about Ruth as an artist. Mae realized now that she'd found Muffie when she found Ruth in her psychic search, but it was such a stretch to connect the two, she couldn't have known it at the time. "I even had my own wires crossed. You did the right thing to bring me here."

They took their seats, and a server brought plates of finger food, and took orders for drinks.

"Get what you want, it's all in the ticket." Jamie put on The Smile, without full light behind it, and looked down, brushing one fist against the other. "Just want you to have a good time."

She asked for a glass of white wine, Jamie ordered a locally brewed beer, and the server left.

"You're not happy," he said.

"I'm mad at Ruth. I can't figure out why she did this ... how can I explain it?" Mae searched for a way to describe the situation at Dada Café. "She started a restaurant *as Muffie*. This nice, artsy vegetarian restaurant. How could she do that as part of a joke?"

"Ruth's a beer heiress," he said. "Beer truck heiress. Smyth Distributors. They bought some of the breweries later. Fucking rich, can do what she wants. Bit much to do a restaurant as Muffie, but she can swing it. Weird, but it doesn't surprise me."

"So the art and the clothing, that's all—what? A hobby?"

"Nah, she makes money at that, too. Her brother-in-law, Alfredo Sanchez—that's him over there—" Jamie nodded toward a table across the room, where a thickly built Hispanic man with a luxuriant moustache and collar-length hair sat with a plump brunette who resembled a younger and healthier Ruth with natural hair and no glasses. "He does the leather design and craft." The man wore a spectacular pair of boots with cacti and mesas on them. "You've got to love the stuff, even if you'd have to be a bloody millionaire to wear it. Ginny, Ruth's sister, is the business brains. They make all the clothes at a little factory in Albuquerque. Sell it in shops here, get those rich Santa Fe style people to wear it. The rich get richer."

Mae watched Ginny and Alfredo Sanchez chat with their server. Ginny wore a simple red dress with subtle silver stars woven into the fabric, and silver jewelry. Luminous, elegant, Sanchez and Smyth. How could Muffie—Ruth—go around telling people they had some spiritual need for the energy essence in these clothes? Couldn't she just market her work honestly?

"She tells people it's good for their aura or something, to wear the clothes," Mae said.

"Well, yeah, the Muffie act."

"But she's got another layer to the act—like it's not an act."

"Yeah, totally deadpan. She never comments on her character when she's in character. Some people around here see her and get pissed off, because the joke's about them, y'know, but fuck, it's about me, too, the sensitive vegan crap, and I think it's funny. Used to, anyway. Not sure I can still laugh at her, after Dusty."

"I'm not explaining this well." How could she expect him to grasp the idea? What he thought of as satirical performance art, complete with its whole pseudo-world of books, guru web site, and art, was being played out as if it were real—and being filmed. Mae cringed at the thought that she might show up on the screen. She'd signed the release, but with the understanding that Bryan was filming a documentary about the restaurant, not a satire on people like herself—a film with a fake psychic at the center. "She tricked people—"

The lights dimmed, and Jamie signaled her to wait and tell him later. A transformed Ruth strode into the room in the same arrogant yet spacey way she'd entered Dada Café. She wore a long, flowing, full-skirted sky-blue dress with patterns of white star-like lines, belted with a Navajo-style concho belt. Heavy silver and turquoise jewelry hung on her neck and ears, and she carried a cream-and-white Western hat with an elaborately beaded band and softly quilted patterns of mountains and clouds in the leather. Her boots matched her hat. Her elaborate eye make-up picked up colors in the clothes.

Mae understood now why all-natural Muffie was so heavily painted. It wasn't just to go with her outfit. The artist used color, shadows, and highlights to practically create a new face. A healthy glow. Fuller cheeks and lips. A sharper nose, a wider jaw, a stronger chin. With her face made up, her blonde wig on, her waist cinched, and hips and bosom padded to full curves, she bore almost no resemblance to Ruth Smyth.

"Nice dress," Alfredo Sanchez said. A few people chuckled.

"Thank you. And this is not tie-dye, by the way." Ruth caressed her skirt, stopping in the middle of the room. "It's *ikat*. I can tell half of you don't know the difference so I'm telling you." She put on the hat, sighed, and took it off. "I'm so torn between Santa Fe style and New Age." She looked around at the crowd as if they weren't laughing, and sighed again. "I guess I'm more Santa Fe style for now, since I'm still Muffie Blanchette." The name itself tickled a few people. "But I hate it when people define me as *Anglo*. Do I *feel* Anglo? No. I am so in touch with animals and the earth." She touched her concho belt, smiled. "I feel more Native."

She sat at Alan Pacheco's table. "I really respect Native culture." Her low, raspy voice droned with a mix of unworldliness and intensity. "I heard some people at the Taos pow-wow talking about me and they called me a Wannabe. No. I know who I am. I was reincarnated here because I was Native before. I don't have to wannabe. In my soul, I *am*."

On a wave of laughter, she rose, moved back to the center of the room.

" And ... oh my god ... Indian men. No, Patel, not you." She tossed a glance at someone in the audience who could be seen to rise halfway, a small East Indian man with a bald head. The face on the cover of Sri Rama Kriya's books. The guru Kenny wanted Mae to meet. The audience laughed more, everyone but Mae and Jamie. "I mean *American* Indian. Oh, that's right, George, you are American. I mean indigenous. I wish I were *indigenous*."

Her eyes passed over the crowds, and seemed to light on Jamie for a moment, as if he might be part of her next joke, but when his sullen glare apparently deterred her, she sat on a tall stool at the end of the room, to one side of the screen, addressing no one in particular. "If I were indigenous, I wouldn't feel so guilty when I wear leather. Because I would have killed it myself." She looked up, rapt and excited, and then snapped out of the apparent trance and said defensively, "I mean, in a sacred manner."

Jamie leaned in to Mae, whispered, "It's like she's making fun of Dusty. Fuck. I know there's a lot of wannabes, but ... How in bloody hell could she do *this* like it wasn't a joke?"

"It's how she ran the restaurant. No one knew she was Ruth."

"What?" The facts seemed to finally sink in. "Like she spent *all day* as *Muffie*?"

The group at the next table gestured for silence, as Muffie talked of a women's earth religion circle that had welcomed her. "They have such powerful female names, like Willow and Starfire. So *goddessy*. I tried out Coyote-Song or Cactus Flower, but it's a neo-Celtic group, and I was still feeling sort of indigenous. We're going to do a ceremony to find my power animal. If you're a neo-Celtic goddess worshipper, I think you still get to have a power animal."

Eyes closed, swaying, Muffie chanted about earth and sky and the waters that rise. She took off her belt and boots and danced, a side-step shuffle, arms upraised—like Dusty's dance. The audience laughed the loudest they had all night. Mae gestured to Jamie to follow her back out to the gallery. He frowned, shook his head, with a quick nod toward Muffie. Mae understood—it would be rude to walk out. As a performer, Jamie would feel obliged to stay, no matter what.

"My circle leader is telling me to look for the animal I love ... I can see it, yes ... So gentle, so giving, so sacred ... the divine feminine. *The cow*." Muffie opened her big brown eyes and stood with her large breasts thrust out, gazing fervently upward. " I am ... a *cow* girl. My totem, my power animal." She closed her eyes and spun, chanting again, this time a song about the gentle mother, the cow. "Oh, they are so abused. Drugged to give milk in factory farms." She sat on the stool and sighed. "My spirit sisters ... My circle leader told me we can't eat our power animals." She looked at her extraordinary tooled boots, rose and picked one up and cradled it. "No wonder I love my boots. I honor the cows with this work of art." She caressed her boots. "No animal could possibly have suffered to make such beautiful boots."

Mae whispered to Jamie, "How long has she been doing this act?" It was hard to imagine no one making the connection and catching on to her. T or C was a three-hour drive, but someone, even one person, from Santa Fe had to have eaten at Dada Café. Ruth shouldn't have been able to pull it off. "Is it famous?"

"Nah. Kind of guerilla art. Like, she'd spring it at her own gallery shows, walk out at the beginning leaving everyone pissed at her, and come back in an hour as Muffie. Or not even show up at all as herself. Inside joke. People who didn't know her took a while to realize Muffie was Ruth. She'd let 'em think she's this New Age flake who wants to meet Ruth Smyth because of the clothes. It got to be a game for people who'd caught on, seeing other people gape at Muffie until they'd get it, too."

"So this is her first real Muffie show?"

"Far as I know."

"And it's all local?"

"Yeah. I heard someone say Ruth was going to T or C, but they figured she'd have a studio there—"

Fierce shushing from the next two tables cut him off as Muffie put her boots, hat, and belt back on, sighing about the inner conflicts of being a walk-in among the crawl-ins who didn't understand her. She rambled about various healers she had been to see to have her aura tuned, her energy balanced, her colon cleansed, her chakras aligned with the planets, an alien intrusion removed from her astral body, and to have her food karma analyzed.

Then the screen came on, opening with a shot of Dada Café. "For those of you who haven't been there, this is my restaurant, where all the food is karmically pure."

Ruth gestured to the screen and stood aside, letting the film take over the show.

The servers, the kitchen staff, and Roseanne gathered for a line-up in the main dining room. Muffie, in her usual commanding style, strode in, and declared, "Jesus is the captain of all the spaceships circling the earth, in contact with the five great mothers who created the universe."

The Santa Fe audience chuckled, as on screen Roseanne seemed to struggle between outrage and laughter, her face growing pink, her lips pressed together, while Frank asked, "Is that what Sri Rama Kriya says?"

Muffie gave a solemn nod, and Kenny uttered a soft, wide-eyed "Wow." The audience exploded in laughter, drowning out half of Muffie's reminders to the staff. Roseanne made a short speech about some practical matters, and let Muffie resume.

"What is our creed?" Muffie raised her arms as if to conduct an orchestra. "Our mantra of work?"

The whole group recited, "To serve is to serve, to feed is to nourish, to clean is to purify," and ended with a long resounding *om*. The camera focused in on Kenny's rapt face, as his strong voice carried over the others, and his *om* lasted the longest. More laughter. Mae felt like standing up and shouting, but she only whispered her outrage to Jamie.

"It's not right. They are *not acting*."

Chapter Twenty-Six

Someone at the next table hushed her again. Mae dug a pen out of her purse and wrote on a napkin: *Staff and customers take her seriously. Short guy with piercings is my neighbor Kenny. He believes in her. She told them documentary, not satire.*

Jamie read, chugged his beer, and failed to silence the usual belch, earning a bug-eyed stare from Muffie. While a new film clip showed Roseanne fuming in the office, he wrote on the napkin. *F!* and drew a frowny sad face. Then he dropped the pen, clutching his beer bottle to drink again.

In the next clip, Muffie wore a black-and-gold skirt and jacket with subtle waves in the fabric and a black T-shirt with a gold sun-like eye in the center. She patted a pinkish man's bald head. "Your aura is wet," she told him, "and your crown chakra is clogged."

Jamie winced, and Mae wondered if the mockery of seeing souls was troubling him, or the meanness of making fools of people. He was sensitive enough, it could be both. She tried to catch his eyes, check in with him, but he was focused on his drink and on Muffie.

The bald man on screen tightened his shoulders around his neck in a turtle-like retreat, stroking his smooth crown. "I can feel these things," Muffie intoned ominously, and drifted to another table, where she closed her eyes and clasped the hands of the couple sitting there. "Oh, oh, too much cheese. The exploited energy of the divine female, the cow, it's heavy. You need," she frowned in concentration, "kale. Kale." She suddenly opened her eyes and began to chat about a recipe, started to walk off, and then looked back at the couple and said, "Remember, I am always right." This got a ripple of snickers and titters from the film's audience.

As the screen went dark, Ruth as Muffie said, "To help spread Sri Rama Kriya's word and wisdom, I have my movie coming out at the Santa Fe film fest. I call it *Sacred Cow Girl*." She waited for the laughter to pass, sat on her stool. "I was inspired when I was visited by beings from the stars. They are with me now."

She rose with a new burst of energy for what seemed like a grand finale and went through the audience, claiming to read their energy and auras. "You have a really soft, soft energy ... You need to cleanse with goji juice, and protect your aura with red shoes. Your feet can take in all sorts of energies from the street and the floor. People *walk* there." After each snip of advice she shuddered as if a spirit had moved through her and she were emerging from a trance, and then proceeded to another person. Jamie tensed and sat rigid in his chair.

Mae wrote on another napkin, *This is what she did in the restaurant, like it was serious.* Jamie looked at Muffie, wrote back another *F!,* and balled up the napkin in his fist.

Bringing her act to an end, Ruth whipped off the Muffie wig, bowed and thanked the audience. Her voice became brisker, perkier, and higher pitched, losing the drawn-out self-importance that was the Muffie character's trademark. "If you liked the outfit, check out the source at Sanchez and Smyth." She took off Muffie's wire rims, traded them for her green glasses. With a grin, Ruth reached in the bosom of her dress and pulled out the pads from her bra, reached under her skirt to wiggle out of Muffie's lower curves, and tossed the false breasts and bottom toward a back exit. "I'd like to thank the Santa Feans who gave my little café some nice online reviews and didn't crack a smile while you were there. You were great." She turned to a table at the back of her performance area, reached into a small bag, and brought out cold cream and tissues. Perched on her tall stool, she proceeded to wipe off Muffie's painted face, dropping the wadded tissues on the floor. "Somebody bring me a brew."

One of the servers delivered a beer. The artist raised it in a toast to herself and called loudly, "Bryan? Bryan Barnes?"

He rose from a table in the far corner of the room and flowed down front to stand by her, smiling.

"My co-creator of *Sacred Cow Girl*, Bryan Barnes."

He took a long, exaggerated bow and smiled.

"I almost had to have him arrested for stealing my image, but I'm sure he'll get an A on his senior thesis, and a prize at our festival."

More applause, from everyone except Mae and Jamie. Mae said, "He played it to me as if *he* didn't take her seriously, but he never made it seem as if his film would make fun of the people in it."

"Are you in it?"

"Yeah, I'm pretty sure I am."

"Fuck. Sue him."

"Can I?" She couldn't afford to, but if Ruth thought someone might, it was worth a shot. "I signed a release. We all did."

"But not for *that*. Jesus. Not to be a bloody mockery." Jamie stood and signaled Bryan with a huge overhead wave, and the tall filmmaker sloped over to their table. "Have a seat, mate." Jamie sounded close to losing his temper. "Remember this lady?"

Bryan did a double-take, then grinned. "Oh—wow. Yeah. Two business cards."

"She needs to talk to you."

Jamie chugged his beer, set the empty bottle down hard, and strode out to the gallery. Mae felt a stab of anger at Bryan mixed with worry about Jamie. Should she go after him? But she had to deal with the film and Dada Café.

Watching Jamie's dramatic exit, Bryan made a face, eyebrows high, mouth twisted. "Charming date you've got there." He sat and smiled. "You know we made your scene the end of the film? You gave us the punch line. It was so perfect. 'Bless your heart, I'm sure you think you are.' "

Dragging her focus away from Jamie, Mae said, "I signed a release for a *documentary*."

"It is. A documentary of a joke." Bryan started to laugh. "Best ending I could have asked for."

"But I don't want any part of making other people look stupid. People are laughing at Kenny, they're laughing at Roseanne for climbing the walls—and to them it's serious."

Still smiling, Bryan slouched low in his chair, almost liquid in his ability to fold his spine into bad posture. "Roseanne said you liked our web site."

"I did not."

"Oh, that's right. You hated our web site. Somebody liked it. Had a lot of hits. Hope you know I did it to keep your little friends employed."

The dismissive reference to Kenny and Frank grated on her. "You did it to keep your *own* job."

"No—I did it for them. And for Roseanne. I like Roseanne." Bryan's face softened as if digressing into a fantasy, and then grew serious. "I took a risk for them. Muffie is Ruth's creation. She really did send a lawyer after me."

"And everybody in your movie might do that next. You lied to us, and so did Ruth. Maybe you should think about not showing this."

Bryan raised his eyebrows and dropped his jaw, acting the caricature of a shocked person, and then turned off the expression and pushed himself out of his slouch. "Nice talking to you." He stood and walked to Ruth with a new energy in his previously languid legs.

What he'd said about keeping her friends employed came back to Mae. Her real goal wasn't to stop the movie. She needed to make sure Kenny and Frank's jobs were safe, and that Roseanne could sign the new lease. Mae stood, hoping to press through the crowd that had gathered around the artist, and ran into Jamie, returning to their table with a new drink.

"Where are you going?" he asked.

Mae took a step in Ruth's direction. "I need to catch Ruth before Bryan warns her not to talk to me."

"I fucked up, didn't I? Bringing you here." Jamie set his beer down and sighed. "It was supposed to be fun, and it's been ugly. Fucking miserable."

"No, sugar, it was a good idea. I need to talk to her. Her restaurant manager can't get hold of her and there's people's jobs on the line."

Trying not to think about the lost look in Jamie's eyes, Mae wedged her way through the admirers around Ruth and her sister and brother-in-law, and interrupted with an extended hand and a smile.

Ruth regarded Mae with a puzzled frown. "I think I should know you."

"Bless your heart, I'm sure you do."

Ruth's face registered recognition. The potential for confrontation caught up with Mae and she wondered if she could handle this. But her anger over the mockery of Kenny drove her on. "If your fans can spare you, I really need to talk to you about my role in your movie. Alone."

Ruth reached into the pocket of her dress, brought out a pack of cigarettes and a lighter. "As long as I can smoke."

She led Mae out the back exit into a small yard of dirt and rocks with the usual adobe wall.

"What about the movie?" Ruth asked, lighting a cigarette and taking a long draw on it. "Don't you dare say you want to get paid for it."

"No." Mae tried to keep her voice calm. "I actually want to talk about Dada Café. What are you gonna do with the restaurant?"

Ruth exhaled smoke and watched it break up into the sky. "When the show is over, you strike the set."

"So you're closing it, then? Some of them trusted you so much they really thought you ascended."

Ruth cackled and coughed, pushed her glasses up, and looked at Mae. "Really? I wish Bryan had kept filming. That would have been great. We shouldn't have cut my ascension speech. There could have been a whole second act."

"You missed my point. You shouldn't show it at all. It's gonna hurt Kenny—and then you'll take away his job on top of that?"

"What else should I do?" Ruth walked away from the building, knocking ash onto the ground. She stopped, turned to face Mae. "Stick around and mother him?"

"Kenny was really vulnerable. He thinks you saved him."

"I know. It's like I created a monster. I thought the staff would all be like Roseanne, put up with Muffie for the money. I wanted to see them faking it, being Dada, part of the act, but Frank seemed to believe it, and then he brings me this little drowned rat of a kid straight out of detox. *Kenny*. Christ, he was so needy. I just handed him the chakra book and improvised."

"You could have dropped the act for him and Frank. Let them in on the joke or something. Not lied to them."

"Why? All my crap gives them something to do besides drugs. And they found a real yoga teacher, didn't they? If I'd blown the cover, they wouldn't have thought the job was *spiritual*." A groan stretched out the word. "And what would that have done to my movie? You've got to admit, they add a lot to it."

"All you're thinking about is your movie. You got people who need to work and a manager who needs to renew a lease. Are you really gonna let the restaurant go, now that you're done with your joke?"

Ruth circled back toward the building and studied Mae. "Miss Kind and Compassionate, what do *you* think I should do?"

"How rich are you?"

"That's a nosy question."

"I'm serious. Because if you're really rich, I think you should give Roseanne the restaurant. You've been mean. I think you owe people."

"I owe people?" Ruth took another breath of smoke and blew it out, watching it float away. "If they want to be fooled, they get fooled. People get what they ask for."

"The people at your restaurant asked for *jobs*. You need to decide. Roseanne has been trying to get hold of you. She needs to know."

"I won't give it to her. That's the stupidest idea I ever heard." Ruth paced away toward the adobe wall. "I'm surprised you didn't want me to give it to your poor baby Kenny."

"He's not a poor baby. He's a better person than you'll ever be. But he has no skills, and he likes that place. I want his job safe."

Ruth dropped her cigarette on the dirt and ground it out. "You don't give up, do you?"

"No, ma'am. I'm stubborn."

"I need to get back to my fans, as you call them. You may not like me or my work, or you may think I'm a rich bitch, but I'm a serious artist and my satires say something that needs to be said. About fools that fall for this kind of crap."

Mae stood in front of the door. "I could sue you over that movie. The whole staff at the restaurant could. Everyone who signed the form can—"

"You wouldn't win." Ruth folded her arms and stared. Mae didn't move. She had to act as if she *thought* she could win. Ruth let out a sharp sigh. "I'll *sell* it to her."

"Cheap. She's not rich."

"For whatever she offers. Now excuse me."

Ruth put a hand on the door handle, but Mae held her ground. She wasn't sure Ruth would do what she said. How could she be sure Ruth's word was good? "I could go tell Alan Pacheco about Frank and Kenny. Ruin your review."

"You want me to sell cheap to Roseanne. I said I'd do it—"

"Call her now, while I can listen, and I won't tell him."

With a hiss between her teeth, Ruth shoved the cigarettes back in her pocket and pulled out her cell phone. Mae leaned against the door and alternately took her weight off one sore leg and then the other while she listened to Ruth's side of the conversation.

As Ruth explained her deception, Mae tried to imagine the irritable Roseanne's reaction. She wouldn't take it well. Apparently she didn't. The negotiation took what felt like an hour, and Mae wished she had dressed for sitting on the ground.

Once she finally heard the price named, and heard Ruth's assurance that she would have her lawyer contact Roseanne in the morning, Mae trusted it was done. Ruth dropped her phone in her pocket and glared at Mae.

"You can use your psychic powers to check up on me, I suppose. Make sure I lose plenty of money on that deal." She put on Muffie's voice to finish. "So that I burn off the karma that's clogging the arteries of my spiritual heart. My *anahata* chakra has atherosclerosis!"

Mae stepped aside and Ruth swung open the door to return to the near empty theater.

Mission accomplished. One mission. Before following the artist inside, Mae started to pick up the cigarette butt for psychic access to Ruth—nasty, but useful—and then realized she didn't have to. She still had the Sanchez and Smyth catalog.

Ready to leave, Mae looked for Jamie. He wasn't in the theater. She hurried out to the gallery. On the serving table, a nearly empty pitcher of margaritas stood by a row of empty beer bottles and picked-clean food platters. Jamie leaned against the wall, telling the bartender a joke. "Eros and Thanatos walk into a bar, and the bartender says, 'Oh God, don't you just love it to death?'"

The bartender frowned, and then chuckled when he got it. Picking up a margarita, Jamie snort-laughed, slurped at the drink, and spilled a splash on the white tablecloth. "Fuck. I'm off my face." He looked at Mae, unfocused. "Sorry. No idea I'd do this."

Drunk. He was staggering, word-slurring drunk.

Chapter Twenty-Seven

A wave of anger, frustration, and guilt washed through Mae. She had left Jamie alone for a long time on what he thought was a date. But it wasn't one, and he knew her issue with Ruth and how urgent it had been to talk to her. Yes, the show had bothered him, in more ways than one, but this was no way to handle it. Was he drowning the loss of his gift? He'd seemed happy about it, then unhappy, and had started hunting for a beer when his mood shifted.

"You shouldn't have given him so much," she said to the bartender. He muttered something about paying guests and began to clean up his station. Mae took the margarita glass out of Jamie's hand, set it down and started for the door. "Let's go, sugar."

Jamie lurched off the wall and followed her. "Never drink tequila." He managed to step ahead to open the door for her, and hung onto it. "Bad idea."

"Is that advice or your story?"

"Both. Jeezus, why did I do that? "

"I wish I knew. I kinda want to smack you upside the head. I won't, but I'm none too happy with you."

As they crossed the graveled lot in the dark, Jamie stumbled on the uneven surface. Mae caught his arm and steadied him. Then he slipped and lost his balance so completely that she almost went down with him, and had to let him go. He landed prone, barely stopping his face from hitting the stones.

"Fuck. Apricots." He sat back on his heels and held up his hands. They were covered in smashed fruit pulp. "I slipped in apricots." He sounded so amazed and offended, as if fruit shouldn't turn against him like that, that Mae lost a little of her anger to the urge to laugh. Wiping his hands on his pants, Jamie immediately put them back in the apricots in his attempt to right himself. "Jesus." He looked down at himself, and then held onto the apricot tree to get to his feet. "They're all over my pants."

"As long as there's none on your ass when you sit in my car." Mae checked him from behind. *What a skinny little ass.* "Good to go."

"Sorry. Really sorry." Falling back against the tree, he looked at her, breathing hard. The comedy was over. "Fuck. I feel like crap."

"Sick? Panic?"

He wiped the smashed fruit off his hands onto his pants again. "Dunno. Just ... crap."

"I'll take you home. Come on. We have to get some things from your van, and then I'll drop you at your place."

"No. You can't." He took her arm for balance, and they walked to her car. He leaned against it while Mae pulled as much of the apricot mess off his pants as she could. He still seemed to be breathing wrong. Could he be having a panic attack even though he was drunk?

"I'll walk," Jamie said.

"Your hip needs a rest."

"Nah. Feeling no pain." He pushed himself off the car and wobbled in place. "I'll walk."

"You haven't done a real good job of that so far." Mae guided him into the passenger seat, relieved when he didn't protest further, and went around to the driver's side, climbed in, and started her car. "I hope you can stay awake while I drive. I don't think I could wake you up if you passed out in my car."

"Just fell down. I'm wide awake." He presented this as if it were a logical sequence.

On the drive to Delgado Street, a short trip the length of Canyon Road, she made an effort to keep Jamie both alert and calm by talking. "Where do you live?"

"I'll walk."

"You keep saying that, but you're in my car, and I'm gonna drive you."

Rolling down the window, Jamie sang a few lines of the Four Seasons' song *Walk Like a Man*, complete with Frankie Valle falsetto. "That hurt." He leaned his head out the window, supporting it on his hand. "Fuck. Are we there yet?"

"You sick?"

"Dunno. Feel like crap. Jesus, I fucked up. Lost everything for bloody fucking nothing."

"What are you talking about?"

Running his hand through his hair, coming fully back into the car, he began to fidget with strange urgency. "Sorry. Just shoot me."

"Breathe slow, sugar. Take it easy."

Jamie continued to squirm, and she sped up a little over the speed limit, hoping he didn't either panic or puke. She didn't know which was coming, and he didn't seem to know either.

She pulled in beside the van, and Jamie let himself out. He stood swaying, and then reached in his pocket and started for the driver's door. Alarmed, Mae grabbed his hand and took the keys from him. "You are not driving. What in the world are you thinking?"

He beat a fist softly on the van's door. "I need stuff."

She remembered he had some kind of jerry-rigged wire fastening the inside of the van's back gate because the latch was broken. He needed his backpack. Or had he left his toothbrush in her house? He'd only come out with the water bottle. Still, he needed his other personal-care things, and she would have to go in and get him his toothbrush. No, he probably had three at home, he was so neurotic about his teeth. Mae walked to the passenger door, unlocked the van, stepped in and started to clamber into the back. "I'll get your stuff."

"No." Jamie still leaned on the van, thumping it weakly. "I have to ... Don't ... don't watch. Let me go."

Sitting and leaning across the seats, she unlocked the driver's door and gave it a little nudge. Jamie nearly fell, but grabbed the handle and opened it.

"You're not making any sense, sugar. What do you need in here? Let's get it so I can take you home."

His huge black eyes stared at her, lost, a fear heavier and sadder than his usual panic seeming to well up and drown him. He climbed in and stumbled to the back of the van, reached into the paper bag and pulled out a knit hat and a heavy flannel shirt. "Go. This is our fucking goodbye. Go."

It was. Mae's heart sank. She was leaving in the morning. They had to have their goodbye tonight, and he was a wreck, the goodbye a disaster. The depth of their friendship suddenly hit her, like one of those unexpected waves at the beach that washed up high and hard. He mattered to her. "I have to get your keys to you. I can leave them in the garden—"

"Leave!" he shouted. "Fuck. Leave me alone."

Mae had never heard Jamie raise his voice like that, no matter how temperamental he'd been, and it struck her like a slap. Why was he yelling at her? Even if he was drunk and couldn't be expected to make sense, it still hurt.

She climbed out of the van and stood a few feet from it while Jamie staggered further into the cargo compartment and struggled with the wires on the back latch. The door shook, but he couldn't get it undone. Finally he emerged from the driver's door, not looking her way, seeming to think she had gone. With his hair stuffed under the knit cap and wearing the big thick shirt, he didn't look like Jamie anymore. He had his backpack on, and carried the sleeping bag, which he tossed out ahead of him. Then he eased himself to the ground without quite falling, picked up the bag, and shoved the door shut.

For a moment Mae stood paralyzed as Jamie started toward the alley. She'd dug up all the wrong secrets. Solved all the wrong problems. He'd been hiding *this*.

Torn between protecting his pride and fearing what he might do, drunk and angry—he'd been drunk when he stabbed himself—she waited, and then followed at a distance as Jamie turned onto Delgado from the alley and tripped on the curb.

"Fuck." Dropping his sleeping bag, he landed on his hands and knees. He crawled to sit on the bag, head in his hands. Mae ran to him, knelt beside him. He shook with a fragile, unreal laughter edging on tears. "I walked into a fucking hole."

"There's no hole, sugar. It was just the sidewalk."

"There is." He rolled up in a ball, arms around his shins. "I fell in a hole."

"Come on, sugar." She took one of his hands, tugging him out of his protective huddle. It wasn't hard. He was easy to lead when drunk, verbally stubborn but physically malleable. Helping him to his feet, Mae picked up his sleeping bag and slipped her free arm around his waist, under the oversized shirt to get a better grip. He was hot and sweaty. Not a good sign. "Better come in. I don't think you should be on your own tonight."

"You shouldn't bring me in," he said, once they were inside.

She took his knit hat off him and helped him out of the flannel shirt. "Why?"

He stared around the room, shivered. "I'm a mentally ill homeless person."

There was something almost funny, yet painfully sad, in the way he said it. How had it sounded to him when she spoke of Dusty that way? "I've had you in here plenty already. You're my friend. Of course, I should bring you in."

He looked into her eyes, then away. "No. Because now you know."

"I'm still your friend."

"But you *know*." He swayed, seemed to watch a slow thought cross his mind. "Fuck. I didn't e-mail the oldies."

"I don't think you'll make much sense if you e-mail them now. Wait 'til you're sober."

"No, I have to. Every day." Leaning against the wall. "They'll worry."

"They don't know you have nowhere to sleep, do they?"

He shook his head. "No one ..." Another shiver. "No. No one."

"Well, someone's gonna have to."

Again he shook his head and pushed off the wall. "Feel like crap." Swaying. "E-mail ..."

If it would make him feel better, she could turn on her laptop and help him type a message. It would be a chance to encourage him to be honest with his parents.

She escorted him to a kitchen chair, opened the laptop on the table, and went to the sink to fill the kettle to make tea. Jamie seemed cold, even though he was hot to touch. He leaned his head in his hands, grabbing at his hair, and mumbled, "Mentally ill homeless person."

"I wish you'd stop saying that, sugar. You like Red Zinger tea?"

"Yeah."

She glanced at him, making sure he was neither panicking nor vomiting, and then looked away long enough to get teabags and put them in mugs, and turn on the burner under the kettle.

Sitting beside Jamie, Mae logged on and asked what e-mail service he used. Once she had brought it up, she turned the computer to him so he could log in to his account. He took three tries to type correctly, going so slowly she wanted to type it for him, and she noticed he had a strange e-mail address with no resemblance to his name, *ct-dmoddw.*

"What's that stand for?

"It's Welsh. Joke. Nah—each time I fell, new nickname. Climbing group ..." He watched his messages appear. "Crash test dummy." A sick hiccup. "Master of Disaster. Last one, they showed up in my hospital room and said they christened me *Death Wish.*"

"I wouldn't want to climb with a guy I called Death Wish."

"Neither do they. Not anymore." He lurched slightly. "Jesus. I can't read." He closed his eyes. "Is there something from my parents? My sister?"

Mae scanned his messages. "Something from Stan Ellerbee."

"Bloody hell." Jamie bolted from the room, hand to his mouth, and she hoped he made it to the bathroom. At least this might put an end to the *feel like crap* mantra.

She rose and followed him partway, making sure he'd reached his destination. "Jamie?"

A loud groan from behind the half-closed door. "I'm puking. Leave me alone."

"I'm gonna check on you if you don't come out soon, though."

"No-o-o." More groans, and the unmistakable sound of his sickness.

Mae returned to the kitchen and sat in front of the computer. He'd wanted her to read him his message from his father, so she opened it. Maybe it would bring good news or some kind of help.

We're still trying to call you. I know you said you have a new number, but it's been over a month. You have to let us know what it is. You don't like it when we have people check up on you, but we're worried. I contacted the people at Soul to see if they had your new number and they said you haven't played there since June. Are you working? Do you need anything? If you're keeping something from us, you don't have to. Please don't ever be afraid to ask for help. Don't wait 'til we get back. We love you. You're not a problem, you're our son.

Saddened, Mae almost wished she hadn't read it. She felt an urge to type back an answer, to tell the truth, to ask for help on Jamie's behalf. If his parents were coming back for the fall semester, which seemed likely, he was bound to see them in two weeks and have to tell them something anyway. Maybe he'd allow her to type something for him.

Noticing that another of his messages was from Wendy, Mae thought Jamie would want her to read that to him, too, and started to open it, but was interrupted by crashing noises, as if something had fallen over. Nothing heavy, but she had to check, and walked to the bathroom. Jamie, on his hands and knees amidst the bottles of lotion, sunscreen, and mouthwash Mae had left on the back of the toilet tank, looked around at her.

"Mouthwash."

She picked up the bottles and put the toilet lid down, grateful he hadn't knocked things into the bowl, and then helped him up, unscrewed the top of the mouthwash, and handed it to him.

"Sorry." He tossed a swig into his mouth, and after a prolonged swish spat into the sink and rinsed it. "I'm disgusting."

Somehow he managed to set the bottle back without knocking it over again, and Mae put its cap on. "Borderline. But for being drunk, not for being homeless." Hearing the kettle whistle, she returned to the kitchen and poured water onto the teabags, trusting Jamie would follow at his stumbling pace. When he arrived, falling into his chair again, she sat with him and read his father's e-mail to him.

"Want me to answer him?"

"Tell him I'm fine."

"You're not."

"Tell him I'm fucking *fine*. Jesus. I'm sick to fucking death of making them worry. I'm twenty-fucking-eight years old, I can't be fucking *rescued* by my fucking parents."

"They love you—"

"And I'm not putting them through any more bloody *rescue* crap. I'm getting by."

"His sabbatical has to be over soon. They're gonna get back and see you all skinny and anxious and figure something's wrong. When does their tenant move out?"

"Dunno. Still there."

Mae typed the reply. It wouldn't meet Jamie's approval, but his parents were already worried, and they needed to be able to reach him and help. *I'm a friend typing for Jamie because he's drunk. He says to tell you that he's fine. You need a second opinion on that. I'll try to make him call you when he's sober, and I'll make sure he's okay tonight.* She gave them her e-mail address and phone number. "I have no idea what time it is in Australia, but we can call them tomorrow on my phone. All right?"

"It's already tomorrow." He folded his arms on the table and laid his head down. "In Australia."

"You have a message from Wendy."

"Who?"

"Wendy Huang. Your future manager. The person who's gonna help you out of this mess."

"Don't tell her."

"What?"

"That I'm a mentally ill homeless person."

It was both funnier and sadder, the way he said it this time. "Of course I won't tell her that, sugar." Mae rubbed his hot, thin back, rose to get the tea, and brought the mugs back to the table. "I'm gonna read her message to you."

No response from the slouched form.

"Here's what she says. I'll tell you again tomorrow when you're sober, but listen. 'I want to see you tomorrow afternoon. Give me a phone number so we can set up a meeting. I still only have this e-mail address. We need to go over a lot of plans and make sure you're ready to sign a contract. I'm excited about what I can do for you. Your new music blew me away.'"

"Tomorrow?" Jamie sat up. "Bloody hell. I'm ... I'll be ... Fuck. I'll be hung over."

Mae nudged the mug of tea toward him. "You'll get better." As the ex-wife of an alcoholic, she knew more than she wanted to about hangovers. "Drink this. Dehydration makes it worse."

He picked up the tea, slurped, apologized. "Move your laptop. Might spill on it."

"Good idea." She turned it off and moved it to the counter. "How'd you end up with nowhere to sleep?"

"I'm a fuck-up."

"No. Come on, what happened?"

"Started with my hip. No—fuck—I dunno. Started when I quit teaching. Lisa was managing my stuff ... I can't do that crap." He slurped the tea again, looked into the mug. Mae sat beside him. "Anyway, it was going all right, I had this gig every Thursday at Soul, and I had the CDs out, played in Albuquerque sometimes. I don't do normal bar music, hard to line up good places, and Lisa ... shit. Quit. I mean, we'd split, but—fuck, that rhymed. I asked her to help ... a little longer." He took a breath, looked at Mae. "I'm not good at anything."

"That's not true. Now what happened?"

His eyes went down to the tea again. "Money. Trying to pay on the fucking medical. And I bought stuff. I'm stupid. I bought—" he gestured a kind of dome, walked his fingers into it and stared at it, as if this object were now in front of him, haunting him with his wasted money.

"Is that a tent? You bought camping gear?"

He nodded. "Bike ... voice lessons ... Thought I'd earn more, but I didn't, y'know? And then Lisa quit. I didn't think she would." Slurping at his tea and spilling a slop of it, he tried to wipe up the mess with his sleeve and sloshed more from the mug. "Jeezus." He looked at the red tea soaking his pink sleeve. "Fuck."

Mae handed him a cloth napkin. "I can make you more tea. And your shirt's fine. You said you didn't think Lisa would quit managing for you."

"Yeah. But she did. No one could order stuff or book me. It was stupid. I'd left it all up to her. And ... fuck, I hate this part ..."

Mae sipped her tea, waited while Jamie fidgeted. He didn't seem ready to speak, close to anxiety in spite of his intoxication. "I don't judge you. My friend Kenny was homeless once."

"He *told* you that?"

Mae thought of Kenny's complete lack of embarrassment about his past. He talked about being a homeless addict with the same accepting frankness with which Mae might talk about getting divorced. "Yeah. Bad stuff happens. He's really open about it."

"Stronger than I am, then. I feel like a failure." Jamie sighed. "My rent check bounced. I got my parents' tenant to let me store stuff—said it was because my new place was small ..." He turned to Mae, and his voice took on a new urgency. "See, I had it figured. I could manage. Get back on my feet. Paid up for the year at the Geneveva back in the winter. I could shower there, y'know? And if I ate less I could eat ... decent."

"So you ate only once a day?"

He nodded. "Still had the gig at Soul, and Lisa had jumped all those hoops with the city for me to do the street stuff. But I had to give up ... give up on the bills. I was in a fucking hole."

"What happened to your work? This place you used to play—Soul?"

"Late. Moving stuff out to Tesuque ... fucking van ..." He laid his head down again for a minute, and then lifted it to finish. "They hired someone else for the summer. See, the phone ..." He rearranged his arms to put his elbows on the table, head in his hands. "Fuck, I had a plan. But William, he was getting all thin and tired. I thought he just missed Lisa and our old place, but ..." Jamie glanced at Mae. "I might cry."

"It's okay."

"I took him to the vet." Jamie squeezed his eyes shut. "William had cancer. I'd been letting my fucking cat die."

"You didn't mean to. Was that while you were homeless?"

"Nah. In the apartment. My first home as a fucking bachelor." He opened his eyes, drank his tea. "I was depressed. All that crap had happened. I thought *William* was depressed. Fucking stupid. Finally took him in. Too late. Terminal. I missed my phone bill, because I had to ... Fuck. First night out of the place, I'm sitting in the van in the parking lot at DeVargas Mall, that was all I could think to do ... and I'm sitting there holding William, and I know he's sick, and I don't want him to die. Just sitting there in the middle of the night, and the poor cat, he starts bleeding out his arse, all over my clothes. Dying on me. But he didn't die. Jesus. I held him all night, and he—fuck—*he still loved me*, and I'd let him down. Took him to the vet in the morning, had him ... y'know. Held him while he died. Fuck. I did wrong by him. Then—Jeezus, the fucking money to eth—euthzan—to kill my dying cat—I couldn't pay for the phone."

"That's awful." Mae wondered if he'd seen the cat's soul go. "When was this?"

"June. Lisa dropped me in May. I fell off fast."

Mae tried to picture his life. The sequence was scrambled by his drunken storytelling, but she had a sense of what had happened. He'd been depressed but functional at the end of the relationship, and then traumatized and blown back into the spirit world by finding Dusty dying. Barely hanging on financially through his limited income from his music, swamped with medical bills for himself and then for a sick pet, not knowing how to master his marketing or to manage his own career, distracted and confused by a spiritual disturbance, he lost control of everything—his mental health as well as his money. The loss of one led to the loss of the other in a vicious circle. Ironically, he'd not even tried to access the same help he'd tried to get for Dusty.

"How do you get by without any help?"

"Hide. The night hat, y'know, so I don't look like me. Swag out late, pack up early. Fuck. Tried to be useful for a while, used to ... used to take the train to Albuquerque, play music in the hospital still, be some use ... It's part of who I am, y'know? But then I couldn't pay for the train."

He'd misunderstood. Told her how he avoided looking like he needed help. "I meant, how do you *live*? What do you *do*?"

"Jesus. You want to know?" With a surge of self-outrage, he straightened himself, arms braced against the table, and glared at the space in front of him, forcing a surprising level of clarity into his speech. "Here's my bloody useless day. Sleep about four hours. Check e-mail at the library. Go the Geneveva and swim and shower, maybe dance. Safe place. Like to stay a long time. Bike if I have to, can't buy gas much, can't fix the bloody van. Play on the street if I think I can handle it, get some cash ... Get a meal at Whole Foods so I don't look homeless, stay sort of healthy, eat while I'm there so I can brush my teeth ... Write some music ... Do laundry at a laundromat ... That's all I can manage. I see too much. I can't think. My head's not clear."

At least she'd freed him of seeing too much, but it wasn't the only reason his head wasn't clear. "It's because you're starving, sugar. And you're tired. Where do you sleep?"

"Gully behind Fort Marcy Park mostly. Up on the hill, those big stairs off Paseo. Top of the city. Nice piece of desert. Smells good.

Pinon, juniper." He drank more tea, set the empty mug down with a clatter. "I'm busy. Takes the whole fucking day just to mind your own business when you don't live anywhere. Find water, find bathrooms, go here to bathe, here to eat, here to use a computer ... Get stuff in and out of the van, move the van so it doesn't get towed ... Busy. I'm bloody fucking busy, and I don't have a fucking thing to do." He let out a short laugh. "At least I'm not depressed."

"You're not?"

"Nah. I'm outdoors. I'm active. Better off than most homeless people, really. Got a place to get clean, got a little income. Can't lie around and brood, can I? Like a fucking wild animal. Survive."

As if the effort to order his story had worn him out, he lay his head on his arms again.

Only one thing still didn't make sense. "How did you make that picnic?"

"Mwizenge's house. He knows I—he saw me crack onto you, y'know?" Without sitting up, Jamie flashed a shy smile like the first time he'd approached her. "I fixed the same lunch for them, made them a cake. As thanks, y'know? For help with the sound files. Said my oven didn't work."

It had taken a surprising amount of planning to bring a cookbook and to figure a way to use his friend's kitchen. It had to have looked odd to Mwizenge and his family. Or had it? Jamie was eccentric enough that peculiar behavior might not raise questions. "If you told a friend, someone like Mwizenge or Alan, I bet they'd give you a place to stay 'til your parents get back."

Jamie propped halfway up on his elbows. "No. I'd rather die. Rather drag my balls through broken glass. It's my bloody fuck-up and I'll fucking un-fuck it."

Finishing her tea, Mae gave up on reasoning with a drunk. She offered a kind untruth instead. "I'm sure you can."

"I can. Work my way out of it, y'know? Bloody hell, Dusty was twice as crazy as I am and—Jeezus, I almost said 'and he lived.' Fuck." Jamie slid lower in the chair. "Fucking Ruth. Did she do it?"

Chapter Twenty-Eight

Mae rested her hand on Jamie's arm. "I couldn't ask her about that. I was trying to get her to take care of her restaurant, not just close it and fire people."

The whole idea that Ruth had owned a business in the role of Muffie seemed to have already dropped from Jamie's mind, he looked so confused. "What?"

"I'll explain it later. It was so Kenny could keep his job. So he wouldn't be homeless again."

"But you got her ... stuff, her ... something. Right? So we can know."

"I have something."

"So you know? Fuck, why didn't you tell me?"

"I haven't done that yet. I'm not going into a trance with you drunk."

"Yeah, you can. I won't bother you. I'll just lie here and be useless." He slumped onto the table and gave her a dazed, pleading look. "Or run off and puke. Y'know. No trouble."

She actually could do the psychic journey now. When it was intentional and not a half-dream journey, she could snap out of it and back to the present if needed. There was an appeal to closure with Ruth. Mae would be leaving in the morning. If she was going to risk upsetting Jamie with whatever she learned, it might as well be now, while she had time to see him through it. Tomorrow, he'd need to focus on getting ready to meet Wendy. "Hang on. I'll be right back."

She quickly got a couple of crystals—amethyst and turquoise, for visions and protection—and the Sanchez and Smyth catalog from the living room, and returned to sit by Jamie. "You need to do anything? Puke? Pee?"

He made a negative sound.

She laid a hand on his back. "I'm gonna take the journey now. It may go fast, or I may be quiet for twenty minutes or so. Hang in there. Interrupt me if you need to, though."

Seeing that Jamie seemed, for him, reasonably stable, she placed one hand on the Sanchez and Smyth catalog and held the crystals in the other, seeking Ruth's energy and asking if she had seen Dusty jump—and done nothing. Mae's concentration felt suctioned by Jamie's proximity, and the tunnel came slowly, but she finally moved through it and into the nighttime garden.

Ruth, still enraged, glared after Dusty, who could be heard grunting and scrambling to his feet on the other side of the wall. She ran to the wall, stepped onto the rock, and pulled herself up on tiptoe to watch his limping sprint away from the house. As she did so, Ruth's hand touched something snagged in the tiny peaks of the rough surface. A speckled feather. She stepped down from the rock, her anger appearing to weaken, and held the feather, her eyes active, her expression shifting from concentration to the dawning of an idea.

Dropping the feather and turning, she walked back to the oval path in the garden and began to imitate Dusty's attempt at a sacred dance. She dissolved into silent laughter. Clapping her hands, she hastened into the house, grabbed a notebook from the chaos of newspapers, books, and magazines on the coffee table, and dug frantically through the heaps, shoving unwashed plates and full ashtrays aside to find a pen, and then sat on the floor and began to scribble in the notebook.

"Muffie as Wannabe. New obsession. Muffie thinks she's a reincarnated Indian. Does this dance. Mix in with her other pagan stuff and lust for Native men. Muffie: 'I don't have to wannabe, I *am*.'" Ruth sketched the dance posture and admired her work, shaking her head with a low chortle.

As a glow of headlights crossed the front window and cut off, she glanced up with a frown, muttered, "Shit," and walked to the front door. Opening it, she met a police woman coming up the walkway. The dog began barking.

"Ms. Smyth?" the officer said. "You reported someone in your garden?"

Ruth waved dismissively and started back into the house. "He's gone."

"Did you get a look at him?"

"Stupid tourist. Gawking at art."

"He was still trespassing. You don't have to go talking to strange men in your yard at night. You did the right thing to call." The officer hesitated, looking into the room behind Ruth. The Chow dog stood a few feet behind its owner, growling. "You sure you want to let this go?"

"Yes." Ruth bristled, hand on the door. "I'm fine. Good night."

When the officer left, Ruth closed the door and returned to the table to look over her notes. She lit a cigarette and nodded, smiling. The dog chased Pie across the room, but Ruth didn't take her eyes off the page. She sat down and resumed writing, laughing to herself, and made another sketch.

Mae pulled out of the vision. Heartless, but not cruel. Ruth had no more concern for a homeless mentally ill person with an injured ankle than she did for a terrorized cat or a messy house or the staff at her restaurant. She hadn't intentionally let Dusty die, but she didn't see him as a human to worry about, either. Once she was inspired to make fun of him, she'd forgotten about everything, even treating the police woman she had summoned as an inconvenience to be gotten rid of.

When Mae opened her eyes, she realized how little time had passed. Jamie hadn't moved other than to turn his head to look at her.

"She got distracted. Stopped in the house to write that sketch we saw tonight. Her wannabe jokes. So she never saw him jump, didn't look where he went past the alley. She even sent the police away. So, in a way it's her fault he died, but not on purpose."

Jamie gazed into her eyes, and then seemed to process something, gears clicking in his alcohol-slowed brain.

Mae asked, "You gonna remember all this tomorrow?"

He sat up, juggled a few imaginary balls, caught one, and watched the rest roll away. He would hold on to enough.

Tired from the psychic work, Mae rose to put the tea mugs in the sink. She needed to use a crystal on herself and go to bed. Time to get Jamie settled for the night, too, while the roller coaster of his emotions had stalled out. She started for the living room to get her grandmother's ruby to cleanse her own energy field.

"Jeeeezus. What's that smell?" At Jamie's exclamation, Mae stopped in the kitchen doorway. He pushed away from the table, regarding his legs with distress and shock. "Did I puke on my pants? Fuck. I'm fucking covered with it. Just shoot me."

"No, sugar." She couldn't help laughing. "You fell in the apricots."

"Oh." He frowned. "Yeah, I did. Fuck. Looks like vomit. Jeezus." He shuddered. "Hope I don't."

"You already did."

"Fuck." He sank low in the chair. "Clean. I need to be clean."

He seemed to be getting less coherent again. Mae knew from living with her first husband that blood alcohol kept going up for a while after rapid drinking. Was Jamie still getting drunker? As sleep deprived as he was, it was hard to sort out fatigue from intoxication.

"I don't trust you in the shower. You might fall down."

"Bath," he said to the table, and then faced her, suddenly anxious. "You don't think—fuck—you don't think I cracked onto you to get a bath, do you?"

"No, of course not. You're the cleanest—" She cut herself off. *Cleanest mentally ill homeless person I've ever met?* "I'll run a bath. Stay put. I don't want you bumping into anything."

Leaving him collapsed at the kitchen table, she crossed the living room to the bathroom. Behind the closed door she shed her clothes and stood at the sink, sponging herself clean of the day's dust while his bath filled. A shallow bath, not deep enough for a drunk to drown in.

Her concern for him hurt. How had Lisa managed to live with him, always worrying what he'd do to himself next? *Crash Test Dummy. Master of Disaster. Death Wish.* Mae didn't want him to be a mentally ill homeless person. He was a fire of life in spite of some strange force driving him toward damage or death. Was there any chance for him to heal? The ordinary existence she took for granted—not rich, not free of struggle or pain, but safe in her own solid, practical mind—would probably feel like some kind of nirvana to him. Had he ever felt that way? Would the fact that she'd closed off his visions help?

Wrapped in a towel, Mae went to the bedroom, closed the door, and got into her nightgown. On her way back to get Jamie, she paused in the living room to take a few conscious breaths and cleanse her energy with her grandmother's ruby. When she returned to the kitchen, she found he had taken his pants off, tossed them across the room, and resumed the same position at the table, in his pink shirt and white jockey shorts that looked too big for him.

Mae tried not to laugh. "What are you doing?"

"The smell. My pants. Didn't want to puke in the sink."

"That was real thoughtful of you." In a way, it was. She picked up the jeans, carried them to the laundry room. The apricots did smell overripe. More laundry. Then she noticed—her clean clothes had been folded into obsessively neat little piles, the cups of her bras tucked into each other, her panties pressed into perfect little colored

squares in a stack, her running clothes in another orderly arrangement, matching colors together. While she'd been in the bedroom
trying to think what to do and he'd been so strangely silent, he'd
folded her clothes. Her *underwear*. So intrusive and personal and yet
so caring. She could almost feel him trying desperately to quiet his
mind, to be useful to her and prove himself a good partner, trying to
make order out of something, anything, after his mood or his visions
had troubled him so much that he couldn't play music on the street.

She left the jeans in the machine and returned to escort him to
the bath, slightly embarrassed at being with him in his underwear.
Jamie had long legs with that same ropy, sculpted look that his upper
body had, as if all the fat had been drained from him. Mae thought
of Hubert's solid, perfectly proportioned body in contrast, and wondered what he would say if he could see her and Jamie.

He wouldn't care. Hubert was probably looking at Jen in her
next to nothings—Mae stopped the thought. She didn't need to go
there. She had enough on her hands and on her mind without that.

"Jamie, when I leave you, can you take off your underwear without falling and hitting your head on anything?"

"Dunno." He sat on the toilet lid while she unbuttoned his shirt.
"You won't help?"

"I know you're drunk, but I really don't want to see your," she
helped him out of his sleeves, "your ... all of that."

"Take a bath in my grundies, then." He moved to the edge of
the tub and lowered himself into the water. "Ah." He sighed, smiled,
wriggled in the water. "Jesus. Fucking back to the womb."

The wet cloth began to be revealing. Mae left the room.

"Let me know you're conscious sugar, make some noise." *Asking*
Jamie to make noise—now that was a new twist. She tucked a sheet
around the sofa cushions, added a pillow from her bed, and a blan-

ket. He seemed to run hot or cold randomly. No telling what he would need. He would want Pie to hold onto. Mae found her in her little cat bed. Once Jamie got settled, she would deliver Pie. They'd both like it, man and cat.

In the bath, he began going through vocal scales. Good sign, not passing out, staying peaceful.

What would Jamie do after she left? She couldn't stand the thought of him sleeping outside, even if he'd blown a lot of money on good camping equipment. It had to be scary out there, and sad and lonely. Maybe she could ask her father and Niall if Jamie could cat-sit a few days. Marty had wanted her to stay longer for Pie, make sure the old girl was all right until the tenants arrived, and Mae—she felt bad about it—hadn't wanted to, because she wanted to get away from Jamie. Hadn't even remembered to arrange for the cat until now, though she'd intended to ask Jamie to visit her.

Mae sat in a chair, thinking. This would work. Pie wouldn't be abandoned. Jamie would have a place for a few nights. He'd be able to eat three meals, sleep better for having Pie with him, and then ... then what?

He had friends he was probably avoiding in order to hide his situation, but he would have to tell someone and ask for a place to stay until his parents got back, and then he'd have to stay with them, pride or no pride. No one would rent to him. His credit was ruined, with unpaid bills and a bad check to a landlord. Even if Wendy got started right away on booking him gigs or new recording sessions, it would be a while before much money started coming in.

Jamie's scales turned into a kind of game, singing the word "high" in his upper range, the word "low" in his lower range. This became a chant, alternating "High aspirations" at the very top notes he could reach, and "low self-esteem" at the bottom. Funny—but it wasn't. It was true. Water sloshed and then began to gurgle.

She fluffed the pillow on the sofa, glanced at Jamie's sleeping bag next to the door. His parents wouldn't want that for him. What would it be like to know your son was sleeping in a park?

A thumping and stumbling broke into her thoughts, and she stood, starting toward the bathroom.

"You all right, sugar?"

"Little slip. Not bad. Vertical now."

"You need a hand?"

Laughter, snorts, and loud hah's. "Fuck. Sorry. Naked. Don't want to see me in the nuddy, do you?"

"Not really. Put your towel on, come on out here. *Carefully.* I made your bed."

He appeared in the bathroom doorway, still damp across the shoulders, holding a towel around his waist with both hands, and wobbled toward the sofa. Mae tried to avoid the scars on his belly, but her eyes were drawn to them. She quickly looked to his eyes instead, and saw the last trace of laughter die hard into darkness.

"Come on, lie down," she said.

"Can't." He stared at the sheets and pillows. "I'm scared."

"Of what?"

He sat on the sofa arm and almost lost the towel, letting it gap across his left thigh and hip, revealing the final scar she'd not yet seen, a surgical scar, and around it the traces of what must have been gashes from rocks or branches. That had been a horrendous fall. She was looking at the root of his slide into homelessness. Jamie could no more pay for that hip joint than fly to the moon, and he'd tried.

He took a slow breath. "Dying."

"Tonight?"

He looked at the couch. "Yeah. Like Hendrix, y'know? Choke on puke. Die like a fucking rock star, and I'm not even famous yet."

"You still feel sick?"

"Dunno." His voice faded out to a hoarse whisper. "Sorry. I'm bloody rotten. I'm ugly." He rubbed the scar on his upper arm, and then spread his fingers over the marks on his belly. "I'm a mentally ill homeless person sitting in your fucking living room, scared to go to sleep, and I'd rather die—I'd rather fucking die than be this. Jeeeezus." A weary rage rose in his voice. "How fucking stupid can I get?" He punched the back of the sofa with one hand while the other worked at the edge of the towel, clutching and releasing repeatedly. "I wish I was dead—and I'm scared I could die."

Chapter Twenty-Nine

Mae moved without trying to reason with herself. No choice. Picking up the pillow, she walked to the bedroom and put it back on the bed. Then she came back into the living room and scooped Pie from her cat bed, holding the cat against her chest as she said to Jamie, "I won't let you die." Her own steadiness surprised her, how calm and sure she sounded. "You can sleep with me."

She didn't watch him follow her. She knew he was there, his normally silent steps heavy.

"Check for scorpions." He sank into the chair by the bed. "Spiders."

"Where?"

"In the bed."

Demonstrating her cooperation, she set Pie by the pillows and flipped the covers back all the way.

"Pillows too," Jamie said. "*Seriously*. Bities get in your bed. I'm not just phobic. They really do."

She checked under each pillow, lifting them high enough to show him all was clear—not that she thought he could see that well—and then walked to the doorway, turned off the overhead light, and turned on the starry ceiling. Jamie would like that.

Mae sat on the bed. "I'm getting in, and I'm not looking at you naked. But it's okay. Get in with me. I'll make sure you don't choke or anything. You'll be all right. No bities, nothing. It's all safe." She slid to the far side of the bed and lay down, her back to Jamie, expecting him to flop beside her. She tried not to think about Mack, about sleeping with a drunk, and reminded herself that Jamie's problems were different.

He didn't move.

"Come to bed," she urged.

His voice came out thick and tight, the one word framed by a gulp and a sniff. "Fuck."

More to take care of.

Mae rose, moved the tissues to the table on Jamie's side of the bed, and walked to where he sat huddled in the chair, rocking, fists pressed to his mouth. His sadness made her heart ache all the way to her hands. She wrapped her arms around him and helped him up, letting his towel fall, and led him to the bed.

The bed. It must be what shook him so—he hadn't slept in one since the first of June.

He sank on the edge of it, and she sat beside him, lightly touching his shoulder. "It's gonna feel nice, sugar. A bed." Crawling across to the far side again, she lay down and patted the place beside her. "Come on. You need to sleep. You'll feel better."

Jamie shook his head and fell onto his side, drawn up in a sobbing ball. He must be so tired he didn't even know what was wrong, like a little kid. Mae curled around his back, making soft, reassuring sounds, stroking his hair as he sweated, shook, and tried to curl up even tighter. The breakdown was even noisier than the previous one, with sobs that bordered on shouts, broken up by vocalized gasps for air. Yet somehow, even while it hurt to ride it out with him, there was more room inside her now to hold his pain. She slid her arms though his and rubbed his belly, touching the scars, and he shuddered, crying more softly.

When Jamie finally quieted, he propped up on one elbow, blew his nose a few times, and lay down on his back. Under the starry ceiling, she could see his eyes, wide open, still wet.

Pie walked over to him and began to knead at his thigh. Resting a hand on the cat, Jamie turned his face to Mae. "I love you." His voice was surprisingly steady. "I want to be the man you danced with, the man who made you laugh while we cleaned this bloody mess, the friend who kept you company and showed you the town ... I want to be ... I want to be ... the best memory of your life when you go." More tears flowed. "Not this."

"Shh." She touched his tears away, kissed him on the forehead. "Go to sleep. It'll be all right. You'll be a beautiful memory. I know you will."

She stayed awake, watching over him, until he faded into a stillness that looked like sleep.

A few hours later, Mae woke to the small, frightened sounds of Jamie's nightmares. She rolled over to reassure him with a light pressure on his shoulder, to stir him out of the bad dream. Without waking fully, he wrapped his arms tightly around her and pressed up against her. The whimpering stopped, and his breathing changed—more rapid, not more relaxed, and he mumbled a question about why she was wearing a nightie. Did he think she was Lisa?

Feeling his erection stir against her, Mae inched away. What had she gotten into? A foolish, reckless situation. Sweet and sad or not, he really *was* a mentally ill homeless person, and a drunken one at that. In her bed, and wanting her.

Mae sat up, and Pie crept into the space she had occupied. Still apparently asleep or close to it, Jamie petted the cat and tugged her against his chest, and she somehow not only tolerated the squeeze, but even answered it with purring.

Rising from the bed, Mae opened the windows and let the cool night air blow in. It had been hot lying next to Jamie. He radiated heat as if sleeping was work.

After checking to see that he was still quiet, she sat in the wooden chair and closed her eyes. Exhaustion flooded her. Her calf muscles were still sore. She should get Jamie to give her a massage before she drove the next day. No, bad idea. She shouldn't.

Sleeping in the chair proved impossible. Best to go to the couch. Mae went to the bed to get a pillow, and noticed that Jamie was starting to cough and retch, not fully waking. She shook him, and he staggered to his feet with a gasping, "Oh fuck," and made a stumbling run for the bathroom.

That's why he's sleeping with me, she reminded herself.

Mae walked to the bedroom door. "You all right, sugar?"

A groan. The toilet flushing. Water running. Jamie returned, smelling like mouthwash, his face wet with cold water. He leaned on her and moaned, "Sorry. I'm disgusting."

She tried to keep her eyes off his long limbs, broad shoulders and narrow hips, but he looked good when it was so dark she couldn't see his bones or all the scars. *Stop. He just got up and puked. This is not sexy.* Disengaging from him, she helped him back to bed.

He fell onto the mattress, and within seconds seemed to sleep again. Lying beside him, Mae rolled him onto his side in case he choked, and Pie slipped between them, finding a spot to nest and purr against Jamie's chest. Mae curled over to face him and took hold of his hand.

He *was* the man who had danced with her, given her a massage, comforted her sorrow, made her laugh, showed her the town, and bared his wounded soul and body. He was worth the trouble of this sorry night. Someday she would hear his new music playing, and know that she'd helped him get there, and be glad.

Light. Light that moved. Mae opened her eyes. She had rolled away from Jamie in her sleep. The sunrise, a thin golden line over the edge of the house next door, showed and then vanished as the curtains seemed to inhale then exhale the morning's arrival. Feeling Jamie's gaze, sensing his alert presence, Mae turned and saw him lying on his side, halfway up, apparently entranced by the movement of the curtains. He looked at her, then at the window, then at her. His expression could only be described as a kind of rapture.

He caressed her face, touched a finger to her lips, and gestured with his hand as if closing her eyes. She closed them. Whatever he was seeing and feeling, it was beautiful, and she should let him have this moment.

When she woke again, the light was brilliant, and she smelled coffee. Jamie, in clean clothes—had he run out to the van naked?—stood holding a steaming mug in each hand.

"G'day, love." He waited for her to sit up, and then handed her a mug and sat at a respectful distance on the bed, his voice and energy subdued. "Hope you slept some."

Mae took a sip of coffee and a deep breath of its aroma. "Thanks for bringing this. Yes, I did. After you got a few things out of your system."

"Sorry." He drank his coffee. "Not my normal. Hard liquor. Jesus. Bloody awful."

"You're gonna see Wendy today. How you feeling?"

"Buggered." A wan smile. "It's all right. Got a bad head, but," the two-part shrug, "I can still cook."

"You don't have to. You've got to focus on your music today. I can—"

"Waffles? Muffins?"

"Do you carry a cookbook around in that backpack?"

He nodded. "I do. Yeah. Get to someone's house and ... you never know. Might have a chance."

"Whatever you feel like, sugar." This obviously meant so much to him, she had to let him do it. "I'm sure I'll love it."

With a faded version of The Smile, he left. Mae rose, drank more of her coffee. While Jamie was cooking, she had a mission to accomplish. After a quick shower, she called her father. Tempted to tell Marty the whole story, but knowing how ashamed Jamie was, she simply asked if he could stay in the house a couple of days while he took care of Pie. He could give the place a final cleaning before the tenants arrived.

"'Course he can, baby, if you need to come back. What's Jamie's number? We should talk to him before Niall comes up to get the new tenants settled in."

"He doesn't have one."

A long silence. "Stan and Addie know?"

"They're about to."

Before sitting down at the table, Mae laid her phone nearby on the counter, hoping Jamie's parents had read the e-mail and would call any minute. Even if she didn't know what time it was in Australia, they had to know what time it was in New Mexico.

As if moving underwater, Jamie served waffles and more coffee. "Lemon corn blueberry," he said. "Let me know if it worked. Can't believe I found all the right stuff to make 'em."

"I can. I bet you shopped for this recipe when we were ..." She didn't finish. Of course he'd fantasized being here for breakfast. The hope-it's-okay version of The Smile admitted as much. Except for the menu, this could hardly be the way he'd imagined waking up with her, though. She tasted a waffle. "This is good, sugar. You're the best cook I've ever met." Meeting his eyes, she saw a mix of relief and sadness as he sat across from her. His last chance to try to impress her. "Can you stay a few days and take care of Pie?"

He nodded and looked down, cut his waffle with atypical neatness, and ate a small piece of it. Swallowed before talking. "Thanks. I'll leave the place perfect. Leave Pie all happy and sweet."

"She loves you. I'm sure you will. Promise me you'll go to some-one's house when you leave, Jamie. You're not going back in some gully—"

"Jesus. You weren't supposed to know that. Can we act like—act like you don't?"

"Not really. You need an address and a phone number. You need three meals a day and eight hours sleep. I can't leave you stranded. I have to know."

"I'm not stranded. I just ... dunno what to do. Yet. I'll figure it out. I'll see Wendy. We'll get a plan."

"*She* needs you to have an address and a phone number, and to get enough to eat. Don't you think you panic more when you're worn out like that? You could have a lot of work coming up, and you can't do it in the shape you're in."

"I've written some great music in the shape I'm in."

A distraction, and she didn't let it snag her. "You have relatives, don't you? Isn't your Dad from here? Family can know."

"I don't, and they can't. My grandparents are dead, and my cousins don't live here. Not that they like me, anyway. All the ones I'm close to are in Oz. Look, I wasn't just talking drunk. I said this is my fucking mess and I'm—"

Her phone rang, and she rose to answer it, saw an unfamiliar number. It had to be, she hoped, his parents.

"Hey. This is Mae."

"This is Stan Ellerbee." A deep, gentle voice with a neutral Amer-ican accent. "I don't know who you are, but thank you for giving us your number."

"I'm Marty Martin's daughter. Doing some work on his and Niall's house."

"Marty." Stan's tone warmed with recognition, and then tight-ened with worry. "Is Jamie all right? Is he— I ... don't know how well you know him."

"Pretty well. He's right here. You can talk to him."

Jamie's eyes grew wide as Mae walked over and proffered the phone. "Fuck. You gave my parents your number?"

"I didn't tell them anything except that you were too drunk to type last night. And my number. And that you *claimed* you were fine."

"Bloody hell." He glared at her, took the phone, and collapsed into a sheltered slump, one hand supporting his head, his voice soft and drained as he said, "G'day, Dad."

Mae began cleaning up the kitchen while she finished her meal at the counter, deliberately making enough noise washing dishes that Jamie could assume she wasn't listening. Occasionally she heard a few words, always in that surrendered, exhausted voice. Enough words to know he'd given up the fight and was telling the truth. *Bad check. William died. Lisa quit.*

Leaving him to finish the long and painful conversation, she went to the laundry room to get her clothes, and then to the bedroom to pack. She didn't know how this would turn out for Jamie, but she felt sure that at least his parents wouldn't let him stay homeless.

Aware that her time here was ending, she slowly folded each dress and blouse. Someone else's hands seemed to be placing the items in her suitcase. *Leaving.* Jamie's pink shirt lay on the floor. She picked it up and hung it on the arm of the chair. Nice to think that he could stay a few days, do his laundry, cook, sleep, shower, even dance and practice his music, all in one place, not be running all over town all day just to take care of ordinary life. She hoped it would be peaceful, and that the break from being desperately busy staying alive would feel safe.

Carrying her purse and suitcase to the back door, she heard Jamie now laughing. "Fuck, Mum, I've been waltzing Matilda ... Nah, no fucking billabong to jump in ..." A roaring laugh. "Jeezus, you're as sick as I am ... Too right ... Nah ..." He sounded subdued again. "She's still half-married ... man back in woop-woop ... "

Mae wished she hadn't heard. Had his mother hoped he'd found someone?

"Yeah. I promise. Told you—I have a manager. I'll be working, might do a tour ... Can I talk to Haley?"

Now he would be on her phone longer, talking to his sister, but this was important, one last thing Mae could do for him. Leaving her suitcase inside so Jamie wouldn't panic and think she'd left without a goodbye, she went out to the garden. A little time with the sage and lavender and the statue would be good for her soul. Finally. Her time alone.

"Thanks."

Deep in contemplation of the gleaming black curves of the statue's hair and blanket and the enigmatic expression on its timeless face, Mae jumped at the sound of Jamie's voice. Where had she been? She seemed to have drifted into a space between her thoughts. He stood near the bench, holding out her phone. She took it from him, slipped it into a pocket, and moved over to let him sit with her. "You don't make a sound."

"Used to be fat, y'know? Had to take dance in college, tried not to be a fucking walrus. Learned to float. Still float." A heavy silence sat between them. He took her hand, and she didn't resist. "Fuck. You've seen everything, haven't you? Past and present. Fat, thin, sick, drunk, crazy, stupid, crying ..."

"I've seen more than that."

"Yeah, but you didn't see," he paused, watching his hand squeeze hers, then looking away, "your equal."

Shocked that he thought she'd looked down on him, Mae protested. "I never said that."

"Didn't have to. It was what you did." He let go of her. "You can handle this—this—" An angry flick of his hand at the space between his eyebrows and then at the crown of his head indicated what he meant. He leaned his elbows on his thighs and spoke to the ground between his feet. "I can't."

He was right that she'd thought he couldn't handle his spiritual gifts right now, but he made it sound like a final verdict, or a matter of finding him lacking in some way. It wasn't. "Not yet. But you could get it back, when you're better. When you get your head on straight."

"It doesn't go on straight. This is it."

"You don't know that."

"I do, love. Come on, so do you." Still avoiding her eyes, he clasped her hand again and turned it over, his long fingers rippling repeatedly across her palm. "It's like my body. I can get to perfect one seventy-five, and I can swim and dance and bike, but I won't get *fixed*. I'll still be full of metal, and scars, and places that hurt. I'll still take my clothes off and scare people, y'know?" A soft laugh. "The mind can get a little better, but not a lot. I live with it, y'know? It's who I am."

"So you don't think you'll ever be ready? Seems you get some kind of gift like that, you're supposed to use it."

"Gift. My bloody curse. Jesus." He met her eyes. "D'you have any idea what I was seeing?"

She shook her head.

"Wish I could tell you." Jamie turned to straddle the bench, and Mae sat more sideways on it to face him, a move that felt strangely like he'd led her in a dance, still holding her hand. "Jesus. It was like ... I'd *know*, but it wasn't words, or ideas—like shapes and lights and even sounds sometimes, but they told me, y'know? *Truths*. In the park yesterday, I fucking couldn't do the music. I could see ..." He shuddered. "Sorry. Something ugly in someone ..." He looked down, released her hand, drummed on the bench. "But I could see stuff so fucking beautiful I could hardly stand it, too. You. And my mates, Mwizenge and Dagmawi—Jesus, their souls when we played together, fucking blinding. Made me fly. But I couldn't turn it off. Sometimes it'd go off when I didn't expect it, then it'd come on again for days, and I'd be in bloody heaven and hell at the same time."

"You could find a teacher, maybe, so you could learn to control it. Your father knows all these medicine people and shamans."

"Put away your tool box. Stop trying to fix me."

"I'm not. I'm trying to tell you—I've kept telling you—I think you're a healer." If he were mentally healthy and could control his gifts, he'd be more than her equal. He'd have powers she couldn't imagine. "A healer shaman."

"And *then* would you see I'm your soul mate? Is that what it'd take?"

"No, that's not why I said that—"

"Because that's what I hoped. That's why I—" He stood, his back to her, and pounded a fist into his hand. "Fuck. That's why I left it to you. To see. If I could. But I can't. You're right." His hands exploded upward, fingers spread, as if tearing a veil from his vision, and then pressed into his temples and burrowed into his hair. "There's not room." He dropped his hands and shoved them in his pockets, walked a few steps along the path and stopped, still with his back to her, shoulders hunched, head down, rubbing the edge of a brick with his heel. "But I'm still the one."

Him? A thousand arguments crossed her mind. Things she could never say to him. She took her time to pull her thoughts together, struggling to assemble both kindness and truth.

"I'm not ready, sugar. I'm taking time out from men. A long time. And ..." It was so hard to hurt him. He'd give her the baby seal eyes and she'd want to comfort him, but they had to make a clean break so he could let go of her. "Even when and if I am ready for a man in my life, it might not be you."

He looked up into the blinding sky, squinting. "Dunno, love. Might change your mind when you hear me on the radio and you wonder if that love song's for you. Wrote one already, y'know." Drifting to the statue, he stroked the sweeping curve of the stone woman's shawl. "Since you closed that door in my head, I've had this music in me, y'know? Woke up when the grog wore off and there it was. Like this *force*. Coming out of everything." He held contact with the statue a moment longer and faced Mae again. "Better get your suitcase, hadn't I?"

With a flash of The Smile, he hurried into the house.

He put her bag in the trunk, and she set her purse in the front seat, keeping her keys out, and took the house key off the ring. She handed it to him. "Niall's coming up to meet the tenants in a couple of days. You got somewhere to go then, 'til your folks get back?"

"Yeah. Alan ..." Jamie jammed the key onto his ring with what Mae now realized must be his parents' house keys. "Mum and Dad are sending money for the van. Y'know, rescue ..." He kicked at the gravel and drew a line in it with his heel. "Thanks for everything, love. You're a fucking angel." Without looking at her, he started away.

"Jamie. Come on, sugar, say goodbye."

"Sorry." He turned around, beginning to laugh. "Fuck."

"What's so funny?"

"I was afraid I'd cry." The snort-laugh. He returned, took her in a ballroom dance position. "That's better. I can do this right." He grinned. "Follow my lead, love, this is a waltz."

"What? Now?"

"Yeah, now. It's all we've got."

He waltzed her into the alley, expanding the sweep and flight of the dance, and began to sing a tender, flowing ballad as they soared and spun.

The curtains breathe
Dawn's golden line
You'll soon be gone
Heartbeat of time.
Your beauty shines
Through heart and mind
So wild and sweet
So strong and kind.

He sang the final verse several times, each repeat reaching further into the seemingly limitless highs and lows of both his voice and his heart.

And though you say
You can't be mine
I'll cherish this
Heartbeat of time.

Crazy. Heart-rending. She felt like a bird flying on the wind, and like a fool dancing in the street with a man singing loud enough to be heard in every house on the block. A love song for her.

On the last notes, he waltzed her back to her car, and with a kiss on the cheek let her go. "Remember me like this."

Mae wasn't sure if she said goodbye. She got in her car and looked out the window at that blazing gold-toothed smile and those deep black eyes, this strange-looking lean brown man with his little dark beard and wild blond hair, walking backwards into the garden. Then she had to look away, and focus on driving. Her eyes were blurring. For the past four days she had been trying, and failing, to get away from him. Now she had, and it hurt.

What could she do with her mind for three hours? Even the red and brown cliffs, the black lava rocks, the startling shapes and colors of the bare bones of the earth along I-25 South didn't stop the tumult inside her. KUNM began to fade. Without taking her eyes off the road, Mae reached for the first CD she could grab.

The last disk of one of the romance novels wrapped up the story with a wedding, as they always seemed to—either that or an engagement, followed by an epilogue describing the happy couple with their two children. *Really? Is that how stories end? Marriage is the golden door people walk through and they live happily ever after. Parents stay together and have perfect children. And the hero of the romance sure isn't crazy, or homeless. Who'd want a story like that? Unemployed personal trainer halfway to second divorce meets mentally ill homeless musician ...* And then? Nothing. Nothing was possible. Jamie, sweet kind Jamie, would drain the life out of her with his endless needs.

She missed Hubert. So calm, so steady. The sound of his slow, Southern speech, the solid feel of his body. If he was here, he'd put on some country music, sing along once in a while—badly—and not say much as they drove. Didn't need to. They'd been comfortable. No noise, no chatter.

Bored shitless. The image of Jamie popped up as if he were there. *Lights are out, love.* He could still see souls when he said that. Her lights. Not a metaphor. Going out. And lighting up for him?

Chapter Thirty

Finally unpacked and settled in her first real place of her own, Mae felt a kind of love for the pea-soup green former trailer and its dirt yard with its strange thorny trees and ants and lizards. She walked through the rooms, imprinting the place as *home*. It felt good, yet the padding of her bare feet echoed, and her own presence took up too much of the space. Something was off, but she couldn't place it. Something empty or missing.

She stepped out to the back yard and the blazing sun. It was too early in the day to use the hot spring, but she wanted to clean the big metal tub for a soak under the stars when the air cooled down after dark, if she could stay awake that long. After the night with Jamie, which seemed like another life, almost a dream, she was as tired as she could remember being in years.

She switched on the pump to release the water from underground. Amazing that under this desert there was all that hot water, waiting to burst up. Mae scrubbed away bird droppings, shoved the windblown grit toward the drain, scooped up the small dry mesquite leaves, and turned off the pump. A noise against the fence drew her attention. A tall ladder knocked against it, and soon Frank appeared among the towering, scraggly sunflowers that peered from his yard into hers. He turned, a precarious move in Mae's opinion, to grab hold of a tall wooden pole decorated with colorful bits of metal. The device for attracting communication from the Pleiades.

"You got it?" Kenny's voice behind the fence. Good. He must be steadying the ladder.

"Yup." Frank hooked the end of a looped piece of twine over the top of the pole and tugged it down to where it caught on some of the metal, and then added another. He faced the fence again and brought the two strands to the boards and hammered nails into his side of the fence. Two strings of small, colorful square flags now waved from the pole to the fence, each flag a different color, decorated with a graceful, curly golden script in some mysterious alphabet.

"Oh, hi." Frank waved. "Hope you like the addition to the view. I'm Frank." The introduction made her realize she'd only met him in a psychic vision, and seen him in Bryan's film. "Kenny told me about you, said we have a cool neighbor."

"Thanks. I think I've got cool neighbors, too. What are you hanging up?"

"Tibetan prayer flags. Each one has a Buddhist prayer on it, and when the wind blows, it sends the prayer, like we never stop praying." He looked down to Kenny. "Any idea what they say?"

"I'm not sure. Peace and happiness to all sentient beings, something like that ... probably."

"Got 'em at a yard sale. Figured we might as well make something of the pole. We've got a lot to pray over. You got some time? Come on by. I've got to go to work soon, but, you're *the source*. We want to talk to you."

The source? Of what? It took a moment to remember her undoing of the Muffie illusion. Mae had been so wrapped up in Jamie, she hadn't thought about Ruth and her restaurant since leaving the gallery the night before. Frank and Kenny seemed okay, but as much as they had invested in Muffie, it still had to have come as a shock that she was a fraud. "Yeah, I'll be right over. Thanks for the invite."

Mae locked her doors and walked around the block to get to her back-door neighbors' front door, again impressed by the smallness of their house. Frank met her on the little shelf of a porch and shook hands. "Now we're officially friends. Got to go prep for dinner. We'll have to work out some sort of fence signal system, like a sign that means drop in if you feel like it."

"I like that. Great idea. Have to ask Niall for a back gate, too."

"We'll figure it out. Kenny's expecting you." Frank pressed his hands together at his heart, made a small bow. "Namaste," he said, and started down the street.

Mae tried saying "Namaste" in response but it sounded funny with her accent. She knocked on the door, and Kenny called to her to come in.

As she stepped into the dim, cool room, her eyes went to the altar. The picture of Sri Rama Kriya—George Patel—was gone. A new set of spiritual teachers now graced the setting for Frank and Kenny's contemplation. Tiny statues of the Buddha and pictures of the Dalai Lama and Mother Teresa.

"I'm in here. Making tea."

In the kitchen, Mae found a barefoot Kenny in tattered cutoffs, looking cheerful. He took some decaffeinated green tea and a jar of agave nectar from the cabinet and filled the kettle. "Hope you like hot tea in hot weather."

It was probably some Muffie idea, but Mae accepted the offer nonetheless. "Thanks. Good to see you. Frank said you wanted to talk to the source."

"Yes. We had a staff meeting about Ruth and her movie today. Roseanne wants us to decide."

"On what?"

"Everything. Like, do we still want it to be Dada Café or change the name, do we want her to fire Bryan or forgive him, and do we want to accept an offer Ruth made, or sue her."

"She's asking you all that?" Rather than sit, Mae used a chair to stretch her legs in several positions. The three-hour drive had left her feeling stiff. "That sounds like a lot's happening with the place."

"We're going to be an employee-owned cooperative. Roseanne's the majority owner when we buy it, but we all buy in. So we get to help with big decisions like these. Feels like *Survivor*, though, if we vote Bryan off the island." Kenny used his arms to hike himself up to sit on the counter, his short legs swinging, and watched the blue flames of the gas burner lick the kettle. "We probably will, though."

"I don't blame you. He wasn't honest with you. Neither was Ruth."

"But she still helped me. Dishwashing may not be a big deal to most people, but she gave that job to *me*. No one else might have given me a chance And she got us into yoga. She really did a lot for us. I don't care if some people think she was making fun of us. I think she really cared about me and Frank, a lot, and didn't dare let anyone know how much. It would have ruined the joke."

Mae wondered if she should tell Kenny any of what Ruth had said about him. Or about the beer and bacon and cigarettes. It might disillusion him too completely. She started with the most obvious. "So you know the aura readings were fake." *But Jamie could really see that.* "And the walking in and walking out." *He could see that, too, in a way. Stop thinking about Jamie.* Kenny nodded assent, untroubled. She went on. "And the nutrition was kind of wacky."

"Yeah." Kenny grinned. "She really got us with that. But I needed to detox, what the heck. No harm done. Drank a bunch of green stuff. I still do. Might keep it up a little longer, 'til I hit my one-year sobriety anniversary."

"I thought you'd be more upset with her. Or with me for finding it all out."

"No. She didn't hurt me. Not at all."

"But I saw clips from the movie, in Santa Fe. She's making fun of everyone who believed her like you did, and of the people who didn't, too. Like Roseanne. For putting up with her."

"That's why Roseanne thinks we could sue her. But I'd rather take the offer."

The kettle whistled, Kenny hopped down, poured the water onto tea bags, and washed the counter where he'd perched. Once a restaurant-kitchen man, always a restaurant-kitchen man. He carried his mug to the table and sat cross-legged on the seat of his chair.

"The offer?" Mae drizzled a little agave nectar into her tea. "Is that what you're praying over, with your flags?"

"How did you know? Yes. That and firing Bryan. And changing the name and theme. Some of it's hard. The Bryan part. But the offer is easy ... I think she did it to," he looked into Mae's eyes, "to thank me. I think it's actually her way of saying I meant something to her, that I reached her heart, even if she didn't mean to get connected."

Ruth, connected? The woman was as unfeeling as a bacterium. Mae waited for Kenny to say more—she couldn't think of a reply.

"If we don't sue her, she'll release the movie locally in Santa Fe, where she has a following, and sell the DVDs at a gallery—oh, and on that web site, too. Bryan will put it back up, without the stuff about the staff, and all the proceeds will go the Interfaith Shelter in Santa Fe." He beamed. "Can you believe that?"

The building with the dinosaurs on the roof. Mae could believe it. Someone more organized and rational had to have come up with the details, but Jamie would have planted the idea to support the shelter. The plan must have gone from Jamie to Alan to Ruth. She needed the art critic's good opinion. It was the logical chain of events, unless Ruth really had that soft spot in her heart for Kenny and all homeless people. Probably not.

"That's a great use of that movie."

"I think so. But I kind of think we should fire Bryan. I hate to judge people, but ..." Kenny fished his teabag out. "He wasn't nice to us."

"Not really. I'd feel better without him around if I were you. What about the name of the place?"

"I think I'll vote to keep it. I mean, look at it. It's Dada. We shouldn't redecorate. We've got a Ruth Smyth design, right? That's pretty cool. Now that we know who she is."

Roseanne had promised Mae, Niall, and Marty dinner on the house at Dada Café as an expression of appreciation for Mae's efforts above and beyond paying for her psychic work. Looking forward to enjoying the food without the Muffie act, and to Niall and Marty's company, Mae approached their house shortly before sunset.

Niall stood by the adobe wall that surrounded the yard, inspecting something and smoking. In the dimming light, the objects embedded in the wall were still visible—broken ceramics, a boat propeller, an aluminum bat, hubcaps with beaded strings of fuses seeming to dangle from them, and other apparently random things arranged in a pattern that ended up both pleasing and puzzling, catching the mind as well as the eye. Beyond the wall, the house glowed, its purple door and red shutters against its red-brown adobe exterior suggesting vibrant life inside.

Mae wanted to make Niall stand straight and to tell him to quit smoking, but she'd known him less than a week. She hoped the urge would fade, and that eventually she could look at him without getting snagged on his bad habits.

"Need to patch this," Niall muttered with barely a glance at Mae, rubbing his hand along a large blue ceramic shard that must have been a bowl in its prior life. "Don't suppose you'd notice it."

"I noticed the wall. I like it."

"I meant this." Addressing her as if she were stupid, Niall tapped a small white spot in the blue glaze. "This is chipped."

"It wasn't supposed to be?"

"Broke in the kiln. Put the good side out. Now it's the bad side, too." He inhaled on his cigarette, exhaled the words as if he wanted to go slowly to keep the smoke in his lungs, and narrowed his eyes behind the thick lens of his glasses. "You got a minute?"

"Aren't y'all ready to go to dinner?"

With a sharp sniff, Niall nodded toward the gate in a *follow-me* gesture and stepped inside. He crossed the bare dirt yard, butted his cigarette in an ashtray on a picnic table, and walked up the steps to his studio, a corrugated metal building that clashed with the aesthetics of the house. Mae followed. She sensed Niall had an agenda.

The interior of the studio was littered with machine parts and old rusted tools on the cement floor, while new, shiny hand tools and power tools, welding masks and torches filled shelves and pegs along the walls above workbenches. A bookshelf lined one wall, and a small refrigerator hummed in a corner.

Niall nudged a set of large rusty gears with his work-booted foot, and paused to examine a work in progress that might be a masked dancer when it was finished, made from pipes and flywheels, rakes and hoes and mufflers. He sat on a wooden stool beside the workbench, and Mae took the only other seat, a paint-splattered chair with an uneven leg, waiting for his speech. Niall seemed to be setting up for something.

He pointed a thumb at the refrigerator. "Soda, beer, if you want it."

"No thanks."

"Probably drink that nasty sweet tea like your father." Niall got up, got himself a cola, popped the can open and took a sip. He set it on his workbench and looked at it as if seeing something more than what was there, and then walked over to his bookshelf. Running a finger along the spines of books, he pulled out a thin paperback. "What'd you think of Jamie Ellerbee?"

Mae found herself locked in by Niall's oddly magnified gaze through his lenses. "I don't know. He ..." Her thoughts about Jamie made even less sense than the man himself. "He's ... intense. Not much of a filter on him."

"That's an understatement." Niall chuckled, and then lost the smile, flipping through the book. "*Storm Child*. Poetry by Adelaide

Ellerbee. Jamie's the light of her life and her worst nightmare all in one." Niall held out the book to Mae. She shook her head—she wasn't ready for Typhoon Jamie yet, even in print—and Niall returned to his stool and picked up his soda again. "She called me today. Glad he's at our place for a few days." Niall glanced at the book of poems, then back at Mae. "And grateful to you. She thanks you for taking care of him."

"I'm glad I could help." Mae stood. "Daddy probably wonders where we got off to. I'm never late."

"I'm not done yet. Addie put in a plug for Jamie. She recommends him to you."

"She doesn't even know me."

"She knows him." Niall drank half the soda. Jamie would have let out a deafening belch if he'd done that. "I'll see him in a couple of days, and you know he'll ask about you."

"Just make sure he met with Wendy Huang and that he's got some kind of plan—"

Niall grinned. "I'll tell him you're thinking about him."

"You'll tell him I wish him well. That's all. And he already knows that."

Niall handed her the book. "Addie wants you to read this."

She didn't look at the book until late at night, under the light of a half moon and a streetlight while soaking in the hot spring.

The cover image showed a stuffed toy kangaroo, battered and lying in the dirt. Mae recognized it as Jamie's roo that still lived in the van, photographed in better days when it still had two ears. The author was A. Nungarrayi. Jamie's mother kept some privacy when she bared her soul, not publishing as Ellerbee.

Careful to keep the pages above the water, Mae flipped through the table of contents. Some of the titles were *Fault Lines, Ecstasy,* and

Sirens. She scanned that one. Ambulances mixed with imagery of the mythical sirens singing sailors to their deaths, *the temptress siren song of death.*

It had to be so hard to be his mother. To be his sister, his father, his friend. His lover. Jamie saw Mae as his soul mate. Addie had probably wanted Mae to read this so she would know what she was in for and see if she could bear it.

<u>*Larger than Life*</u>
"He's larger than life, your boy," a friend said
As your laughter rocked the room.
Bloody stupid, I thought. Life is huge.
So what if you're big and loud and bright?
Life ripped you at the seams like outgrown clothes.
Only death is larger than life. Life is huge
And even your stretched-out soul can't hold it all.
The rest of us stay whole by staying small.

Mae closed the book, gently let it drop onto the path, and sank back into the into the 110-degree water. Resting her head against the rim of the tub, letting her body half float, she watched Frank and Kenny's Tibetan flags flutter prayers across the half-empty cup of the moon.

Was she staying small?

If she pictured her life alone, she had no doubt of her own strength. She could survive without marriage, without a man. Would that be shrinking herself? Or would it be courage? She had to do it to find out.

She sat up and looked at the book cover again, the picture of the fallen toy lying on the ground, and remembered last night in Santa Fe, seeing Jamie stagger out of his van, trying to hide his homelessness. Did he put that roo in his backpack to go sleep in some gulley? That would break his mother's heart.

When Mae had let him into her bed, it hadn't been the match
Niall or Addie had in mind for them, or the kind of love Jamie had
hoped for. It fell short, too, of the deep urge Mae's broken heart had
reached for and couldn't grasp. But it was the kind of love she had to
give right now. She hadn't stayed small. When he'd needed her most,
she'd had room for him.

She sank deep in the water and let go of Jamie as best she could,
looking up to the sky. The brilliant stars of the desert night shone like
openings into another world, where the light was like the eye of some
unimaginable god.

Epilogue

November, Truth or Consequences, NM

The barking of a chorus of dogs came and went, the town grew quiet again, and the cool air of the autumn night floated through the open windows in peace. Kenny lit a candle on the altar. One year without drugs. He really didn't need to make a big deal of it, he'd only been doing what he should have done all along: living a healthy life. So his normal life was the way to celebrate.

Alone, he honored the clean and sober year with an hour of intense vinyasa yoga, stood on his head longer than usual at the end, and then lay in *savasana*, corpse pose, letting the stillness capture him. A year of celibacy, of meditation, of being vegan, of being clean. Of having a job. Of being fully human. He felt both full and empty, a paradox of bliss.

When he rose, he sat to meditate. The old Jangarrai CD, *Sound Bath*, still played, and Kenny let his mind focus on the music. The drone of the didgeridoo, the floating chanting tenor voice, kept him still and took him deeper into his inner peace.

At the end of the last track, he eased his mind back into the ordinary. He'd go to NA in Silver City tomorrow, where he'd first joined. That would be celebration enough, but he also might spend a little money. Frank said Jangarrai had some new music.

Kenny went to the kitchen, turned on the tiny netbook on the table. It was Frank's, but Frank wasn't attached to his stuff. After pouring a glass of iced green tea, Kenny did his gratitude practice. Before shopping for music, he sent a carefully composed and thoughtful e-mail to Ruth Smyth through ruthsmythart.com, letting her know he'd hit the one-year anniversary, and that he still liked the chakra art book, and Dada Café was thriving. She never answered when he contacted her, but it didn't matter. This was his practice. He felt good letting her know.

Virginia Beach, VA

Excited, Deborah bought a copy of the new Jangarrai CD the day it came in at the Healing Balance bookstore, took it up to her office and slid it into her computer.

This was different. Not what she expected, but delightful. Not otherworldly healing music, but powerful drumming, love songs, and blues. Fiery, passionate, and worldly. Some of the songs got her hips and feet dancing, others moved her almost to tears.

This was his best work yet. *Thank me, Jangarrai. Thank me, world. And thank you, Mae. We made this happen.*

Author's notes:

I made a few minor changes in the names or locations of things in Santa Fe.

I changed the houses on the block of Delgado between Palace and Alameda, adding the alley/shared driveway, and breaking up the big white house with the gates in front into two smaller houses for the purpose of my story.

I moved the rocks in the river to the east side of the bridge at Delgado and Alameda. If the rocks were in their real location, only on the west side, that would require Dusty to cross to that side of bridge, and he has no reason to. The rocks have to be there, but he doesn't go looking for them. The soft dirt on the east side of the bridge wouldn't work.

The college where Jamie's father and Alan Pacheco teach is fictitious.

Marisol's is fictitious, in the approximate location of Tomasita's, but smaller and louder and open later.

The dinosaurs are no longer on the roof but they were there in the year in which this book is set. I'm not sure if that building had become the shelter yet in 2010, but for the sake of the story, it had.

I created a slightly different mall in the location of Sanbusco Center: La Villa Real Center. The full name of Santa Fe is La Villa Real de la Santa Fe de San Francisco de Asis.

The cat village at a Ford dealership is actually in Staunton VA, not Santa Fe.

Of course, Dada Café is fictitious, but T or C is delightfully real.

About the Author

Amber Foxx has worked professionally in theater, dance, fitness, yoga, and academia. She has lived in both the Southeast and the Southwest, and calls New Mexico home.

Follow:
> http://amberfoxxmysteries.com
> https://www.goodreads.com/author/show/7554709.Amber_Foxx
> https://www.facebook.com/pages/Amber-Foxx/354071328062619

To purchase other books in the series:
> http://amberfoxxmysteries.com/buy-books-retail-links

Contact:
> mail@amberfoxxmysteries.com

Stay Connected

My newsletter will give you an inside look at my works in progress, notices of sales and new releases, my reading suggestions, the chance to be an advance reviewer when a new book comes out, and a free e-book copy of *The Outlaw Women*, the prequel to the Mae Martin Psychic Mystery Series. Meet Mae at age ten, as seen through the eyes of her grandmother.

http://amberfoxxmysteries.com/subscribe-to-my-newsletter

Also by Amber Foxx

Mae Martin Mysteries
The Calling
Shaman's Blues
Shaman's Blues
Snake Face
Soul Loss
Ghost Sickness
Death Omen
Shadow Family
Gifts and Thefts
Chloride Canyon
The Mae Martin Mysteries Books 1-3

Standalone
The Outlaw Women
Bearing
Small Awakenings

Watch for more at amberfoxxmysteries.com.

Made in the USA
Coppell, TX
15 September 2023

21578721R00215